DRAFTED

The Mostly True Tales of a
Rear Echelon Mother Fu**er

Andrew Atherton

Treehouse Publishing | Blank Slate Press
Saint Louis, MO

Treehouse Publishing Group, an imprint of Blank Slate Press

Published in the United States by Treehouse Publishing Group,
an imprint of Blank Slate Press.
Visit our website at www.blankslatepress.com to learn more.

Cover by Kristina Blank Makansi

Library of Congress Control Number: 2013952940
ISBN: 9780989207911

10 9 8 7 6 5 4 3 2 1

PRINTED IN THE UNITED STATES OF AMERICA

For my wife

DRAFTED

The Mostly True Tales of a
Rear Echelon Mother Fu**er

CONTENTS

AUTHOR'S NOTE

The greatest sacrifice a soldier can make is not his arm or leg, or even his life. It's his soul. His spirit. His hope and belief in himself and humanity, and the possibility of justice. Damage to the spirit occurs at its worst among combat troops. But it's not limited to them. It can happen to rear echelon troops, too.

The vast majority of U.S. soldiers in the Vietnam War—four fifths or more—served in support capacities in the rear echelon. Their stories, many of them fascinating, are seldom told. Perhaps this collection will help correct that oversight.

I wrote these stories many years ago under a pseydonym and fictionalized my experiences. I changed names and details of certain events, used composite characters in some instances, and invented dialogue where my memory, or conversations reported to me, were not word-for-word accurate. The letters to my wife are lightly edited from those she saved "in case you were killed." But while protecting the anonymity of myself and the soldiers with whom I served, my intent was to leave the reader with as accurate an account as possible of the nature of my Vietnam experiences and how they affected me.

Over the years I've rewritten and polished most of these stories, but their content and plot lines remain basically the same as they were back in 1969 and 1970.

If you wish to write to me, my email address is:

andrewatherton1969@gmail.com.

For definitions of military terms and abbreviations, see the Glossary. You will also find discussion questions at the end of the book.

Turns out I'm not humping in the boonies. I'm not using my infantry training, or guarding truck drivers, or scrambling down tunnels looking for VC or even digging ditches. Instead, I'm pushing paper as a clerk in the headquarters office of the 182nd Engineer Battalion at Cu Chi.

If I'd known five months ago I'd end up wielding white-out behind a desk instead of my M16 behind enemy lines, I would have danced in circles, waved my hands in the air, and lit burnt offerings to every deity I could name. Especially Major Roberts.

When I arrived incountry my MOS was Eleven Bravo, meaning I was trained as an infantryman. What a damned farce *that* was. I wasn't even good at pretending to be a grunt in Basic and AIT. I'm not joking. I was fully persuaded I wouldn't return to the States in one piece, if at all. In fact, before I left, I almost told my wife to find another guy, because if I wasn't killed in Nam and I woke up in a hospital without an arm or a leg, I'd blow my brains out. I saw half-bodied men in Madigan Army Medical Center when I got pneumonia in AIT, and I swore I'd never come back like that. So stop loving me, I almost told her, and shack up with somebody who'll stay around for the long haul.

Now I'm glad I didn't tell her that. Of course I could still get my nuts blown off from a mortar round in Base Camp or a land mine on the road when I'm covering a story, but the percentages are a lot better than humping in the boonies.

For the first couple of weeks, I was assigned to perimeter guard duty on Long Binh Base Camp. That was a holding pattern for me and a bunch of other Eleven Bravos. Then thirty of us got reassigned to the 182nd Engineer Battalion here at Cu Chi. Why? Nobody knows. But not knowing in the Army isn't unique. Nobody in the Army knows squat about shit. But in this case you can do a little figuring once you know a little more about the way the Army works.

We newbie grunts were parked for seven weeks in the 182nd because some brass-assed tidy-butt wanted to wait until enough men were killed and injured in the 101st Airborne Division so he could assign thirty hunks of fresh meat, clean and neat, without overloading the 101st Airborne Division's reserves. We were the fresh meat he didn't want clogging up the books.

Anyway, during our processing into the battalion, a personnel clerk was looking through my records and saw I had a college education. He walked into the processing room where I was sitting with the other don't-wanna-be grunts.

Now this is how it was. We were scared shitless. We didn't know what to expect. We were praying to be guards for truck drivers and asphalt pavers. We'd have been happy digging ditches. Anything's better than humping the boonies.

So this clerk walks up to me all crisp and clean and smelling of Old Spice. "You wanna work in battalion headquarters? You got a college education according to this." He waved my personnel file in my face.

I looked around at the other Eleven Bravos sitting at the tables where we'd filled out all those forms. They looked at me like I was a can of piss they had to drink.

Their reaction was to hearing I had a college education, not to the question of whether I wanted to be a clerk. Nobody took that question seriously. It was a joke played on naïve cocksuckers who think their fancy degrees entitle them to safe clerical jobs.

The ones lucky enough to get those safe jobs are called Rear Echelon Mother Fuckers by the grunts. REMFs for short. They're held in high contempt even by the men on road paving crews who are constantly exposed to potential danger. In return, a lot of clerks get mean and cocky with the grunts and paving crew members and any other kind of "field worker."

So, anyway, the other newbie grunts sat there, disgusted by the clerk's privileged smell, and waited for me to lunge for the bait to be just like him—but surprise, surprise—I'd be assigned by this mean-assed cocky clerk to clean shit cans every day, even Sundays, and the grunts would laugh themselves silly. So there was only one answer I could give this loud-talking, sweet-smelling jerk that might save me a place at the table.

"Fuck you, asshole. I'm not grabbing no shit end of a stick."

"No, no, man, this isn't a joke."

The clerk edged me over and sat down beside me, his voice low and confidential. "Our battalion awards clerk in S-1 DEROSED last week, and the colonel says we gotta fill this position ASAP. So if you can read and type and maybe write a little, you've got the job. You want it or not?"

I didn't know what an awards clerk did or what "DEROSED" meant or where S-1 was, but I took a chance and whispered, "Yeah, I want it."

The clerk confirmed his offer by whisking me out of the room and taking me down the hall to S-1, the battalion headquarters office. He introduced me to the other S-1 clerks, as well as to Adjutant Harris and the XO, Major Roberts, who happened to be in the clerical office at the time.

Since that day I've made myself invaluable to the adjutant, the major, and the colonel by editing and typing award citations, letters, memos, or anything else they give me. At first I typed word-for-word what they wrote in longhand and then I typed an edited version of my own. I submitted both, but it was my edited version they always selected. Now I just submit the edited version.

Understand, I'm not the only clerk in S-1 who does this for the top brass. The legal clerk is a dickhead, but he's real brainy and a fast typist, and he edits everything he types, too. Apparently there aren't many of us around here who can read, write, type, and even think at the same time. So when the brass find guys like us, they send the other men out to be killed and save us so they don't have to write and type their own letters, legal briefs, and newspapers.

Mind you, I'm not just a run of the mill clerk. I'm also the editor of the battalion newspaper—*The Road Paver*—except I don't know shit about paving roads.

That's why Colonel Hackett likes my articles so much. I'm so ignorant I write only the basics they spoon-feed me, which is what the folks back home like to read when they get their monthly twelve pages of mimeographed propaganda our men—their sons and husbands—mail to them.

Hackett's no dummy. Once he realized I was doing good work as the new awards clerk, and I asked reasonable questions and could write up the answers, he assigned me as editor of *The Road Paver,* which hadn't been published in eight months.

That plum came with another cut to my integrity, what little I had left. Hackett had me standing at his desk in his air-conditioned office when he laid out my options.

"Specialist Atherton, in addition to being awards clerk, you are now the editor and sole reporter of *The Road Paver*, our battalion newspaper. Congratulations."

"Thank you, Sir, and I consider it a—"

"But if you'd rather do your shitting over a cat hole you've dug in the boonies, then publish *anything* that says one goddamned negative thing about this battalion or any man in this battalion and you'll be out in the razor grass with the bloodsuckers faster than you can whistle Dixie while wiping your ass in one of our six-hole shitters."

"Yes, Sir."

"Good. We understand each other. You're dismissed."

He must have scared the shit out of Major Roberts, too. Roberts previews every article I write. I'm always editing something he thinks might be negatively interpreted. We don't "repair" anything, for example. We "improve" stuff with innovative designs, unless the repairs are needed because of damage caused by the VC. Then I lock and load my adjectives on the VC.

I want to be clear about one thing, though. I'm proud of what the men in my battalion are doing. These guys are working their asses off.

The 182nd paved the Cu Chi airfield and the roads to Trang Bang and Tay Ninh, and now we're paving fifty klicks from Lai Khe to An Loc in the midst of sniper fire and land mines and ambushes here and there along that goddamned road all day long. We're talking quality work these men are doing, most times twelve and sometimes sixteen hours a day, and it's dangerous as all hell. Maybe not as dangerous as being a grunt in the boonies, but it's a helluva lot more dangerous than what I do, which is sitting on my ass in the battalion headquarters office typing memos, articles, and letters.

Four weeks after I started working in S-1, Jerry Maener, my new buddy in Personnel, strolled over to the office and told me my records no longer stated I was trained as an infantryman. I'm now trained, according to my 201 personnel file, as a clerk/typist.

"You're shittin' me! No, wait a minute. Don't kid me like that. That's not—"

"Go look for yourself."

I jogged over to personnel. I asked for my file. All the clerks were grinning but no one said a word. And there it was. "MOS: CLK 71B30."

Jerry said that "correction"—literally a white-out over-type—took place by unofficial directive from Major Roberts.

Three weeks later an order came down from higher headquarters assigning all Eleven Bravos in our battalion to the 101st Airborne Division, an outfit that's famous for combat operations. Within two days, the other twenty-nine guys I'd left behind in the processing room that day were humping in the boonies, and I was still here, safe and sound. I even come back in the office late at night and write letters home—typed ones—and write stories for myself like this one. Or polish articles for *The Road Paver*.

I'm very, very fortunate.

So far.

I say so far just in case my luck turns sour and I'm blown away before I leave this friggin' country. I'm writing this smack-dab in the middle of 1969. Why is that important? Because we're still in the jungle and ain't nobody knows how we're gettin' out unless we're talking about each man's tour when he shouts out the door of the Silver Bird of Paradise, "I'll write you sorry bastards as soon as I get home!"

What I'm saying is this: things aren't going well over here. Don't make no never mind what the big brass tell the press back home, because we flat out don't know what the fuck we're doing.

Nobody has a clue.

Sometimes it's even hard to remember how I got here.

PART ONE

BECOMING A SOLDIER

BASIC TRAINING
Fort Campell, Kentucky

Tuesday, Aug. 27, 1968
Dear Janice:

I miss you. I'm lonely.

I'm doing okay with the physical training. I'm having a tough time with the push-ups and pull-ups, but I'm not dropping out of our morning and afternoon runs as I feared I might.

So far I've met nobody with a college education or anything close to it, nobody with whom I can talk and share my misgivings. In fact, many of the men here don't have high school diplomas. Some were forced into the Army by court judges as an alternative to trial and jail because they were accused of vandalism, rape or some other crime. I feel like I'm over my head in polluted water and wonder how long I can hold my breath.

I love you and think about you constantly....

Love, Andrew

Thursday, Aug. 29, 1968
Dear Janice:

I am sick and tired of hearing people talk about killing and how tough everybody is. Selfishness and hatefulness are expressed in everything everyone does around here.

I have never been with so many ignorant people in my life. Sex and sports. That's the range of topics we discuss while we clean the latrine. Oh, and two other topics: the weather and our training.

Every meal I've eaten I've downed in less than five minutes. More like two. While we're eating the drill sergeants (DIs) walk around yelling at us.

"Get the fuck out of here."

"Get that food in your fucking mouth and get your fat asses outside."

I'm thoroughly disgusted by it all. It's a nightmare.

I think of you every spare moment they give us, and that's not many. Trainees—all of us—are scared, exhausted, and mentally off balance from the time we get up at 4:00 am in the morning until lights out at 9:00 pm. Drill sergeants are yelling at us and intimidating us all the time.

But I can tell you I miss your touch. I miss your kindness. Your thoughtfulness.

They just turned the lights out in the barracks. The drill sergeant will be furious with me in the morning. I spent time writing this letter and didn't have enough time to finish polishing my boots.

Love, Andrew

THE DRAFT NOTICE

On the morning of August 19, I got up early and shaved off my beard. Janice drove me to the outer gates of the Detroit Induction Center with my paper bag of toiletries, two changes of underwear, two pairs of socks, two pipes and a pouch of tobacco, a copy of my birth certificate, and my draft notice. We kissed. I told her I loved her and kissed her again.

My draft notice had arrived in the mail shortly after the Tet Offensive and right before I graduated from college. It was 1968 and I was six months shy of turning twenty-six, the cutoff age for the draft. When I reported to Basic Training, I was seven years older than most other draftees, I was a college graduate with a degree in philosophy and a minor in English and American literature, and I had been married for two years.

I was so much older than the other men in my unit because I'd had three bouts of rheumatic fever when I was a kid and ended up missing so much school I didn't graduate high school until I was twenty. The fever caused no detectable heart damage and the doctor didn't save my medical records, so I couldn't even try to use my medical records as an out. I was older than most draftees, but I was medically fit for combat.

I'd also used my college deferment to stay in school until I was almost twenty-six. I wasn't trying to evade the draft. I was trying to decide what career I wanted and what education I needed. The long and short of it was that I was the last guy Uncle Sam should have wanted on the front lines of any war. But the draft board wasn't interested in what I thought.

Neither were my parents. Or my wife. In fact, everyone in my family was pretty gung ho about the fact I was off to become a soldier and fight the commies over there before we had to fight them over here.

I was raised in the heartland of America by Protestant fundamentalists. They were fine, solid people who provided me with a home full of love. My father was a mail carrier, and my mother was active in the church and taught piano part-time. My older brother became a missionary and then a pastor. Even though I had a lot of questions, I followed right along and was active in the church youth organization. When it came time for college, the logical choice—the only choice my family expected—was the Bible college affiliated with our church's denomination. My brother had attended and graduated there, and it was where my mother had been a student for a brief period of time before I was born. So after high school I packed my bags and headed off to Kings Cross Bible College where I made it all the way through the first semester of my sophomore year.

Asking skeptical questions was frowned upon by the faculty as well as students, and I asked lots of skeptical questions inside and outside of class. But I wasn't expelled just for asking uncomfortable questions about the existence of God and the nature of faith, sin, and forgiveness. I also skipped chapel, smoked a pipe, and was caught eating a hamburger after hours in the campus snack shop I managed. I was quite the sinner.

The dean called me into his office and told me I could finish taking that semester's final exams, but at all other times I was not to "trespass" on the campus grounds. And then, without telling me, he wrote on my transcript that I was expelled "for disciplinary reasons." That meant other colleges, by general agreement, would not accept me as a student without a semester hiatus.

My parents were devastated by my expulsion and my apostasy. They said if I wasn't going to "do the Lord's work," they could no longer financially help me get a college education because they had been giving me their tithe money. I felt badly about this, but I also felt intellectually and emotionally free for the first time in my life. But the fact remained that without God's money, I was on my own.

Through the intervention of one Mrs. Lenora Higgins, the woman Janice did her student teaching under, and her interest-free loan, I was eventually accepted to Western Michigan Christian College. Although a religious school, it encouraged "healthy skepticism," had rigorous academic standards, and believed in second chances. Unfortunately, many of my Bible College course credits were rejected, and others that were accepted had no relevance to any Western Michigan degree program. So it was, essentially, back to square one.

The healthy skepticism transformed me from an obligingly obedient good Christian boy into an aggressive agnostic high on the heady atmosphere of philosophical and literary criticism. Janice, however, remained steadfast in her conservative Christian beliefs. After graduation, we moved to Janice's parents' home outside of Detroit. She got a job in a local school district and soon found an apartment, and I reported to the Induction Center.

Friday, Aug. 30, 1968
Dear Janice:

I'm hanging in there, but it's tough. We're training to run a mile in six minutes and carry a man our own weight one hundred yards in thirty-two seconds.

Lieutenant Kilmore teaches hand-to-hand combat. Earlier today he promised us he'd teach us how to "break every limb on a man's body, take a smoke break, and go back and finish the job in your own sweet time." Nice, huh?

We won't have leave days to go home between Basic and AIT (Advanced Individual Training). Maybe you could come to Ft. Campbell for my graduation from Basic Training in two months. I guess they put on quite a show for the ceremony. We could have one night together.

I need to kiss you and feel you warm against me. I need your love so very much.

Love, Andrew

Saturday, Aug. 31, 1968
Dear Janice:

It's Saturday evening. This afternoon a sergeant and a corporal went around asking for money so they could go to the bar tonight. Each of us had to contribute fifty cents. Hope they have fun.

Hey, I got into a discussion with a guy named Ellison from Arkansas! I told him you were born there. Ellison has a wife and baby, but he enlisted because he wanted to "kill them damn Viet Cong." He also said he was going to kill every farmer he sees over there.

"Why farmers?" I asked.

"I hate f---ing farmers." He didn't explain why. He swears a lot.

Another guy, standing nearby, agreed with Ellison about killing "gooks."

I said I wasn't sure we should be involved in Vietnam, and I wasn't sure "gooks" was an appropriate name for Vietnamese people. The guys were stunned. Shocked speechless. They told me I was un-American.

Love, Andrew

Wednesday, Sept. 4, 1968
Dear Janice:

Today we fired the M14 rifle for the first time. My shot pattern was pretty good.

Punching holes in a distant target gives me a peculiar feeling of power I find difficult to describe. Maybe it's the ability to reach out and destroy things at great distances.

Huh. I guess what I'm talking about is killing people. I didn't think of it that way until right now while writing this letter. I've been thinking about it as target practice. Even so, I'm proud of my accuracy with the M14. It takes skill and concentration.

I've made a few new friends. "Friendly acquaintances" is a better description of them. I still feel like a misfit.

You're always on my mind—behind the stuff they keep pushing in the way. I wish we could spend a night together. I'd play with you. I'd be your Dr. Doctor and you'd be my nurse ... or patient ... whichever ... and I'd diagnose your problem and fix it.

Love, Andrew

PRIVATE DUCHEK

"You love that man you're eye-balling?" Sergeant Akeana shouted.

Every muscle in my body convulsed, snapping my head up, back straight, feet together, eyes wide and uncomprehending. My heart thudded like a piston in an idling diesel. But I hadn't been caught. He wasn't coming for me.

It was late afternoon, and two hundred men in my basic training company sat ramrod rigid on wooden folding chairs in a barn-like building of rough cut boards and thick wooden beams. Lieutenant Nelson was lecturing about MILITARY JUSTICE from a plywood stage. He had printed those words in big block letters on the mobile chalkboard behind him.

That morning we ran a mile as soon as we got out of bed. Two minutes for scrambled eggs later, we were "on line" picking up cigarette butts and other debris with our bare hands in the company area. Then it was on to marching, map reading, and hand-to-hand combat practice followed by a work-out on the PT field. After that, we marched back to the company area and "walked" the overhead monkey bars outside the mess hall as a pre-condition for a two-minute lunch.

In the afternoon, we practiced disassembling our M14 rifles, followed by wall scaling, trench jumping, and rope climbing on the obstacle course. Then, thirty minutes later, physically and mentally exhausted, we sat motionless on hard wooden chairs and listened to Lieutenant Nelson deliver a stream of words as meaningful to us as the sound of water dripping in a dense fog.

I blinked and stretched my eyes wide open, but it didn't help. Lieutenant Nelson looked flat, like a movie actor seen from the far side of the screen. *This is real,* I kept telling myself, *you must keep your eyes open.* I glanced at the drill sergeants standing at parade rest in front of the classroom. They were scanning the assembled trainees looking for sleepers and "star gazers." I quickly returned my gaze to Lieutenant Nelson. The sergeants had cautioned us to keep our eyes and heads "front and center" or we would be punished.

The classroom had no windows. A fan on the stage was aimed at us, but it didn't work. The stifling air was thick with the goatish odor of two hundred heavily perspiring trainees after a day of strenuous labor. Large black flies we dared not swat away for fear of attracting attention to ourselves buzzed our ears and bit our slimy arms and necks.

My eyes rolled and my head bobbed. I desperately tried to stay awake by wiggling my toes and alternating my attention to the left ear and then right ear of the trainee in my line of sight to Lieutenant Nelson: *Left, right, left, right.*

Then I noticed every time I closed my eyes and opened them again the five-hundred watt electric light bulbs blazing overhead formed, on the things around me, a checkered pattern of bleached-out white and sharp-edged black that revolved around me like a circling mobile. I blinked again and concentrated on the shadows. With each blink, my eyelids grew heavier and soon I was in a darkened room sinking into a richly cushioned sofa next to Janice snuggled up against me. We were watching a movie about love and separation and … and … sleep … a little sleep … she won't mind … she won't know ….

Seargeant Akeana was Hispanic or maybe Hawaiian, the toughest and meanest drill instructor we had. He was short and stocky, with pock-marked pudgy cheeks and a beer belly that gave no hint of the power and commitment of a man who exercised with his trainees every day and volunteered—or so we heard—for a second tour in Vietnam after his first taste of combat. He ran across the front of the classroom and yelled at a nineteen-year-old kid near the aisle, grabbed his shirt, and pulled him to his feet. That's when I woke up.

"Private Duchek," he yelled, inches from the boy's face, "I asked if you love that man you were looking at."

Duchek was a tall, thin, stuttering misfit with large, almond-shaped eyes. Nobody liked him because he couldn't follow directions. He bunked over my buddy Henson on the second floor of our barracks.

"Why were you looking at Corporal Eagan when you were supposed to be looking at Lieutenant Nelson?" shouted Akeana. "You want to go to bed with Corporal Eagan?"

"N-n-no, Drill Sergeant."

"Then you hate him? Is that it?"

Duchek violently shook his head. "No."

"If you don't hate him, you must love him. Are you some kind of homo pervert?"

"N-n-n …." Duchek's eyes fluttered as though facing a headwind.

"What the fuck's wrong with you? Can't you ta-ta-talk without stuttering?"

"N-n-no."

"No *what?*"

"N-no, S-S-Sir." His eyes rolled and blinked as he spoke.

"Did you just call me *Sir*, Private Duchek?"

"Y-yes, Sir."

"Sir? *SIR?* Do I look like an officer to you? Are you fucking blind, Duchek? What am I? Officer or drill sergeant?"

Akeana's nose was an inch from Duchek's face. The nose-to-nose confrontation jammed the trainee's gears. He couldn't answer. He just moved his jaw up and down.

"You delay much longer," Akeana yelled in Duchek's face, "and these men will redo this class during free time tonight. Now which is it?"

Duchek stepped back to get more space between himself and Akeana, but he stumbled into a trainee seated behind him.

"God damn it, you piece of dog shit, don't you ever back away from me." Akeana moved into Duchek's face again. "Don't you ever fucking back away from *anything*." Akeana jabbed his index finger against the kid's chest. "You got that trainee?"

"Phu-phu-pheese!" Duchek's wet lips popped saliva on Akeana's face, but Akeana didn't back away or wipe away the spit.

"Did you say please? Oh, God, is he gonna cry, too? Do I see a little tear? Your ass is mine, Duchek. I'll make you a man or have you in a dress within a week." Akeana was still inches from Duchek's face, "Class, what am I?"

Two hundred of us yelled like thunder, "DRILL SERGEANT!"

"You hear that, trainee? Do three stripes and one under tell you anything?"

Duchek shouted, "YES, SIR."

We saw him recognize his mistake. His eyes got big. His body trembled.

Akeana looked puzzled. Then he laughed. "Sir again? Good God, you'll be doing push-ups until your fucking arms fall off. Now tell me what I am. Slowly."

Duchek stretched his neck and lifted his chin. He opened and closed his mouth and blinked his eyes like a baby bird waiting for mama to feed him. Nearby trainees chuckled and shook their heads.

Akeana looked at his watch. "You took too much time, Private Duchek. At 1830 hours this company is marching back here to make up fifteen minutes of class time. If I were a trainee in this company, I'd organize a party for you tonight after Lights Out. Now sit down and pay attention to Lieutenant Nelson."

At 1830 hours, the beginning of our free time, Sergeant Weaver marched us back to the classroom and we recited the Rules of Military Justice over and over for fifteen minutes. When Sergeant Weaver dismissed us back at the barracks a half hour later, we had little time left to shower, clean the barracks, shine our shoes, and write letters home before Lights Out at 2100 hours.

Twenty minutes after Lights Out, Duchek was held captive in his upper bunk by a blanket thrown over him and stretched tight by men on either side pulling down as hard as they could. Other platoon members gathered around and beat Duchek with bars of soap swung inside woolen socks. Duchek screamed the whole time. In his private, thin-walled room thirty feet away, the second-floor platoon corporal apparently didn't hear a thing.

In the morning, we saw black-and-blue welts over Duchek's entire body. His eyes were red and puffy. Nobody talked to him. He wouldn't look at us anyway.

During our pre-breakfast run, Henson—a mild and even-tempered guy who wanted to be a dentist—told me he tried to help Duchek by making his bed for him. But instead of saying thanks, Duchek pulled the blanket off his bed and up-ended his foot locker. Henson asked me what I thought the drill instructors would do when they discovered Duchek's mess. I said I didn't know, but I knew there'd be another party that night.

In the following days, Duchek's erratic behavior continued to cost us time and privileges. He came to formation without his helmet. He didn't button his shirt. He dropped food from his mess hall tray. The platoon was punished each time, and in turn, the platoon punished Duchek brutally after each episode.

Duchek went nuts two weeks later. He ran around the barracks screaming and beating his head against the walls. And then he was gone. We never saw him again.

Near the end of Basic Training, Sergeant Weaver told us that Duchek had been given a medical discharge.

Saturday, Sept. 7, 1968
Dear Janice:

I'm tired of the yelling. I'm tired of hearing war and killing glorified. I'm tired of being told how much we'll enjoy mutilating the enemy.

The drill sergeants tell us they'll make us professional killers in eight weeks. I'm not much of a killer in spirit, but I'm getting pretty damn good at pretending.

I've learned how to cut through a man's neck with a loop of piano wire. I've learned how to kick a man in the groin so when he's groveling on the ground I can crush his skull with what they call a "heel stomp." During bayonet practice, I run full tilt at a dummy yelling "KILL, KILL, KILL" and then ram a bayonet in its chest. This is not me. This is not who I am. I do it because if I don't, the whole platoon will have to come back and do the exercise again—and I'd get the shit beaten out of me that night by the other trainees.

I hate what the Army is trying to turn me into. This is awful, ugly stuff. I hate it. I loathe it. And I hate the drill instructors who teach it. I feel such rage and contempt for what's happening here I'd be frothing at the mouth if I tried to express it all.

Love, Andrew

Sunday, Sept. 8, 1968
Dear Janice:

Roosevelt volunteered to be platoon leader. He's a Negro and a cool head. All the Negro guys are cool and likable. Most are friendly, but they stick together a lot.

I'm losing weight. I keep tightening my belt, but my pants have gotten baggy like a big deflated balloon.

I just wish I were home with you.

I dreamed last night of the two of us playing our game in bed. Gosh we have a lot of fun together. I sometimes wonder if other people have as much fun as we do.

Love, Andrew

Saturday, Sept. 14, 1968
Dear Janice:

We had our first physical training (PT) test this morning. I carried a man one hundred yards in forty-seven seconds. I ran the "run, dodge and jump" course in twenty-five seconds. And—I'm most proud of this—I ran a mile in six minutes.

But I flunked the overhead bar test. The minimum is to "walk" thirty-six bars, but my hands got sweaty and I slipped off the twenty-eighth bar.

I got the cookies! I had as many as I wanted and then I set the box in the middle of the barracks' floor. That's what everybody does with their "care" packages. Moments later, I picked up the mangled box and swept up the crumbs. Needless to say the cookies were delicious.

Love, Andrew

Sunday, Sept. 15, 1968
Dear Janice:

I'm sitting in the dayroom. It's late in a wonderful Sunday afternoon of free time. I'm relaxed and smoking my pipe.

As I write this letter I hear rock and roll on a loud stereo, bouncing ping-pong balls, clacking billiards, a loud TV, and yelling trainees. The air is hot and humid and filled with the smell of perspiration from all the guys.

This amount of locker-room bedlam would ordinarily drive me crazy. But the pressure of training is off my back for a while, and it's nice to be loose and free with the other guys, many of whom have helped me on the PT field and obstacle course.

A guy named Carson and I are on the waiting list for a game of ping-pong sometime in the next hour or two. He's from Tennessee. Several nights ago a blackbird flew in the barracks window and Carson thought it was a sign that one of us would soon die. He was genuinely concerned.

I love and miss you very much.

Love, Andrew

Monday, Sept. 16, 1968
Dear Janice:

Today one of our drill instructors talked to some of us about his experiences in Vietnam. I asked him why we're over there. He looked at me squinty-eyed.

"We're fighting communism."

"But why in Vietnam?" I asked. "Aren't they fighting a civil war there? Do we have any business getting involved in another country's civil war? What if another country stepped in and messed in our civil war?"

He got in my face and said, "France and England and even some of the Indians fought in our Civil War. Besides, that's where our leaders want us to fight, and we do what we're told, and you will, too."

I do not belong here. Blindly following orders goes against everything I believe in. Maybe I should have gone to Canada. I don't know. The only thing I'm sure of is that I love you, and I should be at home with you

Love, Andrew

I AM A MAN

"Stop grazing and sit down!"

The cold authority in Lieutenant Kilmore's command ended our search for a spot near our buddies. We dropped to the grass and sat cross-legged around a knee-high wooden platform the length and width of a small stage.

Kilmore stood at the center of the platform, his hands on his hips and his legs spread apart. He was a symbol of everything the Army wanted us to be.

His shoulders were wide and his back was straight. His broad chest narrowed to a flat stomach and a thin waist without a ripple in his shirt from his chest to his polished buckle and razor-creased starched pants. A glossy black shoulder holster held his nickel-plated .45-caliber semi-automatic pistol. Black dots centered his cobalt blue eyes like the eyes of a wolf, and when he smiled, his lips curled in a snarl.

Kilmore waited until we were all seated before he removed his helmet and shoulder holster. He picked up a rifle in one hand and a bayonet in the other. He pointed with the bayonet at a black trainee seated near me. The trainee was large, physically intimidating.

"What's your name and hometown, trainee?"

The man yelled, "Private Jason Tilson from Atlanta, Georgia, Sir."

"I know people from Georgia who aren't as ugly as you are, Private Tilson, so it can't be where you're from that makes you so ugly." Kilmore cradled the rifle in his left arm and with his right hand he tossed the bayonet in the air, end over end, and caught it while staring at Tilson.

"Maybe ugliness runs in your family. Can you tell us why you're so ugly?"

"I don't know, Sir." Tilson chuckled. "God made me this way, Sir."

We chuckled, too, thinking Kilmore was doing an edgy joke on Tilson. But he followed up with another question.

"Private Tilson, are you as slow as you are big?"

"No, Sir. I can net a ball while I'm in the air catching it, Sir."

A few men cheered, but Kilmore's eyes were cold. "When I asked if you were slow, Tilson, I didn't mean physically."

Tilson re-crossed his legs. A muscle near his left eye started twitching.

Tilson's buddy, Cunningham, sat behind him and loudly whispered, "Hey, man, he jivin' you. Be cool, man, be cool."

"Sir? I don't get your meaning, Sir."

Kilmore snorted and looked at the rest of us as though we were in on the joke. "I'm not surprised you didn't get my meaning, Private."

Tilson nodded and leaned forward, his thick lips pursed, his dark brown eyes squeezed thin for understanding.

"But now I'm wondering." Kilmore smirked and shook his head. "Are you a coward as well as being big, ugly, and stupid?" He attached the bayonet to the end of the rifle with a metallic *click*. "Are you a pussy, Private Tilson?"

Barely audible, Tilson replied, "I'm a man, Sir." He slid his palms up and down his thighs.

The Lieutenant laid the bayoneted rifle on the platform in front of Tilson and walked to the opposite end of the stage. "Private Tilson, are you smart enough to realize I've been insulting your dumb ass in front of your fellow trainees?"

Perspiration beaded on Tilson's face. In a hoarse voice he answered, "Yes, Sir."

"Well, if you're not a pussy," Kilmore called, "I want you to come up here and kill me with that bayonet for insulting you in front of your friends."

"Why you want me to do that, Sir?" Tilson turned and looked in puzzlement at the rest of us.

"Because I'd like to see you dance like a girl with that bayoneted rifle."

Speechless, Tilson got on his knees.

"You can't get in trouble, Tilson. Two platoons heard me insult you and order you to attack me. If you're not a coward, get up here and give it a try."

"No, Sir, I don't play no game like that, Sir."

"I'm not playing a game! I want you to come up here, you dumb ox, and kill me with that bayonet!"

"Sorry Sir, but I don't want nothin' to do with no killin' an officer like yourself, Sir."

"Well, Private," Kilmore smiled his curled smile at the rest of us, but we didn't smile back. "Maybe you'd rather suck me than stab me. Is that what you want?"

Cunningham, behind Tilson, let out a low growl and stood up. He was bigger than Tilson. Much bigger.

Cunningham walked to the stage and picked up the bayoneted rifle. It looked small in the hands of a man at least six feet three and bulging with muscle he'd sculpted in prison, or so I'd heard.

"May' Tilson won't kill you," he said quietly, his voice getting louder as he spoke, "but ah be happy to cut you a new asshole you honka *muthafucka*!"

Cunningham glared at the lieutenant, bowed his head, and charged, the bayonet aimed at Kilmore's chest.

Kilmore hooked his thumbs on his belt, squarely faced the charging trainee, and stared him in the eyes. The bayonet was no more than a foot from Kilmore's chest when he knocked the bayonet off target with an up-swing of his left forearm, swiveled his body sideways like a matador, and swung his right elbow against the side of the passing man's head. We all heard the hollow *conk* of elbow against skull.

Cunningham fell forward, off the platform, and rolled among the scattering trainees. The bayoneted rifle, impaled in the ground next to the stage, swung like a metronome. Holding his head, Cunningham curled into a giant fetus.

"Private Cunningham showed genuine courage," Kilmore announced. "He's my kind of man. Anybody fucks with Cunningham fucks with me. But Cunningham is dead meat in Vietnam unless he learns what an unarmed man can do when properly trained.

"During the next several days, I'll teach you how to defend yourself and do to your attacker what I did to Cunningham. But instead of pulling your punch like I did, you can bust his skull like a melon."

Kilmore looked down at the curled trainee. "You okay? Or should we chalk you up as a casualty of Basic Training?"

Cunningham didn't answer.

The lieutenant waved to Tilson. "Get over here and assist your fellow soldier. You owe him one."

Tilson walked over and helped his buddy stand up and guided him to his seat.

As Cunningham staggered past me, I heard him say, "Ah'ma gonna cut tha muthafucka fi' differn' way."

Tuesday, Sept. 24, 1968
Dear Janice:

We practiced with Pugil Sticks today. They're as long as a rifle with a bayonet attached and they're padded at each end. For protection, we put on football helmets with face protectors, padded gloves, and a groin cup. Then two Pugil Fighters jump to the "On Guard" position and try to jab bayonet thrusts to the upper body of the opponent or beat the opponent's brains out with the butt of the rifle (i.e., the Pugil Stick).

We laugh and strut around like tough guys if we beat the other guy to the ground. It's not a game, of course, but it's hard to remember that when we're laughing and yelling at our buddies, "Kill, kill, kill."

I miss you so very much.

Love, Andrew

Saturday-Sunday, Sept. 28-29, 1968
Dear Janice:

I started this letter Saturday night. Now it's Sunday.

I have free time all afternoon and I have so many things to tell you. First let me tell you about my experience with tear gas. Nasty stuff!

Thursday we started training on the CBR range (chemical, biological, and radiological weapons). After a class about the use of gas masks and different kinds of gas we might encounter, we practiced putting on a gas mask—which is tricky because the mask has to be airtight. Then with our masks on, twelve of us at a time were led into a small, one-room brick building filled with tear gas. Six of us lined up on one side of the room and six on the other side, facing each other.

The tear gas in the building was not cloudy like I thought it would be. It was almost clear. We stood there until the drill instructors (wearing gas masks) were sure our masks were working properly. Then they ordered us to remove our masks, put them back in our mask-pouches, stand at attention, and repeat our names and serial numbers until the drill instructors were sure we'd gotten a full dose of tear gas.

The gas burned my lungs, my face felt like it was on fire, and my nose oozed mucus over my lips and chin. I wanted to run anywhere to get out of that room, but I stayed, and I didn't plead to be released outside like several other guys did.

In fact, I haven't backed down or run away from anything I've encountered or been ordered to do. I've followed orders and accepted every challenge. And that brings me to something I wanted to tell you.

I appreciate your words of support and I know that you sympathize with my dislike of the Army. I appreciate that you understand how difficult this is for me, but I've taken on everything they've dished out so far, and I can take on anything they dish out in the future ... or die trying.

Basic Training isn't really ill treatment. They're preparing us for war. I know it sounds dumb or obvious, but that fact finally dawned on me in the tear gas chamber. I realized I had better know how to put on my gas mask. I had better learn the most effective use of these weapons. I had better learn how to fight, to be an effective soldier for my buddies. If I'm going to war, I know now I have to learn to be a warrior. We're not playing games.

And maybe this sounds like I'm bragging, but I'm doing things I didn't know I could do. It's like Santiago in The Old Man and the Sea. *A man discovers what he's made of by being stretched to his limits. Well, I'm being stretched and I'm not breaking. I'm not doing some of this stuff well, but I'm damn near killing myself trying.*

For instance, I'm a disaster when trying to scale a wall on the obstacle course. I keep running at it and banging flat into it. I can't seem to get my leg up high enough to pole-vault up the wall like we're supposed to do. Sometimes I get over it with help from other trainees pulling and pushing me up the wall, which is terribly embarrassing. The drill instructors finally let them help me after I tried it again and again without success while they laughed their butts off. A couple of the DIs call me "lard ass." But I've done well enough to pass the PT test (or I've shown enough persistence and determination that they're letting me pass).

Never in my wildest dreams did I think I could do some of the things I've done here or shown such resolve about doing things better than I thought was my best. For example—this is going to sound silly to you—if I decide to grab hold of something and not let it go, no matter what, then that's what I'll do. Somebody could rip it out of my hands, but I'll still be gripping it while the ripping is going on. If I decide to run until my heart bursts or I collapse from heat exhaustion, then that's what I'll do. You can stop me physically, but nobody can keep me from trying until I succeed or drop dead. I can't tell you how important that is to me, that I know this about myself.

Another man might jump a broader chasm than I can, but if we need to jump, then I'll jump. And if I'm not sure I can reach the other side, then to hell with it, I'll jump anyway.

Or if a man tries to kill me or hurt me or hurt someone I love, then he better make sure I'm dead, because as long as I have life in me, I can will myself to run, walk, or crawl until I reach him and do whatever I will myself to do to him using whatever strength I have left … or he kills me. Nothing short of that.

I didn't know I was capable of anything like that. I didn't know I had that kind of willpower or that kind of control over my body or my mind. Nor did I know I would ever take pride in having it. I've heard other men talk about this kind of thing, but I dismissed it as macho bravado. But that's not what it is at all. Or at least it shouldn't be. It gives me a sense of dignity and confidence and quiet power I never felt before.

So please don't feel sorry for me. Not everything happening here is bad.

Love, Andrew

Wednesday, Oct. 8, 1968
Dear Janice:

Most of our training yesterday and part of today was devoted to medical care for exposure to poison gases and treatment of wounds.

It was sobering.

The most important part of our training was working with manikins— human-sized dolls with heavy rubber heads and arms and legs—that weighed almost as much as a real person. We practiced, on these manikins, applying bandages for bullet and shrapnel wounds—head, neck, arms, shoulders, torso, legs, feet—and splints for broken or wounded limbs.

One wound we learned to treat was, for me, the most unexpected and frightening of them all. I've never heard of it before. They call it "a sucking chest wound."

If a bullet travels through your chest and punctures a lung, then when you inhale, some of the air will suck through the new hole; and when you exhale, some of the air will blow out the new hole and create little bubbles of blood on your chest and/or back. That's how you discover a wounded man has a "sucking chest wound." The bubbles and the sucking sound. We're supposed to apply a thick wad of bandages over the hole(s) so the air can't go in and out there.

You'd think damage from poisonous gas or being blinded or a head wound would be more frightening, but somehow—maybe because I've never thought *about this kind of wound before—a "sucking chest wound" horrifies me. Makes me want a nice arm or leg wound … if I'm going to be wounded.*

Enough of this. Hope you're having a good day.

Love, Andrew

KENTUCKY DIRT

"How are you getting out of it, Carson?" Beavers turned his pudgy face to me and then back to Carson. "You planning on getting sick?" Beavers' fingers fluttered over his protruding stomach like butterflies.

"I ain't gettin' sick," Carson answered, "and I ain't crawling on no dusty Kentucky field."

Carson and I had chummed together since the third week of basic training. He was a lean, hard-muscled farm boy from Tennessee with a bent beak for a nose and alert blue eyes that tracked the movement of what he watched while his head was still as a stone. It was no surprise to any of us to learn he hunted possum and squirrel "an' anythin' else I kin eat. Raccoon, too."

We were standing on a gravel road waiting our turns to jump on the back of a canvas-covered transport truck that would take us to the infiltration course. Carson handed his M14 up to another trainee and hiked himself over the rear edge of the truck. He looked down at Beavers. "An' ain't nobody gonna make me do it."

Carson grabbed my rifle I held up to him, and he reached down and helped pull me up on the truck. We found two empty seats on the side bench on our right.

Grunting and groaning, Beavers struggled up onto the truck bed by himself and found a seat on the side bench opposite ours. Beavers yelled above the commotion of the other trainees, "You scared those machine guns gonna nail your ass, Carson?"

Trainees kept crowding in. The side benches filled. Men knelt on the floor. Others held their rifles at their sides and grabbed the overhead wooden bars supporting the canvas cover.

"I ain't scared o' nothin'," Carson yelled.

Geason, who had big ears and a pimply face was seated next to Beavers. He yelled over the truck's engine revving up for our trip to the infiltration course, "Either you'll crawl like the rest of us or you'll chicken shit out, one way or the other."

Carson sprang head first between the men in the middle of the truck and hit Geason stiff-armed, slamming him back against the side-board. Carson grabbed Geason's shirt as Carson fell backward—knocking men aside—and pulled Geason over onto Carson's curled-up knees. He held Geason balanced in the air, face to face, Carson holding Geason's shirt in his clenched fists.

Men shouted. Some applauded. Others called for Carson to beat the shit out of Geason.

"Fuck him up, Carson!"

"Goddamn it! You made me drop my rifle!"

"Let go of me," Geason screamed.

"Hey, come on, assholes!"

"Stop horsing around!"

"Take back calling me chicken shit," Carson yelled. He shook Geason so hard Greason's head flopped up and down like he had a rubber neck.

The truck suddenly lurched forward, bouncing us like loose stones in the bed of an empty pick-up. Men braced themselves against other men. Others grabbed the overhead bars and held tight against the men falling against them.

"O-okay, I-I take it b-back," Geason yelled.

Carson shoved Geason off and crawled to his seat. I handed him his rifle. Somebody passed him his helmet. We all settled down while Carson sat glaring at everybody.

I nudged Carson with my elbow. "You thought this through? You have to do the infiltration course same as the rest of us."

"I ain't crawlin' no Kentucky field."

"What's your alternative?"

"They're aimin' to humiliate us."

Dust swirled into the back of the moving truck from white clouds blown up from the gravel road.

"Where'd you get that idea? They aren't trying to humiliate us. They're giving us experience under live fire."

"Sergeant Akeana said he's lookin' forward to watchin' a Tennessee hillbilly crawl in Kentucky dust."

"Good Lord, Carson! That sorry-assed Akeana's just egging you on. You can't let him—"

Carson turned and glared at me.

We sat without speaking to each other until the truck stopped. We waited our turns to jump to the ground.

Baked clay at our feet reflected the blinding sun.

Drill instructors directed us down wooden steps into a narrow trench eight feet deep. We walked single file in the trench to the far end of a field they called the infiltration course. Then we turned left into a wider trench that ran the width of the field.

A flat roof, two feet higher than the surrounding ground, covered the trench. It was open in front so the men could climb over the edge of the trench onto the individual lanes of the infiltration course.

When Carson and I turned the corner into the wider trench, six trainees already stood facing steps that lead, with a leg-up jump, to six lanes laid out across the field. We moved in behind two of the front trainees.

At the other end of the field, facing us, machine guns started firing in a sequential pattern down each lane, one after the other. Each gun, we later saw, was attended by a two-man team.

This was the first time I'd heard real machine gun fire, and it seriously unnerved me. I could get killed today if something went wrong.

A drill sergeant, midway down the trench, yelled, "First line, up and over! Keep your heads down and stay in your own lane!"

The six men ahead of us, separated by white stripes painted on thick wooden steps, hiked up a leg and scrambled to the surface and out of sight.

"Rear line advance to the steps!"

We moved to the bottom step. The muscles in my chest and arms tightened.

Carson suddenly vaulted the steps and landed on the top edge of the trench. He looked down the lane he was about to crawl.

"Hey, trainee, wait for the order!" The sergeant charged past the other men. He grabbed Carson's belt and yanked him down.

"Damn."

"Get your ass back on line with the rest of the men!"

I yelled to Carson, "What'd you see?"

"Buncha damned dirt, not much—"

"First line, up and over! Keep your heads down and stay in your own lane."

We scrambled up the steps and over the edge of the trench and onto the field. At first I was blinded by the sunlight bouncing off the hard, white clay. Our respective lanes, each about eight feet wide, were marked with powdered chalk like a football field.

As I low-crawled, I cradled my rifle in the crooks of my arms. My helmet kept sliding down over my eyes, and I kept stopping to push it back. The sandy, baked clay quickly abraded holes in my fatigues and bloodied my elbows and knees.

At the far end of the field the machine guns continued their metallic chattering. Tracers, like taut red strings, snapped four feet above my head. Simulated mortar explosions in sandbagged emplacements shook the ground. The concussions shook my body and deafened my ears. Stones and sand rained down all around me.

I crawled until I reached a barrier of barbed wire that covered at least eight feet of ground ahead of me. It was constructed of taut, crisscrossed layers of barbed wire held fifteen inches off the ground by metal posts. Coils of wire rose up in the middle like a three-foot pyramid. The barbed-wire barrier extended across all six lanes.

After removing my helmet, I rolled on my back, as I'd been trained, and placed my M14 lengthwise on my stomach. Pushing my helmet ahead of me, I inched forward under the wire. Flat on my back, I was unable to sit up or turn over. Barbs caught on my shirt and rifle, and gouged my hands when I felt around to unhook them. To push myself forward, I cocked my arms and legs sideways and pushed against the ground. Each time I cocked my legs sideways, I snagged a few barbs. I could not reach down to my legs to unhook my pants or my skin, so I ripped my legs free.

After clearing the barbed-wire barrier, I remained on my back and watched the tracers snap overhead. They were fearsome and fascinating to watch. They moved so fast—every fifth round a tracer—they gave no appearance of motion. Sharp red lines, four feet above my head, zapped into existence and then disappeared. Then they stopped appearing and reappeared above the lane on my left.

Rolling on my left side, I looked up and down that lane for Carson. Was he fascinated by the tracers, too? But the lane was empty. He wasn't there.

I yelled as loud as I could, "Carson! Where are you?"

A sharp explosion from a nearby mortar emplacement bounced me on the ground. I curled in a ball and covered my neck and head. Clods of dirt and stone pelted me.

When I looked again, a trainee in Carson's lane, who had completed his crawl under the barbed wire, yelled back at me. But my ears were blown deaf. I heard only *"… passed im … ack … tarted."*

"Yell that again!"

He pointed behind him.

"What's he doing back there?"

"… ead up … ooking—"

We both looked back through the barbed wire and saw Carson running toward us up the lane. He belly-flopped in front of the barbed wire. Moments later, red tracers streaked over my lane for a few moments and then his lane.

He inched his way under the barbed wire. I watched, mesmerized by his reckless courage. Then a trainee in my lane emerged from under the barbed wire, rolled back on his belly, gave me a thumbs-up, and low-crawled past me.

"What the hell are you doing?" I yelled at Carson. "You wanna die out here?"

"… running … lane … Fuck 'um. Fuck 'um all."

"Yell louder! Why aren't you getting shot?"

"… firing … sequence." He made sequential chopping movements on the ground. "… jump up … down …." His hand rode a sharp wave up and down.

I squinted at him. "What if they change their firing patterns?"

"Don't dare. They see … running … pointing at …." He pointed at himself and rolled on his back, kicked up his legs, and let out a, "Whooee!"

He calmed down and lifted his head waist-high to watch the machine guns firing at the end of the field. Red tracers snapped above him. The moment the tracers stopped, he jumped up and ran the next section of lane.

After I finished the course, I discovered Carson in the loading area beside the transport trucks. He was on the ground surrounded by drill instructors and trainees. Sergeant Akeana was stomping his feet and swinging himself around Carson, wild-eyed and swearing, almost tongue-tied. "You … you fucking Dirt Dog! You *did* crawl in that goddamned dust! You had your fucking *nose* in it! You Kentucky dirt dog! Had enough push-ups?"

Carson was in the upright position, supporting himself on trembling arms. "More, Drill Sergeant," he wheezed. "I want more." Then his arms gave out and he fell without catching himself.

Every obscenity and swear word I'd ever heard came out of Akeana's mouth in those next few seconds. His lips curled back and he gritted his teeth and hauled off as if to kick Carson in the ribs, but he stopped in mid-swing.

The rest of us didn't know whether to cheer or run for our lives.

That night, when Carson returned to the barracks from Captain Edmunds's office, we gathered around to find out what they planned to do to him.

"Nothin'. Not a *damn* thing. Said he'd throw me in the brig if I did anything like it again. Said he'd be happy to share a foxhole with me if I learnt not to be so reckless." Carson grinned as if he'd just thrown the winning Super Bowl touchdown pass.

Everybody was silent for a moment. Then we all, even Beavers and Geason, whooped and danced and slapped each other some skin.

Several days later we heard that Captain Edmunds recommended to the base commander that operators of the machine guns should randomize their firing, and trainees should be alerted to that fact.

Monday, Oct. 14, 1968
Dear Janice:

Guess what? I was one of only a few men chosen to qualify with a M16 rifle. We chosen few went to a four-hour class this morning and learned how to tear it down and fire it. We're talking real status now! Ha.
Love, Andrew

Tuesday, Oct. 15, 1968
Dear Janice:

The other night one of the guys got a Playboy Magazine *in the mail. We're not permitted to have anything like that anywhere on the training compound. We all gathered around the guy who was holding the magazine. Some guys got on upper bunks so they could see better. Other guys stood on top of foot lockers. We were jammed body-to-body hooting at pictures of naked women.*

But then Corporal Eagan came in the barracks before we realized he was there. We scattered, of course, and somebody hid the magazine under a bunk mattress. But Eagan found it. The guy who owned the magazine and the guy who sleeps in the bunk where it was hidden were both given extra KP. But they said it was worth every minute of KP to see those pictures.

Everybody here is horny. In the morning, when the drill sergeant comes in and yells for us to get out of bed, we're scared we won't have everything ship-shape in time to make formation, so morning erections don't last but seconds. At night we often hear bunks squeaking, but nobody ever said anything or laughed about it until something happened that broke the ice.

It was in the evening. Who cooked this stunt up I don't know. But after they got ready (hiding under their bunk covers), three guys lined up naked from the waist down and a couple guys tried to whistle Dixie without laughing while these guys kept time with their stiff bobbing peckers—maybe five seconds worth—until everybody lost it from laughing.

Now when we hear a bunk squeaking at night, somebody always calls out, "Get it on, Bro, get it on."

That's probably more than you wanted to know.

Love, Andrew

Wednesday-Thursday, Oct. 16-17, 1968
Dear Janice:

Yesterday morning (Wed) a guy named Lundquist—a tall, fleshy guy who bunks on the ground floor and always looks sad and mopes around a lot during our free time—he was next to me when we lined up at the arsenal to pick up our weapons for target practice. He said he was going to kill himself on the firing range.

I figured if he was looking for sympathy and I gave it to him, he might think he could get more sympathy by actually shooting himself. So I told him Basic Training was a very small part of his life. He could tough it out if he wanted to. But if he killed himself, he'd simply give the rest of us something to write home about.

He didn't kill himself.

Lucky me. Lucky him.

I did well firing the M16. The gun looks and feels like a plastic toy, but it quickly demonstrates it's anything but.

Firing on automatic at 600 rounds a minute is an absolute trip. That's ten rounds a second!! You can empty a twenty-round magazine—zip—just like that. Nudge the trigger and you can't help but shoot three or four rounds like a loud sputter.

The recoil isn't bad. One shot gives a little bump on the shoulder. But firing on automatic, you have to hold the rifle down on the forward guard with your left hand to prevent recoil from climbing the barrel upward and shooting at the sky. But you can control it. Firing on automatic doesn't give you a tight pattern on a bulls eye, but it does a great job spraying rounds in a car-sized area.

I have to say it. The M16 is cool beyond words. It's great fun to fire.

But I'm a little uneasy about the M16 bullet (not the brass casing, but the thing that shoots out the muzzle). It's .22 caliber, and that's an unusually narrow bullet to use in war. And it's unusually long in relation to its diameter. It's fired at very high velocity and set spinning at a high rate by the spiral grooves in the barrel. It can be accurately fired over 400 meters.

Here's what makes me uneasy. The M16 bullet technically meets the Geneva Convention prohibition against bullets that mushroom while traveling through a body (and because of that mushrooming, making a messy exit hole the size of a golf ball). The framers of the Geneva Convention thought it was enough to wound a man without mutilating him too. So bullets used in war, by any of the signatories of the Geneva Convention, are to be covered with a hard metal jacket like copper so the bullet makes a "clean" hole in the body it hits, rather than being made of soft lead or break-apart tips that horribly mutilate the body.

Well, the M16 bullet is designed too long for its width, so it flies through the air straight and true, but when it encounters a little resistance—like flesh—it loses its balance and tumbles. So it's a legal bullet, under Geneva Conventions, but it causes massive destruction similar to a mushrooming bullet, maybe even worse. The DIs told us that a M16 bullet can hit below a man's navel and come tumbling out his thigh or high up his back or even out his neck and make goulash of everything in between.

Sorry to go on like that.

I have nothing in my mind other than this force-fed training. But please know I love you and I wish so very much that I could hold you and that we could be tender and gentle and loving toward each other.

Now I'll catch hell from my platoon sergeant again. He told me if I sacrifice polishing my boots one more time just so I can "write long f--king letters," he'll sic the platoon on me for a blanket party.

Love, Andrew

LOST IN THE WOODS

"All right, listen up! I'm Drill Sergeant Dugan and I've got information you'll wanna hear." Sergeant Dugan did a quick roll of his head and shoulders as though his massive neck and upper torso needed a little workout hefting boulders and throwing tree trunks.

He stood facing us on a three-foot high wooden platform in a narrow clearing between thick forest and a crushed-rock access road. It was early evening. The sun was descending on the horizon. Transport trucks had driven half the company of trainees—about a hundred of us—many miles from our company area.

We stopped our anxious talking, looked up at Dugan, and waited for instructions. But he said nothing more until all but one of our transport trucks revved up, circled at the wide end of the gravel cul-de-sac, and drove off leaving us stranded in the woods.

"I'm gonna say this once! You don't hear me the first time, you're in deep shit."

Behind Sergeant Dugan, red and yellow leaves glowed in the evening sunlight. Beneath them, dark shadows lay deep between the trees along the forest's edge. It was picturesque, peaceful, a perfect place for a campfire with friends. But to us, particularly to me, it was threatening. Ominous beyond words.

"You are escaped prisoners of war! You are to work your way through these woods in the direction you're already facing. You'll come to a gravel road and then friendly lines two miles away. Camp guards carrying rifles loaded with blanks will ambush and attempt to capture you. If you're caught, or if you remain in these woods beyond daybreak and force us to come after you, you will be taken to a POW camp and you will be punished for escaping. Do you understand what I just said?"

We roared back, "Yes, Drill Sergeant!"

I heard the idling engine of the one remaining truck behind us. I turned and looked. The driver was leaning out his window grinning at us.

"Drill Sergeant?" called a trainee near the platform.

Dugan pointed at the trainee. Dugan's hand was curiously small compared to his thick forearm and bulging bicep. "Yes, soldier?"

We all looked at each other. Surprised. Uneasy. The cadre *always* called us "trainee."

"What will they do to us if we're caught?"

"Methods differ, but I guarantee you this." Sergeant Dugan tipped his buzz-cut, bullet-shaped head toward us and squinted over imaginary glasses, which, for some reason, scared the living shit out of me. "You won't forget it until the day you die. I kid you not."

Dugan lifted his head and looked around. "Any more questions?" He paused. "Good luck. You'll need it."

Dugan jumped from his platform and walked to the transport truck. We all watched him climb in next to the driver, and away they drove, leaving us standing there like little lost orphans.

I was scared out of my mind. But now, with no further instructions from Dugan, it was time to start our trek through the woods.

Why was I so scared? Dugan's warning reinforced the rumors we'd heard all week. The two worst, and to me most frightening, rumors were that camp guards would force a captured trainee into a fifty-five-gallon drum, secure the top, and beat on the lid and sides of the drum. Or they'd tie a trainee's arms to his sides and hang him upside down by a rope tied to his ankles and spin him for a circle-puke.

The rumors frightened me, maybe more than most trainees, because I had no sense of direction and very little experience navigating in a forest. This was one exercise I was bound to fail. I would get lost and picked up the next day and physically abused at the POW camp.

The thought of being forced against my will into a fifty-five-gallon drum and having the lid clamped on and not knowing when they'd let me out, and the thought of being tied and spun upside down, awakened in me a latent claustrophobia I didn't know I had. I understood I wouldn't be injured unless I fought the guards and they got too rough with me. And I understood that these punishments for getting caught or lost in the woods were similar to college hazing pranks. But none of that made any difference to me. The prospect of being forced into that drum or being tied and hung upside down generated such terror I'd been having nightmares.

Despite our previous training in how to direct our movements in a woods without a compass—using the sun, moon, and stars; moss growing on sides of trees; sight lines on distant objects—I thought my only hope of locating friendly lines and avoiding capture was to team up with someone who knew his way around a woods. And that was Carson, my nineteen-year-old buddy from Tennessee, who told us about possum and squirrel hunting in the woods near his parents' farm.

When I asked him if I could go with him, he said, "O' course. How else?" Then, still back in the barracks, Robinson asked if he could go with Carson, too. "Even a bro from the Bronx knows when a Tennessee squirrel shooter is a ticket home." We laughed and gave each other high fives.

Carson was our point man. Robinson watched for camp guards in our right and right-rear sectors. I watched in our left and left-rear sectors. Carson waved contemptuously at the men crashing through the underbrush ahead of us. "Too noisy. Moving too fast."

"Maybe they'll draw out the ambush teams," I offered.

"Unless the ambush teams wait for stragglers," Robinson said.

Carson motioned for quiet. We followed him without talking, as quietly as we could, for about forty-five minutes. During that time, clouds moved in and covered the sky. The forest darkened.

We came to a field of waist-high grass. Carson led us into the field and walked us along the left tree line.

I was uneasy about going into the clearing. It was too easy. It was the route a city dweller would choose. But Carson was our woodsman, so I kept my mouth shut. But I squinted and peered extra hard into the black shadows on my left beyond the tree line.

"Ambush!" Robinson shouted. Five guards jumped up from the tall grass on our right.

"Halt," yelled a guard.

"Stop and you won't get hurt," yelled another guard.

I froze for several seconds, petrified. Then instinct kicked in, and I turned and ran into the woods as if fired from a slingshot. I ricocheted from tree to tree. Branches whipped my face and arms with no more feeling than wind on a blustery day. Guards ran close behind, but only at first.

"Damn jack rabbit!" yelled a guard. Rifle blanks popped behind me.

I ran mindlessly. I have no idea how long I ran, but eventually the guards fell behind. My frenzied running ended when I turned to look behind me, missed my footing, slipped on a big mossy log, and fell in a shallow gully on the other side.

I scrambled to my knees, sucking air, trying to get my breath. I stuck my head up and looked around, listened for the guards, but heard only my own panting. I stayed in that position, motionless, until my breathing slowed and I could hear the sounds around me.

I was alone.

I sat down and rested my back against the log. I was physically and emotionally exhausted from my frantic run, but also from a long day of exercises.

I closed my eyes for a moment and wondered how it would end. How all of it would end.

I'm not a hunter. I haven't killed anything other than a bird with a BB gun when I was a kid. Even that made me sick.

A little sparrow. Fell from the branch but wasn't dead. I had to stomp on it in four inches of snow, but it wouldn't die. God, it was awful. "I'm sorry, I'm sorry," I whispered as I stomped it again and again, crying, looking around, hoping nobody saw what I was doing. Never again, I said. Never, ever again, will I kill anything.

Well, mosquitoes and flies. Spiders in the house. Which is a shame, too. Ingenious engineers. Circular strands sticky, anchoring strands not.

Why the hell didn't I go to Canada?

Why? Because I had to prove I wasn't a coward. What a ridiculous reason for going to war! So what happens now? What happens when I get out of these goddamned woods and I'm slogging through some rice paddy in Vietnam? What happens when I have to kill a man? Am I prepared to that? *Can* I do that?

I was so frightened back there. The guard called me a jack rabbit. I'm sure I looked pretty silly running crazy like that. Will I run like that in Vietnam? Like a coward?

But what if they'd caught me? How far would I go to keep from getting stuffed in a fifty-five-gallon drum? If I'm scared shitless of that, how would I feel getting chased through the jungle by Viet Cong?

What will it be like when I'm forced to be a real soldier?

But what about now? How am I going to find my way out of this woods?

And then I woke up.

I couldn't believe it. I'd dozed off! Talk about stupid!

I stood, staggered a moment, and started walking. Then I stopped.

The night was darker than before. I looked up and turned around. Clouds covered the entire sky. Light filtering through the clouds showed a fine-grained mist floating between the trees.

I had no idea which direction I should take. And the light coming through the clouds provided no hint of the positions of the moon or stars.

I started walking again. I walked into so many low-hanging twigs and branches I worried I'd poke my eyes out. So I held my arms out to shield my face.

As I walked, I reflected on what had happened at the ambush. To be captured, the guards had to physically restrain me. Their rifles, loaded with blanks, posed no threat unless they used them as clubs. And that gave me an idea.

I found a small tree limb on the ground. I wedged it between two trees and broke it smaller. The wood was dead, but the limb was heavy and solid, the size of a baseball bat. No guard would take me without a fight.

I began walking through the dark forest again. This time with a weapon. Two hours later—at least it seemed that long—I passed a big mossy log beside a shallow gully. I stopped and took a closer look.

It was the same log. The one I slipped on.

I had walked at least two hours in a perfect circle in a dark forest. I didn't know that was even possible. I was stunned. I would walk in circles all night and in the morning they'd come looking for me.

I resumed walking. Hopeless. Despondent. I tried to imagine what it would be like to be forced into a fifty-five gallon drum, pushing and kicking, trying to get away. Or twisting upside down, hanging from a tree, and throwing up. Getting it in my nose and on my face and in my hair.

And then, ahead of me, I saw what looked like a river of silver behind black silhouetted trees. It was a gravel road reflecting light from the clouds!

Maybe I'll make it out after all... unless it's the same road we started from.

Then I heard a strange sound. A bird whistle? I stood and listened. There it was again. A chirpy whistle. But this time two chirps. I heard nothing more.

I dropped to my belly, cradled the club in my arms, and slowly crawled through dry leaves—as quietly as I could—toward the gravel road. I stopped behind a line of bushes eight feet from the gravel. I watched for movement and listened for sounds. I saw and heard nothing.

I got to my feet. With the club in my right hand, I started running.

But I'd run only several steps when two guards jumped from bushes on the opposite side of the road.

I skidded to a stop on the gravel and crouched in panic. I cocked back my club in self-defense.

"Watch out, he's got a stick," said a voice behind me.

I turned halfway around and at the same time swung the club down and behind, aiming for the man's legs. But I missed. He was too far away.

Frantic, I hopped back and forth, looking front and back.

One of the two guards in front of me threw up his hands in disgust. "We got a live one."

"Throw that thing down," yelled the guard behind me, "you're captured."

"Get away from me." My voice was hoarse, barely audible. My tongue was thick. A high-pitched ringing filled my ears. My body buzzed like a high-voltage transformer.

Suddenly, without thinking, I stepped toward the guard in front of me and swung the club hard, up toward his head. In that split second he looked surprised.

The club hit along his chin and ear, and snapped his head over on his right shoulder. He dropped like a falling tree, without catching himself. I quickly turned to the man behind me. He was standing bug-eyed, open-mouthed, looking at his fallen comrade. I rammed the end of the club into his chest. It hit his sternum with a "crack." He fell backward, his eyes wide and mouth open, clawing at his chest.

I turned toward the third man. He stood slack-jawed, unbelieving. He saw me coming and turned to run, but too late. I dropped the club, ran several steps, and tackled him. He rolled over to defend himself, and I jumped like a frog from his ankles to his waist. As his hands went to my chest, I went for his eyes. I jammed my thumbs in the sockets. He screamed, flipped on his belly beneath me, and kept on screaming. I got up and swung back my boot and kicked him as hard as I could. His ribs snapped like uncooked spaghetti.

"Whoa, fella, we don't want any trouble," the nearest guard said as he backed away from me. He held up his hand like a traffic cop and looked at the other guards. "This guy's lost it. I say let him go."

"Hey, buddy," called the guard behind me. He pointed down the road. "Walk maybe twenty minutes to a winding path on the left that runs perpendicular to the road. Follow it to friendly lines. Okay? Anybody stops you, tell 'em Sergeant Meltzer said to let you go."

I followed the guard's directions, and forty-five minutes later I discovered a field blazing with electric lights powered by portable generators. Trainees milled around collapsible tables loaded with coffee urns and boxes of donuts. Transport trucks waited in the shadows.

Carson and Robinson had arrived an hour earlier. Both men outran the guards at the clearing and proceeded without further trouble.

"How'd it go for you?" Carson asked. He squinted at me. "You run through a briar patch?" His eyes tracked the scratches and dried blood trails on my face.

"I got lost for a while, but I made it out okay. How many men still in the woods?"

"Last I heard it was fourteen," Robinson said. He started speculating about who the guards might have caught.

They questioned me no further. I volunteered nothing. I was too embarrassed to admit how I'd made it to "friendly lines."

Most of the trainees in my transport truck dozed off during our ride back to the barracks. I spent the time thinking about killing the guards.

When the truck arrived at our barracks, my jaw ached from clenching my teeth. My eyes burned. My arms thrummed like power lines in a lightning storm. I had never felt such invincible, destructive power, and I loved it.

Sunday, Oct. 20, 1968
Dear Janice:

Got some bad news. Yesterday they assigned us our MOS (Military Occupational Specialty), and I got assigned 11B10 (we call it "Eleven Bravo"). That means I'll be an infantryman.

I'll be doing my Advanced Individual Training at Fort Lewis, Washington. The forests near Fort Lewis are used as training grounds for infantrymen going to Vietnam. That doesn't necessarily mean I'm going to Vietnam, but ….

Looking forward to seeing you Friday for Graduation Exercises. I can't wait to feel you in my arms … and in my bed ….

Love, Andrew

ADVANCED INDIVIDUAL TRAINING
Fort Lewis, Washington

Tuesday, Oct. 29, 1968
Dear Janice:

AIT here at Fort Lewis is better than Basic Training at Fort Campbell. We're treated with more dignity, and we're encouraged to have pride in being Eleven Bravos.

They told us the emphasis will be less on physical training (PT) and more on weapons, combat techniques, and "live fire" training.

It was great to see you at Basic Training Graduation last weekend. You looked spectacular. Being in bed with you was wonderful and I miss you already. And I'm sorry I upset you. But we did have fun. Didn't we? You and the Nipple Nibbler? Huh? Yes?

Are you really proud of me? You said you are. Do you mean it?

Love, Andrew

Tuesday, Nov. 5, 1968
Dear Janice:

Sorry I haven't written for a few days, but they're keeping us very busy. Lots of classes and training in the woods. And we're spending much of our time on target practice firing the M16 and other weapons.

I know I upset you when you came to Fort Campbell, and I said I was sorry. I don't want to dwell on what happened. Just know that I was excited to see you and be with you, and I'm glad you came.

We're being told most of us will go to Vietnam. The company in the barracks next to ours received their orders yesterday. Every one of them is going.

Love, Andrew

Thursday-Friday, Nov. 7-8, 1968
Dear Janice:

In your last letter you said you want more communication from me. I haven't written every night because there's not much to tell, and sometimes I'm just too tired. All I do is go to class, train with weapons, and do PT.

I guess I could tell you about the weapons we're learning to use. Actually, they're quite interesting. Here's some info about the weapons we trained with so far this week.

Monday morning we trained with the M-79 Grenade Launcher. It's a nifty weapon. The M-79 is about the length of a man's arm. It looks like a pregnant shotgun. The grenade it fires is a little smaller than a man's fist and explodes into hundreds of jagged pieces that produce casualties within a five-meter radius.

Tuesday and Wednesday we had classes on explosives and booby traps. We started off with TNT, plastic explosives, and det-cord.

Det-cord is an explosive that feels and looks like plastic clothesline but explodes at five miles a second. It's used to detonate a collection of explosive charges all at the same time, each charge at a different place (like bridge trusses), by stringing det-cord from one charge to another and then attaching a blasting cap to any one of the explosives. We all took turns rigging charges of TNT and plastic explosives. It was a boy's dream come true. The explosions were great!

We also learned about Claymore anti-personnel mines. A Claymore is the size of a thick paperback, but curved or bent round a little bit, and has a hard plastic casing. You set the Claymore on its edge (on little metal fold-out feet), the convex side facing the enemy, and you insert a blasting cap in one of two holes in the top edge. Then you run electrical wires from the blasting cap back to your foxhole, or wherever you're going to hide, and connect the wires to a "clacker" (a hand-operated detonator). A Claymore is packed with a pound of plastic explosive. In front of the plastic explosive are layers of steel balls. Since the Claymore is shaped like a crescent moon, the plastic explosive blows the steel balls outward, left-middle-right, while the concave shape in the back blows part of the explosion against itself, reducing the effects of the backside concussion. So the soldier who squeezes the "clacker" fifty feet behind the Claymore is safe as long as he keeps his head down. Anything in the left-to-right arc out in front of the Claymore is blown apart or pepper-shot with shrapnel.

Took two earlier drafts to get the descriptions right. Hope it's interesting to you.
Love, Andrew

Sunday, Nov. 10, 1968

Dear Janice:

Yesterday I pulled KP all day. In a way, that was good. Every time I looked outside I saw drizzly rain. The other guys told me training was especially cold and miserable.

Friday we had a class on the M-72 LAW (Light Anti-Tank Weapon). We went out in a field after class and fired the LAW at old tanks and personnel carriers.

The LAW is constructed of two plastic telescoping tubes (about 2½ inches in diameter) with a rocket fixed inside at the end of the rear tube. When the tubes are nested with the caps on, the whole thing is under three feet long and weighs about 5½ pounds, so it's easy to sling its strap over your shoulder and carry it on your back.

To fire the LAW you pull the caps off the tubes, telescope the tubes out, rest them on your shoulder, make sure your buddies are clear of the blast area behind you, aim, and press the trigger-button on top. The rocket fires its entire propellant charge while still in the tube, so the backward blast of the propellant doesn't flash out in front as the rocket leaves the tubes and burn the face of the guy who fired it. The effective range of the rocket is about 200 meters. Once it's launched, the plastic tubes are discarded.

When the rocket hits the tank, the shaped charge in the rocket focuses the explosion to the size of a silver dollar and punches a hole through the armor plating. This "deactivates the crew with flying fragments and explosive forces bouncing inside the tank like a clapper in a giant bell" (that's our drill sergeant's description—he's cool). The LAW is our version of the VC's RPG (rocket propelled grenade).

Do you find this stuff interesting? Took me a couple drafts to get the LAW description right. It's really the only kind of thing I think about these days. Not much time or energy for anything else.

Except you. I always miss you.

Love, Andrew

Tuesday, Nov. 12, 1968

Dear Janice:

The weather is turning cold. We don't feel it at first when we leave the barracks, and it doesn't bother us when we're marching or running, but when we sit in the bleachers for an outdoor class, the cold seeps into our bones like ice water. Particularly after we've worked up a sweat from PT.

You keep saying I'm not writing frequently enough and I'm not telling you what I'm really thinking. You keep bringing up the Ft. Campbell graduation and how upset you still are by my behavior. I know we didn't have the best time, and I've already told you I'm sorry. And I'm sorry you don't like the way I speak now. But how could it be otherwise? I don't know what else to tell you.

Love, Andrew

Thursday, Nov. 14, 1968
Dear Janice:

I've got a sore throat and a runny nose. Coughing a lot. We lie on the ground at the firing range or out in the woods and the damp ground sucks all the heat out of us.

Why are you still writing about Fort Campbell? And why are you so concerned about my swearing during your visit and my "new fascination" with weapons? I've always been curious about guns and explosives, ever since I was a little boy. I'm training to be a soldier—I am a soldier. You said you wanted to know what's going on in my mind while I'm away from you, so that's what I've been writing about.

What do you want me to write about?

How's the car doing? You never talk about the car. Why don't you talk about the car? I want to know your deepest thoughts about the car.

Love, Andrew

I AIN'T COMIN' BACK LIKE THAT

Four of us were polishing our boots in the barracks on a Sunday afternoon—my buddy Carson; Roosevelt, who was now our platoon leader; Shaughnessy, a bull-necked, red headed Texan boy of few words; and me. We formed a half circle on the floor around Roosevelt who sat cross-legged above us on his lower-level bunk.

Among the other men, several lay on their bunks reading. Others slept. Still others wrote letters. A lucky few, on weekend passes, made love to visiting women in off-base motels. A half dozen men from our platoon watched *King Kong* at the Fort Lewis Movie Theater.

A blustery November wind smacked rain and flecks of ice against the windows. It was getting dark earlier now, and the sky was already black. A storm was moving in and the rain was getting louder and more insistent against the window panes. It was a free day and I was trying to be cheerful, but it wasn't easy. I had a lot on my mind.

We had pooled our money and given it to Toby, a boy who got on everyone's nerves. Must have been an only child. Complains and whines about everything. He's short and tubby, and has a pug nose.

We'd dumped the contents of a nearly empty washing detergent box into the crapper and handed the box and a laundry bag to Toby who then left the barracks and walked off the training grounds, illegally, to a donut shop. As we waited for him to return, we polished our boots.

We called it *polishing*, but we didn't use brushes or polishing rags. We used spit. We wet the tips of our index and middle fingers on our tongues, rubbed our fingers on a cake of black wax in a can of Kiwi Shoe Polish, and rubbed the waxy mixture on our boots, using fast circular motions, applying more spit and then more wax, until our boots were glassy-smooth, and a thin smear of wax on a heel or a toe disappeared under our fast moving fingers like steam evaporating off a black mirror.

Eventually, Toby snuck back in, dripping wet, shivering and cursing, with five dozen glazed donuts at the bottom of the laundry bag and nine cups of coffee and cola in stiff paper cups with plastic lids, the cups stacked in the washing detergent box.

"You guys b-better appreciate this 'cause I'm f-f-fuckin' f-f-freezing."

"Gotta make sacrifices," Shaughnessy said, studying the floor, his face turning pink to match his red hair. Carson grabbed the laundry bag and Shaughnessy grabbed the detergent box and balanced it on a wastepaper basket from the latrine. The box dripped rain puddles on the floor. Shaughnessy handed out our cups of coffee and no-brand cola.

At the same time, Roosevelt, a natural born leader who looked like Bill Cosby, helped Toby with a towel and a little praise, since the rest of us said "thanks" without another word or pat on the back because Toby was a whiny little weasel who tried to brown-nose his way into our group. So we used him.

"You got the shit past the guard," Roosevelt said, rubbing Toby's head with the towel, "and you're our main man for today, and that's for sure."

Carson shook the paper bags of glazed donuts from the wet laundry bag onto two towels I'd spread on the floor. Then we shook the donuts out of the paper bags.

The donuts were flattened and squeezed together in odd shapes, and had to be pulled apart. They were heavy and slimy with grease and melted sugar-glaze, but they were marvelously illegal and wondrous to behold, resting misshapen on the floor on sheets of writing paper next to our cups of cold coffee and warm cola.

The cadre were gone for the day. The barracks was unsupervised all afternoon. We were in paradise.

But Toby wasn't happy. Exiled to his bunk and shivering, he complained about his thin blanket. Then he whined about the cold coffee and complained about how greasy the donuts were—donuts he hadn't paid for. We rolled our eyes.

Henson stopped reading, jumped off his bunk, and declared it'd be funny if Toby "died from pneumonia in a Washington winter while training for war in the tropics of Vietnam."

Henson, who looked older than the rest of us, earned a donut for that one even though the joke was old. It was originally used on Carson and me. The two of us had spent the previous week sick from pneumonia in nearby

Madigan Army Medical Center.

We'd missed a few grenade-throwing exercises, but more importantly, we missed training with the M60 machine gun. Our sergeants told us we probably should take AIT over again, but we were bright, they said, and we could pick-up the M60's operating characteristics along the way, "at least good enough to get by." We knew they were sacrificing us for their trainee quota lists, but we had more disturbing issues on our minds. We hadn't mentioned them to our buddies during the two days we'd been back in the barracks because we were embarrassed by how much they'd frightened us.

After Carson and I woke up in the hospital from our fever-induced delirium, we did double-takes at the other patients. They weren't sick. They were broken. Or burned. Or missing limbs. Many of them horribly scarred. We saw big white casts everywhere. Lunch in the cafeteria was an exercise in not looking. Madigan Medical Center was the U.S. Army's primary facility for treating and rehabilitating men who had been wounded in Vietnam.

"One guy I saw in the cafeteria didn't have a jaw," Carson said, after we admitted what was bothering us. "Bottom half of his face hung in folds. I didn't get a good look at it 'cause he hid it with his hands when he pulled back the bandage. He used his fingers to squeeze his lips around a straw."

Shaughnessy spit on his boot. "What's he doing in the fucking cafeteria without a jaw?"

"Aah, that's all crap," Roosevelt said, waving his brown fingers that didn't show the polish. "You ain't seen nothin'. That's full o' shit."

"You sayin' I ain't seen nothin'?" Carson thrust his face toward Roosevelt. "You think I'm full o' shit? I'll tell you something, smartass, I seen men without arms and legs. Is that good enough for you? I seen men with sewn-up wounds you wouldn't believe. So you tell me what I saw. Go ahead. Tell me what I saw."

"He's not bullshitting," I said. "I saw the same things he did. An orderly told me they even have a ward for guys with their balls shot off."

"I ain't comin' back like that." Roosevelt stuck out his lip and shook his head and swirled a touch more wax on the toe of his boot. "All my parts come home hangin' where they belong or I ain't comin' back."

"You got that right, motherfucker," said Quenton, another black guy, walking up the aisle next to the windows.

Roosevelt rolled off his bunk and slapped Quenton some skin and got some back.

Then he grabbed his crotch and jerked it up and down. "Ain't nobody doin' no tongue job in this nigga's bed." They collapsed in laughter, got all loose-limbed, and gave each other a black brothers' handshake.

"Preach the truth, my Righteous Brother," proclaimed Quentin loud enough to fill the barracks. He turned, laughing, still not looking at the rest of us, and walked along the windows to the latrine. Roosevelt settled back on his bunk, grinning to himself, and resumed his boot polishing.

I was curious about how serious Roosevelt was, so I asked, "What will you do if you lose an arm or a leg?"

He looked up, irritated. "I tol' you. I ain't comin' home 'less everything hangs the way it was before."

"So you'll kill yourself?"

"What'd I say? How many times I gotta say it?"

"What if you can't do it and you wake up in the hospital and you can't move?"

"Then I'll *ask* somebody, just *do* the thing."

"But what if you're messed up and you can't tell people what you want?"

"*Fuck,* man!" Roosevelt dropped his boot in his lap and looked at me like I was the dumbest asshole he'd ever seen. "Then *you* shoot me! Damn, if I'm that bad. Send me to Jesus."

Everybody laughed.

"No, man, I'm serious."

"So am I. You guys gotta swear you'll shoot me if I'm all fucked up," I blurted. Everybody looked at me. I was surprised, too. I'd reported a decision I didn't know I'd made. Now I needed to explain it ... even to myself. "I'm not coming back like those men I saw. Not like that. Life isn't worth it."

Carson nodded his head. "I'm for that."

Shaughnessy nodded, too.

"If it's right for you, my brothers, it's right for you." Roosevelt focused on his boot. "If it's gotta be done, then we do the hard thing."

The rest of us looked at each other in confirmation of our agreement. None of us said a word about the shooter and the problems he might have.

So we all agreed: if we're bloody and broken and can't do it ourselves, we want our friends to shoot us.

Maybe gathered around us. In a circle.

In *my* mind, anyway, a circle. Looking down at me. Tears welling in their eyes.

Monday, Nov. 25, 1968
Dear Janice:

We've had a great Thanksgiving. Turkey. Dressing. Pumpkin pie. The works. The mess hall was decorated. We had the whole day off.

I'm pretty much back to normal from my bout with pneumonia. A little weak, but getting stronger. Carson is better, too. Our free day, today, helped a lot.

You're right, lately I haven't been talking in my letters about much of anything except my training. I'm sorry about writing in that letter that I wanted to hear your deepest thoughts about the car. That was mean-spirited. I'm sorry.

You know I love you. If you don't know that by now, then I don't know how to say it any plainer. I love you.

But I'm struggling to … I'm just struggling. There are some things I can't put in words. I'm conflicted. I'm not sure what I think.

But know that I love you and miss you so much that I ache inside.

Love, Andrew

Wednesday-Friday, Nov. 27-29, 1968
Dear Janice:

You keep asking about what's going on in my mind, so I'm going to tell you.

This letter will take a few nights to write, but I can't help that. I can't write reflectively under these conditions without taking a lot of time doing it.

Honey, I'm becoming a soldier. Training to be a soldier isn't just learning how to shoot a weapon. The training is designed to alter our minds and make us psychologically strong enough to withstand horrible conditions and the possible abuse we'll face if we're captured. Most of all, it prepares us to kill and maim other human beings.

You keep making a big deal about the vulgar language I used when you visited me at Fort Campbell. I say "fuck" and "shit" and "cocksucker" all the time. Maybe that's not needed. You're right. Maybe I should learn how to shoot, stab, burn, and blow a person's guts out without cursing. But that's the way I'm being trained. Vulgarity is a tool we use to prepare ourselves to kill. We have to become hard and insensitive. We have to build a barrier around our minds to prevent us from thinking about the people we'll kill and the families who'll miss them. Killing is vulgar and using vulgarity helps to separate us from the men we once were and mold us into the soldiers we must become. Honey, consider what I'm training to do.

We both agreed, if you remember, that I could not claim conscientious objector status. I believe some wars are justified. Like World War II. So when my draft number came up, I didn't run to Canada. Right? We talked about all this. Remember? And I also believe my country's leaders might know more than I do about large-scale political and military situations. If South Vietnam is fighting to be independent of the North, and if North Vietnam is trying to force communism on the South, and if we can stop it from happening, shouldn't we?

Everybody said that doing what my country is asking me to do is right and proper and honorable. Mom even wrote that she's praying I'll be a good soldier. (She hasn't a clue what she's praying for.) So I'm learning how to kill, because that's what it means to be a soldier.

And you keep objecting to the <u>words</u> I use to harden me to do the killing? Maybe I shouldn't have exposed you to that language. But I haven't learned, yet, how to be a "motherfucking killer" during the day, ready to jab out a man's eyes or blow off his head, and then transform myself in the evening and make soft cooing noises to my visiting wife. I am immersed in the culture of killing every second of the day and I haven't yet found the switch that turns off the soldier and turns on the sensitive husband who can write flowery love letters. I hope someday I find that switch, but you not understanding doesn't help.

I know I spoke and acted badly at Fort Campbell. But when you said, "That isn't the way a Christian should talk," I went nuts. How many times do I have to say I'm sorry? But I was angry, and I still am. My pious, sanctimonious family wants me to be a patriotic skull crusher. They want me to stab people in the chest with bayonets and learn how to use explosives that will blow a person's body into so many pieces their own relatives couldn't find them all or recognize them even if they did. You want me to salute the flag and kill the enemy, but you don't want me to say "fuck." Heavens no! So I took my anger out on you at Ft. Campbell, and I shouldn't have. I'm sorry. Please forgive me. But it wasn't only that.

You were from another place in my life. You seemed foreign. You were beautiful and good and wonderful and totally out of place in the ugliness I'd grown accustomed to. I felt coarse and crude around you. I'd become proud of doing things I never wanted to do—things I never want you to see me do. That's why I acted distant. That's why I didn't want you to come here to Fort Lewis. And

I still don't want you here.

I struggle with the morality of all this. Independent of whatever else is happening in the world, my basic training calls for me to be willing to kill people. Anybody they point to. I must be ready to do unspeakably violent things to other human beings upon the command of my superiors. The moral justification for this killing or that killing is not relevant when I'm training to be a state-sanctioned killer.

I now realize it's the political neutrality of Basic Training and AIT that's crucial for preparing me and other morally and politically uncertain men for fighting in Vietnam. Once I allowed myself to be inducted into Basic Training and allowed myself to become a trained soldier committed to trusting my superior's orders, I'm in less of a position than I was before to make fine-tuned political and moral decisions.

So ... you wanted to know what I'm really thinking.

Love, Andrew

Sunday, Dec. 1, 1968
Dear Janice:

I know that last letter must have been disturbing to you, and we can talk about it when I'm home at Xmas. But there are a few more things I might as well explain.

I worry that my participation in the Vietnam War will be morally wrong, but I can't come to any definite conclusion about it. I've talked to captains and sergeants and anybody I think might have an informed opinion, but all they say is, "A soldier does what his government tells him to do."

Here's the example they use to justify doing whatever we're told to do. Suppose your sergeant says, "We've been ordered to take that hill." But as far as you can tell, that hill is of no military value and attacking it will cause pointless deaths and injuries among your buddies and nearby civilians.

Question: Should you refuse to obey the order?

Set aside that you'll be court-martialed if you refuse. Should you refuse to obey the order if you're <u>convinced</u> the attack will result in nothing of value?

Answer: You obey the order.

Why? You don't know enough of the larger picture to make an informed decision. As far as you know, the attack might be part of a diversionary operation that will save many more lives than the casualties you suffer and the people you and your buddies kill.

Despite all my reading about the flaws in our Vietnam policies, I assume my government and my military leaders see the big picture better than I do. On the other hand, maybe they don't. I don't know. But I do know that U.S. involvement in Vietnam is not for economic gain or political power. And North Vietnam attacked us in the Gulf of Tonkin. So shouldn't I give my government the benefit of the doubt and hope they know what they're doing?

I'm caught in a conflict of issues over life and death more basic than anything I'll face the rest of my life. I've found no secure position. But my dilemma goes even deeper.

Suppose I decide our involvement in Vietnam is unjustified. I don't know if I can bring myself to refuse to go. I don't know if I have the courage to stand up against my buddies, the Army, the government, society, and my family all at the same time.

I would be called a coward. I would go to a military jail. Any future career I might hope for as a teacher would be compromised.

And what would your dad say?

What would your granddad say if I refuse to go to Vietnam but say I'm willing to go to Germany or some other safe place? I respect your granddad more than any man I've ever known, a man who confided in me about the things he saw and did in the trenches of France. He advised me to "do what you have to do." What would <u>he</u> *say?*

And what would <u>my</u> *parents and grandparents say? Grandpa Atherton already wrote me in Basic Training to "buck up" and stop complaining and learn to defend my country, the one God blessed and appointed as a "beacon unto the world."*

And it's not just our families. It's you, too. You'd all say, "You should do God's will, and that's to fight godless communism," and since you're all convinced you know God's will and you think I do too, you'd think I was a coward. You'd say, "We still love you," but deep down you wouldn't respect me. And deep down I'd wonder if you're right. I wouldn't have any way of proving or knowing, <u>even for</u> <u>myself,</u> *that you were wrong.*

I can't tolerate the thought of that. Do you understand? And then I put up with your complaints about swearing at Fort Campbell!

When I think about coming home at Christmas and being with people I've known all my life, I want to go somewhere and hide. Or go somewhere with other soldiers.

I still love you and miss you and need you, but sometimes I wish you didn't love me. I feel like everything that came before is from another life. I don't want to be loved anymore. I feel twisted inside. Morally perverse. I just want all this over with. One way or another.

Andrew

LAND MINE COURSE

Sitting on bleachers in the middle of a training field, we huddled against a cold wind. We leaned forward, cupping our hands to our ears, trying to hear Sergeant Lopez as he swaggered across the wooden stage in front of us, the wind whipping away his words. He was near the end of his briefing on what we were to do at the Land Mine Course.

"Oh, one last thing. The pseudo land mine you dig up tonight might be booby-trapped with a CS gas grenade." Lopez turned at the far side of the stage and swaggered back in the opposite direction. His head down, he talked off-handedly, as if bored by his memorized lecture. "So, if you find a grenade under or next to your mine, secure the lever and raise your hand. One of the drill instructors will come over and insert the safety pin." Lopez stopped talking.

Was he done? He strolled across the stage with a sarcastic grin on his face. He turned to us, shrugged his shoulders, and raised his hands palms up, as though saying, "That's it. You want more?"

We waited. We looked at each other. A trainee on the bottom bench couldn't take it anymore and called out, "What do we do if we pop the grenade?" Lopez looked at him in mock surprise, as though the one bright bulb in the class finally clicked on.

"It won't explode, you know. Just hisses." His purple lips stretched into a grin that put dimples in his yellowish brown cheeks. He was enjoying this. "As you know, CS is stronger than tear gas, but it's not lethal. So if you fumble and pop your grenade, crawl to the windward side. You can withstand a lot of that stuff if your life depends on it, and that's what you gotta imagine for this exercise. So don't stand up and don't crawl away. That makes you a more visible target. You're supposed to be in the perimeter kill zone of an enemy camp. And remember: a soldier without his rifle is worse than dead. He's a liability to his platoon."

Later in the day, a corporal gave us another suggestion for coping with the gas. Days earlier we had been issued woolen gloves. It was early December, so there was frost on the ground every morning and the wind whipped us with icy flecks of snow. The corporal said we should take our gloves with us that night, and if exposed to the gas, we should spit on a glove and hold it over our faces.

Late that night, after standing in line for our rifles at the armory, we rode transport trucks to the Land Mine Course. It looked like a miniature football field lit with flood lights on telephone poles. The field was divided into four-foot wide lanes drawn with powdered lime. Drill sergeants instructed us to line up at the ends of the lanes.

Breaking away from the other men, I ran down the side of the field to a lane not yet selected by other trainees. I wanted to be first in line. My fellow trainees probably thought I was putting on a good show of "gung-ho" confidence. But I was motivated not by courage, but by fear and desperation.

I wasn't a failure, but neither was I successful at most of what I was being trained to do. Although accurate with a rifle, I was physically awkward and made numerous mistakes—like not seeing booby traps and getting lost in the woods—mistakes that would be fatal in the jungles of Vietnam. Because my fear of failure was enormous and I had an excellent imagination, I was scared shitless most of the time. So I tried even harder to overcome my faults and face my fears without hesitation. Whenever I ended up at the end of the line and had to watch everyone go through an exercise before me, I imagined a hundred different ways I could screw up, a hundred different ways I could get killed—and get my buddies killed. So I always tried to be the first one out, the first one in line. That way I wouldn't have time to get too worked up.

While the other men were still assembling at the ends of other lanes, I waited anxiously on my belly for the exercise to begin. I had my gloves tucked in my fatigue pockets.

The freezing night air was foggy. The sandy ground in front of my face sparkled gauzy white from overhead flood lamps on either side of the field. A column of mist floated on a soft breeze down the center of the field like a blue ghost.

Sergeant Lopez fired the starting pistol.

I low-crawled down the lane. I held a bayonet in my right hand and I held my M16 as I was instructed: balanced parallel on my left forearm, the stock in the crook of my arm and the barrel in the crook of my thumb—with my thumb held up and bent sideways over the barrel—which, after five minutes, induced thumb cramps and pain, then numbness.

Every few feet—holding the bayonet along the length of my open right hand, my thumb pressing the handle against my upright palm—I gently pushed the point of the bayonet at a backward slant into the ground directly in front of me. Then again on the left and on the right, the width of my crawling body. Feeling nothing resist the thrust of the blade, I crawled about one foot forward and repeated the process. In this way I "cleared" the lane, one foot at a time, halfway across the field.

Then my bayonet struck something hard an inch below the ground. I yanked the bayonet back as if shocked by a live wire.

Laying the bayonet aside, I carefully brushed loose dirt off the top of the mine. It was dark green and made of sheet metal, the size and shape of a round coffee cake tin. The trigger on top was a circular pressure plate.

After digging a little trench around it, an inch or two deeper than the thickness of the mine, I scooped dirt from under the mine's right edge while holding the mine steady with my left hand so it wouldn't tip into the cavity. I continued scooping out dirt until I was sure there was no CS gas grenade underneath with its spring-loaded safety lever pressing up against the bottom of the mine.

I lifted the mine from the hole and set it on my mound of excavated dirt and raised my hand. A drill instructor strolled over and approved my work and ordered me to wait for the all clear.

I laid there for several minutes. Then I heard a popping sound followed by hissing about five lanes upwind from me. Then two more pops. I raised my head and saw white clouds of CS gas drifting my way.

I frantically pulled out a woolen glove, cursing myself for not having done so already. I tried to spit on it, but my mouth was dry. I couldn't work up any spit. I sucked in a chest full of air and covered my face with the dry glove.

Then a thought came to me like a shout: *Put your head in the hole! The gas will blow over it!*

It wasn't until after the training exercise that I realized my mistake. CS gas is heavier than air; it's manufactured to be that way. So the gas would flow down into the cavity I'd dug, displace whatever good air was down there, and I would be exposed to a higher concentration of the gas than if I had kept my head above ground.

I pulled forward, removed my helmet, closed my eyes, and pressed my face, covered with the glove, against the bottom of the hole. I held my breath.

My neck thumped with blood. My heart thudded against my chest.

Already I needed air!

Five more seconds. Count slowly. One ... Two ... Three ... Four ... Five ....

My abdominal muscles convulsed. I had to breathe! My body was fighting for air!

No! Count five more seconds again: One ... Two ... Three ... Four ... Five ....

I took a shallow breath to test the air.

It felt like steaming acid searing my throat and lungs! My eyes flew open. For a split second I saw what looked like white cotton. Then my eyes caught fire. I gasped and pulled in a chest full of gas. The pain was instant and overwelming. I yanked my head out of the hole.

My lungs and throat locked up. I couldn't breathe even when I tried!

I had to get out of the gas. I had to have air!

I jumped to my feet and stumbled on something, but I staggered forward.

Intense claustrophobia closed in on me. I had to find my way out of the gas! Blinded, stretching out my arms, I tried to feel my way. I shuffled around, still unable to breathe, lost my balance, and fell to the ground semiconscious.

I revived moments later. I was on my side. Totally disoriented. I had no idea where I was. Rusty razor blades filled my lungs. Sharp pain cut my breath to quick, shallow gasps. My face burned like fire. My eyes were covered with hot sand. Mucus, moist and slimy, dripped over my lips.

Where was I? What happened? I tipped back my head and tried to see. Muscles over which I had no control were squeezing my eyes tightly shut. Leaning on my left elbow, I pulled my eyelids open with my fingers.

Thin slits of light. Watering. Burning.

I was in a field lit by floodlights. Men lay motionless all around me. Others writhed and gagged and cried out in agony. Smoke drifted over the battlefield.

Suddenly I understood. We were in the perimeter of the enemy's camp! We had been machine gunned down! Men lying all around me had been shot!

But the battle was over. The enemy defeated. Medics wandered among the fallen, ministering to the wounded.

I felt for my rifle. I couldn't find it.

Then I realized I was one of the bodies on the ground.

Oh my God! I must have been hit! But where? I felt my legs. No, no, not my legs. It's my chest! I've been wounded in my chest! I could hardly breathe! Oh Jesus, Jesus, I've got a sucking chest wound!

I tried to yell "Medic!", but I doubled up, wheezing and coughing.

I pressed my hand to my chest and tried yelling again. "Somebody help me." My voice was hoarse from my chest wound. "I've been shot," I called.

Little time was left. Blood was filling my lungs.

"Help," I wheezed. "I'm dying."

A medic walked in my direction, ducking around and below the clouds of smoke. I waved him over.

He came closer and shouted, "Shut the fuck up, asshole." His face, without a gas mask, glowed like a cherry in the sun. Tears streamed down his cheeks.

"You abandoned your weapon." He kicked my leg. Hard. "Get back in your lane and stay on the ground before I beat the shit out of you."

We all assembled after the exercise. Two other trainees had abandoned their rifles. We had disgraced our platoons.

Our punishment was to low-crawl in front of everyone, retrieve our weapons from where they were stacked thirty feet away, and crawl back to the starting line.

The three of us reached our rifles at the same time. As we pulled them from the stack, a hidden CS gas grenade popped in our faces.

Saturday, Dec. 7, 1968
Dear Janice:

Yesterday we simulated a raid on a Viet Cong village. We had blanks in our M16s. Members of the cadre wore black pajamas and pretended to be Viet Cong.

I might have injured one of the Viet Cong pretenders. He was in an underground tunnel and flipped open the trapdoor just as I entered the hooch. I was so hopped up I stuck the muzzle of my M16 in his face and fired a blank and ran to the next hooch before I remembered he wasn't a real VC.

The reason I'm concerned is that the muzzle blast and wadding from a blank round, fired up close, can cause considerable injury, especially if fired in a person's face. I told one of the sergeants about it, but he said not to worry.

When I come home at Christmas time, let's play lots of games in bed. Okay?

Love, Andrew

Wednesday, Dec. 9-11, 1968

Dear Janice:

We've been doing live-fire exercises the last few days. The DIs give us live ammunition and we practice advancing, on line, firing our weapons. The ammunition we use includes tracers. We load a tracer in our magazines every fifth round.

One of the live-fire exercises goes like this. If we're ambushed, we're not supposed to drop to the ground. We're supposed to remain standing and move on line toward the enemy. The idea is to use superior fire power to keep the enemy's heads down until we walk up to their position and kill them. In each squad, one or two men fire automatic bursts. The other men fire individual shots.

I can't imagine this working in a jungle situation. Not only would we instinctively drop to the ground if ambushed, but I can't imagine how we could see where the enemy is nor advance through jungle vegetation "on line," granted we could advance at all. There has to be something here I don't understand. I asked a drill sergeant about it and he said, "Do as you're trained and adapt as conditions warrant."

Anyway, the effect of live-fire exercises at night is surreal. M16 muzzle flashes are star-shaped and rapid like strobe lights. The noise is sharp and metallic like high-performance motor bikes without mufflers. The streaking tracers, some of them ricocheting off rocks, are so beautiful it's hard to focus on what I'm supposed to be doing. It's like fireworks on the 4th of July.

One time I got so excited I advanced too fast and got ahead of the line. A sergeant ran up and grabbed hold of my belt and pulled me back.

He yelled, "Ya dumb fuck, you're gonna get shot by your own platoon!"

There's another exercise they call "leap frogging," at least some instructors call it that. It does make sense, but it's scary. Here's how it works:

We move in squads. The main part of the squad stays behind and two guys advance ahead to a predetermined point where there's cover (protection from enemy fire) and where the others can join them. But while the two guys are running ahead and the other guys are in protected places behind them, the protected guys are supposed to fire their weapons past the running guys to "cover" (or protect) them by forcing the enemy to keep their heads down. Then the two forward guys fire "cover" so their buddies can run up to the forward position.

It's the first run—by the two guys running ahead—that's scary. If the guys behind them aren't careful, they can shoot those two forward-running guys. I've seen tracers streak past me and I've wanted to turn around and yell, "Watch it, assholes!"

One of the sergeants told me that in real combat, the forward-running team often gets shot in the gut by the enemy or shot in the back by their friends. A no-win situation. But I can't imagine any better way a squad could advance under enemy fire while risking minimum casualties.

Graduation exercises are December 19. I'll get plane tickets for a flight home leaving that afternoon.

I'm excited about coming home. I still don't know where I'll be assigned. Hope it's Germany.

Love, Andrew

Tuesday, Dec. 17, 1968
Dear Janice:

My plane tickets are all screwed up. You'll probably get this before I'm home.

My plane tickets are for the 21st. So I have to hang around after graduation (which is on the 19th) until the 21st. Then, on the 21st, I don't depart until evening … and I have a layover between flights. So I won't arrive in Detroit until the afternoon of December 22.

I'm coming in on Delta Flight #4423 and landing at Metro at 4:05 pm—but the flight number and arrival time will probably change by then so I'll call from my layover airport as soon as I know for sure.

We have until January 9 to be together. That's the day I report to Oakland Army Base in San Francisco.

I received my orders today.

I'm going to Vietnam.

Andrew

THE FLIGHT TO WAR

Thursday, Jan 9, 1969 - San Francisco
Dear Janice:

It's late in the evening and I haven't reported to Oakland Army Base yet.

After my plane landed in San Francisco, I ran into Eric Becker at the airport terminal. He was in my training company in AIT but in another platoon. We didn't see much of each other.

His last day for reporting to Oakland is Saturday. Mine is today.

He wanted us to rent a hotel room and bum around San Francisco together until Saturday. Sounded like a great idea. What can the Army do to me? Send me to Vietnam? So we went outside and flagged a taxi and asked the driver to find us a cheap hotel. He did. The place is a dump, but it's good enough for us.

San Francisco is beautiful. You'd love it. We must have walked ten miles today just looking around. Took the trolley down the hills to the wharf. It's like in the movies. We looked around the docks, then rode the trolley back up again.

We stopped at a wonderful hole-in-the-wall used bookstore run by a little old lady who talked about Hemingway and Faulkner and Virginia Woolf as though they were old friends. Becker held up his end of the discussion pretty good, too. Turns out he has a few years of college and is quite well-read. So the three of us talked for two hours about novels we'd read and writers we liked. I bought a book of short stories and a magazine for the plane trip.

I loved being with you during Christmas and New Year's!

My God, you're beautiful when you're naked.

Your parents were so good to me. Your granddad is a great man. I love and admire him more than any man I know.

When we visited my folks ... I hope you had a good time like you said you did. I was pleased to hear from Mom about my brother's missionary activities, but I think her feelings were hurt when I said I didn't want to read his letters she handed me. So you took them and read a few. Thanks. And it was awkward when Dad said grace at every meal. It's nice I guess. That's one thing I appreciate about you and your family. Good Christians, but you don't say grace every frigging time you eat a snack.

I'm not sure it's a good thing being home two weeks prior to going to Vietnam. I didn't want to leave you. I was almost ready to ask you to go to Canada with me.

But all that doesn't change the fact that today, here in San Francisco, it's been a great day!

I love you so much, Andrew

Friday, Jan. 10, 1969 - San Francisco
Dear Janice:

It's Friday evening. I'm at Oakland Army Base. I changed my plans. I reported for duty this afternoon rather than wait another day.

I'm sitting on a cot in a mammoth warehouse. There must be over a thousand cots in here with a soldier or a duffle bag on every one. Everybody's waiting to go to Vietnam.

Today Eric and I were in a Chinese restaurant in Chinatown for lunch when I started feeling strange. I realize now I was getting scared, but at the time I didn't know it. Couldn't get my breath. Started sweating. It was bizarre. Never in my life have I had a feeling like that.

I tried to stay seated, but I had to move. I had to knock over a table, kick a chair, break a window. Do something. So I got up, paid for both our meals, and darn near ran out of the restaurant.

I knew I had to face this thing and not put it off. Putting it off would just make it worse. I had to face it.

I went back to the hotel. Left money on the bed for my part of the bill. Grabbed my duffel bag. Called a taxi. And told the driver to get me to Oakland Army Base. Fast!

I'm calm now, but I still feel funny. Nothing seems real. It's like a dream. I keep shaking my head. I can't believe this is happening.

If you were here, I could talk to you and hold you and walk around with you, and maybe that would help. But you're not here, and the feeling—I'll be honest with you—the feeling hasn't left yet. It's like a pressure on my chest. It comes with a "thud" every time I think about what's waiting for me.

Love, Andrew

Sunday, Jan. 12, 1969 - Flight to Vietnam
Dear Janice:

I'm on a plane bound for Anchorage, Alaska.

I spent two nights on a cot in that huge warehouse waiting to board a plane to go to war. It was awful. Lights on all the time.

They told us if we missed hearing our manifest number we'd sit on our cots another twenty-four hours.

My stomach stayed clenched the whole time. I barely slept.

The plane we're in is commercial. It carries 219 soldiers (or so they told us) plus stewardesses and pilots. Every seat is filled. So far I haven't seen anybody on the plane I recognize.

Everybody's jittery. The stewardesses are friendly and pretty, but too happy-happy. The guys are talking 'em up a lot, so maybe I'm being unfair.

After breakfast I read a long article in The New Yorker *I purchased in San Francisco. It was about protesting the war. The guy on my right next to the window leaned over and said, "They should be lined up and shot." I asked what he was talking about and he said, "Them, the protestors."*

If I hadn't been drafted, I might have been one of those protesters. Strange world.

I'm bored.

Hi again. We're beginning our descent into Anchorage. We've been told the total trip to Vietnam, including stops for fuel, will take 23 hours.

I'll write more later.

We're back in the air and on our way to Japan.

We didn't get off the plane back in Anchorage. It was just a fuel stop.

The book of short stories I bought in San Francisco is a hit among the other guys. Few if any of them brought reading material and now they're going crazy strapped in their seats with nothing to do. I have my New Yorker *so I'm letting the book circulate.*

It's Sunday. I hope you're having a good day.

I guess I'll read some more. By the time we get to Japan—certainly by the time we get to Vietnam—I will have read every word of every article and advertisement in The New Yorker *five or six times, probably more. Actually, the advertisements are quite interesting. Everything is presented as the optimum in casual sophistication. It's nauseating, but enticing, too.*

I'm alternating between feeling giddy, fearful, excited, and needing to go to the bathroom.

Be back in a few.

I'm back. Actually I've been back for quite awhile.

Drank a couple cups of coffee in the last thirty minutes. Woowie! I'm in the stratosphere. Higher than the plane. Way too much coffee. Been asking for extra cups the last few hours. Gotta stay awake for Vietnam. Why? I don't know. No, I do know. Don't want Vietnam sneaking up on me. Of course, we're not even to Japan yet, so I don't know how that could happen....

We landed in Japan. I'm writing this at a table in the airport. We've got a 90-minute layover here in Yokota.

The mountains of Japan are staggeringly beautiful. The most beautiful are sharp jagged edges rising up out of the ground. We saw Mount Fuji. It was more cone-shaped, like most volcanoes.

Japan would be a great place for a vacation.

Here in the airport, the designs of everything—tables, chairs, decorative things—are uniquely (we'd say) oriental. Bamboo, fish, and cloud-shrouded distant mountains are the primary motifs I can see from this table. Lovely stuff.

Back in the plane. Next stop Vietnam.

Everybody is tense and bored, too. My book of short stories circulated back to me a while ago. I tried to read a short story or two, but I can't hold onto the meaning of the words. They look like black marks on paper. I've flipped from one story to another, but I can't find anything that holds my attention. I put the book down ... well, in the pocket of the seat in front of me, and then I pull it out again.

Writing helps pass the time, but I have nothing else to say. Guess I'll write you something a little later.

Hi again. I've been getting leg cramps. Dad called them "Charlie horses." Even my arms are getting cramps in them. I guess it's from the stress of ... what? Maybe flying to war?

I'm going to get up and walk to the bathroom. Might help. We'll talk later.

I've been back awhile. Decided to write a little more.

Everybody's coiled tight as a spring.

Seems hot in here. Maybe that's just me. The guy next to me is shivering.

Hold on … A stewardess started crying! Unbelievable! Hugged a guy in the aisle … mascara's dripping down her cheeks. Walked to the rear of the plane. Hands over her face.

This her first trip? Not good.

Hot news: Blond stewardess walked down the aisle holding the hand of a guy walking behind her. What's that about? Now a bunch of guys are raising their hands and wanting to hold the blond stewardess's hand walking up and down the aisle.

Ha! And she's doing it. Taking turns with them.

Just woke up.

Everybody's talking really loud. Excited. Must be close.

How would they know? Maybe the pilot announced something while I was asleep?

Guy in the seat next to me, on the aisle side, grinned and told me he's going to call the stewardess ….

Oops! Cancel that.

Pilot announced we're off the coast of South Vietnam!!

Our plane is descending. Men piling up at windows.

Wow. Hope you can read this.

I've been looking out the window.

Hazy air. Wispy clouds.

Looks like a rumpled green blanket down there. Tiny little fires like sparks. Smoke columns trailing up.

Winding river. Maybe Saigon River??

Now I can see helicopters. Way, way down there … like low flying insects.

Wish me luck.

Andrew

PART TWO
VIETNAM

INCOUNTRY

Monday, Jan. 13, 1969 - Long Binh Base Camp
Dear Janice:

We landed on an airstrip at Bien Hoa Air Force Base. It's pronounced "Ben Whah."

The humidity and heat hit us like a wall when we walked off the plane. It was early evening. Still light. Humidity so thick I couldn't get my breath.

Looked around in all directions. Saw lots of planes on the tarmac. Jets. Cargo carriers. Helicopters further off from the runway protected by free-standing, six-foot-high walls on either side of every chopper. Hueys with side doors off or slid back. Giant double-rotor Chinooks. Jeeps and gas tankers and tool trucks running everywhere.

Further off, lots of Quonset huts and one-story wood buildings. Screened windows run the full length of the wood buildings and downward slanted wood slats cover the screens for protection from sun and rain.

Men walking around without weapons. Must be safe here?

Workers pulled our duffle bags from the plane's cargo locker and dumped them on the tarmac a little distance from the plane. They turned on two mobile flood lights—getting dark fast—and set us loose looking for our duffle bags.

Carrying our duffles, we boarded seven buses. A sergeant in our bus stood up front and yelled, "We're driving between base camps to Long Binh." He pronounced it "Long Ben."

Guy in the back of the bus yelled, "Why you got heavy fence mesh over the windows for?"

Sergeant yelled back, "So the VC can't throw a grenade through the windows, Private Low-Watt." The sergeant must hear that question every trip.

Black tape on the bus headlights reduced them to bright slits. An armored jeep with a M60 machine gun mounted on a post led the way. Another jeep, similarly equipped, followed at the rear.

Took at least forty-five long minutes in the dark driving to Long Binh. They assigned us barracks. Said we'd stay at Long Binh at least a week doing perimeter guard duty until we're assigned our permanent units somewhere out across the countryside.

Love, Andrew

Monday, Feb. 10, 1969 - Cu Chi Base Camp
Dear Janice:

Got your letters. Dozens of them! Had a great time reading them, smelling the Tabu Perfume, kissing your lipstick smootches. Here are the answers to your questions.

The office I work in (S-1) is the central office of the 182nd Engineer Battalion that's comprised of seven hundred men organized into six companies designated by letters of the alphabet (except for Headquarters Company I'm in). We refer to those companies by using short-wave radio designators for the letters. Alpha Company, Bravo Company, etc.

Our building has a cement floor. The walls are plaster board and painted light green. In our office we have five green metal desks that have four-inch deep rectangular depressions in them for our Remington Manual Typewriters. My desk is at the back of the office, furthest from the door.

Behind my desk a short hall leads to a narrow room containing ditto and mimeograph machines on a long, narrow table. The rest of the room is filled with reams of paper and double-sheeted ditto and stencil masters, and cans of chemicals for the duplicating machines.

The open doorway at the front of our office leads to a corridor and an outside screen door. Follow the corridor to the left and it takes you to the Personnel Office. That office maintains personnel files on all the men assigned to our battalion, including the colonel and the major. Personnel has ten desks for nine clerks and a warrant officer who's in charge of the office.

Cu Chi Base Camp gets its name from the nearby town of Cu Chi. The camp itself is enormous. Must be over a mile across. Studded with barracks and office buildings. Mess halls. Outhouses. Machine shops. Repair shops. Medical services. An asphalt plant. Heavy equipment yards. Truck yards. Howitzer enclaves. Ammo dumps. Chopper pads. Plane hangers. And a runway in the middle of the camp!

The 25th Infantry Division (also called "Tropic Lightning") is the main military unit at our base camp. I've been told Tropic Lightning has thirteen thousand men in it, but most of them are out in the boonies or stationed at fire bases. Fire bases are small camps with big artillery guns that provide support for infantry in the field.

Our battalion provides engineering support for Tropic Lightning by paving roads, building chopper walls ("revetments"), constructing buildings, and paving and repairing the base camp's runway for fixed-wing aircraft (vs. helicopters).

No, our letters aren't censored like GI mail in WWII. At least that's what the adjutant told me.

Yes, I come back to the office at night to type my letters. The adjutant and Major Roberts said it's okay.

Love, Andrew

UGLY TRUTH, UGLY JUSTICE

"Specialist Jones died proudly serving in America's military struggle against communism and for the preservation of freedom for the South Vietnamese people and the citizens of the United States of America." That's the kind of thing I type over the signature of the colonel to the family members of men who've died as a result of enemy action—even if enemy action means the poor guy was stoned and stumbled into a known enemy minefield to take a piss.

Being in charge of processing awards is interesting, frustrating, and emotionally challenging work. I know who, when, where, how, and why any man in our battalion is killed or injured by accident or by enemy activity. I help type letters of condolence to the families of those men, and I type Purple Heart recommendations for men injured but not killed by enemy fire (KIAs are automatically issued Purple Hearts by higher headquarters based on the "cause of death" listed on their death certificates). I also review, edit, and often compose and type (for illiterate NCOs and officers) recommendations for medals awarded to our men for meritorious achievement and heroic action.

Letters of condolence are the worst things I deal with because they're the most troubling and troublesome to edit and type. The colonel and his editor/typists (we clerks) bury ugly truth under euphemisms and generalities in our letters to grieving families. Some people might call those letters "cover-ups," especially when we obscure facts about men who died from friendly fire (that's when GIs mistakenly fire on their buddies).

Most people don't realize friendly fire happens all the time in a war zone. When we tell these naïve civilians that their son or husband was killed by friendly fire, they get outraged and want to know how this could possibly happen. But it's not difficult to figure out if they'd stop and think about it a minute or two.

Imagine how many mistakes are made each day by professionals in a big corporate headquarters building or a big department store. Not everybody, but a few of those people make fairly serious mistakes every day. Not enough to screw up the whole corporate operation, but enough to fuck up a shipment, or screw up a contract, or shelve the wrong gadgets on the wrong shelf and create serious problems for at least a handful of people. I'm not saying this because I've taken a survey or read about it somewhere. I'm saying this because it's been true everywhere I've worked, and everyone I've talked to says it's true everywhere they've worked. People are prone to making mistakes. I figure I'm doing well if I get away with two fuck-ups a week, and often it's more than that. Now multiply two fuck-ups a week times the number of people who work around you, and you have your average fucked-up day. And you *know* a lot of people make mistakes every day driving the highways of most cities because you hear the ambulance sirens.

Now imagine how often mistakes are made by heavily armed soldiers juiced up with fear and excitement. Their blood pressure pops out their face and neck veins, they have tunnel vision, some are pissing their pants, and they're so strung out they can forget to flip off the safety on their M16s and can't figure out why their rifle won't fire. Combine that with the fact that grunts out in the boonies often can't see past the foliage in front of them and will fire at almost anything that moves or makes a sound, including a lost GI squad that's trying to follow a map in a thick jungle. Now add on the mistakes made by officers and NCOs planning military operations and calculating artillery and bombing coordinates. So injuries and death from friendly fire are fairly common. Civilians back in the States don't hear much about it because everybody in a combat zone wants to save the guy who killed his buddies from punishment and further disgrace. They figure he'll be fucked-up for life anyway. And it could just as easily have been them. So the guy's buddies cook up a story in the field and higher headquarters never finds out what actually happened, and a Purple Heart is issued for the injured or killed victim.

So, we write letters of condolence to the families of guys we know died from friendly fire, but we don't award them Purple Hearts—and I therefore don't have to type the their recommendations—because one of the criteria for receiving a Purple Heart is that injury or death must come from enemy fire. You'd think that would be a big clue to the families of guys killed by friendly fire—why no Purple Heart?—but you'd be surprised how many families don't pick up on it.

Anyway, our so-called "cover-ups" in condolence letters for friendly-fire casualties (and stupid accidents not related to friendly fire), are acts of kindness for the families, not just acts of bureaucratic self-protection. When we receive letters from home asking for more information, and we seldom get such inquires, we send back additional facts in measured doses commensurate with the demand.

Here's the core of the problem I'm trying to get at. How can a parent, wife, or child share with family and friends the obscenity and indignity, even stupidity, of how some of these men die? Imagine a mourning widow telling her husband's parents, "The Army says he died when he broke his neck falling off the back of a truck while returning from the local massage parlor." In many cases, it would be downright cruel to tell family members the truth. So we don't. We obfuscate the hell out of it.

Compared to infantry units, we have few combat casualties. Those that occur at night are from attacks on the base camp. Those that occur during the day are from snipers and booby traps at construction sites on the road. We've had a few "holy shit" exceptions to the rule, including a booby trap planted in one of our six-hole shitters—more about that in a minute.

While we don't have as many combat casualties as infantry units do, we have construction accidents infantry units don't have. Oh, and we have our share of meaningless, stupid deaths common to all military units in a combat zone.

But regardless of how our men die, we always, in our letters of condolence, describe a dead GI as having died in the performance of his duty, no matter how remote from duty his death might be, like the aforementioned classic of walking into a *known* minefield to take a leak. Any idiot who did that in our unit, we'd give him a Purple Heart. Not for stupidity, but for death caused by enemy action—the planted enemy land mine—and we wouldn't mention that the minefield was known or marked. Here's a real-life example of what I'm talking about.

One of our guys got killed by a boom-boom girl. We gave him a Purple Heart for death by enemy action "while investigating hostile activity in a hooch near his work site." The whore *didi-maued* out a back window, but we know how it happened because his work buddies knew why he went in there and they went after him when he didn't come out. They found him with his pants down and his throat slit. The guy's buddies won't expose our "cover-up" because they liked the guy and they hope the same kindness will be shown to their families, too, if needed.

We typed our worst batch of condolence letters soon after I joined the battalion. It was one of those "holy shit" incidents. Four men were killed and three injured by a booby trap planted in Bravo Company's six-hole shitter located near one of Bravo's pissers. The bomb went off one evening after supper. Two of the injured men were standing near the pisser. The bomb was a quart-sized orange juice can filled with plastic explosive that was planted and triggered under the crapping hole opposite the door to the shitter, a hole seldom used unless most holes are already occupied. This location for the booby trap provided reasonable assurance that the bomb would not go off until after supper when the crapper was in maximum use and the VC bitch who planted the bomb would be safely off the base camp with all the other Vietnamese day workers.

We think we know how the device was triggered. But first a few words about shitters and pissers.

A shitter (some guys call it a "crapper") is not equipped to handle a lot of liquid, so a soldier on a base camp is supposed to piss, when at all convenient, in a pisser, not a shitter. A pisser is a fifty-five gallon steel drum open at both ends and buried vertically within two or three inches of its top edge. Water is then poured in the barrel and topped off with several inches of oil. Streams of urine sink through the floating oil and gradually soak, with the water, into the soil below. Each pisser is surrounded, for privacy, by shoulder-high corrugated galvanized sheet-steel with an overlapping entry way or a spring-hinged door.

The holes in the battalion's six-hole shitters are about four feet off the ground. Steps lead up to a door somewhere in the middle of the front wall of a six-hole shitter. Between the waist-high front wall and the six-hole seat-box there's a narrow walkway that runs the length of the building. The waist-high front wall allows for a little privacy, and comfort level is increased by a mosquito screen that runs from the waist-high wall up to the roof. Guys sitting in the crapper can look through the screen and see anybody in the area, but people in the area can't easily see the seated guys through the screen. So you can read and relieve yourself at your leisure, with a little privacy, and without too many mosquitoes except for those pesky little devils who come up the back way and bite you in the ass.

Shitter buildings are fully enclosed except in back, below the crapping holes, where cut-off ends of fifty-five gallon drums, one for each hole, collect droppings. Butt cheeks and balls can be seen pooching down through the crapping holes by mama-sans who, once a day, bend over and look up at each crapper hole to make sure it's not occupied before using long steel hooks to pull out full barrel ends and replace them with empty ones. The mama-sans haul the full barrel ends on a flatbed wagon to a far corner of an equipment yard, at the edge of the base camp, and burn the shit with kerosene.

A conscientious practice for a GI about to take a shit during the day (when the mama-sans are on the base camp) is to look through his selected crapping hole to ensure a mama-san isn't in the process of removing the shit can. If he sees a mama-san through the hole looking up or pulling out a full can, as sometimes happens, the man uses another hole or, if he's a mean bastard, he calls hello and turns around and does his business.

The center holes are never used during the day because the door, when opened, exposes the bare legs and pants-at-the-ankles of any man sitting there. But all six holes are occupied many evenings after our men come in from a hard day's work, eat a big supper, and go for a leisurely crap.

The bomb was set off, or so we believe, by three or four wires stretched close together and roughly parallel across a shit can under one of the center holes. Those wires were attached to a triggering device on the orange juice can that was positioned out of sight under the crapper's walkway. The wires—not easily seen in the shadows—were jerked by crap falling from a height of four feet. That's what triggered the bomb.

I talked to a man who was in the shithouse, seated at the end, at the time of the explosion. He miraculously escaped serious injury. He told me, months later when he could hear again, that after the explosion he *felt* a thick silence (probably from damaged eardrums and the residual tactile effects of blast pressure). And as he lay with his pants around his ankles amidst the smoke and scattered boards and bodies in this thick molasses silence, he saw the man next to him look in astonishment at scattered pieces of himself before he died.

After the injured were medevaced and driven to hospital units, men from other companies went over to help Bravo clean up the mess. They burned what was left of the shitter and built a new one.

The colonel wrote up a letter of condolence for the four families of the men who were killed. But when the head clerk got the handwritten draft, the rest of us agreed it needed revision. The colonel was so outraged he couldn't keep his language in check. He alluded to the circumstances of the deaths in ways that would prompt readers to ask too many questions, and this was one story we definitely didn't want the families of those men to hear. So the head clerk typed up another version that included our recommended changes, most of which the colonel accepted.

The final letter included sentences like the one I mentioned earlier: "Specialist Jones died proudly serving in America's military struggle against communism and for the preservation of freedom for the South Vietnamese people and the citizens of the United States of America." I'd like to put a footnote of apology on every letter of that kind I type, but I also understand the need for boilerplate phrases that honor the dead while hiding the details that no sane family wants to know.

We clerks typed that bullshit over and over. We had to produce one original and four duplicates for each of the four letters. That meant each letter had to be typed perfectly two times, once with two carbons and once with one carbon, since four sheets of carbon paper and four sheets of typing paper under a master sheet won't stay aligned when the typewriter's platen rolls up the paper for the next line of type.

Typing those condolence letters was tedious and emotionally exhausting. Of course, that's true for all condolence letters. I know grieving family members will hold and read the very piece of paper I'm typing and rolling out of the typewriter, so I'm fully sympathetic to the fact that condolence letters can't have a single mistake or white-carbon correction on the original.

And since I'm the awards clerk, I was responsible for typing three Purple Heart recommendations for the surviving injured men. As I mentioned earlier, Purple Hearts for our dead GIs would be awarded and sent to the families by higher headquarters.

Even though I understand the need to shield family members from the truth, I was outraged by the obfuscating dishonesty of the condolence letters and I was incensed by the ludicrous nature of the Purple Heart recommendations. Giving a medal to a soldier for being wounded or killed while taking a crap is an affront to the man's dignity. That's why we fudged the details in the condolence letters. How could a grieving parent, wife, brother or sister, tell friends something like that about the man they loved? Or the guy's kids? It's not something any man would want them to know. There's no good way to tell a man's family he was blown up while taking a leisurely shit and reading a magazine.

I'm not sure what it was—nerves? rage?—but I'd screw up the typing of those letters and recommendations on my Remington Manual Typewriter time after time. I'd get close to the end of a perfectly typed letter, and then, in the last line or in the colonel's signature block, I'd fuck it up again. Or I'd forget to wipe the damned sweat off my hands and forearms—we work in the tropics without air conditioners, so I keep a rag in my desk for that little chore—and I'd leave a sweaty thumb print on the original or drip sweat off my forearm onto the letter when I laid the letter on the desk to separate out the carbons.

The mama-san everybody thought set the booby trap was caught three days after the explosion. An officer from Charlie Company, Lieutenant Archie Armstrong—a weasel of a man with thin, hairless arms and thin fingers with long nails—told three of us clerks about the captured mama-san a week later when he made an unusual visit to our hooch with a bottle of Jack Daniels.

Since officers seldom fraternize with the troops, the whole situation was odd and made us uncomfortable. We figured he wanted to do some bragging and wanted us enlisted men to boost him up and be in awe of what he helped to do. What can I say? He's an asshole. Anyway, we laid around on our cots, drank his booze and listened. He didn't spare any details, and the drunker he got, the more he talked.

Archie said he'd gone over to Bravo Company's headquarters office to talk with Captain Larson about the explosion in Bravo's shit house when Colonel Hackett charged in. Hackett, who has deep-set dark eyes and a jutting lower jaw that make him formidable when angry, told them the mama-san responsible for the booby trap had been caught on a road we were repairing near Tay Ninh. Two men from Bravo Company recognized her and chased her down the road and across a field. Hackett said she was being held in battalion headquarters and that he was taking her on a chopper ride. He poked his finger at Larson and said he needed to come along and do his duty for the men he'd lost.

Then Hackett looked at Archie as though he'd just noticed Archie was in the room. Hackett said Archie should come along because he might be needed. Archie said okay and away they went.

Hackett was pumped, Archie said. The whole time they were getting Mama-san out of the office and into the jeep, and then on the way to the chopper, he kept talking about justice being served. But Larson said nothing. He kept looking at Mama-san and frowning, shaking his head.

Archie didn't know why, but Hackett didn't have Mama-san tied up or shackled, so when they arrived at the air field, she pushed away and refused to get on the chopper. She kept saying, "Mama-san no go, Mama-san no go."

Hackett and Archie gave their M16s to Larson and they tried picking up

Mama-san to throw her through the Huey's open side door. But she wiggled and squirmed and rolled and grabbed at their shirts or anything she could get her hands on to keep from being thrown in that chopper.

Finally, Hackett pulled away from the struggle with Mama-san and she fell to the ground. He pulled his .45 semi-automatic from his holster, locked and loaded, and aimed it at her chest.

"You bitch, you fight us one more second and I'll blow a hole the size of my fist between your fucking tits. Now climb on that chopper or so help me God I'll kill you right now."

Mama-san remained on the ground staring at Hackett. Silent. Unmoving.

"Larson! Archie! Pick this bitch up and throw her on the chopper. Punch her in the face if you have to. Break her jaw."

Captain Larson was trembling. His thin lips, sensitive eyes, and steel-rimmed spectacles were those of a frightened librarian. Hackett looked at him. "What the fuck's wrong with you? Help Archie! Larson?" But Larson was focused on Archie.

Archie had pulled Mama-san to her feet and slugged her, knocking her to the ground. He dragged the limp and dazed sixty-pound woman to the chopper. Hackett went over and helped Archie pick her up and roll her through the open side door of the Huey. They pushed her to the middle of the floor in front of the four canvas seats attached to the motor housing.

Hackett and Archie retrieved their M16s from Larson and waited for Larson to hop on the chopper. Then they followed him and strapped themselves in. Mama-san was still dazed and lying on the floor in front of them. Hackett yelled at the pilot to take off, and the chopper started its run and lifted into the sky.

Once they were in the air, Archie said he was positive Hackett was going to dump Mama-san out one of the open side doors of the Huey. Hackett kept kicking her, from his belted seat, toward one open door and then the other open door as she rolled about, trying to get oriented. He yelled at her, calling her a goddamned murdering bitch who ought to suck air. But throwing her out would have been difficult, even dangerous, because she had fought them like a wild cat, and she could take one of them over the edge with her.

As it turned out, Hackett had already talked to the pilot about where to go. The pilot set the chopper down in a field not far from Cu Chi. Hackett jumped out of the chopper and turned around and yelled at Larson.

"So what are you going to do?"

But Hackett didn't wait for Larson to reply. He walked away from the chopper, looking here and there, acting as though things were taking place behind him in accord with his implied order. But Archie, Larson, and the Mama-san stayed put. Archie said he lost sight of Hackett when Hackett walked back behind the chopper's tail rotor.

Mama-san couldn't understand or speak English very well, but she understood the situation. Her face was smeared with dirt and tears, and a red-veined lump had swelled from her nose and eye to her left ear. Her eye was swelling shut.

She locked her arms around Larson's leg and rocked back and forth. She cried out above the *whump-whump-whump* of the chopper blades and roar of the motor: "Big GI no hurt Mama-san! No hurt Mama-san!" Then, "Big GI fuck Mama-san? You like fuck Mama-san!"

She yelled that over and over. Archie said her voice started cracking and went all high and squeaky. Within moments her voice was gone, or the chopper drowned out whatever voice she had left.

But here's the kicker, Archie said. The moment Hackett disappeared behind the Huey, Mama-san started caressing Larson between his legs. Larson pushed her hand away, but Mama-san didn't let up.

Archie said it was the damnedest thing he ever saw. He figured Larson had been humping Mama-san since he'd arrived incountry.

Moments later, when Hackett came back from behind the chopper, he saw what Mama-san was doing. His lips pulled back from clenched teeth and he leaned through the door of the chopper and hit her on the head with the butt of his M16. She rolled on the floor moaning, holding both hands to her head.

Hackett yelled at Larson. "So what's it gonna be?"

Larson yelled back, "I'm not sure, Sir."

"What the fuck do you mean you're not sure?"

"I know what I want to do, Sir, but I'm not easy about it."

"You think you're going to let this VC bitch go?"

"But how can we be sure Mama-san did it?"

"What kind of candy-ass are you?" Hackett was twisting and turning with rage. "Get your fucking ass out here and do what you need to do for the honor of your men!"

Larson didn't move. Archie said Larson's hands were porcelain white from gripping his M16. His eyes were bugging out at Hackett.

Hackett turned and walked straight away from the chopper's open door.

He looked up through the whirling chopper blades and held out his hands, palms up, as if beseeching God. Then he did an about-face and stormed back to the chopper.

Larson yelled as Hackett approached. "We can't know she's the mama-san who did it!"

"She's the only goddamned Vietnamese day worker assigned to Bravo Company's shit house who didn't show up the day after the explosion or any day since, you fucking jackass! And that's by your own goddamned account." Hackett was going hoarse from all the yelling.

"Jesus fucking Christ, man, this woman murdered four of your men and sent three young boys out on medevac! You have responsibility to seek justice for *dead* men, butchered men, men who *trusted* you as their officer. God damn it, Larson, *do* something about it!"

Hackett's face had turned purple.

Larson didn't move. Mama-san didn't move. All they heard, said Archie, was the *whump-whump-whump* of the rotor blades and the roar of the chopper's motor.

Suddenly Hackett lunged and grabbed Mama-san's ankle and yanked her off the chopper. She slashed her arm on the edge of the floor and thudded her head on the chopper's runner.

Hackett kicked her. "Get up. Stand up."

He locked and loaded his M16.

"Get up you fucking VC cunt! Start running!"

Mama-san got up and stood shaking within arm's length of Hackett. Her head was bloody and her arm was bleeding. She wasn't crying anymore. Her one open eye was round with fear. The bottom of her dress was wet, but not with blood.

Hackett palm punched her shoulder, and her arms swung like a soggy rag doll. Hackett pointed across the field. "Run, you cocksucking VC!"

Mama-san jumped past Hackett, stumbled, caught herself, and ran.

Archie said she got no more than twenty feet away when Hackett shot from the hip and emptied a full clip on automatic that started in her ass, climbed up her back, and blew open her head. Hackett reloaded, walked up to the body, and pulped her with another clip.

Larson unbuckled and jumped out the other side of the chopper and threw up.

———————

Back in the hooch, we clerks waited for Archie to continue his story, but he stopped and looked at the floor. He reached for the bottle of Jack Daniels, poured himself a quarter tumbler of whiskey, and slowly recapped the empty bottle. He appeared to be reflecting on something. Then he chugged the booze in one swallow as though it were beer.

I grimaced. "You okay, Archie?"

"Yeah, I'm ... ah ...." He waved his hand as though I were far away. "Woozy, that's all."

"You talk to Larson since this happened?"

"Nope. Larson won't ... talk. He's history around ... anyway. He'll be ... he'll ... shhhhipp off soon as ...."

I waited for Archie to collect his thoughts. Then I asked, "You think Mama-san planted the booby-trap?"

"Huh? Wha...?"

"You think she really did it? Maybe another mama-san did it and your mama-san knew about it and didn't show up the next day because she knew how the guys might react. Maybe the real VC is still pulling shit cans from Bravo Company's new shitter."

"I ... ah ... humm." Archie shook his head to clear his eyes and his confusion over his inability to read his watch. Finally he looked up.

"The mama-san? Fuck ... I dohn know." His tongue and lips weren't working right. "Good sssstory for the kids back home, though."

Archie got up and staggered out the hooch door. He stumbled into the waist-high wall of sandbags and fell to the ground in a drunken stupor.

We decided to let him sleep it off.

"He'll be okay out there."

"Yeah, bring him in the hooch and he'll throw up on our cots."

After Archie collapsed outside there wasn't much of anything we wanted to talk about. I walked to my bunk and lay down with my boots on and stared at the tin roof overhead. The other men went to their bunks, too. One man turned off the overhead lights at our end of the hooch, so all the hooch lights were off.

As soon as the lights went out I knew I'd had too much to drink. I needed light to keep my head from spinning.

I got up, staggered in the dark to the screen door, and stepped outside.

The moonlight was blue and the air chilly. I looked up at the sky. I quickly stepped back, unsteady, and walked to the end of the hooch and threw up.

I sat on the sandbags awhile. How long I don't know.

At some point I must have scooted down between the hooch and the sandbags and fallen asleep. That's where I found myself in the morning. Archie was gone.

———————

Saturday, Mar. 8, 1969 - Cu Chi Base Camp
Dear Janice:

Happy Birthday! I forgot until this morning that today is your birthday. Sorry. But I'll make it up to you with presents fit for a queen! Let me explain.

There's a giant PX commissary on the base camp and they sell everything a soldier could possibly want. Jim Beam. Crown Royal. Wild Turkey. Smirnoff. Beefeater. All for the equivalent of four dollars a quart. Not a fifth. A quart!

Har har, me matey, and a wee bit of rum, too!

But seriously, they have toothpaste, deodorant, bars of soap, shaving lotion, all basic-needs stuff I can buy with my monthly pay … which comes in Military Payment Certificates (MPC) so the VC and NVA don't acquire American greenbacks for use on the international black market.

That reminds me. When I signed up for my pay, after getting assigned to the 182nd Engineer Battalion, I specified that half my month's pay be automatically sent home to you. If we save all of it while I'm over here, we should have enough to buy a used car for me and you can use your Mustang for whatever you want.

Now back to your birthday presents.

The PX has a mail-order catalog in which high-quality merchandise is half-price or less with free shipping. Charges are deducted from my pay here in Vietnam. So I'll order for delivery to you an eight-place set of Noritake China (black rimmed white porcelain with gold edges), eight gold-rimmed lead-glass water goblets, a moonstone bracelet, and four yards of heavy silk cloth of shimmering green and gold for a sexy, sleeveless, sheath dress. I'll let you know when you can start looking for the Parcel Post truck.

You asked about my sleeping quarters. We call it a hooch. It's a wood-frame building with a galvanized tin roof, a cement floor, and it's divided by interior plywood walls into two-man rooms. Each room has enough space for two cots, two footlockers, and two upright steel lockers. One end of the room is the outside hooch wall, and the other end opens to the hooch's center walkway. Most guys hang bead curtains across those openings for additional privacy.

Love, Andrew

BRONZE STARS & PURPLE HEARTS

Real heroes deserve more than medals. They deserve open-mouthed wonder and quiet, heartfelt thanks and praise. There's no meaningful comparison between a medal and what some of these men do. But standing them in front of a formation and pinning a medal on their chests is what we have to give them.

Bronze Stars. Purple Hearts. Army Commendation Medals. Those are the most common medals we award our men. Sometimes I have stacks of them on my desk waiting for our official awards ceremonies. You'd think the ceremonies—the most revered ceremonies of all time, honoring war heroes—would be the high point of my work, but they're not. For me, they're a time of deep embarrassment.

The medals we hand out are cheap alloy and plastic hanging on a ribbon with a safety pin on the back. It isn't that the medals should be made better or the metal should be more expensive or the ribbon of higher quality. It's that there's something ludicrous—inherently absurd—about giving a man a little medal for having his leg blown off or risking his life for his buddies or killing an exceptional number of VC while putting his life in great danger.

The ceremonies are phony, too. More than once I've stood next to the colonel in front of rows of men standing at attention and looked down at my awards list and the medals I'm holding to make sure I'm handing the colonel the right medal for the right man—he seldom knows who's getting what—and my helmet slides down my sweaty forehead. I always catch it with the hand that's holding the awards list and push the helmet back on my head, but I have visions of it falling and rolling between the colonel and the winner of a Bronze Star for Valor.

And the men standing in formation? They're hot, sweaty, and bored out of their fucking minds. In the opinion of most draftees, an award is like a little gold stick-um star on the foreheads of chumps who've risked their lives in a war we can't win, can't manage, and shouldn't have entered in the first place. That might be irritating or upsetting for some people to hear, but it's how most of the men in our battalion see these medals—unless they're awarded one.

As for myself, even if I set aside my low opinion of this ridiculous war, I'm still ambivalent about these medals. I don't see how these cheap things can represent what heroes do. So the bottom line of my rant is that I'm proud to do my job to the best of my ability and help get meaningless medals for true heroes.

The guy who did this job before I got here didn't care at all about the work he did. He had no filing or tracking system whatsoever. When I first arrived, all I had to work with was a disorganized pile of carbon copies of the original award recommendations he forwarded to higher headquarters. I found the pile in one of my desk drawers.

The problem wasn't only that the copies were disorganized. The guy left no indication of their current status: pending, rejected, or approved. Some copies had big X's scrawled on them and some did not. Some had little checks at the top and some did not. Some were dated recently, some almost a year ago. He apparently discarded the original copies that came back from higher headquarters with "approved" or "rejected" checked in the appropriate boxes. Why discard them? I guess because they were rejected (so why keep them?), or, they were approved and came with the medals requested (so, again, why keep them?).

I don't know how he got away with it.

On the *third* day I worked in S-1, Colonel Hackett came out of his office early in the morning, walked over to my desk, and stood looking at me. I hesitated a moment, then I jumped up, knocking over my chair, and stood at attention.

"Yes, Sir?"

"How many awards we got pending, young man?" Hackett was so close he was looking at the pores on my nose.

"I don't know, Sir, but I'll—"

"What do you mean you don't know?" His jutting jaw and dark eyes were fearsome.

"I mean—"

"Isn't that your job?"

"Yes Sir, but the filing system is screwed up, and it'll—"

"Then unscrew it. I want that information after lunch."

I worked through the morning and my lunch break frantically studying a year's worth of paperwork, trying to detect some kind of sorting system. I was interrupted every few minutes when I had to answer one of three phones on my desk—an assignment the other clerks gave me as a "learn-the-ropes" job. They had the same phones on their desks, and they answered a phone only when two calls came in at the same time. I scrambled for information, misdirected phone calls, and randomly punched buttons. I was scared out of my wits. Any problems created by my confused phone work were directly attributable to me, of course, and by the end of the day I'd been reamed a new asshole by several sergeants and a couple officers. I also finished a priority typing assignment for Major Roberts given to me by Adjutant Harris. I didn't dare ask the other clerks for help during my first week on the job for fear of creating suspicion I was trying for a short-cut to paying my dues.

After a couple of hours sorting through the pile of award recommendations, I finally concluded there was no way to know, judging from the papers in my desk, how many were pending. I asked Adjutant Harris about it. He said the only award records S-1 had should be in my desk. The personnel office had records, he went on to say, both of submitted recommendations and received awards, scattered throughout the personnel files. But locating them would entail a week's worth of searching, and Chief Warrant Officer Prescott, the man in charge of personnel—an all business and no-nonsense guy—would never allow it. Not for me, anyway. A newbie.

I had no choice but to call the awards office in Group Headquarters at Long Binh and find out from them how many awards were pending for our battalion, and assume that neither Roberts nor Hackett were sitting on award recommendations not yet sent to higher headquarters.

The sergeant in the awards office at Group Headquarters expressed contempt for my "newbie ignorance"—he thoroughly rattled me—but he gave me what I thought was sufficient information to satisfy Hackett. I typed it on a piece of paper and had it ready to hand Hackett when he walked in the door.

But Hackett didn't return to the office after lunch or later in the afternoon.

Just before quitting time at 6:00 p.m., David Connors, S-1's legal clerk, told me that Hackett had scheduled the afternoon for inspecting road construction sites and had no intention of returning to the office any time after lunch. So I placed the memo on Hackett's desk.

He never mentioned it.

But the problem wasn't solved. The sergeant at Group Headquarters only gave me the number of awards still pending. I was so nervous and intimidated I forgot to ask him the names of the men and the medals for which they'd been recommended.

The next day I told Adjutant Harris about the mistake I'd made and asked him what I should do about it. He said I had no choice but to call Group Headquarters again and get the missing information.

The sarcasm and verbal abuse I took during that second phone call were withering.

After the reaming I got that first week, I swore I would never be caught without complete and correct information again. So I created a kickass filing system using one file drawer in my desk and one wooden card catalog on top of my desk.

The file drawer holds the carbon copies of award recommendations, each in its own manila folder, filed alphabetically by the man's last name.

The card catalog has five sections corresponding to each ascending stage in the award assessment process: (1) Major; (2) Colonel; (3) Higher Headquarters; (4) Approved; and (5) Rejected. Each of those sections is subdivided into medal titles: Army Commendation Medal, Bronze Star, Purple Heart, etc. I make a 3x5 card for each man recommended for a medal and file it in the appropriate medal subdivision starting in the major's section. If and when the major approves it, I move it forward to the appropriate subdivision of the colonel's section—and so on—as the assessment process proceeds. Using this system I can easily track and count every award recommendation throughout the assessment process.

After two months on the job, Hackett ordered me to start *screening* award recommendations. That kind of pre-judging for rejects ordinarily should have been done by an awards officer or NCO, but S-1 didn't have one because we were understaffed.

So Hackett called me into his office one day and upbraided me for passing on to Roberts and himself award recommendations he said I "damn well knew" were poorly written or cited actions inappropriate for the medal being recommended. He said he wanted me to bounce those recommendations back to the recommending officer or NCO with suggestions for improvement.

Thanks a lot.

A SPC-4 clerk needs United Nations level diplomatic skills to tell officers and NCOs they don't write well, or that the award candidate's actions, described in the recommendation, aren't worth a medal.

But that's what I've been doing. Following Hackett's guidelines, I've been screening and sometimes editing every award recommendation received by our office. I reject, with explanatory notes and suggestions for improvement, award recommendations that fail minimum standards of coherent writing or that fail minimum standards of meritorious action (as specified by Hackett and Army REGS criteria). If I have doubts about a submitted recommendation, I check with Hackett or Roberts. Any officer or NCO can bypass me and submit an award recommendation directly to Roberts or Hackett, but they have to justify to Hackett why I'm being bypassed.

It takes a lot of time writing a diplomatic explanation for a recommendation's rejection and then suggestions for improvement. I think I'm getting better at it. One of my standard openings has become, "Thank you for your concern that (man's name) be recognized for his (bravery / performance). Unfortunately, for this recommendation to be approved, we need … Perhaps when you resubmit it, you might …."

All the officers and NCOs in the battalion know what I'm doing and many of them deeply resent it. I've been told my rejections have ignited fury in some of our seasoned sergeants and officers that should frighten the hell out of me. It's a wonder I haven't had the crap kicked out of me behind the shitters. Hackett's support of my editorial decisions is my only protection.

After being awards clerk for awhile and returning and editing quite a few award recommendations, I typed up a list of adjectives that headquarters officers like to see in award recommendations, words like *outstanding, unrelenting,* and *extreme diligence.* I titled the list *Our Dictionary of Army Superlatives.* Believe it or not, adding a handful of grandiose superlatives increases the number of approved awards.

Before I realized the importance of superlatives to the awards granting process, Roberts and Hackett were bouncing back award recommendations on which they'd written, "More outstandings!" or "Punch up the adjectives!" When I told the submitting officers and NCOs about it and we added superlatives to a handful of rejected recommendations, they were approved all the way up the line. No other wording was changed.

So now I give *Our Dictionary of Army Superlatives* to officers and NCOs who are writing up recommendations. It's a just single page I staple to an additional page of suggestions for writing vivid and detailed descriptions of what a soldier did to merit a medal. The superlatives don't add any content to good descriptions—in fact they clutter them with bloated verbiage—but that's what the top brass want so that's what we give them.

Occasionally I receive a poorly written award recommendation for a cited action that appears to have merit. When that happens, I get approval to interview the recommended medal recipient and I try to write a better account of the guy's actions. Then I submit my edited version of the recommendation back to the initiating officer or NCO for his approval.

Every three weeks—give or take a few days—our courier returns from Long Binh with a canvas bag full of medals. Often I have on my desk ten or even a dozen Bronze Stars, Purple Hearts, and Army Commendation Medals. Each medal comes in its own presentation box with an accompanying green plastic folder that contains an award citation suitable for framing. I double-check each citation for correct spelling of the man's name, and then I double-check each medal to make sure the safety pin in back is functional and all the parts are intact and properly constructed.

One time a Bronze Star arrived with one of its points missing. Occasionally the ribbons the medals hang from are frayed or creased. One of the Purple Hearts had its purple plastic chipped. When I discover flawed medals like that, we delay the ceremony for those awards, ship them back, and wait for a new batch.

When we award Purple Hearts in our ceremonies, reaction among the ranks is sometimes unpleasant because they don't know the criteria for that award. When draftees arrive incountry, they think a man has to be killed or gut-shot, or lose an arm or a leg to get a Purple Heart, but that's not true. Any injury that requires medical treatment and that results from interaction with the enemy under combat conditions can earn a man a Purple Heart. Concussions and hearing loss can merit Purple Hearts. A lightly injured man can return from the dispensary the same day, or from the camp hospital within a day or two, bandages showing and sometimes not, and weeks later have a Purple Heart pinned on his chest while his buddies are smirking at the rear of the formation. Purple Hearts for superficial wounds in the ass are classic for generating smirks in formation and hilarity back at the hooch. Regardless, some guys still want those Purple Hearts. Why, you ask?

Superficial wound or not, medals are no laughing matter to a lifer. For lifers, a medal is a big deal. 'Lifer' is a prejudicial term of contempt, when used by draftees, for any man who makes a career out of service in the military. Lifers hope for at least one medal during their tour in Vietnam because lifers returning from Vietnam without a Purple Heart or a medal for outstanding service or achievement, if not for valor, are assumed to be screw-ups and low achievers, and their chances for advancement are sharply reduced. Their hope of advancement is so strong that some lifers use the buddy system to help each other get medals. And since their claims are often difficult and awkward to confirm, they get their medals almost every time.

The Army Commendation Medal is a favorite for lifers. ACMs are given for valor or for service. It was originally intended to be a serious award. Now it's nothing special at all—at least not in our battalion. All our clerks, NCOs, and officers are given ACMs for service unless they have bad work records or they've been court-martialed. We hand out ACMs like candy to kindergartners on Halloween. So if a man is awarded an ACM for an act of *genuine* valor or *legitimate* achievement, it means very little, except to lifers who use it as a stepping stone to promotion.

And then there's the Bronze Star for Meritorious Service. We hand those out, too. We're not talking about valor or heroics, but excellent work. Maybe I'm not sufficiently acquainted with the history of Army medals, and I guess I'm not, but in any account of warfare, or in any literature of any kind I've ever read that includes a discussion of awards granted to soldiers, a Bronze Star is spoken of with reverence and respect as a medal for bravery and heroism, not excellent paperwork or superior organizational achievement. We can canvas a thousand people in any western city in the world and ask them what merits a Bronze Star and they'll say, unless they're in the military and aware of the awards system, that it must be something brave and heroic. Period.

The thing that really irritates me is that whatever recognition we can give a man who has done something genuinely and marvelously heroic, and granted I've already said that a little brass star strikes me as ludicrously inadequate, but if that's the system of recognition we're using, then we should not debase and cheapen that recognition by also giving it for excellent planning or superior office work.

When I visited Long Binh not long ago for a briefing on award application procedures, I met an awards clerk from another unit who told me they give a Bronze Star for Meritorious Service to every officer who DEROSs from their battalion. I'd think a Certificate of Merit—something they can hang on a wall—would have greater legitimacy than a Bronze Star for good work. You'd have to explain your Bronze Star every time a civilian asked about it.

"Oh!" they'd exclaim after hearing your explanation. They'd pooch out their lips and raise their eyebrows, and say, "I guess that's a good reason for receiving a Bronze Star, too. I didn't know you could get one for that."

Pretty soon you'd give up explaining it and let people come to their own conclusions.

"Hey, I heard you got a Bronze Star in 'Nam! Wow. What's it for?"

"Nah. I can't talk about it. Know what I mean?"

Even I've been recommended for a medal! An Army Commendation Medal for Service. I'll probably receive it at the end of my tour. The only thing I can say for myself is that I neither submitted nor processed the recommendation. That was the work of Command Sergeant Major Mollema.

Mollema is short and soft-spoken. Thin lips. A little pudgy. Buttery-brown skin. I think he's Pilipino. He always carries a tube of lip balm in his pocket. He pulls it out, uncaps it, and swipes his lips with a left-right movement a hundred times a day, even when he's talking. I like him. He's a decent lifer. He was so pleased when he told us he was recommending all the S-1 clerks for ACMs that I couldn't show him disrespect by telling him what I thought about the idea. The other guys thought it was "cool."

The standard citation that comes with every Army Commendation Medal for Service says the soldier "*distinguished himself by exceptionally meritorious service,*" and goes on to say:

> *...he astutely surmounted extremely adverse conditions to obtain consistently superior results. Through diligence and determination he invariably accomplished every task with dispatch and efficiency. His unrelenting loyalty, initiative, and perseverance brought him wide acclaim and inspired others to strive for maximum achievement. Selflessly working long and arduous hours, he has contributed significantly to the success of the allied effort.*

Yep, that's me! And if that doesn't prove the awards system is debased, here's something that will, at least for our battalion.

Not long ago Adjutant Harris was under pressure to get more awards granted for the men in our battalion. So he had me type up the following memo and send it for distribution to all our officers and first sergeants.

> *1) One of the best ways to give credit for a man's year of service in Vietnam is to recommend him for an award.*

*2)	The year 1969 should be one in which we can shake each man's right hand while placing an award of commendation in his left hand.*

*3)	The following personnel under your command/supervision are leaving during the month of _____. Request you forward their Recommendations for Award (USARV Form 157-R) to the S-1 Section.*

From now on, at the beginning of every month, I'll have to go to personnel and get the names of men who will DEROS in two months and type those names into a form I'll send to every officer and sergeant in command over them. That's a hell of a lot of work. And notice, in the bottom line, the battalion adjutant is telling these officers and sergeants he's *expecting* and *requesting* they comply!

What a bunch of bullshit.

Some of the *real* workers in our battalion sweat through sixteen-hour days building security revetments for helicopter pads or paving roads and landing strips vital to military transport activities. These men do this exhausting work while exposed to threat from enemy fire and booby traps. They deserve recognition far more than I do, but I sometimes wonder if a medal is appropriate even for them.

Here's why handing out medals for just doing your job sits wrong with me: if anybody—me or somebody on a paving crew—doesn't do his assignments as ordered, putting out maximum effort, he'll be written up for dereliction of duty. The guys out on the work crews do what they're ordered to do under threat of an Article 15 or court-martial or dishonorable discharge.

Maybe they merit a medal because they work with enthusiasm. I'm not sure anymore. I don't begrudge them their medals. Not at all. And maybe I'm too involved in the award-granting process to make a fair judgment. But if I were told, back in the States, that I was about to meet a decorated war veteran, I would expect somebody who had done something more than pave roads with e thusiasm, even if he worked sixteen hours a day doing it. Granted, they're working harder and in far more dangerous conditions than I am. No contest there.

When I receive my medal—if I do—I won't deserve it. Not for typing and filing forms in an office. I'll be embarrassed having the thing pinned on my chest.

But, like I said, there are real heroes out there doing genuinely heroic things—things that deserve to be written up in history books. In some cases, I'll go out on my own time to interview the guy to make sure the recommendation is as thorough and well-written as we can make it.

For example, Lieutenant Ferguson is a functional illiterate who submitted a recommendation for a Bronze Star for Valor for Raymond Landers. Once I understood what Landers had done, I knew I had to help him get a medal.

So I got approval from Lieutenant Ferguson and went to Raymond Landers' hooch one night with a few beers in a little blue and white plastic cooler I borrowed from the colonel's driver. The plan was to talk with Landers and his work buddies about what had happened so I could get an angle or two that might enhance the narrative on the award recommendation. At the same time, I hoped I'd be spending an interesting evening with a genuine hero. I wasn't disappointed.

Raymond Landers and his buddy Nitro were sitting in green vinyl-webbed aluminum lawn chairs backed up against the side of Landers' cot. The cot was covered with a rumpled green Army blanket. Left of Landers, his short-timer's calendar, two-thirds full, was taped to a gray metal locker standing against the wall at the end of his cot.

Right of Landers and Nitro, I sat with Marvin Simmons on a wooden footlocker. We all had cans of beer from the plastic cooler I brought with me. My yellow legal pad was resting on my knees and I was scribbling notes.

"I love my dozer and I love my job," Landers said, his brown eyes proud and confident, daring me to mock him.

Nitro nodded and grinned. "We been clearing jungle during the last couple weeks." His long nose was greasy, his lips full, the upper lip line dented in the middle. "Ray goes crazy if the 25th Infantry Division's mine sweeps delay us getting out there in the morning." Nitro's bare chest looked like a centurion's breastplate covered with black hair.

"We cut down whole jungles for the Man," Marvin Simmons said in a low, gravely voice. We all looked at him. His open hand sliced the air like a black scythe cutting down wheat. His very black skin had a blue sheen like a skim of oil on a puddle of water. His eyelids drooped half-closed and his lower lip hung heavy from his half-open mouth. He looked bored, but that was his usual expression.

Landers turned his attention back to me. "Guys like us get off on heavy equipment." He took a drag on his cigarette and forcefully blew a stream of smoke high in the air. His face was broad and heavily pockmarked. His thick, tangled hair and even his eyelashes were bleached yellow from the sun.

"We got Rome Plows on our dozers," Landers continued. "Biggest damn blades you ever saw." He looked with pride at Simmons and Nitro as if they were members of his private club. "We doze down underbrush, trees, cane fields, anything and everything. Scrape it clean to the ground. We get our dozers lined up, step-staggered in a diagonal line, sometimes five at a time," Landers grinned and nodded as he spoke, "and plow the fuck out of the jungle. Trees and undergrowth rolling over in front of us and flat ground opening up behind us. Nobody hides or stages ambushes out there after we sweep through with"—and here he thrust his pelvis to the beat of the words—"our gallon-a-minute, turbocharged, diesel dozers."

"Man's a poet, too," Simmons said. He shook his head in mock amazement.

Landers tipped back and howled like a dog baying at the moon. Then he chugged the remains of his beer. We toasted him with ours.

I looked in my plastic cooler next to the wooden footlocker. "One can left," I announced.

Simmons and Nitro shook their heads no.

"Hey, you got me there." Landers held out his hands to catch the beer. I leaned over and handed it to him. I wasn't confident about my left-handed tossing skills.

"You hit any landmines? Booby traps?"

"Hell, that's part of the job description." Landers held the can out from between his legs, popped the tab, and bent down and slurped the suds foaming up and out the hole. "We're fucking mine sweeps." He wiped beer froth off his mouth with the back of his free hand so his cigarette remained undisturbed between his fingers. "It's like the colonel said at the work site the other day, 'You got a better way to clear these woods?' And then he said, 'I appreciate you men.'"

"The threat must be pretty high for him to come out and talk to you guys like that. I thought ambushes and snipers would be your biggest problems, not mines."

Simmons shook his head. "Anti-personnel go poof under the tracks." At the word "poof" he spread his long black fingers parallel with the floor and gave a little upward bounce. "Beats walkin' through that shit."

"Okay, sure," Nitro waved to quiet Simmons while looking at Landers. "Tell this clerk, Ray, what you hit last week."

"Yeah, I hit a tank mine last week. Must have been a twenty-pounder. Blew five links off my right track and broke the drive chain." Landers' hands broke the drive chain. "Keeps us alert."

We nodded our heads and grinned at each other, all except Simmons. He studied Landers.

"Our main worry when we're cutting through a forest," Nitro said, "is anti-personnel mines rigged in the trees."

"Haven't hit any yet," Landers said. He pressed his chin on his chest so he could look down and brush cigarette ashes off his green T-shirt.

"Tha's why we got mesh shit welded on our cabs," Simmons said.

"BOOM," Landers whispered, all bug-eyed, leaning toward Simmons, his hands flying apart like an explosion.

"Is that why Lieutenant Ferguson recommended you for a medal?" I asked. "Maybe I should hear more about the land mine thing so I can—"

Landers shook his head. "That award shit don't have nothin' to do with mines."

"Oh, really? I didn't bring the papers with me, but—"

"Hell, all dozer operators hit mines," Landers said. He pointed at Simmons. "You hit a big mine. When was that? June? July?"

"Gradin' side of a road," Simmons said quietly, nodding his head.

"I need to get this straight." Looking at Landers, I pushed for more. "What happened that made Ferguson put you up for an award? Something about saving a woman?"

He shook his head. "Listen. I dragged a gook into a ditch. She got caught in the line of fire. All that happened a long time ago."

"Five days ago," Nitro said.

"How'd the woman get in the line of fire?"

"Happened in the morning," Nitro said. He ran his hand through the curly black hair on his head and scratched his chest. "We were transporting our dozers in a convoy to the work site. Supposedly a friendly area. Had security from the 25th. APCs front and back of the convoy mounted with quad-fifties. Fuckers hit us from huts two hundred meters out from the road. Two rockets fell short, but one hit the lead APC. Then the VC opened up with automatic fire."

I turned to Simmons. "You there too?"

"Miss' all that shit, man." He waved it from his face as though shooing a fly.

Just then whoops and yells erupted from a group of men standing in the aisle at the end of the hooch. They were passing around photographs. Landers and Nitro whooped and raised their fists in reply. Simmons smiled and raised his fist, too, but casually, without exuberance.

Somebody turned up the volume on Marvin Gaye's "I Heard It Through The Grapevine."

"Go on," I said, leaning toward Nitro. "What happened?"

"We were passing a gook family on our left going in the opposite direction. Couple of them pulling one of those wooden carts piled with blankets and tools and shit, kids running alongside. But the VC in the hooches across the field didn't care. They had their ambush set up and they opened fire anyway. We couldn't get our carriers around the forward APC and we couldn't back up fast enough, so we jumped out of our cabs and ran past the wooden cart to the ditch. The gook family got there first."

"It was crazy," Landers said quietly. He looked at his boots. "Down in that ditch with all those gooks jabbering, kids crying, everybody shouting, returning fire. And the rear APC firing its quad-fifties. A regular circus."

"Water in the ditch?" I asked.

"Hell no, not in the dry season."

"We could hear rounds pinging off our dozers," Nitro said. "Hell, they popped several of my carrier's tires. 'Any more tires blow,' I thought to myself, 'and the carrier's gonna roll over and bury me under my own dozer.'"

"Gooks in the ditch right next to me." Landers spread his arms, appealing to common sense, his cigarette in one hand and his beer in the other. "All of them jabbering, pointing to a mama-san on the road next to my carrier."

"Must have got confused," Nitro said. "Ran toward the carriers." He shrugged his shoulders. "Heading for the ditch on the other side? Scared of being with GIs? Maybe hit right away and crawled to those big tires for protection? Who knows?"

"Got hit in the leg," Landers said to himself. He looked up. "I mean, I saw her … watched her dragging around. But I thought the gooks with me in the ditch, I don't know …." He shook his head. "Or maybe … but that's stupid, with the kids …."

"Those fuckers are dedicated," Nitro said. "Nobody knows what they might do."

"Some my women I know is like that," Simmons chuckled. He looked over his shoulder at the men passing around photographs and hee-hawing together.

Landers shrugged and looked at us. "So I ran out there and pulled her back in the ditch. Wasn't any big deal."

"Huh," Nitro snorted. He jabbed his finger toward Landers. "It was a fucking big deal. Hell, man, you ran out there without telling us what you were doing." Nitro turned to me. "At first we just stared. 'What the fuck?' Then we laid down cover. But Jesus, I never saw anything like it."

Landers looked like he had indigestion. "It's funny. All of a sudden I was out there. Wasn't even afraid."

"Wha' happen' nex'?" Simmons's eyes were big.

Landers looked at Simmons. "You'd know what happened, wise guy, if you'd been there." He looked at me and jerked his thumb toward Simmons. "Mama's boy back here with phony diarrhea."

"So what did happen?" I asked.

Landers flushed. "Our air support came in and the VC stopped firing."

Nitro said, "The medic worked on the guys in the forward APC. They were pretty messed up. Then he checked the woman. We already had a compress on her leg, but she'd lost a lot of blood. The dust-off took all four of them."

Simmons was chuckling. "Tha's not the story what Nitro tol' me couple nights ago."

Nitro waved "no" with both hands to quiet Simmons, but Nitro was laughing, too.

"What'd he tell you?" Landers swiveled to Nitro. "What bullshit you passing around?"

"Come on, Ray, other guys were out there too, okay? It's no secret."

"You son-of-a-bitch! Some fucking friend!"

"Shit, man, we jus' havin' *fun* wit' you, tha's all." Simmons was laughing out loud now.

Landers got up from his lawn chair, his face flushed. "You guys think you're so fucking funny." He stalked into the aisle, poked his finger at us, and yelled, "I don't give no goddamn rat's ass about no medal."

Everybody in the hooch looked up at Landers. He swept his arm in dismissal. "All you fuckers can go to hell!" He stomped down the aisle to the end of the hooch, hit the screen door with the palm of his hand, and walked out.

I shook my head. "What'd you guys say that worked him up like that?"

Nitro looked at Simmons. "Why'd you have to go and do that with this clerk here and everything?"

Simmons shrugged his shoulders. "Listen, I got somethin' comin' down with a bro in Delta." Simmons turned to me. "You write that shit good so our man get his medal." He stood up, raised his fist in a casual belt-level salute, and walked down the aisle and out the door.

I sat with Nitro and nursed my beer.

Finally I said, "Would you mind telling me what's going on here?"

"Nothing, really." He looked down the aisle and then leaned in toward me. "After Ray dragged the woman back to the ditch and we patched her up, we were on our knees watching the choppers take out the hooches. Mini-gun fire. Rockets. All that good shit. And all of a sudden Ray fell on his face. Just like that. Fell over and laid there. Scared the shit out of me. I thought a sniper hit him. I yelled 'Incoming! Incoming!' and everybody flattened down in the ditch again. But when I rolled him over to look for a wound, he woke up." Nitro grinned. "He'd fainted. Don't make what he did any less amazing, but that's what happened, and some of the guys won't let him forget it."

Three weeks later I received in the courier's satchel Raymond Landers' Bronze Star for Valor. I was pleased. I double-checked the citation, inspected the medal, returned it to its presentation case and stacked it with the others.

Monday, Apr. 21, 1969 - Cu Chi Base Camp
Dear Janice:

Guess what! I can call you on the phone!

There's a special phoning service at Long Binh that uses ham radio operators who work with the military so we can phone home from Vietnam. It's called MARS (an acronym for Military Affiliate Radio System).

The way it's been described to me, I stand in line waiting my turn for an hour or two. Then I enter a plywood booth. I pick up a phone receiver and give the operator the phone number I want called. I wait two or three minutes. When I'm given the go-ahead, I talk for a short time and say "over." That cues a technician to flip a switch that reverses the transmission from "send" to "receive." After a five second delay I hear your reply and then you say "over" and wait five seconds to hear me talk again. Back and forth.

I'll tell you when I can get to Long Binh so you'll be home when I call. I'll work out time differences so I don't call you in what for you would be the middle of the night.

By the way, be thinking about where and when you'd like to meet me for R & R. I can spend one week in Thailand or Hong Kong or Australia or a few other places including Hawaii. The Army pays my travel expenses, but not yours. Hawaii is probably the best choice, unless we want to rack up a big debt.

Love you, Andrew

DE-DRUMMING

"The other man is up there hacking drums," Staff Sergeant Brogan growled at me, "and you meander in here like you're going to a goddamned Sunday school picnic."

Sergeant Brogan is a human bulldog well-suited to managing men from every company in the 182nd Engineer Battalion on their one-night-a-month assignment in Alpha Company's asphalt plant. His bald head is mounted on a thick neck. His bulging chest and beer belly are always covered with a sweat-stained T-shirt torn free of sleeves and streaked with tar and a week's worth of grime. His upper arms are slabs of flesh that taper to massive forearms and pudgy hands and thick short fingers. A slick of sweat covers his pink scalp and hangs in droplets from black hair protruding from his arm pits.

Brogan took down a clipboard from a hook on the outside of his aluminum shed. He looked at the name on my fatigues and ran his finger down the roster.

"What company you from?"

I looked around as I answered and tried to appear unconcerned. "Headquarters."

"That figures." He checked off my name with a pencil tied by a dirty string to the clipboard. He glared at me with disdain and curiosity. "You one of those hotshots hung over from drinking beer and fucking that Delta Company prostitute all night?"

"Driver had trouble with his jeep. Otherwise I'd have been here early."

"My ass." Brogan slapped the clipboard back on the wall hook and turned and glared at me. "We got a lot of tar to melt tonight. You done this before?"

I smiled at Brogan. "I've had the pleasure of your company on several occasions."

Brogan squinted at me with puzzled contempt. Then he let out a snort. "Get your smart ass up there and get to work."

I slung my M16 on my shoulder and climbed the corner ladder of the three-story, open-frame structure that supported the tar furnace and other machinery for making asphalt. When I reached the second floor, I stepped around and off the ladder onto tar-streaked wooden planks. I turned and looked at the equipment yard down below.

Far to the left, three deuce-and-a-halfs bounced off a dirt road into the yard, their truck beds banging and gate chains jangling as they braked to a stop, one after the other, under the giant mixer. Sparkling black asphalt slid down the chute, smoking hot, into the oily bed of the truck first in line.

At the far edge of the yard, a front-end loader scooped sand into a truck from a sparkling brown pile as big as a house. Resting next to it was an equally large pile of crushed rock. Off to the right, a forklift weaved between old tires and rusted truck parts toward a wall of fifty-five-gallon drums, neatly stacked four pallets high. In the field behind the wall of drums, a mountain of discarded barrels oozed pools of tar. A plume of black smoke from the tar furnace momentarily obscured my view of the yard's blinding-white gravel and blistering-hot equipment.

Then I noticed, underlying the sounds of roaring engines and clanking machinery, a relentless hissing, like a compressor hose but more throaty. It came from the gas burners in the tar furnace. My call to hard labor.

"Hey, man, the work is over here."

I turned around, befuddled, waking from my reverie. I looked to see who yelled.

He was a nineteen-year-old boy, short and stocky, with fuzz on his chin. His blond hair was pulled back in a stubby pony tail. He stood, legs spread, on top of the nearest of twenty fifty-five gallon drums wedged side-by-side. He held an ax resting on his right shoulder.

"How's it going?" I asked.

"I'll tell you how it's going." He swung the head of the ax down and propped it at his feet, and leaned on the handle as though it were a dancing cane. "It's the hottest season of the year and I'm de-drumming tar with a guy who shows up late for the hottest part of the shift."

"Do much work yet?"

"I hacked a few holes in this drum after Sergeant Numb-Nuts got pushy. This ax ain't worth shit. But don't worry. I didn't soak up your share of the gravy."

"Any drums in the furnace?"

"Nope." He dropped the ax and jumped to the floor. "Been waiting for you."

He hunkered down and lit a cigarette with a one-snap-flourish of his Zippo lighter and blew smoke in an upward stream from the side of his mouth. He looked up at me and nodded his head with a grimace on his face. Apparently I confirmed his worst expectations.

I hung my cloth jungle hat, my rifle, my bandoleer of M16 magazines, and my web belt with three canteens of water on bolts protruding from a metal I-beam rising to the wooden planks of the third floor overhead. I turned and leaned my backside against a barrel and slid down to a squatting position facing my new companion.

"I wish they'd start this de-drumming shift after sundown instead of in the middle of the afternoon," I said. "This heat and humidity, and shoving 400-pound drums into that tar furnace, could kill us as easily as— "

My companion jabbed his finger toward the ladder I had just climbed. "Heads up," he said in a loud whisper.

We stood and turned just as Brogan stepped off the ladder onto our second floor platform. A green towel hung around his neck. He wiped his dripping face and bald head as he walked to where we were standing.

"You two clowns need to get something very clear," Brogan said, his hands pulling at the towel around his neck, "because if you don't, we're gonna have trouble."

"You got my attention," my fellow de-drummer said. I nodded agreement.

"Okay, here it is." Brogan spread his legs like stanchions under his massive body. "If we don't melt enough tar tonight, we won't have enough asphalt for the paving crews in the morning. That fucks up the entire battalion, and Colonel Hackett will court-martial me for dereliction of duty. So if I come up here one more time and see an empty furnace without drums draining hot tar while you two are playing kissy-face, I'll break your legs with a two-by-four and throw you off this scaffolding. That'll be my excuse. Two clumsy fuck-ups fell and broke their legs. And if you don't think I'll do it, then keep your thumbs up your asses until I check on you again." Brogan turned and walked heavily to the ladder. Floorboards groaned under his feet. He descended to the ground floor without a backward glance.

I looked at my work companion and rolled my eyes in mock alarm over

Brogan's performance. "So what did you say your name was?"

"I didn't. My name's Waller. Derek Waller. You think maybe Sergeant Brogan's a hard ass?"

"I think maybe we should get to work. Want me to hack with that ax for a while?"

"There's another set of gloves on the ledge by the furnace."

I found the gloves and hiked myself up on the drums. Waller handed me the ax and backed off, standing a safe distance away.

The ax handle was a solid metal bar welded to an ax head half its weight, making the ax unwieldy and slippery to swing. Several layers of black friction tape were wrapped at the handle's end to prevent the ax from slinging out of our hands with every swing. A wooden handle, apparently, was too easily broken by men frustrated with opening steel drumheads with an ax.

With my feet spread apart on two adjacent drums, I aimed the ax blade at the nearest end of the chopped line in the drumhead started by Waller. I swung hard, and the ax blade cut another inch in the ragged line along the steel rim. I swung again and again, repositioning my feet each time, building up accuracy and rhythm. The ax hit the rim several times, once springing out of my hands. Another time I overshot the end of the cut and the ax head wedged itself in the drum, two inches deep in tar. I pried out the ax, wiped it with a rag, and continued hacking until I'd hacked a jagged line half way around the barrel's rim. Then I chopped three holes in the middle of the lid's uncut side and tossed the ax on the lids of nearby barrels. The hacking was done.

I jumped off the drums to the floor. Waller helped me tip the 400-pound barrel and balance it on its edge. I rolled it on its edge to the tar-sticky floor in front of the furnace and let the 400-pound barrel fall on its side, pivoting over a wooden fence post Waller had positioned on the floor near the base of the drum. Stepping to the uncut end of the barrel elevated by the post, we stooped shoulder-to-shoulder and lifted up on the drum's bottom lip. Grunting involuntarily, we heaved the barrel up most of the way—Waller kicked the wooden post to one side—and switched from lifting to pushing during the split second when inertia held the barrel suspended on its edge. The barrel dropped solidly, no rocking, with the hacked end down.

Speed and efficiency were now crucial, since tar in the drum would sag out the hacked lid within minutes and glue the drum to the floor. We rocked and slid the drum across five feet of tar-blackened floor to the open mouth of the furnace.

The mouth of the furnace belched flame from the burners and smoke from residue of months of melting tar. The black smoke was oily and thick with greasy soot. Inhaling it was like inhaling glue or gasoline fumes. Many men hallucinated during their night of de-drumming. We all tasted the oily slick at the back of our throats and coughed up brown-streaked phlegm.

The furnace accommodated two drums at a time, the mouth being as wide and high as the front of a jeep. The floor of the furnace mouth was an iron grating on which we slid the upended drums the remaining few feet by sitting on the floor and pushing the drums with our boots, the gas-fed burners throwing a yellow glow on our boots and ankles. Tar from the drums would melt in thirty minutes and drain through the grating into a heated vat.

Four hours later, the sun sinking on the horizon, we had passed Brogan's inspection several times. We felt safe. We took a break after working extra hard and loading the furnace and rolling two lid-hacked drums next in line.

I had cottonmouth. Everything shimmered with a luminescent glow around the edges. My head was a balloon floating above the hands and legs that moved the drums. I drank half a canteen of warm water. I chewed two salt tablets from a bottle near the furnace and took another slug of water and collapsed to the floor with my back against a drum. My fatigues were soaked with perspiration and black with tar. I wiped away the sweat dripping from my face and hair. I looked at Waller. He was sitting on the floor opposite me, his head tilted back, resting against a drum. His moist white face looked like a grime-smeared ball of Ivory soap gone soft in a tub of bath water.

"Makes me appreciate my 290 earthmover," Waller said.

I massaged my sore arms. "You operate heavy equipment for Bravo Company?"

"Best job I ever had. I love it." He was silent a few moments, his head resting against the drum. "Aren't you some kind of clerk? I think I saw you in a ceremony handing medals to the colonel."

"I do what they tell me to do. Mostly typing in the S-1 office. Where you from?"

"Ohio. My dad works in a steel mill at Steubenville. My older brother works in a coal mine." He tipped his head forward and looked at me. "They work like this all the time. Hell, I'd kill myself. I'm gonna get me a job with the state highway department operating a 290 earthmover. Then I'll buy a house with a big yard."

"You married?"

"Draft notice came three weeks after the ceremony." Waller looked at me from the corners of his eyes without moving his head. "How 'bout you?"

"I was married two years, then got drafted."

We sat without talking for a few minutes. Then I asked, "Did you hear anything about a prostitute in Delta Company last night? I was over there talking to a guy about an award recommendation we're submitting for him and on my way back I saw men lined up behind a canvas-covered truck. Must have been at least ten of them."

"Heard about it."

"Somebody told me she was fourteen years old."

"How'd you know she was fourteen?"

"I don't. That's what I was told."

"We better get back to work," Waller said. "Those drums must be drained by now."

We got up, stiff and aching. We pulled the empty drums out of the furnace with a three-foot metal hook snagged on their bottom edge. We flipped them on their sides and rolled them, still smoking, off the edge of the second floor. They fell, booming and banging, into a disposal truck down below. We upended the two hacked drums next in line and shoved them in the furnace.

Four or five hours after night fall, exhausted from the work and inebriated from inhaling tar and oil fumes, I looked out at the yard from our well-lit, second-floor work platform and stared in amazement. Heavy clouds had covered the night sky and descended into our work yard as black-mist darkness. I could feel the moist cloud as it nestled against the open framework of the second floor. The mist would drift several feet into our work area where bright lights turned it smoky-white before it dissipated into the air. But the true marvels lay out in the yard.

Out in the yard's darkness sat huge yellow cones fifteen feet high and, at their base, at least twenty feet in diameter. The tips of the cones were capped with hooded bug bulbs hanging by electric wires from long wooden arms attached to telephone poles. But none of that structure was visible except the very bottom of each pole. Yellow light from the hoods, shinning down in the fog, made each cone glow like ectoplasm from the spirit world.

That surreal image launched me into a world of dreams where heat and exhaustion and fumes from the furnace loosed phantoms as real as objects I touched everyday.

I was hallucinating, and I knew I was hallucinating because I kept hacking and rolling drums, but I *saw* a fourteen-year-old girl in front of me. She couldn't see me, but I could see her. I could have touched her if I'd wanted to, but I was hacking drums.

She was sweeping a path to her thatched-roof hooch. It was early morning. The air was humid, but fresh with the earthy smell of dew on the ground. The sun shone yellow on the tops of nearby trees.

She was a typical Vietnamese girl. Coal black hair. Cinnamon brown skin. Dark narrow eyes. Breasts mere bumps on a thin cage of ribs under a white cotton blouse. Her head barely reached my chin.

But my vision of her in sunlight changed to a vision of her in darkness. She was lying in the back of a covered truck. Her blouse was pulled up to her neck and her pants were pulled free of her feet and lay crumpled on the floor of the truck. One GI after another crawled over the truck's tailgate and felt for her bare legs. Then they pulled down their pants and pushed into her without a word. They laid heavily on her. They bounced her head with the force of their thrusts. I wondered how sore she was. I wondered if her flesh was tearing. I wondered how she would feel in the morning about her father and her brothers, her mother and herself.

Then the girl's arms, legs, and breasts began to swell with soft flesh, smooth and cool to the touch. She began whining and moaning and begging for more as men pushed into her and other men cheered them on.

I could feel a loosening in my groin and a swelling between my legs as I watched the girl's torment twist into pleasure. I knew this was wrong. I knew a fourteen-year-old girl could not enjoy intercourse with ten men. I shook my head to clear my mind. I tried to focus on the drums, the hacking, the tar, but it did no good.

The scene changed again. I saw her struggling to free herself. She was fighting a stocky, blond-haired GI. He laid his full weight on her. His lips curled back from teeth he clenched against her head. His saliva sprayed her hair as he pounded her into submission.

I was like a dog cowering in the corner of the truck. Watching. Trembling. Smelling the semen. Seeing the shine in the eyes of the men. Hearing them pant and grunt and push against the body of the little girl.

I found myself sitting on the tar-covered platform in front of the furnace pushing with my boots against a drum. When the drum reached the hot grating, it slid smoothly into the furnace. I got up, my trousers pulling free of the tar on the floor. I walked slowly to where Waller was standing on the drumheads hacking another drum.

It will soon be my turn and I don't think I can do it.

Waller stopped hacking and stared down at me for a moment with a puzzled look on his face. He looked at my pants and grinned.

"You're not keeping your mind on your work, are you big guy? You should've got some pussy last night. Is that what you're thinking about? Huh?" He grabbed his crotch and jiggled it up and down. "You need a little poontang?"

Blood thudded in my neck from humiliation. I shook myself as if preparing for an obstacle course. I focused on Waller's question. My arousal was gone.

"You're right. I've been thinking about the prostitute. But not because I wanted to fuck her. How can anybody do that to a fourteen-year-old girl?"

"Do what?"

"Gang-rape a fourteen-year-old girl."

"She wasn't raped," Waller said. "Nobody held her down. She got paid for it. Hell, her own mama-san was standing at the end of the truck collecting money."

"A fourteen-year-old girl does not decide to become a prostitute."

"Says who? You? Lots of girls that age get married in these Asian countries, so why can't they decide to be prostitutes, too?"

"Those are arranged marriages. Their parents make those decisions."

"So this was arranged prostitution. What's the difference?"

"How could you possibly know the mama-san was the girl's mother and not some old whore that got her hands on a kid?"

"Because she told us, you dumb ass. Why would she lie about something like that?"

"So you were part of this? You got in line to fuck a fourteen-year-old girl?"

Waller looked at me, stone cold. He dropped the ax on the drums where he was standing and jumped to the floor. He removed his gloves and crouched down on his haunches.

"We really didn't know how old she was." He looked at the palm of his right hand and pulled at a broken blister. He looked up. "It was hard to tell."

"Why was it hard to tell?"

"Well, we didn't have a goddamn night-light in the truck, you know."

"And she was laying naked, on her back, on the floor of the truck?"

"No, she was on a mattress. What the hell difference does it make to you?"

"Was she crying?"

"No."

"Did she say anything?"

"What the fuck…? No, she didn't say anything. What difference does it make to you?"

"Did you say anything?"

"What kind of dumb question is that? What would I say to her?"

"So you crawled in there and felt around until you found this little girl with her legs spread apart and you fucked her without even acknowledging she was alive?"

"Hey, she got her money. She and her mama-san got enough money in one night to buy food and clothes for six months, probably enough for their whole family."

"That was a little girl you screwed."

"Hey, fuck you!" Waller stood up and faced me. "I'm not proud of what I did, but I didn't force myself on her. It wasn't rape. And I paid for what I got."

"You better hope you don't get VD." I grabbed the ax off the barrels. "You use a rubber?"

"Didn't have one." Waller looked off in the darkness of the equipment yard. "Most of us didn't."

"Jesus Christ." I grimaced and shook my head. "If I were you, I'd get shots or something from the medic in the morning."

"You think shots will knock out VD if you get them in time?"

"Depends."

Waller stared at the floor and started nodding his head. "It *was* pretty disgusting." He looked up at me while feeling the back of his head for his stubby ponytail.

"So why did you go through with it?"

"It started out as a joke. Somebody said there was a prostitute in Delta Company, so a bunch of us walked over there. Mama-san was outside the truck collecting money. Some of us got in line. She kept smiling and saying, 'Baby-san boom-boom.' Somebody asked how old the girl was and Mama-san counted fourteen on her fingers." Waller threw up his hands. "Who knows what she meant? But the girl wasn't tied down or anything. And her mother was collecting the money so it seemed okay. And I wasn't about to back off at the last minute. So I did my thing and got out."

I stared at Derek Waller.

"Hey, the hell with you," he yelled. "Who made you the judge and jury of everybody else? If you're so righteous, why are you in Vietnam? Nobody even knows why we're here. You came over here ready to kill women and children because otherwise you'd go to jail. Right? And now you get high and mighty because I fucked a prostitute and gave her the money she asked for? I didn't kill her. I fucked her. But you, you asshole, you won't fuck her. Oh, no, but you come over here ready to kill her. And then you get a hard-on thinking about what you condemn the rest of us for doing. At least I'm not a fucking hypocrite. God, you make me sick."

I studied Waller's pale moist face several moments before I realized I had nothing to say. I turned and tossed the ax on the drums and hiked myself up on a lid. I grabbed the ax, positioned myself, and swung as hard as I could. The blade cut a two-inch gash in the steel drumhead.

"This ax is fucked up."

Waller lit a cigarette and blew smoke toward the rafters overhead. "Hell, the whole Army's fucked up."

"Don't forget the U.S. government." I swung the ax so hard I grunted when it hit the drumhead.

"You got that right." Waller spit out a fleck of tobacco.

We didn't talk much after that. We worked through the night on a platform floating in darkness. We cursed and swore at the drums, the war, and each other while flames from the furnace danced on our faces and drained from the drums the black tar for the roads of Vietnam.

Tuesday, June 10, 1969 - Cu Chi Base Camp
Dear Janice:

A few days ago we had our battalion's yearly AIG inspection by higher headquarters at Long Binh. "AIG" stands for Army Inspector General.

We in S-1 and Personnel made sure all our files were ready for inspection. We couldn't be sure what they'd inspect in depth, so everything had to be properly organized, straightened, and cleaned.

There's a rumor that sergeants in one of our companies wanted a small-bucket excavator they couldn't get through the ordinary procurement process, so, sometime in the previous year, they traded with a unit outside our battalion in exchange for a couple trucks. But the ID number on the excavator wasn't listed on the company inventory, and inventories are difficult to jigger because they specify sources and procurement dates that can be checked. In preparation for the AIG Inspection, according to the rumor, the sergeants buried the excavator and claimed one truck they traded away was destroyed by a mortar shell and the other truck was destroyed by a land mine alongside the road.

Our hooches got a bad gig. Remember the plywood walls I told you about that separate each hooch into two-man rooms? Well, those walls have to go. The hooches aren't to have any impediment to us "moving out" fast when the attack siren blows.

Love, Andrew

Monday, June 16, 1969 - Cu Chi Base Camp
Dear Janice:

We've had racial fighting in Delta Company. David Connors, our legal eagle and head clerk, is typing court-martial documents against three men—two blacks and one white—involved in a brawl over Martin Luther King's death and the riots back home. Several other men drew knives on each other. Fortunately nobody was seriously injured.

We don't have anything going on like that here, but there is a down side to HQ Company's racial mix. Most of our men are white. That's because far more whites than blacks have the education and requisite skills for working in an office. There are reasons for that, of course, which have nothing to do with the intrinsic nature of being black or white. Doesn't make any difference. The imbalance could stir up emotions between us and other companies. A few officers voiced their worry, here in S-1, about a battalion-wide race riot among heavily armed men!

Love, Andrew

Wednesday, June 25, 1969 - Cu Chi Base Camp
Dear Janice:

Hi beautiful. How are things at home?

DRAFTED

Back when I helped Adjutant Harris hook up his new hi-fi equipment, I began thinking about buying my own stuff and sending it home. Otherwise I'll never be able to afford the quality hi-fi equipment I can buy over here through the PX catalog.

I decided I'd order an Automatic Record-Changing Garrard Turntable. An Akai Reel-to-Reel Auto-Reversing Tape Deck. A Pioneer Tuner/Amplifier. And two sets of Pioneer Speakers, one set small enough to rest on bookcase shelves in my study, and the other set big enough to double for lamp tables in the living room. I'll place my order in a couple months.

Love, Andrew

R & R

Jerry Maener and I walked over to the EM Club for a few beers and to see a rock-and-roll band of four Filipino girls swing their tight little butts to the beat of the music. But when they started singing Tom Jones' "Green, Green Grass of Home" in squeaky, Asian-accented voices to the discordant sounds of a lead guitarist who couldn't lead and a drummer who couldn't drum, Jerry and I got up and walked out without saying a word.

We walked slowly in the moonlight—slapping at mosquitoes—toward the headquarters company formation yard. We were at loose ends. Disappointed. Unsure what to do with ourselves.

Jerry is a good friend. He works in the personnel office down the hall from where I work in S-1. He's thin, medium height, and has sandy brown hair. Gold-rimmed spectacles frame his brown eyes that look out at the world with quiet, unassuming intelligence. There is a gentleness in appearance and manner about Jerry that makes him appear more fragile than he really is. He got his bachelor's degree in classics from the University of Chicago and is, for me, an oasis of intelligence and sensitivity in a desert of ignorance and machismo. We'd probably spend more time together if we weren't such obsessive readers.

I do an enormous amount of reading and writing in the evenings. As soon as I get off work at six o'clock (1800 hours military time)—unless I'm assigned KP, guard duty, CQ runner, or de-drumming detail, and if I'm not chasing information so I can rewrite an award recommendation—I immediately take a shower and head to the mess hall for dinner. Then I go down in an underground bunker with a lawn chair, a thermos of coffee, my M16, a bandoleer of ammunition, a book, and a notepad. I turn on the bunker's electric lights and read and write into the night. Down here, beneath the worst of the humidity and heat, is the only place I can get away from all the loud talking and rock-and-roll and country-western music blaring from hi-fi speakers the size of end tables. Even down in the bunker I can feel a thudding beat when somebody cranks up Iron Butterfly's "Inna-Gadda-Da-Vida."

Early in my tour, after I realized I'd be a clerk on a secure base camp, I wrote and asked Janice to send me paperback books of one specified kind or another. I also subscribed to the Book-of-the-Month Club and asked them to send me Will Durant's *The Story of Civilization*. I've read half of Durant's ten-volume history, as well as novels by Updike, Faulkner, Mailer, Dickens, and many others. I've read quite a few short story anthologies, and right now I'm reading the philosophical essays of William James. At lunch or dinner, or an occasional evening at the EM Club, I meet Jerry to talk about books we've been reading or the Army's latest fuck-up.

We'd both read about the cruelty and insanity of the world around us, but at some deep level we both continued to believe that intelligence, hard work, and good intentions could overcome the world's pain, poverty, and injustice. The Army, Vietnam, and the realities of war popped that naïve idealism like an overblown balloon.

"Did you hear what happened to that poor asshole in Delta Company?" Jerry asked. We were walking across the company formation yard after leaving the EM Club. It was eight o'clock at night and electric lights on telephone poles spaced around the yard created a bubble of illumination in darkness that swallowed the base camp.

"Yeah," I replied. "I typed the condolence letter to the man's family. I never found out exactly what happened, but you're the second person I've heard describe the guy as an asshole. Was he some kind of jerk?"

"I don't know. But I guess he was acting like a macho hotshot, sitting on the edge of his truck bed while it was being loaded under the asphalt chute. Apparently he lost his balance, and in all that noise and confusion, nobody noticed. They filled his truck and looked around for the driver, but he'd disappeared."

Jerry and I looked at each other and burst out laughing.

"But if he hadn't slipped," I said "he'd still be a macho hotshot. Is this true?"

Jerry pondered the question. "I believe you're right."

"That means we're calling him an asshole because he was clumsy, maybe even drunk. Now there's a question for you. Why does clumsiness, whether inherited or from booze, make him an asshole?"

"An excellent question, my dear Watson," Jerry puffed on his corncob pipe, his eyes bright with the pleasure of relegating me to second fiddle. "Indeed, it strikes at the heart of our Vietnam experience."

"Watson?" I exclaimed with feigned outrage. "I beg your pardon. I was interrogating to illuminate and inform, not seek enlightenment from a superior. Besides, you're smoking a corncob, and Holmes never smoked a corncob."

"I believe he did."

"Doyle wouldn't have made him stoop so low. Holmes smoked a calabash."

Jerry suddenly became very serious. "Not once. Not in a single story."

"That's beside the point anyway." I waved hello to Connors, the head clerk in S-1, as he walked past us in the direction of the EM Club. "Why does my question about calling a man an asshole go to the heart of our Vietnam experience?"

"Elementary, my dear Watson—"

"I wish you'd stop acting superior. It's the worst kind of posturing because it's true and we both know it."

Jerry turned and looked at me with a grin. "Touché."

I shot a fake smile back at him.

"As I was about to say, before your rude interruption," Jerry lifted his chin above the rude interruption but dropped the faux-British tone and talked normally again. "Similar clumsiness elsewhere would not qualify a man as an asshole." Jerry puffed thoughtfully on his pipe.

"Go on," I said, "I'm waiting."

"Well, if a man doesn't understand, prior to coming over here, that we're fighting without clear strategy or rationale, those facts become obvious to him when he sees firsthand that we're not fighting a war we can win, and the only criteria for success—the kill count—is wholly unreliable. Even the ARVN's have no stomach for this war. The South Vietnamese government is thoroughly corrupt, a dictatorship feeding at the trough of American wealth and power, and it's not worth dying for."

"I presume we're coming to the point where the clumsy man becomes an asshole?"

Just then Doug Stevens, who works in personnel with Jerry, walked past us about twenty feet away. Doug was wearing a flower-embossed Hawaiian sport shirt billowing loose from red Bermuda shorts. Jerry waved.

"How was R & R?" Jerry called. "When'd you get back?"

"This afternoon," Doug shouted, and gave a thumbs up without interrupting his walk to the EM club.

"Please continue," I said to Jerry. "I need amusement."

Jerry stopped walking and looked down at the ground in concentration. I waited a few feet ahead of him. We had crossed the formation yard and stood under a floodlight at the beginning of the path to our hooches among the trees.

"The soldier in Vietnam," Jerry said, "now fully aware he has no moral justification for being here, should lay down his weapon and say: *this killing is wrong because I no longer know why I'm doing it.*' But he doesn't do that. He continues his part in the war. He thereby compromises himself in the most fundamental way possible."

"And that is?"

"You don't see it? He violates his own humanity by mindlessly killing other human beings."

"And that makes him an asshole? That's not the connotation of 'asshole' used around here. Besides, it's not even relevant to—"

"Will you let me finish?" Jerry put his hands on his hips and raised his eyebrows like a peevish school teacher. "If you don't mind?"

"Point taken." I crossed my arms and waited.

Jerry resumed in a tone of exasperation, but he quickly focused his full attention on his exposition. "As I was saying, when the truth dawns on our soldier that he's killing people without good reason for doing so—except for fear of incarceration by his own government—his compassion and concern for others drains away. Thus, a soldier in Vietnam who foolishly causes his own death has destroyed the one thing his fellow soldiers know he values above everything else, including women and children and moral principle of any kind."

"Himself!"

"Exactly. So they judge him a dumb fuck."

"Which is loosely synonymous with 'asshole'."

"Indeed." Jerry looked at me as pleased as if he were Plato parsing the meaning of *justice*.

We began a leisurely walk down the path toward our hooches.

Jerry suddenly turned and asked, "You ever smoke anything other than pipe tobacco?"

"Cigarettes, occasionally. But I love my briars. And Hayward Pipe Tobacco. Nothing fancy. Basic Virginias and burleys laced with latakia and perique. A good smoke."

Jerry grinned as though I said something funny. He swaggered and swung his shoulders as we walked, which was uncharacteristic of Jerry.

"Okay, what's so funny?" I asked.

"You wanna get out of here for a few hours? Fly away on R & R?"

"What are you talking about?"

"I'll bet you never did any drugs when you were back in the States, did you?"

"I never had the opportunity. Nor the desire." I paused and considered what I'd just said. "No, that's not entirely true. I was intrigued by Aldous Huxley's *Doors of Perception* and his other book *Heaven and Hell*. And I read a few essays by Timothy Leary. Oh, and I read *Confessions of an Opium Eater*. But nobody I knew used drugs, so far as I know."

"Would you smoke a little grass if you had the chance?"

"I'd give it a try. But I'd worry about having a bad trip."

"People don't have bad trips smoking grass. LSD or mushrooms, but not grass. Of course, some people don't like being high. But you enjoy booze, so…?" He shrugged his shoulders and looked at me.

"You've smoked pot?"

"A few times." Jerry smiled.

"And you haven't had bad experiences with it?"

"Not once."

"Well, maybe someday I'll give it a try." I lit my pipe with my Zippo lighter.

"Would you like to give it a try right now?"

I turned and looked at him. He was grinning at me. "You have pot?" I was incredulous. Stunned. "Here? In Vietnam? On a military base camp?"

"Better than anything I smoked in the States."

"How did you get it?"

"The Vietnamese sell it at fruit juice stands along the road. Men on the paving crew buy it any day of the week. A couple truck drivers I know occasionally buy for me. You can buy a Kools pack of ready rolls for two dollars."

"What's a ready-roll?"

"It's a joint. You get twenty of them in a Kools pack. The Vietnamese roll an ordinary Kools cigarette between their hands until the tobacco falls out. That leaves a paper tube with a filter at one end. Then they fill the tube with finely cleaned pot and twist the end shut. You wanna try one?"

"What's it like being high?"

"You can hear counterpoint in Mozart you haven't heard before." Jerry raised and lowered his eyebrows like Groucho Marx.

"You listen to Mozart stoned?"

"When you're stoned you hear Mozart the way musicians hear Mozart. Same with colors. Seeing a landscape while stoned is seeing it like Van Gogh saw it."

"Sounds incredible."

"It could take you away from this place for a while."

"I'm all for that." I knocked out my pipe. "Let's give it a try."

We walked beyond the hooches to a dirt road between two heavy equipment yards. Jerry lit one of the ready rolls, inhaled, held the smoke for a moment, and released it with a cough.

"That's the way you smoke a joint," Jerry said. "You take a deep drag and hold it as long as you can."

Jerry handed me the joint. I sucked down a chest full of smoke and held it for a few moments but expelled it in a spasm of coughing. Jerry chuckled. We continued walking down the dirt road.

"Take another hit and pass it back to me," Jerry said. "Always keep a joint moving. Don't jones the joint. It's considered bad manners."

I took another drag. This time I held the smoke down and handed the joint back to Jerry. I tried speaking while expelling the least amount of smoke possible. "Sorry," I wheezed. "I didn't know I was jonesing anything." I watched Jerry take a deep inhalation and wave the joint under his nose, sniffing up more smoke. I exhaled just as Jerry passed the joint back to me. I took a deep hit and wheezed, "You sure this stuff isn't ground up pine cone?" A curl of smoke drifted from my mouth.

Jerry laughed and choked on his smoke. "That's the Kools filter you're tasting."

We passed the joint back and forth and ambled along the road between equipment yards.

I looked around and checked inside myself, trying to detect the effects of the smoke. Vision. Thoughts. Perception of the environment.

We were walking on a deeply rutted dirt road. The full moon was golden and large on the horizon ahead of us. Trucks and bulldozers and earthmovers rested heavily in yards adjacent to the road, their upper edges glowing yellow from the moon.

Suddenly Jerry waived hello to a guard who appeared in the middle of the yard on our right. I quickly pulled the joint from my mouth and tried to hide it in my palm, but Jerry said, "Don't worry, he's cool."

We continued walking and sharing the smoke.

"So when does this stuff start working? Maybe it isn't any good."

Jerry laughed. "Trust me, this is good reefer. Here, finish this. I'll fire up another one."

We stopped while he fished in his shirt pocket and pulled out the Kools pack and tapped out another ready-roll. I took a hit on the joint he told me to finish and flipped the filtered end to the side of the road. Jerry handed me number two. We passed it back and forth, and inhaled deeply each time it returned to us.

"Notice anything yet?" Jerry asked.

I did another internal check of my thoughts and sensations. The back of my head felt peculiar. And there was something faintly ominous about the black shadows along the road. I wasn't worried about yard guards or VC. It was something else. Something lurking behind the scenes. Maybe it was just my head. I felt light-headed.

"I'm a little woozy from sucking in so much smoke," I said. But now my voice sounded strange to me. "It's like I'm listening to somebody else. Is that the marijuana kicking in?"

"Could be." Jerry sounded pleased with himself.

"Oh, wow," I exclaimed. "The ruts in the road look like mountains. It's like we're ten miles tall and walking over mountains!"

I started taking giant steps to clear the tops of the mountains.

Then I looked ahead of us at the moon on the horizon we were walking toward. "Oh my God. I feel like I'm flying toward the moon. This is incredible."

Jerry said, "Hey, look at me."

I stopped taking giant steps and began turning toward Jerry. As I turned—feeling a little unsteady—I looked at the dirt road directly in front of my boots.

My attention locked on a palm-size flat white stone. It was pressed level with the ground at the bottom of a tire rut. It twinkled with reflected moonlight.

That rock astounded me. It was inexplicable. Not just as a rock, but its very existence, its physical stuff. Why does this rock exist rather than not exist? Why does anything exist? Do causal links from everything else create and sustain this rock? Wouldn't that make this rock the center of the world? Or is each thing the center?

I was sure no one had ever noticed this rock before—no one had really seen it—until now. It had existed unobserved for thousands and thousands, maybe millions of years. Without reason, without explanation. A lump of opaque beingness that defies rational understanding.

I completed my turn toward Jerry.

His face looked like a grinning mask.

Jerry laid his open right hand on his mask and pulled his hand straight out while bringing his fingers together. It looked like he pulled his rubbery nose and face to a point. It was the funniest thing I'd ever seen. I bent double laughing.

"Any of that joint left?" Jerry asked.

"Ah, no. Better light another one."

"Maybe not. I'll have to lead you back to the hooch as it is. Let's head on back."

Jerry led us back to a hooch. I wasn't sure which hooch it was, but it wasn't mine and it wasn't Jerry's.

When we walked through the door of the hooch, white spikes sticking out from overhead light bulbs stabbed me in the eyes. I ducked my head and shielded my face with both hands. Moments later, when I cautiously lifted my hands and looked up, the spikes had disintegrated into blue smoke.

I looked around in the smoke and I was amazed to see a translucent surface inches from my face. It was like a stained glass window constructed of brilliantly colored miniature mosaics. Little army cots. Tiny lawn chairs. Footlockers. Miniature men in T-shirts and fatigues. Each mosaic was colored in glowing yellows, greens, browns, and grays. Some moved and some stood still, but they all fit neatly against each other with razor-sharp precision in a flat, two-dimensional composition. I was stunned by the picture's crisp artistry. With great pleasure, as if in an art museum, I locked my attention on one mosaic after another. If I moved my eyes too quickly, the images snapped across my visual field like slides in a projector.

And then, out of nowhere, I heard a woman in cowboy boots in a field of sagebrush singing over a wailing, moaning, electric guitar that made outrageous parody of her stilted delivery and sing-song lyrics of Patsy Cline's "Walking After Midnight." I chuckled at the delicious send-up of country-western music.

Then I saw the flat, distorted faces of four or five men staring at us as if we were freaks in a county fair. I knew my face was distorted, too, just like theirs, so I grinned at them to acknowledge our shared condition.

"Here come a couple more heads," somebody yelled. The voice was like a slap in the face. It swatted away my pretense of normality. I was exposed. Everything was moving in slow motion. I was teetering, unsteady, in front of these men. I turned to look at Jerry for how I should react. But Jerry was flat as a pancake. No wonder they knew we were stoned.

I followed Jerry to a cluster of five men sitting on the floor around an electric hot plate. A teapot was on the hot plate. Each man had a porcelain teacup.

Across the hooch, in a corner, men were drinking beer and playing cards. One man had a bottle of Jim Beam. "Fucking dope heads," one of them yelled. They pulled at their ears and stuck out their tongues and wagged their heads with wide-open eyes. Their hostility hit me like a physical assault. They were dangerous men.

"They're juicers," Jerry said quietly. "Stay out of their way and they won't hurt you."

"Hey, Jerry," one of the juicers called, "Come over here. I got a joint you guys can suck on." All the men in the corner laughed, but the men around the teapot did not laugh. Two of them nodded their heads and smiled. Jerry waved at the juicers. Then he turned his attention to the tea drinkers.

"You guys have extra tea?"

"Sure. Always room for two more." The man closest to the teapot waved his arm for us to sit down and join them. Several men moved over and made space for Jerry and me. We sat cross-legged on a thin straw mat that covered the concrete floor between the cots.

Somebody handed me a tiny porcelain cup without a handle. Another man picked up the pot and poured tea in my cup. His face was kind, but serious. Beads of red, yellow, and green sparkled with exotic beauty around his neck.

I moved my gaze from the colored beads and looked to my left. Two men nodded at me and smiled knowingly from behind mirrored aviator sunglasses. They looked like cops.

I waited for instructions.

"You ever had jasmine tea?"

Jerry's question, whispered in my ear, seemed to come from inside my head. I answered *No* in my mind.

I looked down and saw tiny purple flowers floating in my tea.

"Put your nose to the cup and smell the tea," the voice whispered.

I did as the voice suggested.

An essence of lavender and scented silk garments of oriental women permeated every cell of my body.

"This is beautiful," I whispered. "Lovely."

Waves of water distorted my vision and I feared I was drowning in jasmine tea. I looked up, out of the cup, and I saw we were all drowning in jasmine tea.

"I don't care," I said. "It's all so beautiful."

———————

Sunday, May 18, 1969 - Cu Chi Base Camp
Dear Janice:

Glad to hear your birthday presents arrived in good condition. I was a bit worried about the china being damaged. I'm happy you're pleased with it all.

Thanks for asking about my story writing. I've been taking notes, making outlines, writing rough drafts. But writing is in competition with my off-hours reading and the nights I return to the office to finish typing jobs I don't get done during the day.

Yesterday I went on a road trip in a jeep with Chaplain O'Donnell. Just the two of us. He wanted to visit a number of firebases and conduct religious services for the men, and he asked me if I'd like to come along and write an article about it. He said the roads we'd be driving were safe.

Chaplain O'Donnell is a nice guy. He's about thirty-eight. Warm brown eyes. Easy smile. But he's convinced our war in Vietnam is sanctioned by God because we're fighting Godless communism. I asked him which method of killing Jesus would use. O'Donnell just smiled.

Love, Andrew

Saturday, May 31, 1969 - Cu Chi Base Camp
Dear Janice:

It was wonderful talking with you on the MARS hook-up.

But I didn't like having short-wave operators listening to us. And waiting five seconds to hear each other's replies made conversation stilted and less personal than I thought it would be.

If it's okay with you, I'd rather not do the MARS thing again. I love hearing your voice, but not under those conditions. I'd rather get more Tabu perfumed letters with lipstick smooches on them.

Captain Davis of Alpha Company is the guy I mentioned who took me to Long Binh with him so I could phone you. He had to attend an asphalt conference.

I wrote a short piece for the paper about "Talking on MARS" and another piece about "Asphalt vs. Concrete" from info Captain Davis gave me.

Love, Andrew

Perilous Foundations

Three months reporting and writing for the battalion newspaper and it went straight to my head. I started seeing myself as a reporter of facts. A digger for truth. An explainer of issues. *A journalist.* So I did a story on Buddhism after hearing an NCO call one of the most prevalent religions of Vietnam "a bunch of bullshit." Then I did an editorial on the protestors back home. I said they aren't idiots or evil, just misguided.

The earlier stories came in under the radar, but the protestor story caught Colonel Hackett's attention. He called me in, cautioned me, and reminded me on which side my bread was being buttered.

But that warning didn't hold me back when I thought I was on the road to the biggest story of my Vietnam tour as editor of *The Road Paver*. Even at its best, *The Road Paver* is a dozen pages of pure brainwash, but this story would be different. It would be *real* news. Good God, it would be *The Truth*. And Hackett couldn't touch me when Stars and Stripes picked up the story and full national attention was on my side. Why I thought that puzzles me even now. How could I be so blind?

Well, my big news story, with the "help" of Major Roberts, turned into a two-sentence news release that was rejected by *Stars and Stripes* for having no merit whatsoever. That dashed my hope of being a "true journalist" then and there.

So to hell with journalistic integrity. Since Major Roberts robbed me of my chance at a Pulitzer, this time I'll tell the story the way I want. I'll use the techniques of a new kind of journalism and describe scenes and events I've heard about from reliable witnesses, but I'll describe them as though I saw and heard them myself, like an unseen fly on the wall. If Truman Capote can do it *In Cold Blood*, then I can do it too. Here goes.

"Hey, Marko, wake up," Dawson called.

"Huh? What?" Markowski lifted his sweaty head off his damp pillow. "Wadda ya want?" He looked around. Mid-morning sunlight filtered through window slats and mosquito screening, and colored everything in the hooch muddy yellow.

"You hear anything?" Dawson asked. "Anything strange?" Dawson sat on the edge of his cot at the far end of the hooch. His beer belly hung over his boxer shorts. His pink skin dripped with perspiration.

"Do I hear anything?" Markowski raised up on one elbow. "What the hell do you mean, do I hear anything? I hear you, you asshole. Why'd you wake me up?" He plopped his head back on the damp pillow.

Heat waves rippled under the scorching hot galvanized tin roof. Oscillating fans resting on ammo boxes rolled humid air like warm blankets over the sweating bodies of Dawson and Markowski. The previous night Dawson had been on de-drumming detail at the asphalt plant and Markowski had been on perimeter guard duty. Now they had the day off and were alone in the hooch for needed sleep ... alone until three hooch mama-sans arrived with their mid-morning chatter while gathering laundry bags, sweeping the hooch, straightening blankets, fluffing pillows, and gathering everybody's extra set of boots to polish later in the day. They finally left to do the wash at the shower building.

Ten minutes after the mama-sans left, Dawson called again. "Marko, you still awake?" Dawson walked barefoot down the aisle past cots, footlockers, fans, and Conroy's waist-high fridge toward Markowski's bunk in the middle of the hooch. "I need to turn off these fans so we can listen—"

"What the hell are you talking about?" Markowski raised up on both elbows. "And leave my damn fan alone." He pulled the tip of his walrus mustache down from where it had curled up on his nose. "Goddamn it. Between you and the hooch girls ...." Markowski leaned to one side and punched his pillow. "Now I'm wide awake." He swung his legs over the edge of his cot and sat up, giving a quick adjustment at the crotch of his jockey shorts. His brown hair stuck out on either side of his broad head like wings.

"Listen to me," Dawson said. He was now standing in the aisle next to the wooden footlocker at the end of Markowski's cot. His round, pudgy cheeks were copies of his round, pudgy belly. "I think I hear digging or scraping, and it sounds like it's coming from under the hooch."

Markowski closed his eyes to focus his thoughts. "You're hearing the

Vietnamese day workers filling sandbags outside."

"No I'm not. I heard scraping sounds even when they took a break."

Markowski opened his eyes, raised his thick brown eyebrows, and looked around as though sound could be seen in the air. "I don't hear anything."

"Put your ear on the frame of your cot," Dawson said. "That's how I heard it the first time. Better yet, get down and put your ear on the floor."

"What the hell, I'm not laying on the damn floor to hear *scraping sounds*." Markowski pronounced "scraping sounds" in a high, baby voice.

"Marko, I'm telling you, I think somebody is digging under our hooch."

Markowski groaned and stood up. He rolled back a thin straw mat in front of his cot. He turned and glared at Dawson. Then he and Dawson got down on their stomachs and put their ears to the exposed concrete floor.

"I still don't hear anything," Markowski said, his head resting on the floor next to Dawson's.

"I know," Dawson whispered. "I don't either."

Markowski got to his feet and tried to brush the sand off his sweaty chest and belly. "I can't believe you woke me up so I could get down on that goddamned sandy floor. Oughta fire those fucking hooch girls. They never sweep under the matts."

Dawson sat on the floor with his legs folded like a meditating pudgy Buddha. He squinted and scanned the concrete. "Before I woke you up, before the mama-sans came in and after they left, I heard scraping for maybe ten seconds, then nothing, and then more scraping. It's gone on like that … must be over an hour by now. I'm not imagining this."

Markowski rolled his eyes and shook his head. "Christ. Okay, let's try again. But this time let's listen at your end of the hooch. And turn off the fans," he waved his hand to encompass the hooch, "and unplug Conroy's fridge. I wanna hear what you're talking about."

Dawson smiled, got up and brushed off the sand, and walked down the aisle and unplugged Conroy's fridge. Markowski turned off the fan on the ammo box next to his cot and headed for the four-foot-high plastic oscillating pedestal fan three cots further down the aisle.

"Hey, I got an idea," Markowski said as he padded on bare feet behind Dawson. "Put a drinking glass on the floor and press your ear in the glass." He tipped his head sideways toward his cupped hand. "My brother and I did that on my parents' bedroom wall."

"That's disgusting," Dawson called over his shoulder. "You're one sick pervert."

"Nah. Just curious. All that grunting and groaning." Markowski chuckled. "When Dad got going, he talked dirty in Polish."

"What about plastic tumblers from the mess hall?" Dawson called from the end of the hooch. "I got some in my locker."

Within minutes, Markowski and Dawson were on the floor again, this time beside Dawson's cot. But then the hooch door squeaked open and banged shut. Carl Zimmer, the Headquarters Company clerk, sauntered down the aisle, whistling as he walked, until he came opposite Markowski and Dawson stretched out on the floor.

"Hey, what are you guys doing?" He squinted and leaned his head forward. He looked quizzically—suspiciously—at the two sandy-legged men clad only in their under shorts.

"Quiet, Zipper." Dawson glared at him. "We're trying to hear something. Okay?"

Carl Zimmer was a fundamentalist Christian from Indiana who talked about Jesus every chance he got until one night three men pushed him into a corner of the hooch and told him to "Zip it up about Jesus or we'll squirt Deep Heat up your butt." Everybody called him Zipper after that.

"You drunk again?" Zipper asked.

Nobody said anything for a few moments.

"There!" Dawson whispered. "Put your tumbler down, Marko, and listen to that. *That's* what I heard!"

Markowski was lying on his side pretending he was looking at Zipper through the plastic tumbler like a telescope. Markowski rolled over on his stomach and put the tumbler on the concrete floor and listened. He looked up. "I still can't hear anything." He put his finger in his ear and skewered it back and forth as though reaming a clogged sewer line. "Shared a bunker on the perimeter line last night with a guy from Charlie Company. Damn asshole fired several rounds with the muzzle near my ear. Still ringing—"

"God *damn* it," Dawson yelled. "Damn it all to hell. Why didn't you tell me that before? Jesus Christ."

"What are you guys talking about?" Zipper asked. "And do you have to use the Lord's name—?"

"Come over here, Zipper," Dawson said, "and put your ear in this tumbler and tell me if you hear anything."

Zipper hesitated, but Dawson was apparently serious, so Zipper got down on his belly and pressed his ear into the plastic tumbler. He looked up.

"What am I supposed to—?"

"Just listen," Dawson said.

Zipper pressed his ear in the tumbler again and listened. He squeezed his eyes shut in concentration. "Well, I think …." He lifted his head and looked at Dawson. "Sounds like scratching or scraping. Sort of thunking, too. Is this a trick or something?"

Dawson jumped to his feet. "I'm reporting this to First Sergeant Watkins. The fucking VC are digging a tunnel under our hooch!"

Delta Company's Lieutenant Redding—a blond-haired, blue-eyed, ROTC graduate from the University of Georgia—walked double-time next to Specialist Dawson toward Delta Company's hooches. First Sergeant Watkins walked a slower pace behind them. Watkins' brown head was shaved and oiled. His portly frame and brown eyes were confident and steady with twenty-eight years of experience in the Army.

The company area was deserted except for Vietnamese day workers filling sandbags. The truckers of Delta Company were out hauling laterite and asphalt for Charlie Company's paving crew working on a side road off QL-13.

After listening to the scraping sounds coming from the hooch floor, Lieutenant Redding and First Sergeant Watkins walked outside. They looked toward the perimeter line a quarter mile away and then back toward the center of the base camp and the nearby chopper pads and especially the heavy equipment yard next door.

"Bet they're planning to surface some night in Charlie Company's equipment yard," Redding said to nobody in particular.

Watkins raised his eyebrows and tipped his head to one side, granting qualified plausibility to Redding's idea. He waved his hand toward the cluster of Vietnamese sandbaggers moving to another work site. "Day workers could calculate the distance to the equipment yard or any other damn thing in the base camp. Never trusted those little bastards."

"If we dig at the end of the hooch nearest the perimeter," Redding continued, shading his eyes as he looked at the distant perimeter bunkers, "I'll bet we find the tunnel." He turned to see who was standing nearby. "Hey

Dawson, go over to Charlie Company and ask First Sergeant Taylor for a backhoe and start digging at the end of this hooch. ASAP."

"Sir, I'm a truck driver." Dawson hiked up his pants from under his bare, sagging belly. "I don't know anything about backhoes."

"Then tell Taylor I need an operator, too. On the double."

When the backhoe and heavy equipment operator arrived and began excavating at the end of the hooch, nobody thought to arm himself. The idea of VC digging a tunnel under the base camp was so audacious it seemed like wild speculation. But when the backhoe operator broke through the top of a tunnel four feet below ground, everybody got serious.

"Hey, Markowski," Lieutenant Redding yelled. "Get your weapon and stand guard over this hole. We don't want VC popping up and firing at us. You too, Dawson."

"Lieutenant, can I speak to you a moment?" First Sergeant Watkins walked slowly away from the excavation site and stopped to confer. Redding followed and stood close to Watkins.

"Digging that hole, Sir," Watkins bobbed his head and raised his eyebrows in admiration, "was a sign of real leadership."

"Why thank you, Watkins." Redding's young face turned pink.

"But now somebody's gotta explore and blow that tunnel, and none of our boys is trained for that kind of operation." Watkins rubbed his hand over his smooth, brown head. He looked up. "But we could ask the 25th Infantry Division, right here on our own base camp, to send us a tunnel rat. They got a tunnel school that trains men for that kind of thing. We'd be smart, though," he squinted at the sky, "if we clear our request through Colonel—"

"Wouldn't that make us look like we can't take care of our own backyard?"

"Sir, with all due respect, are you going down that tunnel?"

"No, but that's not my area of responsibility. Nor is it yours."

"Well, Sir, you go right ahead and send one of our boys down there, but you best tie a rope around his leg because he won't be coming out alive."

"Shouldn't we at least ask for a volunteer?"

"Sir, none of our men will volunteer for that job. And if they did, we'd be irresponsible if we let 'em do it when experienced men might be available."

"Okay, call Colonel Hackett and see what he says about your idea. But make sure he knows it's *your* idea."

———

I reached for the receiver resting in the cradle of the ringing black phone to the left of two other phones on my desk in the battalion headquarters office.

"182nd Engineer Battalion, S-1 Office, Specialist Atherton speaking."

"This is Watkins in Delta. We got a VC tunnel being dug under one of our hooches and I gotta talk to Colonel Hackett right now, if he's available."

I put Watkins on hold and walked to the closed door of Hackett's air-conditioned office and knocked. I opened the door as Hackett called, "Come in." Cool air, smoky and rancid from Hackett's cigar, cascaded over my face and arms.

"First Sergeant Watkins from Delta Company on the battalion phone for you, Sir. Apparently they found a VC tunnel under one of their hooches."

Hackett jerked back from his papers as though buzzed by a wasp. He dropped his cigar in the ashtray and grabbed the receiver off his battalion phone and yelled, "What's going on Watkins?"

I retreated to my desk in the main office. Three minutes later the battalion phone rang again. I picked up the receiver.

"182nd Engineer Ba—"

"Get me someone on the horn from Tunnels, Mines, and Booby Traps. ASAP."

"Yes, Sir. And where—?" Hackett hung up.

I looked at the hunched back of David Connors, our head clerk—known as "Dickhead" behind his back—leaning over his typewriter two desks ahead of me. "Hey, Connors. Hackett wants me to phone something called Tunnels, Mines, and Booby Traps. You know anything about that? Who do I call?"

"25th Infantry Division."

Connors sounded irritated. Impatient. He was making a typing correction on a court-martial document by over-typing his mistake on a tiny sheet of white carbon he was holding against the document as he struck a word's worth of keys. So I knew my question wasn't the primary source of his anger. The tight-assed little Dickhead was irritated because each of two carbon copies below his original would reveal his whole-word fuck-up as a black-blob over-type.

I waited a few moments and asked, "Why would I call the 25th Infantry Division?"

Connors answered into his typewriter, his voice going higher and louder as he spoke. "Because a school for training tunnel rats is here on our base camp and it's run by the 25th Infantry Division."

"Really? They have a school for that?"

Connors spit out the words: "Will you let me do my goddamned work?"

"Ah ... any special way of getting hold of the 25th? I haven't called them before."

Connors turned in his swivel chair and looked at me over his clear-plastic-framed glasses. "You pick up the base camp phone, not the battalion phone or field phone, and you ask the base camp commo operator to connect you with an operator for the 25th. Then ask the 25th's operator to connect you with the tunnel school. Got it? Oh, and by the way, I hope someday you'll stop announcing the name of our battalion when you answer the battalion phone. Anybody calling on the battalion phone is in our battalion"—Connors' eyes got big—"and he needn't be told what unit he's in." He forced a wide smile, rapidly blinked his eyes, and turned back to his typewriter.

Asshole. Dickhead.

Five minutes later I was routed through the necessary phone connections and got a sergeant from the tunnel school and put him on hold. I walked over and opened Colonel Hackett's door and said, "Staff Sergeant Albers from Tunnels, Mines, and Booby Traps on the base camp phone for you, Sir."

I returned to my desk and tapped a pencil's eraser on my typewriter for a minute or two. Then I got up and walked to the adjutant's desk in the rear-left corner of the office.

"Lieutenant Harris?" I said quietly. "There's a story developing in Delta Company I'd like to cover for the battalion newspaper and maybe for release to *Stars and Stripes*." I reiterated what Watkins told me, and I explained that Hackett, at that very moment, was very likely asking the 25th Infantry Division's tunnel school for a tunnel rat.

Harris's eyebrows shot up. "What's your typing load? Anything you need to finish today?"

"Two easy letters and a long memo for Major Roberts. Nothing urgent. Corrections and margin edits are done on the Roberts thing. Ready for typing."

"Okay. Ah ... Bonky is loaded for the day, so give that stuff to Connors, and tell him I said he should stay after hours, if necessary, to get them typed."

"Oh my goodness, I'd hate for—" I shook my head and frowned. "This might be a hot story in Delta, but I can patch it together tomorrow after it gets cold."

Harris grinned. "Atherton, get the hell out of here."

"Yes, Sir."

I grabbed the two yellow legal pad pages off my desk. They had Major Roberts' indecipherable scrawl on them and my red corrections and rewordings on the margins of each page. I took the yellow sheets and crumpled them together, twisting them like a yellow rope. Then I flattened them out and carried the wrinkled pages to Connors' desk. He had been taking phone calls while I was talking to Harris.

"Harris wants you to type this stuff for Roberts." I spread out the wrinkled yellow pages in front of Connors. "Gotta be perfect. Without correction over-types. Gotta be done today."

"What the hell …?"

"Hey, ask Harris. I'm only telling you what he told me."

"Why are these pages wrinkled?"

"Major Roberts must have wadded them in his pocket."

"Wait a minute. This is *your* work. Why aren't you typing this stuff?"

"Beats me. Harris said I can take the rest of the day off. Oh, and he wants you to type the two rough drafts in my inbox, too."

"What the …? That's bullshit!"

I shrugged and returned to my desk while Connors hustled over to Harris. I slid the gray plastic cover over my typewriter, grabbed my M16 and ammo bandoleer off a wall hook, and walked out the door.

———————

I stopped by my hootch and picked up five small pads of lined paper and stuffed them in my pockets together with three pens. Then I walked to Delta Company. I passed Delta's HQ building and walked a dirt road to the hooches that sat in a grove of young trees at the edge of a flat field that extended a quarter mile out to the perimeter.

I didn't have a problem finding the right hooch. It had a backhoe parked at the building's end facing the perimeter, and there was a truck-size pile of dirt off to the side. A dozen men from companies all over the battalion were walking around the excavation site talking and pointing and looking down at the tunnel hole at the bottom of the excavation. Most of Delta's men were still out with their trucks hauling asphalt or laterite for a paving operation.

When I asked a couple of men standing at the site how the tunnel was discovered, they directed me to Dawson and Markowski. I questioned them and got notes for the beginning of this story. Then I talked to First Sergeant Watkins who told me how they decided to dig at that particular spot. I made a note to talk to Lieutenant Redding later. He was standing on the hootch-road talking to several other officers.

Then Colonel Hackett arrived.

I pulled back and stayed out of his way. He inspected the excavation site and talked briefly with Lieutenant Redding. Then he returned to the office. Lieutenant Redding and Sergeant Watkins walked to a nearby equipment yard scouting likely spots where the VC might have intended to surface.

It was then that the tunnel team from 25th Infantry Division pulled up like movie stars wearing sunglasses in a shiny new Tropic Lightning jeep. Staff Sergeant Albers, the driver, had a florid, patrician face topped with an Australian bushman's hat that made him look like an Englishman on safari. Corporal Petty, in the passenger's seat, was a short and skinny, sunburned nineteen-year-old with buzz-cut newbie hair. But the guy sitting in the back seat with a case of C-4 plastic explosive was the man who caught our attention.

He looked like a Latino street thug. Short, muscular, and slender. Not an ounce of fat. He wore blue-tinted sunglasses and a faded black bandana tied on his head for a doo-rag. When he turned a certain way in the sun, prominent bones below his eyes cast shadows in his hollow, olive-colored cheeks. As soon as the jeep stopped, he jumped over the side to the ground. His faded fatigues were tailored tight to his waist and legs. His nickname, Reeko, was sewn on his fatigue shirt. His jungle boots were scruffy brown without a trace of polish.

Reeko walked straight to the excavation. His right hand rested on the handle of a .38-caliber Smith & Wesson revolver in a holster tied at the bottom with rawhide to his thigh. He studied the tunnel hole, walked around to a spot between the excavation and the hooch, and studied it some more.

Staff Sergeant Albers walked to the side of the excavation opposite Reeko and the hooch and stood near the backhoe operator. To their right, between them and the backhoe and the huge mound of dirt, Dawson and Markowski stood with M16s slung on their shoulders.

Corporal Petty remained at the jeep fastening a KA-BAR combat knife and its leather sheath to his belt. Then he walked to the excavation with his hand on his holstered revolver and stood next to Reeko and stared down at the hole.

As each of these men joined the group, we looked at them and they looked at us, and then we all looked back at the hole again. Our visiting tunnel experts saw nobody of rank to whom they should report, so they waited for the officer or NCO in charge to appear.

After a few minutes, Lieutenant Redding and Sergeant Watkins returned from up the road where they'd been surveying the equipment yard. Sergeant Albers walked over to meet them and the three of them walked back up the road, presumably to scout the terrain and discuss what should be done.

Reeko was clearly agitated. He walked up the road past the hooch to where Redding, Watkins, and Albers were talking. I followed from a distance, pen and paper at the ready.

Lieutenant Redding was talking to Sergeant Albers and pointing to the equipment yard. Reeko caught Sergeant Watkins' eye and brought him over with an uplift of his chin. They talked. Reeko returned to the excavation. I did, too.

"First Sergeant Watkins said nobody has been in this tunnel," Reeko said quietly to the men around the excavation. "Is this true?"

We all nodded. Reeko spoke with a musical upswing in his voice. Sounded Puerto Rican. Not a surprise.

"Anybody look in this tunnel?"

We all shook our heads no.

Reeko slid down the side of the four-foot deep excavation and stood on a cleared space next to the tunnel hole. The backhoe operator, under the direction of Lieutenant Redding, had dug three feet of standing-room on the east side of the tunnel—assuming the tunnel ran south, directly from the hooch to the perimeter. Reeko removed his sunglasses, tucked them in his shirt pocket, and buttoned the flap. He squinted up at Petty. "Get me a frag."

Petty jogged back to the jeep and returned with a fragmentation grenade. He tossed it down to Reeko.

Reeko straightened the pin and set the grenade upright in the loose dirt next to the hole. Then he got down on his belly with his head and shoulders over the hole, and his boots angled up the side of the excavation. Pulling a small round mirror and flashlight from his side pocket, Reeko extended the mirror's telescoping arm. Hanging his head and shoulders partway down the hole, he held the mirror and flashlight in the tunnel. He turned them back and forth, looking in both directions. Collapsing the mirror and putting it and the flashlight pack in his pocket, Reeko rolled on his side and looked up at Petty. "Pull me up when I toss the frag."

Petty nodded and yelled, "Fire in the hole."

Rolling back on his stomach with his head and shoulders over the hole, Reeko pulled the pin and threw the grenade in the tunnel in the direction of the perimeter. In one smooth motion he jackknifed to his knees and then to his feet, and scrambled toward Petty, who pulled him up to ground level.

Lieutenant Redding, Sergeant Albers, and Sergeant Watkins heard Petty yell and came jogging around the hooch just as the rest of us were crouched down with our backs to the excavation. In that split second, the grenade went off. All three men flinched and dropped to the ground in front of us. The explosion in the tunnel wasn't dangerous to them, so they looked foolish flinch-ducking and hitting the dirt. None of us dared laugh.

The explosion was muffled but impressive. Especially when I considered the shock wave it must have sent down the tunnel. I intended to ask Reeko if he'd ever been in a tunnel when a grenade went off further down the line, but I never got a chance. I was too busy watching and taking notes.

Reeko walked back and sat with his legs over the edge of the excavation. He waved for Petty to join him. Smoke and dust coiled up from the tunnel hole. Sergeant Albers glared at Reeko's back. Lieutenant Redding and Sergeant Watkins looked puzzled, unsure of who was in charge.

"You tell your *muchacha* like I say?" Reeko asked Petty. "You tell her you ask for this shit?" Reeko was speaking quietly, as though he and Petty were alone.

Petty hung his head. "She got whacked outta shape."

Sergeant Albers walked up behind Reeko and Petty. "So you men are anxious to go down the tunnel?" His voice was twisted with anger and sarcasm.

"Waitin' for the air to clear," Reeko said without looking at Albers. "Frags use a lot of air."

"I know that." Sergeant Albers voice was a loud hissing whisper. "Proceed when ready." He walked from the excavation site, past Redding, Watkins, and me toward the jeep. His neck veins bulging.

Reeko pulled his .38-caliber Smith & Wesson from his holster. Petty did the same with his .22-long-caliber Colt. Both men swung open the cylinders, spun them, snapped them shut, and returned the revolvers to their holsters. Reeko felt for the sheath-covered bayonet hanging from his belt and tied to his leg. Petty looked down at his new KA-BAR knife. They pulled flashlights from their side pants pockets and checked to see they worked.

"You do this all the time?" Markowski asked, looking at Reeko. Markowski and Dawson had returned, after the grenade explosion, to their earlier positions next to the backhoe.

Reeko didn't look up. "My company discovers a tunnel? They call me." He pulled out a compass, looked around, checked the perimeter against the compass, and returned it to his pants pocket. Petty did the same.

Markowski pulled at the hairs of his walrus mustache and asked, "So you're ordinarily out in the boonies with an infantry unit?"

Reeko looked contemptuously at Markowski. Petty grinned and kicked dirt with his boot.

"Okay, how'd you end up here then?" Dawson asked, scratching his bulbous belly. "I thought Watkins, or whoever, phoned a tunnel school on the base camp."

"Our company pulled in for downtime. I was delivering my main man to the tunnel school"—Reeko tipped his head back and smiled at Petty like a man showing off his son—"when your call came in. So we come over for some live-action training."

Reeko slid down the excavation to the tunnel hole. He waved for Petty who slid down next to him. Reeko then eased himself into the tunnel, his face in the direction of the hooch. With only his head and shoulders above ground, he motioned with his hand to Petty, *Stop there*. Reeko ducked into the tunnel and was gone for five minutes, maybe a few minutes longer. When he reappeared—head and shoulders dusty, face dripping sweat—he spoke loudly to nobody in particular. "This tunnel ends twenty feet under the hooch. When we come back, we yell before we come out. Don't shoot us."

He looked sharply at Petty. "Know your job?" Petty nodded.

Reeko disappeared down the tunnel heading toward the perimeter. Moments later, Petty dropped in the tunnel but remained standing in place several minutes. Then Petty disappeared down the tunnel, too.

Almost an hour passed. We started to get anxious.

Finally we heard Petty yell from inside the tunnel. Our rats were back.

When they crawled out of the tunnel their faces were thick with grime. Sweat dripped from their hair and faces. Their fatigues were black with perspiration and dirt.

Reeko brushed himself off, smeared sweat from his face, and leaned against one of the big tires on the backhoe. He started, without preliminary announcement, to brief us about their exploration. We gathered in a half circle around him.

I was scribbling notes like crazy. I was worried I'd run out of paper. I'd scrawled notes on every page of my five pads and was already on the unused back-side pages of my first pad. I had to write smaller.

Reeko said the tunnel walls near the hole had broken up—but not a lot—from the grenade explosion. He dug through the clods of dirt and continued down the tunnel. Petty followed six meters behind so any exploding booby trap Reeko triggered would have less chance of seriously injuring Petty too. The tunnel, Reeko said, was dug in a zigzag pattern.

We all expressed surprise.

"This is done," Reeko explained, "so rounds can't travel all the way—"

"More importantly," Albers interrupted, "it reduces effects of explosions further down the line and provides hiding places for VC attacks."

"If you would like to do so," Reeko melodramatically waved at us while looking at Albers, "you can explain what else I found."

Albers' face flamed red, but he remained silent. Petty, leaning against the front backhoe tire near Reeko, looked off to the side with a grin on his face.

Reeko continued. "The tunnel goes a long way toward the perimeter, but it ends in a deep shaft. Straight down and wide as the tunnel, and filled with water. When I found the water, I called Petty and told him to turn around and crawl back to the entry hole."

Dawson blurted, "How wide's the tunnel?"

"About two feet," Reeko answered, "and three feet high."

"So how'd Petty turn around?" Dawson asked, and pulled up his pants from where they'd slid down the underside of his protruding belly.

"Rolled over on his back, walked his feet on the ceiling, and flopped over. But I crawled backward on the return trip so I could face the water-end of the tunnel. We found no trap doors, no booby traps, and no VC."

Reeko barely finished his sentence when Albers called out, "Okay, let's blow the tunnel." Reeko glared at him.

Albers waved for Petty to follow him. They walked to the jeep and brought back the case of C-4, a coil of det-cord, a small box of blasting caps, two-stranded electrical wire, and a detonator.

Reeko and Petty crawled back down the tunnel and positioned packets of C-4 at three locations and strung them together with det-cord so they'd explode simultaneously. Down in the tunnel, near the entrance hole, Reeko molded a blasting cap to the end of the det-cord with a gob of C-4 plastic explosive. He connected electrical wires to the blasting cap and ran the wire about twenty yards from the excavation and connected the wire to a hand-held detonator called a clacker. He handed the clacker to Petty and nodded.

Petty yelled, "Fire in the hole." Everybody crouched down as the air pulsed and the ground thudded with a powerful *WHUMP*. Dirt popped up from the surface of the ground at three sites about fifty feet apart, each one progressively closer to the perimeter.

Lieutenant Redding ordered the tunnel hole filled with dirt and the excavation leveled. The backhoe operator dropped a few buckets of dirt directly over the hole in the tunnel. Then he called to Redding and said he was returning the backhoe to Charlie Company and he'd return with a small dozer as soon as he got the okay from Charlie Company's first sergeant.

Lieutenant Redding shook hands with Staff Sergeant Albers and declared the operation a success. First Sergeant Watkins stood back and smiled as Reeko and Petty carried the remaining C-4, det-cord, blasting caps, and clacker back to the jeep while talking together about their work as tunnel rats. Redding and Watkins walked over and commended them for an "outstanding job."

By then it was early in the evening, and the men who had gathered around the excavation drifted away and several dozen new men arrived to see where the tunnel was and hear the story first hand. Lieutenant Redding relieved Dawson and Markowski from guard duty. Redding then returned to Delta's HQ to phone in his report to Colonel Hackett who was probably no longer at the office.

––––––––––––

The next day, while working on the story, I phoned Staff Sergeant Albers at the tunnel school. I asked him how I could get in contact with Reeko. Albers said Reeko had returned to the field that morning.

"What about Corporal Petty?"

"He's still here, but he's out on a training exercise. What do you want?"

"I'm writing an article for our battalion newspaper and I didn't get a chance to ask Reeko about the empty tunnel. Where'd the VC go? And what'd they do with the dirt from digging the tunnel?"

Albers laughed. "They carry the dirt back through the tunnel in canvas bags. And where'd they go? The water at the end of the tunnel wasn't ground water. It was a water trap, like the U-shaped drain trap under a kitchen sink."

"The tunnel walls don't collapse from the water?"

"Older tunnels in this area have walls hard as rock from laterite in the soil. Moisture in the air apparently hardens it. I'd guess the VC started this tunnel a few years ago—maybe longer—and recently resumed digging for a sapper attack on the base camp."

"Okay, but what happened to the VC? Who dug the tunnel?"

"That's what I'm telling you. The VC ducked back through the water trap when you guys found the tunnel. They were waiting on the other side of the trap, ready to kill anybody who came up from the water. Either that or they were long gone."

"So why didn't Reeko swim the trap?"

"Our men don't swim water traps. It's a suicide mission if they do. Swim one of those traps and you come up the other side blinded by water and without a clue which direction to point your flashlight, let alone your weapon. You're defenseless against VC just waiting to pop you. Some tunnel rats swim water traps, but they're crazy if they do. Odds are they'll end up dead. Our job is to render the tunnels inoperable. We blow 'em and plug 'em. That's what the 25th did when they built this camp in '66. The engineers found lots of tunnels, apparently from the war against the French colonists or even earlier. So the engineers blew the tunnels and bulldozed the openings full of dirt. Some of those tunnels we kept open for our tunnel school."

"But couldn't the VC dig out the collapsed tunnels?"

"Sure, and they did. First twelve to fourteen months after the camp was built we took quite a few attacks from the tunnels. But we kept blowing and plugging until the VC got tired of it."

"Let me get this straight. You're telling me the top brass knew all along they were building Cu Chi Base Camp on a nest of VC tunnels, and they did it anyway?"

"The risk was worth it. This is a perfect place for a base camp. The land is high and dry even during monsoons. The ground is firm, solid from laterite, good for heavy equipment and runways."

"Huh. And my engineering unit has no institutional memory of this because it was deployed here a little less than two years ago?"

147

"Sounds about right, but your top officers know about it."

"So why didn't the 25th fully destroy the tunnels right from the start?"

"How? The only way to do that is bomb them. Pulverize them with craters ten feet deep or more. But you can't easily build a base camp on land cratered like that. Besides, in 1966 they didn't know how extensive the tunnels were. We've since found tunnels in this area that have second and third levels. I'm talking about munitions rooms, sleeping quarters, assembly halls, hospitals, storage facilities, and ventilation shafts up to camouflaged openings at ground level."

"That's another thing. How'd they have enough air? I mean in the tunnel under Delta Company. They didn't have surface vents—"

"Actually, there's a lot of air in that tunnel. And the water in the trap might have been added after you started digging. It'd sure make the VC's job of hauling back dirt a lot easier it they didn't have to lug it through the water. The other side of that trap there might be any number of intersecting tunnels and air shafts."

"You're making me feel very uneasy."

"Don't be. Did you feel safe before you found out about this?"

"Except for occasional mortar rounds and harassing attacks on the perimeter. I've been telling everybody back home that Cu Chi is the safest place in Vietnam."

"It is. And nothing's different now that you know about the tunnels. We might get a little harassment from the tunnels once and awhile, but we have overwhelming force here. Nobody's gonna overrun us by crawling up a few tunnels."

"So why are you telling me all this? What if I put this in a news release? What if the media back home hear about it? Or the troops find out? No matter how you justify it, building a base camp on a bunch of enemy tunnels sounds wacko. More than that. Irresponsible."

Albers laughed. "I get a kick out of talking to you. Smart kid. College, right?"

"Yeah."

"But dumber than a box of rocks. Look, you'll never print this stuff. Your superiors won't allow it. And the story sure as fuck won't get stateside. But just so you know: if by some miracle you do publish this and you quote me, I'll come over there some night with a couple buddies and we'll beat the living shit out of you."

I wrote my expose about the tunnels under Cu Chi Base Camp. For the lead I used "Reeko the Rat" and the tunnel he explored under Delta. Three tight pages of my best writing. Front page stuff for *The Road Paver*. Slam-dunk for *Stars and Stripes*. I credited "background sources" for information about the tunnel network so I didn't step on Albers' toes. I claimed it was all widely known by officers in higher headquarters.

Major Roberts rejected it.

He said our battalion paper should not alarm the families of men who mail the paper back home. But he said a version of the article, if properly edited, could be submitted to *Stars and Stripes*.

I revised the article, aiming it specifically for *Stars and Stripes*.

Roberts rejected it.

He said I should eliminate what he called "speculation" and stick with "substantiated facts." But I couldn't substantiate the facts because nobody would go on record about them.

So I tried another angle: "If one tunnel, why not more?"

Roberts rejected it again. Said it was *pure* speculation this time, unworthy of responsible reporting in a war zone.

"Then that's it," I said. "I'm done. This is a waste of time."

"No, keep working on it." He handed the article back to me.

"No point in trying, Sir. You'll reject anything on this topic I write."

"You don't understand. I'm *ordering* you to work on it until it passes my inspection."

So I cut the damned thing to a two-sentence news release of "substantiated facts" for which I had *beaucoup* witnesses:

HEADING: "Perilous Foundations." 18 April 1969 a tunnel was discovered under a hooch in the 182nd Engineer Battalion located at Cu Chi Base Camp. The tunnel was destroyed without further incident.

Roberts chortled and praised it as a marvel of journalistic precision. He said it was still inappropriate for our newspaper, but he insisted we send it to *Stars and Stripes*.

"They won't accept it."

"Don't be so negative." He grinned. "Send it anyway. It's really good."

Stars and Stripes sent it back with this note: "Lacks lively writing and relevance to the ongoing war effort."

I'd been diddled. Made the butt of hee-haws at the officer's club.
Actually, I was lucky. Roberts could have reassigned me to the boonies.

―――――――――

Friday, July 18, 1969 - Cu Chi Base Camp
Dear Janice:

We're in the monsoon season. It's worse during the months of July, August, and September. The poor guys in the boonies must be suffering.

We had a visitor in our hooch last night. Ray Gunderson is a friend of Curt Myers in personnel. Ray was heading for the 90th Replacement Center at Long Binh and decided to stop by and say hello to Curt before flying back to the States.

Ray's face is pock-marked on the right side. So is his right arm and leg. The marks are deep and disfiguring. There's a pink scar where his right eyebrow should be. After Ray knocked back five or six gulps of Jim Beam from a quart bottle Curt had stashed in his locker, he told us how he got the pock marks.

He said the VC used fishnet to tie a U.S. fragmentation grenade at waist level to a tree trunk and fastened the loosened pin to a trip wire. Ray said the grenade's time-lapse chemical fuse must have been replaced with an instantly exploding percussive fuse. Leaves hid the grenade. The explosion killed the point man and peppered Ray with sharp-edged, BB-sized shrapnel. When Ray came back from a hospital in Japan, his company, at his request, made him their interrogator.

He said his best interrogations were with two or more suspected or confirmed VC. Ray said he'd tie them to trees at some distance apart but so they could see each other. Then he'd wrap det-cord around their necks, attach fuse-detonators, and ask the first guy to give him information about whatever Ray wanted to know. If the guy didn't talk, Ray ignited the fuse and the det-cord popped the man's head up in the trees "like a cork out of a bottle of spurting cherry soda." Then Ray went to the next guy who'd already be jabbering whatever Ray wanted to hear.

Love, Andrew

INTERVENTION

"Where's the guy who handles award recommendations?" asked a bull-necked junior officer as he swaggered into the S-1 office and stood over Dickhead Connor's desk.

"That would be Specialist Atherton." Connors jerked his thumb over his shoulder in my direction.

The lieutenant strode back to my desk. "You the awards clerk?"

"Yes, Sir. What can I do for you, Sir?" I looked up but remained seated and did not salute, which is technically acceptable for a clerk sitting at his desk in an office and responding to a junior officer. Not standing was a little cheeky, maybe even rude, but the guy's swagger and pushy voice irritated me.

"I'm First Lieutenant Douglas Paddington, Commander of Echo Company."

He was a typical football playing frat boy. Wide head. Thick neck. Muscled biceps. Closely spaced eyes. ROTC without a doubt. I was sure the only reason he'd been given command of an entire company was because captains for engineering companies are in short supply.

Paddington squinted at the papers on my desk. He tipped his head and turned with one finger a memo in my in-box so he could read the subject heading. While still looking at the memo he said, "I'd like to recommend some of my road crew for awards."

His behavior infuriated me. I used two fingers to straighten the memo back the way it was.

Paddington's eyebrows arched. "I've been told you'll write the award recommendations."

"That's technically the responsibility of the recommending officer or NCO, but I'll be glad to help any way I can, Lieutenant Paddington. Please pull up a chair so we can talk."

Paddington pursed his lips and flicked his eyes up and down our poster of Vietnam we had tacked on the wall. He acted as though his two "louie" bars gave him the authority to assess our operation. The colonel's approval apparently wasn't good enough.

"Sir? There's a chair right there beside my desk, if you'd like to sit down."

He settled in the chair and I took notes as he briefly described a fire that occurred the previous day at Sáng Mât Trâng Village. The fire halted his paving crew's work on a road that bisected the town. Paddington summarized, in very broad terms, the actions of eight of his men who joined the villagers to fight the fire and said he wanted to recommend them for Bronze Stars, especially Staff Sergeant Miller.

Bronze Stars? *Eight of them?* I was stunned. We award Bronze Stars for *exceptional* valor and *outstanding* achievement. The actions Paddington briefly described were commendable, but they didn't come close to meriting Bronze Stars for achievement, and certainly not for valor against an enemy.

Paddington's request was peculiar, and it made me uneasy. After months of handling award recommendations, I knew an officer or NCO can have ulterior motives for recommending medals for his men. Recommendations can be used to mollify angry or contemptuous subordinates and help suppress rumors of the superior's incompetence. There was more to Paddington's recommendations than he was telling me.

"You have rough drafts that describe each man's actions?"

"Ah, no. I didn't— "

"We can't just say they all risked their lives fighting a fire, you know."

"I realize that, Specialist Atherton. That's why— "

"You have notes, anything at all, about the actions of these men?"

"No, but— "

"Then how can we inform higher headquarters that these men merit Bronze Stars?"

"Goddamn it, that's why I'm coming to you. I can write memos about regulations and Army policies, but describing what these men did in a way that conveys their bravery requires a special kind of writing that Colonel Hackett thinks you're good at. That's why I'm giving you the names. I want help with this! Here's the list." He removed a spiral notebook from his shirt pocket and tore out a sheet of paper and handed it to me.

After each hand-printed name he'd written a hooch number. "Ahh … Lieutenant, you're asking me to do a hell of a lot of work that's technically your responsibility."

"As I understand it, *Specialist* Atherton, Colonel Hackett lets you reject recommendations you think aren't—"

"They can always be revised or resubmitted over my—"

"Do *not* interrupt me!" snarled Paddington. He glanced over his shoulder. Then low and husky, "Before you waste *my* time rejecting *my* recommendations, I expect you to help me get these awards for my men." Paddington pushed his face close to mine and spoke low and threatening. "Do we understand each other?"

"Yes, Sir. Fully understood. I'll write rough drafts for your review. But I'll need to interview the men. I guess that's what these hooch numbers are for."

"You got it." He leaned back in his chair. "I'm proud of my men. They risked their lives to help those villagers. I want maximum effort on this."

"I'll do my best, Lieutenant Paddington."

That evening I visited two of the listed hooches and was rerouted to the EM bar. I had a quick beer with Sergeant Miller and another one with Specialists Gallagher and Kohler. They gave me accounts of the fire and their respective roles in helping the villagers. But they were embarrassed by the whole episode and asked me to spike any medals Paddington might request for them. Sergeant Miller said I might want to talk with the RTO, a guy by the name of Donaldson. His name was not on Paddington's list.

The following night I tracked down RTO Donaldson, the unit's on-site radio operator. He gave me his account and told me how to locate the helicopter pilot, Captain Steuben, whose name was also not on Paddington's list. Later that night I bummed a ride halfway across the base camp to a pilots' club where I found and interviewed Steuben.

Those five interviews gave me enough information to understand what had happened at Sáng Mât Trâng and why it was unlikely that any of Paddington's men, as laudable as their actions were, would get a Bronze Star.

Sáng Mât Trâng Village was a small but growing center of commerce. In addition to thatched huts, it had several cinderblock warehouses and three or four wood-framed buildings on each side of the main road that bisected the town.

We were paving that bisecting road, QL-14, at the request of the 25th Infantry Division so they'd have faster access to their western artillery bases. Echo Company's paving of QL-14 would also improve the commercial traffic in and out of Sáng Mât Trâng Village, which delighted the merchants.

The day of the fire, early in the morning, Lieutenant Paddington, Staff Sergeant Miller, and RTO Donaldson stood at the rear of Paddington's jeep. They had parked in the middle of town alongside a stretch of QL-14 where gravel-laced laterite had been spread and leveled by bull dozers. Water tankers were now spraying the mixture and road rollers were compressing it in preparation for the asphalt paver advancing slowly from the east. Far ahead, beyond the western edge of the village, dump trucks and bulldozers were spreading the gravel and laterite mixture over the dirt road that was cut smooth several inches below the surrounding surface by giant earth movers working even further up the line.

Staff Sergeant Miller was a stringy, energetic man who couldn't hold still when he spoke. He was medium height. High forehead. Dark thinning hair and fast growing black whiskers. Men respected him as the brains behind Echo Company's paving operations. Although Paddington had formal command of the unit, Miller regularly made recommendations to Paddington and, for all intents and purposes, controlled the day-to-day operations. He stood beside Paddington and studied the spec sheets they'd unrolled over the back of the jeep.

At the same time, RTO Donaldson—a soft, fleshy young man, maybe nineteen or twenty, with ruddy cheeks and a stubby pink nose—was installing a new battery in his PRC 25 portable radio. The radio was vital for calling in dust-offs. Echo's road medic was a good man, but working with heavy equipment produces injuries needing far more than roadside medical attention. A PRC 25 and a radio operator were also necessary for requesting combat support in case of an attack. But the likelihood of a VC attack, in this case, was low. Sáng Mât Trâng had no history of VC activity. It was a friendly village. And with Echo Company improving commercial access and boosting trade, the villagers had good reason to resist VC activity.

Miller looked up from his spec sheets and leaned back to stretch his neck and shoulders. But he also looked up because he'd heard a distant "poof," like a gas stove burner igniting. He saw, over the tops of nearby huts and buildings, a rising cloud of smoke less than a quarter-mile north of the road, smoke that hadn't been there moments earlier.

"Goddamn, look at that," Miller said.

Donaldson looked up. "Got themselves a fire. No explosions. No gunfire."

"Northeast corner of town," Paddington said. "Must be the kilns."

At the edge of town, twelve clay kilns formed the basis of Sáng Mât Trâng's charcoal industry. The clay kilns were bleached white from heat and domed like Quonset huts twenty feet long, eight feet wide, and five feet high. Villagers cut and trimmed tree trunks and limbs two and three inches in diameter and dragged them behind water buffalo from the forest to the kilns. They cut the limbs and split the cut trunks into chunks, positioned the chunks in the kilns, and burned them in restricted airflow for seven days. The villagers then sealed the kilns and allowed them to cool another seven days before workers emptied and restocked them. Vendors bundled the resulting charcoal in gunnysacks for sale as heating and cooking fuel as far away as Saigon.

The citizens of Sáng Mât Trâng Village built the kiln field a safe distance from town, but the town had grown. Villagers built thatched huts in all directions out from town, and they built along the edge of the kiln field, too.

On a previous day, Paddington and Miller had walked around the town and took note of thatched huts built next to the kiln yard. So they recognized the danger the fire posed for the town.

Miller looked at Paddington. "Should we offer help?"

Paddington grimaced and nodded his head, but he was slow to recognize the implications of his decision. Miller was not. If they shut down and sent men from either laterite operation, that would soon halt the asphalt paver.

Assuming he had Paddington's full approval, Miller ran to the nearest road roller and motioned for the operator, Specialist Kohler, to turn off his machine and follow him. Miller pointed to the smoke rising in the sky across town. Then he ran to a dump truck loaded with laterite and idling alongside the road.

"Help me alert the other men! We have to help put out the fire," Miller shouted through the truck's open window to Specialist Gallagher. "The whole town could burn down."

Miller's shouted warning scared Gallagher, and he stuck his head out and yelled, "What fire? Should we take our weapons?" But Miller didn't hear him. Men were already gathering around Miller without their weapons so Gallagher, a fine-boned, lightskinned, Bible believing Missouri boy who thought he was daring by growing a scraggly blond mustache, turned off his truck's engine and breathed a quick prayer for safety and guidance. He left his weapon in the truck and joined the others.

While the men gathered around Miller, Paddington stood next to his jeep with his mouth gaping. Miller was redirecting the entire laterite crew! Of course Miller knew far more about engineering than Paddington, and Miller regularly made engineering decisions for him, but halting the entire laterite operation was going too far. Paddington turned to RTO Donaldson and growled, "Someday I'm gonna court-martial that son-of-a-bitch for insubordination."

Laterite operations on QL-14 quickly ceased and seven men led by Miller ran toward the fire. While they were running, Miller yelled to Specialist Kohler, "Go back and alert Paddington to be ready for an attack in case this is a diversionary tactic of the VC." Miller wasn't worried there'd be an attack. He was just covering all the bases his newbie commander might not think about.

When Miller and his men arrived at the fire, they were transfixed in wonder. The smoke Miller had seen ten minutes earlier had come from a collapsed kiln that had been in use. It was also coming from the roofs of nearby huts built side-by-side that were set ablaze by the kiln's explosive burst of combustible gases and superheated charcoal. The remaining charcoal in the kiln glowed with hellish intensity, but it was no longer a danger to the town. Flaming ash from the burning huts was the real danger.

The huts' roofs were grass thatching. The frames were bamboo. The walls were slats of wood patched together with dried mud. Everything but the mud was kindling that was now burning with increasing intensity. The fire sucked air from all sides and formed a vertical blowtorch that blew flaming thatch and glowing cinders high in the sky to float down on other huts. A nearby hut caught fire while Miller and his men stood paralyzed by lack of equipment and the apparent inevitability of the disaster.

Women gathered in clusters watching their homes burn. Children squealed and jumped and ran with excitement. Other children held tightly to weeping mama-sans. Men of the village scrambled up bamboo ladders to the roofs of nearby huts and were beating smoldering embers with wet towels. A line of women formed a bucket brigade to bring water from the village wells for moistening towels and dousing sparks and cinders.

The fire consuming the huts quickly settled into a blast furnace of burning sticks, wood slats, and straw thatching. Waves of heat and swirling sparks roiled around a cauldron of combustion, a boiling red glow topped with immense yellow flames that leaped free of their source and flew up in the sky before flicking out. The heat was so intense the villagers were shielding their faces and turning their backs while beating out fires on nearby huts.

Suddenly Miller turned to his men. "Get on the roofs," he yelled. "Do what they're doing."

The men from Echo Company swung into action. Village women held out buckets of water for the GIs to soak their shirts for flogging sparks and cinders. The GIs hoisted each other up on hootch roofs by making slings with their hands. Miller remained on the ground.

"You guys up there," Miller yelled. "Be careful you step only on cross-supports! That thatching might support villagers but not you!"

"Get the water tankers," one man yelled.

"The equipment stays on the road," Miller yelled. "Tankers can't get in here anyway."

"Fuck!" yelled a heavyset GI when his right leg crunched through thatching up to his crotch. He tried to pull himself free, but he grew desperate after pulling out handfuls of thatching from the upward-sloping roof in front of him. He quickly realized what he had to do. He tipped far to one side and brought his free left leg up into a kneeling position. Then he rolled to the left, over his kneeling leg, and pulled his right leg out of the hole and promptly rolled off the roof. He fell to the ground, rolling as he hit.

Miller shook his head and passed along a bucket of water. "Get stuck up there," he yelled, "and you'll get barbecued."

While the other men extinguished burning embers, truck driver Gallagher jumped to the ground and ran back toward Paddington's jeep. He had what he thought was a great idea, an idea God had just given him, an idea that needed immediate action.

"Lieutenant Paddington!" Gallagher yelled while yet thirty feet away. "Chopper with water tank … before the fire spreads."

Paddington assumed Gallagher was conveying a request from Miller. He instructed Donaldson to radio Tropic Lightning on Cu Chi Base Camp for an emergency mission by an appropriately equipped Chinook helicopter.

Gallagher ran back to the firefighting crew and told Miller what he'd done. Miller immediately recognized the breakdown in command structure but thought Gallagher's idea was a good one. Distracted by the whirl of activity and the necessity of putting out the fire before it spread any further, he quickly forgot about it.

An hour later five huts were piles of glowing embers emitting thick smoke high in the sky. Several men had minor burns and other men had sprained ankles, but the GIs and citizens of Sáng Mât Trâng Village were beaming at each other from roofs of huts in a broad half-circle around the collapsed kiln. Miraculously, nobody had fallen or been seriously burned.

And then they heard the sound of a Chinook helicopter. The heavy thudding of its double rotors got closer. Men looked at each other and frowned. They pointed as the Chinook appeared, a huge water bucket slung beneath it.

"Is he coming here?" yelled a road-roller operator sitting on a roof.

"We don't need no fucking water dropped on us *now!*" yelled another man.

Captain Steuben flew the Chinook in at 500 feet. At first, he was guided by smoke from the charred huts no longer burning with visible flame. Then he saw the smokeless red glow of the kiln fire nearby. Uncertain, Steuben radioed Paddington and asked, "Where you want this water dumped?" He assumed Paddington was at the site of the fire.

According to RTO Donaldson, when Steuben's call came in, Paddington, back on Route QL-14, rolled his eyes and repeated Steuben's question to Donaldson. Then Paddington spoke in the PRC 25's handset to Steuben, "Try dropping the water on the worst part of the fire." After a long pause, Steuben radioed back, "You got a Roger on that."

Captain Steuben prided himself on his intelligence and his four years at the University of Colorado, and he deeply resented the sarcasm in Paddington's reply. To his copilot, Steuben said, "Let's make sure we hit what that asshole wants us to hit."

The worst part of the fire viewed from the air—the only fire that could be seen—was the red glow from the collapsed kiln. It was a small target when seen from the sky and surprisingly difficult to hit with water falling from a tank hanging below the middle of the Chinook, particularly since Steuben and his copilot were not experienced dropping water.

Then smoke from the burned huts obscured the kiln.

To recover the target's visibility, Steuben slowly lowered the Chinook over the kiln field opposite the burned huts. Wash from the rotors cleared the smoke and made the target visible again. But the chopper's downdraft blew more than just smoke. Ashes and burning embers flew over huts that previously had been in no danger.

Kohler, a weight-lifting black kid, was sitting on a thatched roof and could not believe what he was seeing. He yelled, "That dinky-dao pilot don't know what the fuck he's doing!" Kohler held his arms over his face for protection against the smoke and cinders.

Villagers and men of Echo Company shouted and cursed and waved the pilot away, but smoke hid many of them from Steuben's view. The few people Steuben saw waving he assumed were waving their welcome to him and their relief at his arrival. And Steuben assumed he'd be alerted by radio if there were a problem. From his chopper, he couldn't distinguish smoke from scattering embers.

Steuben, now oriented to a flight path, raised the Chinook and flew over the kiln and smoking huts and released the water. But when the water hit the kiln's super-heated clay and glowing charcoal, they exploded in clouds of steam and flying embers that blew in all directions like tracers from a firefight.

Steuben radioed Paddington for confirmation that the first drop was successful. Paddington thanked him and requested another load of water, since Paddington now saw more smoke than before. Steuben turned and flew back toward Cu Chi.

When the Chinook left, the villagers and GIs, many of them now wet, brushed cinders from their hair and clothing and looked around. Despite the shower of water, they saw glowing coals on thatched roofs all around them.

They renewed their efforts. They worked as fast as they could, but too many huts were catching fire. Two or three small fires would spring to life on a hut's thatching and rush together and engulf the roof in a roaring inferno. Several men were almost trapped by roof fires.

The GIs and villagers pulled back their firefighting operation to where Route QL-14 bisected the town. Women screamed for their children. Men ran from hut to hut looking for elderly parents.

The villagers and engineers now worried the blaze would jump the road to the south side of town. Several GIs drove two water tankers to the south side of QL-14. Using hoses at the rear corners of the tankers, they sprayed roofs and buildings closest to the road to prevent them from catching fire from falling embers. Other GIs and villagers hoisted each other onto thatched roofs of huts and ran up stairs to roofs of buildings to beat out sparks and glowing cinders.

In the end, a gentle wind began blowing the airborne sparks back toward the burning side of town. Nothing on the south side of QL-14 caught fire.

Then the men heard the Chinook flying in with its second load of water. Lieutenant Paddington, who had by now learned about the disastrous consequences of the chopper's first visit, radioed Steuben.

"Wash from your chopper blew fire all over town," Paddington shouted in the PRC's handheld mike. "Maintain higher altitude and scatter water over fire closest to the road."

Three hours later, nearly half the town on the north side of QL-14 was a steaming pile of damp ash and gutted wood-frame and brick structures. The heat was sufficiently reduced to allow GIs and villagers to walk through the devastation, so Paddington ordered his men to look for casualties.

Gallagher and Kohler discovered an elderly man who apparently had been trapped by fire on all sides of him. He had wrapped himself around the base of a waist-high stone ancestor shrine for as much protection as possible. His hair was singed off except for his stringy white beard. The backs of his arms, legs, and head were badly burned. His plaid shirt was fused with the skin on his back. But he was still alive.

"Run and get the medic," Gallagher yelled to Kohler. "And radio for a dust-off."

While Kohler ran for the medic, Gallagher sat cross-legged on the warm ground next to the burned man. The yelling had roused the man and he sat up.

He seemed unnaturally alert but unaware of how burned he was. Gallagher said his eyes shone like the eyes of church members filled with the Holy Spirit Gallagher remembered seeing back home. Gallagher started praying aloud for the man, and the man started talking in Vietnamese.

Days later, during my interview with him, Gallagher said he was sure God was there with them—"I could feel His presence"—and he was sure the old man felt it too. God's grace, Gallagher said, enabled the man to "speak words of forgiveness to me."

While the old man and Gallagher were communing with each other, a young village woman came running between the smoking ruins of the town and found them. When she saw the man's face and hideously burned body, she started wailing and slapping her hands against her thighs. The old man waved for her to be quiet.

Despite protestations from Gallagher and the woman and other villagers who had gathered around them, the burned man slowly got to his feet and staggered toward the distant road. Not even the woman dared touch him. His body oozed water and blood from charred skin and broken blisters. He walked fifteen or twenty feet, Gallagher said, before he crumpled as though his legs had lost air pressure. He fell on his side without catching himself.

The woman danced from foot to foot while pulling out handfuls of her hair. Her mouth was open as if she were screaming, but no sound came out. Gallagher said he again prayed for God's help and called to the woman. He told her a dust-off was on its way, but she ignored him.

At this point, Gallagher stopped praying and stared motionless at the ground, stunned by a frightening thought. He jumped up and ran toward the road. He passed Kohler and the medic running with a stretcher in the direction of the old man.

"Lieutenant Paddington," Gallagher yelled as he approached Paddington's jeep. "Radio the dust-off. Warn him about the downdraft!"

Five minutes later the dust-off landed further west, in a clearing, beside Route QL-14. The burned villager had been carried on the stretcher to the road and now he lay across the back of Paddington's jeep as the medic drove him and the young woman to the dust-off. Both medics—Echo Company's medic and the dustoff medic—said the man was already dead, but they loaded the body on the chopper anyway and took the grieving woman with them.

The day after my two evenings of interviews, I tried phoning Paddington in the late afternoon, but he hadn't come in off the road. I left a message for him with Echo Company's clerk. Paddington returned my call a few minutes before quitting time at 6:00 p.m. He asked if the rough drafts were ready for his review.

"Sir, regarding those recommendations, I seriously doubt Bronze Stars will be approved for your men. We have a better chance if we try for Army Commendation Medals for Achievement. But even for ACMs, we might consider attaching a note about the politically sensitive nature of the fire and how it spread. That way Colonel Hackett and Major Roberts, as well as higher headquarters, will have all the facts when they make their decisions."

"What are you saying?" Paddington's voice was brittle. "Are you saying my men didn't act heroically? Or they did something wrong?"

"No, Sir. Not at all. What I'm trying to say, and this is just my opinion, but if the full story of the Sáng Mặt Trăng fire were picked up by *Stars and Stripes* or the press back home, your medal winners might appear foolish despite their obvious heroism. I know you wouldn't want that. And Sir, I should inform you that your men do not want these awards."

"They said that?"

"Yes, Sir."

Paddington was silent for almost fifteen seconds. I had to break the tension.

"Look, Sir, I stepped way out of line. I'll start writing your recommendations right away."

"No, no, I see your point. Hold off on the write-ups and let me think about this. I'll get back to you later."

"Yes, Sir. Whatever you think best, Sir."

And that was that. I never heard another word from Paddington about those bullshit Bronze Stars.

Saturday, Aug. 9, 1969 - Cu Chi Base Camp
Dear Janice:
Every day we're getting heavy rain. We have a few hours when it isn't raining, then it starts up again.

Been thinking about you. I wish we could go for a walk together. And hold each other. I miss you.

Love, Andrew

KP WITH BRUNO, TWEEZE, & BERRY

I pulled up from my run in the morning darkness across our company's formation yard and yanked on the wooden handle of the screen door to the mess hall kitchen.

The door wouldn't budge.

I refocused and realized Sergeant Bruno Dretchler, the first-shift cook, was standing in front of me on the other side of the screen. He was holding the inside handle so I couldn't open the door. I threw up my arms in frustration. Here we go again.

I looked at my watch in the light coming from the kitchen door. It was 4:26 in the morning. I'd made it with four minutes to spare.

"You trying to test me?" Dretchler asked, and grunted his question again. "Your buddy is here, but the other KP is sick. So that means you guys got a lot of work to do. So why aren't you on this side of the door where you're supposed to be? A man proud of his work comes early to pick up the slack if it's needed."

"I hear you, Sarge." No sense arguing with him.

Dretchler let loose of the door handle and moved aside. I quickly opened the screen door and squeezed past him into the kitchen. Seemed like I often had to squeeze past him.

Dretchler forced that kind of chicken shit on all his KP workers, and it drove me nuts. I'd never met a man who repelled me more than Bruno Dretchler. He was at least six-foot two-inches. Huge chest. Firm tub of a stomach. Massive hands. His cheeks pushed up against deep-set, dark eyes too close together, so he looked like a giant pig sizing you up before he mashes you against the stall.

And Dretchler stunk. If I smelled his body odor long enough, working next to him at the serving line, I'd get sick to my stomach. He *might* be a person with exceptionally funky perspiration, but he didn't help it any by wearing the same T-shirt all week long. Any Saturday you could read the previous week's menus off his shirt. That's a *Sad Sack* cartoon joke, I know, but it's no joke with Dretchler. And every day he worked in that hot kitchen his T-shirt was *soaked* with sweat.

Inside the kitchen I was pleased to see Tweeze. He nodded and smiled. He was one of our company mechanics, an all-round fix-it guy. He even fixed my typewriter once. We worked KP well together, anticipating each other's actions, accommodating each other's strengths—Tweeze was a better egg cracker, I was a better bread toaster—and having a blast turning KP into high-quality team-work of which we were proud, and it made the time pass quickly too.

"Third KP's sick?" I asked.

Tweeze tipped his head down and glared at me. "Got my Superman cape on."

Tweeze was a proud lifer, far more experienced than most KPs. He was thin. A little on the short side. Narrow nose and face. Narrow head for that matter. Brown hair. Gray eyes.

At first I thought his nickname was due to his thin physique, but that didn't initiate the name. The story was that Tweeze dropped a screw in a tight place working on a jeep. He worked five minutes trying to get the screw out. Finally he walked to his tool box he kept locked when he wasn't on duty, pulled out surgical tweezers he'd recently "borrowed" from the medics, and said with a grin, "I'll tweeze it out." After that everybody called him Tweeze. Fits his personality too. He'd been busted from sergeant several times because he smarted-off to superiors. Just tweezing. Not taking any shit.

I liked Tweeze. I did not like Dretchler.

Dretchler walked to the stainless steel table at the center of the kitchen, leaned his backside against it, and looked at me. "What's your name? Hey, hey, turn n' lemmie see your .... Oooh, that's right. *Atherton*. Ain't you special? What a royal fart in the dark that is." He laughed.

I didn't respond.

"Okay, fun and games is over. Fancy-Pants and Tweezy-Tit. You guys are carrying the ball by yourselves. No third—"

"Come on, Serge," Tweeze interrupted, "call me Tweeze or I'm leaving."

Dretchler moved in so close his protruding stomach touched Tweeze's chest, but Tweeze stood his ground. "What do I got here? A mutiny? An insurrection? You wanna fight me? You gonna disagree with everything I say right off? Go ahead. Throw a punch, you skinny turd that can't hold his rank."

Tweeze said, "So let's get to work if there's so much of it."

Dretchler smirked and backed off. "Okay, now here's the rules. This is my kitchen, *Mr.* Tweeze, and you answer to what I call you. Got it? Now these are the jobs you guys got for breakfast." And he gave us assignments as though laying down the law to KP first-timers when we already knew what had to be done.

"And while you're doing that," he pulled a pack of Camel cigarettes from his chef's apron, "I'm going for a smoke. And remember, I got special projects for loafers."

The standard breakfast menu for the a-la-carte serving line was scrambled eggs, bacon, toast, chipped-beef gravy over toast, French toast, cold cereal, coffee and milk. Dretchler ran the stove—frying, baking, cooking of any kind—and we ran support.

Dretchler's shift started at 4:00 a.m., thirty minutes before ours, but he must have come in even earlier. He'd loaded and plugged in the big coffee canister. The red "perking" light was on. He'd poured water in the steam tables and turned on the electric heaters. The water was already sending up little curls of steam. He'd mixed the milk and flour gravy, and added the chipped beef. Three empty gallon milk containers, a ripped-open cardboard box, and a balled-up plastic bag were beside the gravy bowl for us to throw away. The fourth milk container, half full, we'd leave on the table to be used later. We knew Dretchler had mixed two palms of coarse-ground black pepper and a palm of salt in the gravy because the quart-sized plastic containers of salt and pepper sat beside the bowl, and we saw pepper in the gravy. Last but not least, he'd perked the cook's ten-cup coffee pot.

So we were off and running in what we called "The KP Race to Stardom" for which every move is synchronized and choreographed to feed a mess hall full of cranky, ravenous men on time and without a hitch. Usually.

Tweeze jogged to the bowl of chipped beef gravy, carried it to the serving table, held it balanced on the table's edge as he pulled an empty tray from a lower shelf and dropped the tray on the serving table over the steaming water, poured the gravy in the serving tray, and slapped a lid on it. He carried the empty mixing bowl to the big, square, galvanized steel sinks, dropped the bowl in the left basin—*BONG*—and ran warm water in the bowl. He jogged to the walk-in cooler.

While Tweeze did that, I pulled two, four-slot toasters to the center of the stainless steel table across the kitchen from the six-burner gas stove. I grabbed a butter brush from a hook on the wall behind my table and reached down for a cookie sheet on which I'd butter the toast and carry them to the steam table.

I crossed the kitchen. Poured two half-cups of black coffee for Tweeze and me we wouldn't have time to drink. Maybe a swallow. I threw the empty milk cartons, torn cardboard box, and balled-up plastic bag in the gray plastic waste barrel in the corner of the kitchen. Grabbed a damp wash cloth off a hook above the sink and wiped up flour and drops of milk and gravy off the stainless steel table where Dretchler did his mixing. Rinsed and re-hung the wash cloth. Then I jogged into the cooler and passed Tweeze walking out.

Tweeze was carrying six square, cardboard egg cartons, each holding three dozen eggs. He set the cartons on the stainless steel table I'd wiped clean, about three feet to the right of the gas stove. Tweeze pulled down, from an overhead hook, a stainless steel mixing bowl and started breaking eggs in it, one egg in each hand, and threw the shells in the covers of the egg cartons.

He broke thirteen-and-a-half dozen eggs. Threw in palms of salt and a big palm of fine-grained black pepper. Anybody wants more, they can sprinkle it on their eggs with their hot sauce. He added a glug of milk from the half-full carton Dretchler left on the table, and then grabbed a metal whisk from an upper hook and beat the fuck out of the eggs. Then he pulled down a giant iron skillet for the scrambled eggs and slid it on the cold right-front burner ready for Dretchler.

While Tweeze was breaking and whisking eggs for the scrambled, I grabbed from the cooler three cardboard boxes of bacon—five pounds each— and dropped them on the stainless steel table on the left side of the stove. I jogged to the steel table at the center of the kitchen, pulled down a giant skillet from the overhead hooks, jogged back and slid the skillet over the cold left-front burner and flopped in a handful of bacon.

We assumed, from breakfasts in the past, that most men would want bacon along with four scrambled eggs. A few men would pass up the eggs for the French toast or the chipped beef gravy on toast, or even cold cereal. So thirteen-and-a-half dozen eggs more than covered forty men. That was the rule. Most mornings forty men showed up for breakfast from Headquarters Company's roster of a hundred GIs.

An exceptional breakfast was when we had an early morning rocket or mortar attack. Everybody hurriedly donned their gear and hunkered down in defensive positions. But when morning light dispersed the darkness as well as danger, *everybody* came to breakfast and ate like starved fools until stuffed. But that wouldn't be this morning—judging from recent enemy inactivity—so we were ready, scrambled wise, for our breakfast eaters.

Of the remaining four-and-a-half dozen eggs, one of us, likely Dretchler, would break three dozen for the French toast. The last dozen-and-a-half eggs were for over-easy frying orders from the top brass and Sergeant Major Mollema, if they showed up.

Where'd Tweeze go? I looked around while jogging to the sink to wash my hands. Usually nobody worries about washing hands on KP, but with my hands covered in bacon grease, I wouldn't be able to hold on to anything. Hands dried, I jogged toward the pantry. And there was Dretchler leaning against the wall between the pantry and the cooler watching me!

"Cook's on deck!" I yelled as I ran into the pantry.

Tweeze yelled back from inside the mess hall, "Hit the fucker with a frying pan!"

I laughed as Dretchler followed me into the pantry. In a low voice he said, "You stupid fucks." A grin turned up a corner of his mouth, but his eyes were hard, staring at me.

I grabbed six long loaves of sandwich bread, three under each arm, and jogged into the kitchen. Dropped four loaves next to my toasters and carried the two remaining loaves across the kitchen to the stove side and plopped them on the stainless steel table four feet to the right of the bowl of scrambled waiting for Dretchler.

I pulled a knife from its wooden block on the wall behind the table. Slit the cellophane on the two loaves for the French toast. Dropped the knife back in its slot. Jogged to my toast station across the kitchen and pulled a knife from the wooden block on my wall, and slit the cellophane wrappers on the four loaves. I dropped eight breads into my two toasters and depressed the levers. I glanced over at the steam table.

Damn. So do it before you forget it!

I jogged to the steam table and pulled three trays, one at a time, from a stack on the lower shelf and slid them on the table, over gently bubbling water, on my right of the gravy tray. Now we had one heated serving tray for scrambled. One for bacon. One for toast. Gravy tray's filled and covered. I slid two more trays on my left end of the steam table: one for French toast and one for extra bacon and scrambled.

My toast popped up. I jogged to my toast station.

Damn! I forgot the butter.

I pulled out the popped toast and dropped them on the cookie sheet. Dropped eight more breads in the toasters and ran for the cooler.

Grabbed three waxed-paper covered bricks of butter—one for Dretchler, two for me—and jogged into the kitchen.

Dropped the butter on the steel table left of the stove. Bumped two sauce pans off overhead hooks, fumbled one, dropped it on the floor—*bing-bang-bong*—scooped it up and placed both pans on the table. Unwrapped the butter bricks. Dropped two in my pan, one in Dretchler's pan. Set the pans on back burners and turned on low heat under both and low heat under Dretchler's empty frying pans so they'd be ready for him.

Dretchler walked into the kitchen toward the six-burner gas stove. He'd start frying now. But as I jogged to my toast station while glancing behind me, Dretchler spotted our two half-cups of coffee at the far end of the stainless steel table with the big square wash sinks. I stopped at my table and watched as he lumbered to our cups and held them high in the air—uncontestable evidence of our crime.

"Who poured from my private pot and didn't even drink it?" He dumped our coffee.

I returned my attention to my toaster and pulled out eight popped toasts and dropped them, cold and hard, on the cookie sheet where I'd butter them. Cold and hard wasn't a problem. The serving table would steam and heat them like it did all our toast. Turns them into warm little rubber bath mats moist on the back when you pick them up. I reloaded the toasters with eight fresh breads. As I slapped down the levers on the two toasters, the kitchen suddenly filled with Dretchler's roar.

"What fucker put two unattended pans of butter on the back burners to boil all over my goddamned stove?"

Shit! The butter!

I jogged over as Dretchler, hot pad in each hand, moved the two sauce pans, frothing and dripping butter across the stove, to the safety of the left-side steel table.

"Am I looking at the knucklehead who did this? Don't ever leave unattended butter on a burner! If that stuff caught fire, I'd have you court-martialed."

"You're right, Sarge. But look. *Two* butter pans. One for me and one for you, too."

"You think that's the end of it?" And in a mocking voice as he wagged his head, "You melted butter for my scrambled? I'll have you scrubbing this stove all afternoon!"

I heard my toast pop up.

I used a pad to carry my pan of butter to the toasters. I loaded eight more breads. Unbuttered toast was piling up, but now I had my melted butter and my wide butter brush. Buttering one toast takes two seconds. One to dip. One to brush. Wouldn't be but minutes before I caught up.

Tweeze finally returned to the kitchen from the mess hall. I called to him as he passed me, "Had enough time with your girly magazine out there, Tweeze?"

He was carrying two empty five-gallon plastic milk bags, each in its own special cardboard box with a rubber spigot sticking out the bottom edge, one box under each arm. But he managed to flip me the bird anyway. He later told me he'd been restocking the milk dispenser and the jelly packets on the tables out in the mess hall, jobs that should have been done last night. Good thing Tweeze checked them out or we'd have had forty GIs screaming at us alongside Dretchler.

Dretchler turned up the fire under the egg and bacon frying pans. Poured one-third cup of butter in the egg pan. Swirled it and let it bubble for a moment. Pulled down a steel ladle from a hook above the stove. Scooped up a ladle full of gooey scrambled eggs and poured them in the skillet. He jiggled the bacon pan over the fire he'd turned up, and with his right hand he pulled down a spatula for the scrambled. But he kept glancing up at those overhead hooks.

"Where's the tongs for the bacon!' Dretchler bellowed. "And get me trays for carrying bacon and scrambled to the steam table! Get your thumb outa your ass!"

And on and on it went throughout breakfast.

After breakfast we scraped food off the dishes and silverware, rinsed them, and packed the first batch in a big commercial washer. But when the wash cycle ended and we pulled out the dishes on the wire rack on rollers, they were rinsed of soap but cold and greasy. We told Dretchler hot water was not getting to the washer.

"Do the dishes anyway," Dretchler said. "They'll dry and nobody will notice. We're one KP short and we don't have time to wash dishes by hand.

And maintenance won't come until tomorrow. I'll fill out an urgent request form after my smoke break."

We finished "washing" the dishes, and, as always, handwashed the stainless steel serving trays, frying pans, and cook's utensils, dried them, and put them back in their proper places. We retrieved the red plastic meal trays stacked outside where each man had dipped his tray in a galvanized trash bucket filled with scalding hot water and disinfectant heated by a waterproof kerosene stove hooked on the indside edge of the bucket. We slid the wet trays into vertical wooden racks at the far-end wall of the mess hall where the men pull them out while waiting their turn at the serving line.

Our last clean-up job was the concrete floor. We swept up crushed egg shells, pieces of cardboard, powdered sugar, drips of milk, egg, grease, and French toast dip. We sprinkled disinfectant on the floor and hosed it down. We sluiced the brown caustic water toward the drains with push-broom-sized rubber squeegees.

We sat down at nine o'clock for our first break that morning. Ate sandwiches—made by Dretchler, no less—and drank cups of his burned black coffee. After our fifteen-minute break, we started peeling spuds outside in the shade of the mess hall.

And then—happy days are here again—the second shift cook, Staff Sergeant Faulkenberry, showed up at 9:30. The real fun would now begin.

His nickname was Berry. But he told his friends and any KPs who worked for him that we could call him Berry-Ain't-Cherry, "since da' Lord *know* I like sweet pussy."

Berry outranked Dretchler and was in charge of the kitchen from the moment he showed up until 8:30 that night. All Dretchler's put-downs and verbal abuse ended. Berry-Ain't-Cherry wouldn't tolerate it. "All my KP is top of the cream, and they don't need no lashin' to make 'em better." Dretchler didn't say a word the rest of his shift unless it was needed to get the work done.

Berry was almost as tall as Dretchler, but thin and angular, and he moved with the grace and elegance of a male model on Fifth Avenue in a photo shoot for *Ebony Magazine*. He loved jazz and rock-and-roll, and his wit and jive were worthy of a stage. When he talked, he focused on our eyes and took our measure as he joked and made us laugh. At heart, he was an entertainer. He said he loved to see people laugh and dance. He even looked the part since his lean frame and pencil-thin mustache reminded us white guys of Sammy

Davis Jr.

The first thing Berry did, whenever he arrived in the mess hall, was turn on his Teac Reel-to-Reel, Self-Reversing Tape Deck jacked into a top-of-the-line Pioneer Amplifier and two kick-ass-big speakers. Berry had asked Tweeze, early in their tours, if he'd attach shelves to the kitchen walls for Berry's hi-fi equipment and install conduit for the wires so the installation would pass an IG Inspection. Tweeze finished the work in one night after waiting four days for replies to his "unofficial call" for conduit, wooden shelves, and metal brackets.

Tweeze wouldn't take payment for his work, but Berry insisted. Tweeze finally accepted Berry's offer of a Kools pack of ready rolls. Even so, Tweeze made a point of smoking the entire pack, over a period of several weeks, with Berry. After Berry's shift ended, they'd go between the heavy equipment yards and smoke a few and then come back to their concert-hall kitchen and jam the night away on rock-n-roll.

Tweeze told me that every night they shared a joint or two, Berry would ask him what kind of music he wanted to hear. But Tweeze was stoned, and he thought he was being asked what kind of rock-n-roll he wanted to hear. Tweeze knew nothing about jazz, and at one time or other he must have said something negative about it in front of Berry. So Berry set aside consideration of his own preferences to please his friend. Tweeze told me he didn't clue-up to it until that very afternoon the dishwasher broke down. Here's how it happened.

Soon after Berry arrived in the kitchen that morning, we pulled him aside and told him about the broken dishwasher. Berry said it was a serious health hazard and he'd get it fixed immediately, even if he had to hammer on the doors of Colonel Hackett and Major Roberts to do it. So he walked over to battalion headquarters office and asked for help from the top NCO of the battalion, Sergeant Major Mollema.

When Berry returned from the sergeant major's office, he was ecstatic. "Gotta know how to use your motherfuckin' connections," he said, and burst out laughing. And when the maintenance men showed up fifteen minutes later, Tweeze and I slapped each other a high five and got happy, too. But Dretchler shook his head and walked away. He later told Tweeze, "You know that's racial, that's all it is. Berry and Mollema doin' favors for each other. You or I couldn't do that. They get anything they want."

"What kinda music you wanna listen to *now*?" Berry asked us as the dishwasher started back up.

Tweeze and I looked at each other and I said, "Let's go with your jazz shit this time." Tweeze agreed.

So Berry cranked out Charlie Parker. Miles Davis. Thelonious Monk. Billie Holiday. John Coltrane. And Dizzy Gillespie. He had other performers recorded, but those are the names I jotted down from the list of artists he'd printed on the label of a tape reel.

I'd watched Louis Armstrong on *The Ed Sullivan Show*, but Armstrong made me uncomfortable. Sometimes he seemed to be acting out a white man's cliché of a black jazz musician. But the music of Parker, Davis, Monk, or Billie Holiday was a world far removed from white-bread suburbia where *The Ed Sullivan Show* was most at home. Their creativity, unfettered expression and ability to improvise such complex music astounded me. I'd never heard anything like it.

In the late afternoon, after Bruno Dretchler finished his shift at three o'clock, Tweeze and I were in the pantry getting supplies for supper and digging the jazz. We laughed as we showed each other how we thought black people slow danced at night clubs where jazz was being played. Our embarrassing behavior resembled a cross between Hispanic zoot-suit strutting and the funky chicken. The music's high volume created a cocoon around us, so we didn't notice Berry standing in the kitchen watching us through the pantry door.

He startled and embarrassed us when he walked into the pantry. He wasn't laughing or smiling, but dead serious.

"No, my brothers, this is the way you wanna move to my lady Holiday's grooves." And he closed his eyes and slow danced, alone, under what we imagined was a blue moon. His movements were smooth and fluid. Tweeze and I watched with our mouths open. Mesmerized.

Wednesday, Aug. 20, 1969 - Cu Chi Base Camp
Dear Janice:
Today we typed and sent to all the companies Colonel Hackett's formal announcement that we'll be moving to Lai Khe in late November or early December.

Echo Company was sent up there last week to construct hooches and offices and maintenance buildings for when the rest of us make the move. Vietnamese day workers are helping.

I'll soon go up there for a "look-see" and to write an article about the progress of the construction. I'll take some photos and send them home with all the others.

Lai Khe is about 18 miles northeast of Cu Chi. It's the home of the 1st Infantry Division ("Big Red One"). We'll be doing engineering work for Big Red One.

Lai Khe has a history of receiving lots of incoming rockets, so it's nicknamed "Rocket City." But Major Roberts told me they haven't had much action recently, so that's good.

Love, Andrew

RIDING HIGH WITH MANGUS

Paving roads in a guerrilla war zone is one of the lunacies about Vietnam that can make you smile. Charlie knows where we are and what we're doing, and he knows we're focused on our equipment and not on him. And Charlie can't miss the equipment. It's big.

Asphalt pavers. Bulldozers. Road graders. Earth movers. Oil sprayers and water-weighted road rollers. Fuel tankers. Asphalt haulers. And the men operating all that heavy equipment, their shirts off, sweat glinting in the tropical sun, sit high in the cabs of their machines and muscle the wheels and gears of bellowing engines, pushing dirt with their dozers, peeling ground with their graders, trucking asphalt to the pavers, and waiting to get slapped in the head by a bullet from a rice-paddy dike four hundred meters out from either side of the road.

One God-awful hot afternoon, while I was checking out new roadway for a story Major Roberts asked me to write for *The Road Paver*, the entire road crew went nuts from the uncertainty and tension. I had hopped a ride out to the site with an asphalt trucker named Mangus and we were in line with the other asphalt haulers waiting to hook up and funnel our load into the paver. The air in the cab was thick with the smell of hot tar and high quality reefer.

I'd asked Mangus a few questions when I first got in the truck, but he waved them away and shook his head, so I backed off and sat silent for awhile. He didn't say anything until we stopped for a few ready rolls, and then he spoke only to ask if I wanted some reefer. "Sure," I said, hoping smoking together would loosen him up. I figured I wouldn't ask any questions until he gave me a sign he was willing to talk.

By the time we got to the paving site and pulled in line behind the other waiting truckers, we'd finished a Kool's pack ready-roll that Mangus had declared was "good shit," definitely better than any state-side dope he'd ever smoked. It was get-it-on-the-edge, kick-ass grass of the highest Vietnam quality. You could focus on a nit's nose on a bug's ass thirty feet away and watch it wiggle.

After we sat waiting a few minutes behind the other asphalt haulers, Mangus glanced at me with an appraising look and then turned away. "You be honest with me if I ask you something?"

His black, peat moss chest, muscular shoulders, and thick contoured biceps sparkled with rivulets of perspiration as he leaned against the steering wheel, craning his head back and forth, looking through the windshield and then through the side windows in constant survey of the countryside.

"You a smart man, that right?" He still wasn't looking at me.

"No smarter than you. I'm here, aren't I?"

"Don't mess with me, man. You got a college education and you're working at battalion headquarters, right?"

As he spoke, the trucks in front of us moved one length ahead toward the asphalt paver. Mangus depressed the clutch and throttled the engine two belching roars, yanked down on the gearshift post, and moved us up the line one more notch.

"I'm not walking that road, Mangus. We're doing just fine. You got us some good shit, but now you're fucking with my mind."

"I'm not fucking with you, man, I'm asking a question, and you know so much you think you know what I'm gonna ask."

"God it's hot. And the smell of that asphalt ... whew! What'd you do back in the States, Mangus?"

"Don't you want to hear my question?"

"Sure. I want to hear your question. What's your question?" I'd gotten better at recognizing and controlling my high since I first smoked with Jerry, but high is high, and I left myself open when I told Mangus I wanted to hear his question.

He turned his head and squinted at me. "Why do you white dudes like pussy licking so much? No, no, I'm serious. Why don't you just fuck the bitch? Why you gotta stick your nose up her snatch? All you white dudes be the same. Always smellin' it. Makes me sick."

"You're fucking with me, Mangus."

"I told you, I'm not fucking with you. I never asked a white college boy this before and I thought you could explain to me why every white boy I meet is a pussy licker or a cocksucker."

"Mangus, is this shit making you wacko or something? Or maybe there's something about pussy licking you need to get off your chest? Maybe you tried it and you got the wrong hole? What's your problem?"

"I got no problem, Office Boy, and any problem I do got, I can blow away and toss in the trash."

"Look, Mangus, I can't help I'm not a Brother, okay?"

Mangus gave me one of those you're-a-piece-of-shit stares, hawked up a gob from the back of his throat, and spit over his left shoulder out the window.

Forgetting I was high and maybe lacking good judgment, I lifted my M16 from where it leaned in the corner between the dashboard and the door, raised it vertically between my legs, and clunked the butt on the cab floor.

"Is that the problem? Is that it? You want us to go out there in the field and blow each other away? Is that what you want? Okay, let's do it, if that's what you want. I don't have anything against black fuckers, particularly a black fucker who shares good shit with me. But if you want us to blow each other away, then let's go do it right now. Let's go. Let's get it over with."

Mangus looked at me. Hard. Uncertain.

"But you better know this before you step in that field." I looked him square in the face. "Before I kill you, I'm gonna blow your nuts off."

Mangus burst out laughing, and I did too. "You ain't nothin' but a piece a Wonderbread," he said. Then we did the handshake thing, which I screwed up.

But then he froze. He stared past me out my window at the tree line four hundred meters out from the road. I snapped my head around and looked out my window.

"What'd you see?"

"A flash. Those fuckers are sniping us again. Goddamned motherfuckers. Those cocksuckers ...." Mangus grabbed his M16 leaning against the seat between us and opened his door and jumped out. "I'm gonna kill those slant-eyed motherfuckers."

I tipped my M16's muzzle to the floor, locked and loaded, and scrunched down as low as I could go while looking over the edge of the window at the wood line. My heart was beating so hard and so fast I was gasping for air.

I was about to crawl across the seat to Mangus's open door and jump to the safety of the ditch when I looked through the windshield and saw Mangus on the hood of the truck. I stared at him, my mouth open, stunned by his full-body exposure to enemy fire.

He had his right foot on the wheel fender and his left foot up on the hood. I leaned forward so I could see him better through the windshield. He raised his M16 horizontally, high in the air, like a salute to a passing general, and started yelling. "Come on you motherfuckers. Kill me. You got your chance." Mangus lowered his M16 and jabbed the air with the middle finger of his left hand. "You cocksuckers! You fucking slope heads!"

He looked down and saw me staring at him through the windshield, then locked and loaded and raised his M16 to his shoulder and fired on full automatic toward the woods. The recoil knocked him off balance, and he fell backward, off the truck, and sprayed M16 rounds in a semicircle from one side of the road, up and over, to the other side. It happened so fast, I didn't have the sense to duck.

I jumped out of the cab and ran around to see how he was. He'd landed on his shoulder and his right elbow was bleeding, but he seemed okay. I put my hand out and he grabbed it and pulled himself up. We laughed while he picked up and checked out his M16. We got back in the truck.

"So did you see anything or not?" I asked.

"Didn't see a fucking thing, but I scared your lily white ass, didn't I?"

But by then the guys in the other asphalt trucks had spooked on Mangus's joke. They assumed Mangus was returning received fire, and they fired randomly toward the woods at an increasing rate as more and more men fired their weapons out of the need to shoot at what they feared but couldn't see.

Then our heavy equipment operators heard the truckers firing and stopped work and everybody got low and fired their weapons. We got real noisy when Tropic Lightning's half-track, at the rear of the construction site, opened up with its quad-fifties. That's always a special sight to see: four 50-caliber machine guns all firing at the same time. Gives a man a feeling of accomplishment.

I tried hitting a few nearby trees while Mangus merrily blew off three more magazines of ammo. But then I crouched low in the cab and waited for a bullet to ricochet through the door. Some of the men were shooting at nearby rocks, and tracers were twanging away in every direction. Assholes probably high on dope.

After the firing stopped, a sergeant walked down the line and asked everybody what started all the shooting. Mangus said we saw a couple muzzle flashes along the wood line. "Somebody else must have seen them, too," he said. I nodded, eyes all wide and fearful, like the office-clerk-ride-along I really was.

During the trip back to the base camp for another load of asphalt, Mangus and I got along fine. He was funny. And smart. He answered all my questions about the ups and downs of driving an asphalt truck in a guerrilla war zone.

After I got the road project's big picture from the officer in charge, I wrote the article using Mangus as the lead-in to what I saw the pavers doing on the road. I didn't write anything about smoking dope, of course, but I wrote a few lines about the "sniping" and our superior fire power response. Then I switched over to the project officer. I reported what he said about the over-all road plan and threw in a few details he gave me about the technical stuff. I liked the article and submitted it to Major Roberts for his approval.

Roberts liked it, too.

It was the lead story in the next edition of *The Road Paver*.

———————

Saturday, Sept. 6, - Cu Chi Base Camp
Dear Janice:

Tonight I'm CQ runner for HQ Company. I have tomorrow off to get some sleep.

A "Charge of Quarters runner" is the eyes and ears of his unit while everybody else is asleep. Each night there's a CQ runner in every company's HQ office, every battalion's HQ office, and every division's HQ office. If there's an emergency or the Sergeant of the Guard calls and says there's an assault on the perimeter, the CQ Runner runs around and wakes up everybody to do what needs to be done, including starting the siren if needed. Then the CQ Runner goes back to the office and waits for something else to run around about.

Hope you're having a good day. So far, I'm having a good night.

Love, Andrew.

Friday, Sept. 19, 1969 - Cu Chi Base Camp
Dear Janice:

Won't be long before we're together on R & R in Hawaii.

When I think about how warm and snuggly you are naked in bed, and we're arm-in-arm together, and every place I touch you you're silky smooth, and I slide my hand up and down your back, and over your butt and ....

Oh, God, help the needy! Help the needy!

Love, Andrew

GOING OUT IN TRUCKS

After a busy day at the office and early release time for collecting gear back at the hooch, I was outfitted for war. I wore a standard issue, three-pound helmet; a flack jacket with grenades hung from its shoulder clips; two cloth ammo bandoleers crisscrossed on my chest; an equipment belt hooked around my waist with attached water canteen, rain poncho, and a pouch for my gas mask; and, finally, my M16 slung on my shoulder with its safety on and a full, eighteen-round magazine slapped in its receiver.

I walked with other off-duty Headquarters Company clerks, cooks, and motor pool mechanics to the late-afternoon briefing of the perimeter guards. A similar briefing was held every day in front of the communications bunker at 1700 hours (or, as draftees say, 5:00 p.m.). But off-duty personnel, like me that night, are called to the briefing only when a night attack is expected.

Perimeter guards aren't needed during the day. A few lookouts are sufficient because our roving Cobra gunships can spot the enemy from the air before they get near the perimeter and can annihilate them with rockets, mini-gun fire, and grenades from automatic grenade launchers. But the VC and NVA own the night.

We joined other off-duty soldiers from every company in the battalion and stood behind a rag-tag formation of unlucky men whose duty rotations assigned them perimeter guard duty the night of an expected attack. Standing in front of that loose formation, the Officer of the Guard called the guards to attention in the style commonly used in a combat zone.

"All right, listen up," he yelled. He had his hands on his hips and his feet spread apart. He was outfitted like the rest of us with a helmet, a flack jacket with attached grenades, ammo bandoleers, and a M16 hung on his shoulder.

"I'm Captain Blaine from Charlie Company and I'm your Officer of the Guard tonight. The 25th Infantry Division informed us that NVA activity has been detected during the last several days at scattered points north of Cu Chi. An NVA scout was captured last night by an ambush patrol one klick out from the camp and he gave up an assault plan during his interrogation."

Blaine stopped talking. He paced back and forth looking at the ground, pursing his lips. We stared at him. Tracked him with our eyes. He was tall. His face long, finely chiseled and aristocratic. He turned and faced us.

"We're not sure they'll attack tonight, but if they do, expect mortar and sapper attacks followed by an assault on the perimeter. Phone the Sergeant of the Guard as soon as you detect movement so we can call up the Cobras for suppressing fire before the NVA get too close."

Blaine paused again and surveyed his troops. He had our full attention.

"We just discovered that communications with bunkers four, five, and six are down. We're not sure why, but we think Vietnamese day workers cut the commo lines. We've got a team working to get those bunkers plugged back in the system. If you men in those bunkers see movement beyond accurate firing range, pop smoke and I'll send a runner for details. Otherwise, the roving guard will keep you tied in with info."

One of the perimeter guards raised his hand. "Captain Blaine?"

"Yes, you in back."

"Are we getting reinforcements?"

"Reinforcements will be deployed by order of Major Roberts in the commo bunker if an attack occurs." Another soldier raised his hand. "Yes, you at the end."

"We getting extra ammo? And what's the password?"

"The password is *Fair Weather*. I repeat, the password is *Fair Weather*. Pick up extra ammo, flares, and grenades from the supply truck by the commo bunker on your walk out to the perimeter. As always, a roving guard—ah, Specialist Peters—will be walking back and forth along the supply road behind the bunkers checking for sappers. He will periodically visit your bunker and announce himself with the password. Those of you not assigned regular guard duty are to reassemble, immediately after this briefing, in front of your company headquarters buildings for further instructions. Any other questions?" Blaine looked gravely at the guards. "Good. Stay alert. Challenge anyone approaching your bunker. If they don't stop or don't know the password, blow 'em away. You're dismissed."

The other off-duty Headquarters Company personnel and I headed back to the Headquarters Company HQ building.

When we got there, Emanuel Tibbot, our new first sergeant, was standing on an empty ammo box at the head of the formation yard. Apparently he wanted to make sure everybody could see him. Tibbot was short and paunchy. He looked even shorter with his helmet off and us with our helmets on. His helmet was between his feet on the ammo box. Several men chuckled as we walked toward him.

"Give him a little push and he'll fall over."

"Gather 'round," Tibbot called. His face was round, his eyes squeezed thin by puffy cheeks. His voice was pitched higher than usual. He waved us toward him, his plump little hands whirling and waving over his head like a choirmaster drawing more volume from the tenors. "Don't be afraid to move a little closer," he called. A tiny gold Crucifix we'd named *Jesus' Bull's Eye* glinted from the buttoned flap over his left shirt pocket.

We formed a circle around Tibbot, about sixty of us. Somebody said quietly, "Now this is scary." Nobody laughed. We looked with uncertainty at each other. Where was Captain Kirby? Or Lieutenant Ashley?

We knew from Tibbot's personnel file that this was his first assignment in a combat zone. Which meant he had no combat experience whatsoever, since we'd had no enemy activity at the base camp during the previous three weeks that Tibbot was in our battalion. We also knew that Tibbot's original MOS was Chaplain's Assistant, but he'd been assigned outside that MOS for ten years prior to his current assignment with us. He had been a warehouse supply manager at Fort Benning, Georgia.

Three days after Tibbot arrived in our battalion he started stopping us in the company area and asking, "Where's your hat soldier?" or "You ever polish that belt buckle?" You don't ask that kind of chicken shit stuff of heavily armed soldiers in a war zone—unless you're stationed with MACV at Tan Son Nhut Air Force Base, or you're working in the offices of some other high-level command like the Big Red One at Lai Khe or Tropic Lightning here at Cu Chi.

"Our assignment," Tibbot shouted, perspiration dripping off his chin despite the evening breeze, "is to provide reinforcements to our sector of the perimeter."

We knew that. It was our Standard Operating Procedure (SOP). Our company was one of two companies in our battalion closest to the perimeter.

"You can return to your hooches," Tibbot announced, "but sleep with your boots on and laces tied. When you hear the Full Alert siren, get over here in front of HQ on the double in your combat gear. The first thirty-two of you—four reinforcements for each bunker—will board trucks and be driven out to the perimeter. The rest of us will wait in the company's underground bunker until I receive further deployment orders from Major Roberts. Any questions?"

What the hell? We looked at each other. This was all wrong. And coming from an inexperienced newbie—a chaplain's assistant/warehouse bureaucrat no less—who didn't ask questions to find out what he didn't know.

"Where's Captain Kirby?" somebody yelled.

Tibbot squinted at us. "Captain Kirby put me in charge. He and Lieutenant Ashley have commo training and Major Roberts asked them to work with the commo crew on the down phone lines to the perimeter bunkers."

"First Sergeant Tibbot?"

"Yes ... ah, Specialist Pochanski."

"Why are the reinforcements going out in trucks?"

Tibbot put his hands on his hips and replied from the corner of his mouth, "It's the fastest way to get there, partner."

Gerhardt, one of our general maintenance mechanics—a man of thuggish character and appearance—called out from behind Tibbot, "Who decided we'd go out in trucks rather than run out there?"

Tibbot stepped off his ammo box and disappeared from view, except for those of us near the front. He turned and faced the men behind him. "I did."

"First Sergeant Tibbot," Berry-Ain't-Cherry said, his brown eyes flicking among the men affirming our common concern. Tibbot turned and clearly recognized him with a big smile as our fun-loving, second-shift cook. But Berry looked at Tibbot without smiling. "Sappers hit trucks one, two, three, RPG, just like that." Berry snapped his brown fingers three times. Several men nodded. Everyone liked Berry and knew him to be wise to the issues.

"Our first responsibility," Tibbot replied, the pitch of his voice going still higher, "is to reinforce the perimeter as fast as we can, and that's what we're going to do!"

"But if sappers are in the area," Berry said, "we won't be reinforcin' nothin' if we get our motherfuckin' asses blown off in a fuckin' truck."

"Major Roberts personally told me he wants reinforcements moved out there as fast as possible," Tibbot said, his lips tight, "so we're going out in trucks!"

Everybody groaned and shifted around.

Bruno Dretchler, our other Headquarters Company cook, called out from behind me, "Roberts *say* to go out in trucks?"

Tibbot glared at us and said nothing.

It occurred to me that Tibbot didn't understand the tactical advantage of our improvised SOP for ground assaults. I raised my hand and called out, "First Sergeant Tibbot?"

The man in front of me stepped aside and Tibbot gave me a smile of recognition. "Yes, Specialist Atherton." Tibbot thought he was better acquainted with me than with the other men. When he first arrived in the battalion, I was ordered by Adjutant Harris to walk Tibbot over to Headquarters Company and introduce him to the company commander and the office staff.

Trying to sound reasonable and even friendly, I said, "If our reinforcement teams have perimeter bunkers assigned to them, they can run the quarter mile from their hooches directly to the perimeter. That's actually faster than loading up on trucks and driving out there. The password identifies us to the guards as reinforcements, and our run sweeps the area for sappers. Like Faulkenberry said, we don't use trucks."

Tibbot's gaze drifted unfocused for a moment. Then he looked at me as though I were far away. "This is a different kind of situation," he said. He wiped his forehead with the tips of his fingers and shook the perspiration to the ground. "Communications with three bunkers are down, and we've been ordered to move out as fast as possible."

"First Sergeant Tibbot," I said, "this is unnecessarily dangerous. Please do not order us out in trucks to a ground assault. That bunches us into ideal targets. We'll be ducks in a shooting gallery if sappers get past the perimeter in our area."

Tibbot's face reddened. "Specialist Atherton, I'm in charge here, and you'll do as I say."

I had not intended my answer to be heard, but I said out loud what I was thinking: "Well, I'm not getting on a fucking truck."

Tibbot's response was immediate. "You'll get on that truck, soldier, if I order you on that truck!" Tibbot's hand moved to his holstered .45-caliber semi-automatic pistol.

My reaction was instant, without thought or premeditation. I locked and loaded my M16 and flipped the safety to automatic. I held the rifle at my waist and aimed it at Tibbot's feet. My finger was on the trigger ready to walk the firing rifle up the asshole's body. The other men backed away on either side of us.

Tibbot moved his hand slowly from his .45 and pointed his finger at me. "Atherton," his voice cracking, "I'm charging you with insubordination and threatening a superior."

From a great distance, and in slow motion, I saw myself raise the muzzle of my M16 in the air, flip the safety back on, release and drop the magazine, and eject the chambered round. Everybody seemed to calm down except for me.

I'm ready to die if I have to, but not for this stupid fuck.

Tibbot took a deep breath and rubbed his hands together. His eyes darted from man to man.

Corrigan, a friend of mine from Personnel, came up beside me and put his hand on my arm. I jumped. "You okay?" he whispered. I glared at him and started trembling.

"All right," Tibbot said in a hollow voice. "I need eight volunteers to carry M60s and eight volunteers to carry their ammo." He paused, noting the raised hands. "Okay, good. You volunteers pick up your equipment at the armory as soon as we're done. Any questions?" Nobody said anything. Everybody looked at the ground or glanced at each other from the corners of their eyes. "Okay, you're dismissed. And Atherton! You report to my office in the morning."

As we walked back to our hooches, Corrigan, his face dotted with red acne, told me I shouldn't worry. A couple other guys heard Corrigan and agreed. Tibbot was an asshole. Nobody would testify against me. I said "Thanks," but I knew too many men had seen the confrontation. With sufficient threat, at least a few of the men would testify. I would be charged, court-martialed, and sentenced to the LBJ at Long Binh for the duration of the war.

Later that evening, sitting on my cot around nine o'clock, I wrote a letter to a friend back home. I detached the two grenades from the clips on my flack jacket and rolled them back and forth on my cot while I described in the letter my fascination with the fearsome power in these objects the size of baseballs. After finishing the letter with a little bragging about my standoff with Tibbot—"I almost pulled the trigger"—I decided to get a few hours sleep. The attack, if there was one, probably wouldn't occur until the middle of the night.

I arranged my helmet, my flack jacket, and my M16 on the floor beside my cot. My bandoleers and grenades I positioned on the floor near my feet. Then I lay on my back, my hands behind my head, and reflected on what had happened between Tibbot and me.

I had become a different person than I was before being drafted. Back then, I had no idea I could be a killer. Yet now I had no doubt that, in the emotion of the moment, I would have wasted Tibbot if he had tried to draw his weapon. I would have regretted it, but not because of the presumed immorality of killing a fellow American soldier. I would have regretted it because I would have forfeited my freedom and maybe my life. Tibbot had made himself a needless danger to me and to the other men in my unit. Killing him would have been morally questionable, but no more so than killing VC. Many VC were fighting to avenge the families and villages we destroyed with our indiscriminate bombing and free-fire-zone killing. And other VC were fighting for national unity and freedom from decades, even lifetimes, of foreign occupation. Tibbot was an asshole who was endangering his own men. Killing him would therefore be as defensible as killing any other threat to the lives of American soldiers.

Even if the only motive of the VC and NVA was to enforce communism on South Vietnam, we'd still be engaged in a monumental compromise with evil. We're doing the devil's work at the same time we're fighting him, and here's why.

Nobody I know, here in the Army or at home in the States, gives a damn about the Vietnamese people. We traveled halfway around the world to kill citizens and destroy property of another country so we can be safe from the threat of communism. This war is about us, not about them. Thus it follows, by the logic of *self-preservation at any cost*, if Tibbot is a danger to me and my military unit, particularly if that danger is due to his arrogance and stupidity, I or any other man can justifiably blow him away.

The question now was what should I do if Tibbot ordered me on one of those trucks? And if he didn't order me onto a truck, he'd order me into an underground bunker with the second wave reinforcements—a less dangerous idea, but almost as stupid as his truck idea. His order for the second wave reinforcements to wait in an underground bunker was consistent with Army SOP, but it wasn't the way we, in this company and battalion, did it because we had a safer, more effective procedure.

When preparing for a ground assault, a number of men from every company are assigned as additional guards to the perimeter bunkers while others remain behind in their company areas. Those who stay behind position themselves behind waist-high walls of sandbags we all have around our hooches. That puts them at greater individual risk from rockets and mortars— even friendly crossfire—but the risks are worth it. That way, the company area is guarded and the men aren't clumped together in underground bunkers in locations known by every Vietnamese day worker employed in the vicinity, which means the VC also know where the underground bunkers are. So if we follow regular Army SOP, any VC sapper who encounters no resistance will immediately know we're in the company's underground bunker. He'll know where it is and he'll shoot the bunker lookout and lob a grenade or satchel charge down the bunker steps. One sapper could kill or injure forty or more men that way.

With Tibbot in charge, maybe the best thing for me to do, if the attack came, was to run straight to the perimeter line and avoid Tibbot entirely. In all the confusion, he'd think I'd gone out on one of the trucks.

One thing was certain. In the morning, I'd either be a casualty or I'd be court-martialed. Probably both. *What the hell, why not kick off my boots and enjoy these last few hours?*

So I took off my boots, laid back, and fell into a deep sleep.

I awoke with a jolt. The hooch was dark. My heart was pounding. I looked at my watch. It was 1:20 in the morning.

At that precise moment concussive air pressure from an explosion hit my ears like nails rammed in my eardrums. I found myself on the floor with my arms over my head. I had no idea how I got there. A mortar round had exploded near the hooch.

Everything was still pitch dark. My ears were ringing from the explosion. But I could faintly hear, at a great distance on the other side of the ringing, men yelling and cursing, pulling on gear, and stumbling for the door. Then the Full Alert siren started wailing.

On my knees, beside my cot, I fumbled in the dark for my boots. They weren't there. I felt under the cot. I swept the floor with my arms. I found one boot near my foot locker at the end of my cot, and the other boot near the hooch wall at the head of my cot.

I pulled on my boots and laced them in the dark. Kneeling, I found my flack jacket and bandoleers and put them on. Again I swept the floor with my arms, searching desperately for the grenades. My fingertips hit a smooth, round, metal object and sent it skittering across the concrete floor. I crawled under the cot, raising it with my head and shoulders, and found the grenades. I threw the cot off me and, sitting on the floor, I tried to hook the grenades to my flack jacket clips, but my hands were shaking and I couldn't work the clips. In frustration, I stuffed them in the lower leg pockets of my fatigues.

Another explosion slammed at the hooch. It sounded metallic. Must have hit a tin roof.

I stood up, bent over, and stepped backward while brushing the floor with my fingers for my rifle, and fell over my cot. As I got up, I found the rifle. The clip was in and the safety was on. I bumped my helmet with my boot. I kicked the stupid thing toward the wall.

Then, in dim light now filtering through the window screens from overhead flares, I ran down the aisle in the middle of the hooch. Halfway to the door I stepped on a bottle, turned my ankle, and fell in front of Ken Latimer running behind me.

Latimer, tall, thin, and usually stoned, pitched over me and yelled, "Whoa, what the hell?" We scattered fans and toiletries in all directions, and knocked over somebody's reel-to-reel tape deck that was sitting on his foot locker.

"You okay?" I yelled.

"God, you're worse than the VC."

"Come on," I said. "Let's get out of here." We were the last ones in the hooch. He pulled me up and we ran out the door. My ankle hurt like hell.

Outside, the world looked like an old-time tintype photograph. Everything was either opaque black or glowing silver in the light of magnesium flares floating in the sky on little white parachutes.

Another explosion shook the ground.

I ran with Latimer between the hooches on a silver-colored dirt road. As I ran, the grenades in my leg pockets bounced against my shins like wrecking balls.

"Go on," I yelled to Latimer, "I'll catch up."

I stopped, laid my M16 across the toes of my boots, fished the grenades from my lower pants pockets, and snapped them onto my jacket clips. I picked up my M16 and started running—hobbling—again.

Setting aside my resolve to run to the perimeter line, I hobbled toward the Headquarters Company formation yard. Two trucks were moving out to the perimeter. Men in trucks. Were they nuts?

"All right," Tibbot yelled, "the rest of you, down—"

An explosion slapped at us. I fell to the ground and stayed there to survey the situation. I didn't see where the mortar shell hit or any damage it caused. Must have landed behind nearby hooches or the motor pool buildings.

Tibbot jumped up before I did and yelled, "Is that you, Atherton?"

I stood up and limped toward Tibbot.

"Where's your helmet?" Tibbot yelled.

"Couldn't find it in the dark."

"What's wrong with your leg?"

"Sprained my ankle."

"Then get in the bunker with the second wave reinforcements."

"Sergeant Tibbot, we'd be better off—"

A mortar round exploded over in Delta Company. We hit the ground anyway. Shrapnel can travel a long way.

Tibbot was on his feet within seconds yelling at men running past us toward the perimeter. I jumped to my feet, uncertain what to do. I looked around.

The blackest shadows I'd ever seen were spreading on the ground from buildings and trees like flowing puddles of India ink. When new flares popped overhead, the shadows disappeared and new shadows started pooling out again as the new flares floated closer to the ground.

Silver-colored soldiers—glowing, dream-like figures—ran across the formation yard. The only colors in the landscape were red and green tracers streaking high overhead among the flares. I could hear M16 fire, chattering M60 machine guns, and exploding claymores out on the perimeter line. Cobra mini-guns started roaring like locomotives—6,000 rounds a minute—their tracers weaving sensuous red ribbons I could see above the trees.

The NVA ground assault had begun under the arching mortar rounds.

Then I realized Tibbot was yelling and waving his arms at me. "Don't you hear me?" He jabbed his finger toward the tunnel entrance across the formation yard. "Get your ass in that bunker ASAP!"

A mortar round exploded in Charlie Company. The NVA were zigzagging the rounds back and forth across the battalion. The rounds were coming our way again.

Ignoring the pain in my ankle, I ran for the bunker. Tibbot followed.

We climbed down the bunker steps. The mortar explosions became distant thunder.

The tunnel was about fifty feet long and lined with hardwood beams. Three low-watt light bulbs, spaced evenly along the upper edge of one wall, provided barely enough light. Men sat opposite each other on thick wooden benches that extended out from the walls. A space of two feet separated opposing knees, a space filled at floor level with boots and legs extended across the aisle. The air was stuffy—dusty, earthy—smelling of sweat and oiled metal.

I squeezed past a dozen men to an empty spot on the right-hand bench. I sat down and rubbed my swelling ankle through the tight upper canvas of my boot.

Entering the bunker had been a big mistake. Helmets, flack jackets, bandoleers, M16s, M60 machine guns, and ammo chains bulked up the men sitting on either side of me. We were crowded together like cattle waiting for slaughter. If a grenade or satchel charge were thrown down either exit, I would not be able to get out of the tunnel fast enough to escape harm. I was trapped in the middle.

Lookouts at the tunnel exits periodically yelled down descriptions of what they saw up on ground level. The first two lookouts were assigned by Tibbot and were to alternate with other men every twenty minutes. Everyone wanted to be near an exit. Everyone but Tibbot knew we were in a death trap.

Tibbot removed his helmet and picked up the field phone next to the steps and listened for sit-reps from the command bunker.

Dretchler, several men down from me on my right, stood up—bending so he didn't hit his head—and yelled, "First Sergeant Tibbot. One grenade or satchel charge from one single sapper and we're all dead meat. We need to get out of here."

A thought surfaced in my mind and I quickly looked up and down the two rows of men for our other cook, Berry-Ain't-Cherry. I didn't see him. Fuck. Berry was on a truck. This was particularly disturbing to me because Berry, like a few other NCOs, often joined the reserve guards during an unexpected attack on the perimeter even though his rank exempted him from such duty.

Suddenly I had a premonition. It was eerie. Frightening. I could *feel* the future and it wasn't good. I couldn't get my breath. I started to panic.

I pulled myself together. *He's okay. I'm okay.*

I turned my attention back to the bunker.

While I was thinking about Berry, several guys had said, "Yeah, man," agreeing with Bruno's call to get out of the bunker. I looked at Tibbot for his reaction.

A red strap mark from his helmet ran across his sweaty pink forehead. He cupped his hand over the phone's receiver and yelled, "Bruno, sit down."

Bruno did not sit down. Several more men stood up. I did, too.

"We stay topside behind hooch sandbags during ground assaults," Bruno loudly explained. "If reinforcements are needed on the perimeter, they send us a runner who calls out the password so we know he's okay."

"I'm telling you one last time," Tibbot shouted, "sit down and shut up."

We did not sit down.

Tibbot yelled, "You men at the exits." He waited for a reply, glared at us, and yelled again, this time louder. "Hey, you lookouts at the exits, answer me!"

"Yes, First Sergeant," they called back in unison.

"Don't let anybody leave this bunker until I give the order."

"Oh, sure," one lookout yelled back. "I got my safety off right now."

The other lookout yelled, "I'll kick their dinky-dong asses back down the steps."

We all laughed. Several men hooted and thumped the floor with their boots. Bruno sat down, laughing, shaking his head in disbelief. The rest of us sat down, too.

I was relieved. I wanted out of the bunker, but—

The lights went out.

"What the hell—"

"Oh, shit."

"Anybody got a flashlight?"

"I got one, but the stupid—"

"Turn on the emergency lights!"

"Anybody got a flashlight?"

"Shut the fuck up, okay? If anybody's got a flashlight they'll turn it on."

"Eat a big one, dick head."

Several men flicked on their cigarette lighters, but that didn't last long.

We sat several long moments in the dark, yelling and cursing at each other. Then a light blinked on at Tibbot's end of the tunnel. Tibbot had located the switch on a battery-operated emergency light on the endwall of the bunker beside the steps. But the battery was old and corroded by the tropical climate. The light was dim.

"Everybody stay where you are," Tibbot yelled. "You at the other end, turn on the battery light."

"I'm trying to," Corrigan yelled, "but it won't come on."

When our eyes adjusted, we saw silver light flickering down the bunker exits from flares floating into our company area that were popped by men up on ground level in other companies.

"Hey," Bruno whispered. "You guys hear Tibbot assign anybody topside to guard the company area?"

"I didn't," somebody whispered.

Logan, the colonel's driver, sitting opposite me said, "I didn't either."

"Then sappers could be in the company area," Bruno said quietly, "and we wouldn't know it."

Somebody at the dark end of the tunnel whispered loudly, "I gotta get out of here. This is crazy."

"You didn't complain when Tibbot was telling us his asshole plan," Bruno said.

"Hey, you didn't either."

"Hell, I thought Atherton was gonna blow him into hamburger."

The guy on my left leaned against me and whispered, "You shoulda done it."

"Let's grease Tibbot and get the fuck out of here," Gerhardt whispered. Gerhardt was a mechanic who looked like a Cro-Magnon exhibit at the Smithsonian.

I suddenly yelled, "Hey Tweeze, you down here?" Tweeze was another mechanic, a friend of mine.

"You bring your grease gun?" somebody asked Gerhardt with a chuckle.

"You're fucking A-right I brought my grease gun."

"Tweeze boarded one of the trucks," yelled a guy down the line.

"You guys do that in the bunker," Logan whispered, "and all of us'll be court-martialed."

Frank Hensley, ordinarily a quiet, rather mousy personnel clerk, said, "Let's hold off a while and see what happens."

"Oh, that's a good idea," Bruno said. He leaned forward in the dim light and spit between his legs. "Let's just sit here and wait for a grenade to come bouncing down the stairs. Any other suggestions, Einstein?"

"Maybe the guy nearest the grenade could chuck it out the door."

Gerhardt snorted with derision. "The guy's pissing his pants, scared shitless, and he's gonna feel around in the dark for the fucking grenade."

"So you come up with a better plan since you know it all."

"I say move out of here right now," Gerhardt whispered in a hoarse voice. "If Tibbot tries to stop us, we walk his ass topside and waste him up there."

"Hey, I'm tired of talking," Bruno said. "Let's get the hell out of here."

Gerhardt stood up. "Let's do it." He locked and loaded his M16. Then Bruno stood up, too.

"Wait a minute," I whispered, motioning for everybody to calm down. "Why haven't I heard incoming for a while?"

Gerhardt grunted. "Figure it out. The gooks pushed through the perimeter. They don't wanna mortar their own men."

"Jesus," somebody said quietly.

"Fuck this shit," Bruno said, "I'm getting out of here."

Several more men rose to their feet.

"First Sergeant Tibbot," Gerhardt shouted, "we're going topside."

"Shut up so I can hear the phone," Tibbot yelled. "I'm getting a status report from Major Roberts right now."

"Hold off until he finishes listening to Roberts," I said quietly. I stood up with the others, sweat dripping in my eyes.

"One more minute, phone or no phone," Gerhardt said, "and I'm going up those goddamned steps."

"I'm with you," Bruno said.

Tibbot hung up the phone. "Okay, listen up," he yelled. All of us were standing. "The perimeter is secure. Fighting has ended for the time being. Sappers were reported in Echo Company, but they—"

"Sappers are in the base camp?" Gerhardt shouted.

"Major Roberts just received the reported sighting and he—"

"If sappers are in the area," Bruno yelled, "why aren't you ordering us the fuck out of here?"

"I've given you all … If Major Roberts wants—"

"Fuck this shit," Gerhardt yelled, "I am not gonna die down here with this motherfucker. Let's get out of this goddamn bunker."

Men started walking up the stairs, shoving heavily past Tibbot.

"Okay, everybody topside," Tibbot yelled. "Search the area—"

Tibbot was still shouting orders in the bunker as I hobbled, in the light of overhead flares, toward a wall of waist-high sandbags circling the nearest hooch. My M16 was locked and loaded and flipped on automatic, and I was ready to shoot any moving figure who didn't shout *Fair Weather* when challenged.

The attack lasted only forty-five minutes. We found no sappers in our company area. A hooch in Headquarters Company had taken a direct hit from a mortar round and was now a pile of mangled tin and scattered boots, fans, cots, blankets, and hi-fi equipment. The generator shed was hit too. Rumor was that four men had been injured by the mortar rounds, but that wasn't confirmed until later in the morning. Soon after daybreak a runner informed us to "stand down" and assemble in front of our company's HQ building at 0700 hours.

We assembled in early morning sunlight. The air was warming. Everything was damp. We were tired but catching our second wind and happy to be alive.

Captain Kirby stood fully erect and dignified at the head of our formation yard, a somber look on his dirty face. He called for us to quiet down and listen up. First Sergeant Tibbot and Lieutenant Ashley stood off to one side. Tibbot's face was washed and he'd changed into clean fatigues. Lieutenant Ashley's face, like Captain Kirby's, was dusty and streaked with sweat. The fatigues of both Kirby and Ashley were caked with dirt and black with perspiration.

"Cu Chi Base Camp was attacked by one, maybe two harassing companies of NVA," Kirby announced. "One contact point was our three bunkers with cut commo lines. Lieutenant Ashley and I would have returned from our temporary assignments to be with you men, but we encountered commo glitches and then other problems I'm not at liberty to discuss. We suspect this sabotage was done by Vietnamese day workers who were possibly coerced into doing it by the VC—if they aren't VC themselves. Interrogations begin later today when workers arrive on base."

Kirby paused. He looked at us and nodded his approval. "I want you men to know I'm proud of you." Then his face turned grim. "Now the bad news. Headquarters Company sustained four minor injuries from a mortar round hitting a hooch. Those men are being treated at the dispensary right now. But our worst casualties are indeed grievous. Two men were killed and seven injured—three severely—when sappers attacked reinforcements on their way to the perimeter. Their truck was hit by RPGs and small arms fire." Kirby read the names of the casualties from a piece of paper he had in his hand. One of the men killed was Jeremiah Faulkenberry.

Tweeze was okay—his name wasn't on Kirby's list—but Berry-Ain't-Cherry was dead!

I turned and stumbled out of formation before we were dismissed. If somebody called after me I didn't hear him.

I knew what Kirby said—the words circled round and round in my head—but they didn't mean anything to me. What could it possibly mean that Berry was dead? How could the world be without Berry?

I walked around the company area until I found myself leaning against the outer wall of the mess hall kitchen. I was trying to fit Berry's death into my head, but I couldn't fit it in there. Everywhere I turned his death was already there sucking out meaning and value—trees, grass, hooches, other men. Everything soon meant nothing to me.

I didn't know him well, but he was one of the bright spots in my Vietnam life. A source of fun and happiness every time I saw him. Never again would I be served chipped beef gravy by a man who could make me laugh every time I saw him.

"Ain't gettin' none this good shit no place 'cept here, ean' yo mama's kitchen."

I walked around about an hour. Got chewed out by the adjutant for reporting to work later than everybody else. Stayed for thirty minutes and left. Told Adjutant Harris I was sick.

I again walked around the company grounds. I began to form the idea that if I took my bayonet and placed its point against my chest, left of my solar plexus, and pulled it straight in, hard and quick with both fists on the handle, I could get Berry's death in there with the steel.

The loss I felt for this man was so deep and hurt so much I couldn't hold still. For long moments I felt like I was drowning and couldn't get my breath. Then I'd hold still, motionless for twenty minutes at a time, thinking about Berry-Ain't-Cherry entertaining the men lined up in the mess hall. KP with Berry in charge was like being a straight man for a comedian. He never turned off. Until now.

I'll miss you, Berry-Ain't-Cherry. And if it weren't for your mention of belief in a black Jesus—"he be a Jew, but some a' them motherfuckers be black like me, too"—I'd cuss God from now until my last breath for sleeping on the job when He could have been protecting you.

Jeremiah? Jeremiah Faulkenberry?

Huh. No wonder the crazy fucker made up a name for himself.

Later, in the S-1 office, David Connors, our head clerk, called the medics for updates regarding the wounded. One man would likely lose an eye. Another man might lose a leg. Yet another was near death. These men were dusted off to Long Binh. From there they'd be flown to Japan or to a hospital ship off the coast.

I didn't report to Tibbot's office that morning as he had ordered me to. I was afraid I'd lose control. If he wanted to court-martial me, he knew where to find me.

He never came looking.

Two days after the attack a story floated around Headquarters Company that Tibbot found a fragmentation grenade in the bottom drawer of his desk. The straightened pin, according to the story, was nearly pulled from the grenade by a string tied to a crossbar above the drawer. Several men winked and nodded at me during conversations about the rumor. I pleaded innocent but confessed disappointment it hadn't worked.

First Sergeant Tibbot never charged me or anybody else in our company with insubordination or threatening a superior. Nor did he ever again send us out to the perimeter in trucks. One week after the NVA ground assault, Tibbot was reassigned out of our battalion.

Sunday, Oct. 5, 1969 - Cu Chi Base Camp
Dear Janice:

I've been rereading The Plague *by Albert Camus. It's a powerful and disturbing book. Particularly in light of what's going on over here.*

We're infected with a sickness that blinds us to the sick things it causes us to do. Neither the men over here nor the people at home appear to comprehend what we're really doing ... until somebody we care about gets mangled or killed.

I look forward to us holding each other.

Love, Andrew

Friday, Oct. 25, 1969 - Cu Chi Base Camp
Dear Janice:

What did I like most about R & R in Hawaii? YOU!!

You looked fantastic! I missed you so much, and suddenly you were in my arms. What a great time we had. Let's do a lot more of that when I get back home!

Love, Andrew

PURE DUMB LUCK

We banked hard to the left and dropped like a stone. From the open side door of the Huey, I looked straight down through four thousand feet of air at rice paddies the size of postage stamps.

I braced my feet on the tilted floor, pushed back against the motor housing, and gripped the belt that held my courier satchel to the canvas seat on my right. But I wasn't in any danger. My seat belt held me securely to the motor housing. I could not fall out.

But Captain Harbury, the newbie courier for the 25th Infantry Division, had not fastened his seat belt when he boarded the chopper. He had been seated on my left, beside the open door and empty space. I yelled at him before we lifted off, "I always fasten my seat belt," but he ignored me.

Was he trying to be macho? Did he think this flight was always *el primo* smooth because it was scheduled primarily for the 25th Infantry Division's courier? Did he think he was too important to take a friendly warning from a piggyback-riding, SPC-4 battalion courier? I don't know.

The moment the chopper banked to the left, Harbury flopped over and grabbed my legs like a drowning man clutching a floating log. I reached over his back and grabbed his belt. His silver tinted aviator sunglasses flipped off his face and fell out the door along with his new glossy helmet with lightning bolts painted on the sides. He had trouble keeping his knees from slipping toward the edge of the floor. He wasn't getting much traction, but he sure was getting religion, because I could hear him calling into my lap, "Jesus, Jesus, oh Jesus."

Nobody except me noticed what was happening. Or maybe somebody noticed and thought Harbury was hanging on to me and I was hanging on to him good enough. But I'm pretty sure the left door gunner didn't see Harbury because I looked back and he was suspended almost face down with his feet crossed and braced against the M60 gun post yelling, "Get that fucker! Get that fucker!"

The rice paddies were getting bigger. I pulled harder on Harbury's belt. Maybe the clutch housing was hit. Maybe the Jesus nut was cracked. But the chopper's rotor was forcefully beating the air with unusual force, *WACK-WACK-WACK,* as we dropped and circled to the left.

At the last moment, when I could see individual clods of dirt on rice paddy dikes down below, we straightened our forward motion and leveled out. As was later explained to me, we had circled back two miles and were now flying our original flight path again.

Harbury held onto my legs while he swiveled his butt up on the steel-framed canvas seat. He fastened his seat belt and half-turned and looked up at the steel engine housing we were seated against to make sure his courier pouch was still hanging on the spring-loaded hook used by medics to hang their IV bags. Then he turned to me and shook my hand, his face white as typing paper.

The left door gunner yelled, "Bring him on. His ass is mine."

That's when I knew for sure we'd taken fire from the ground. Somebody in the chopper must have seen muzzle flashes in the brush far below or maybe tracer rounds streaking up at us, since the distant sound of firing could not be heard through all the noise from the rotor and motor and rushing wind. Even the sound of rounds striking the chopper—*tick, tick*—could be missed in all the commotion.

The chopper tipped forward and accelerated to maximum speed, over one hundred miles an hour. We were no more than fifteen feet above rice paddy water. At the last second we rose up over trees bordering the paddies and then dropped back down to water-skimming again.

The door gunner had his M60 machine gun angled forward. He began firing and quickly swung the gun to the rear. A stand of trees flashed by, strafed by the gunner's string of red tracers. He stopped firing, leaned out the gun well against his anchoring strap, and raised his middle finger toward the clump of trees now far behind us.

"Okay, okay, I know," he yelled in his helmet mike. He dropped back in his gunner's seat and saluted the copilot who turned and looked back at him with a grin on his face. The chopper was flying straight ahead and gaining altitude.

The door gunner leaned his head forward so he could see us better and tapped us on our shoulders. Painted on his helmet were the words *Chief Hot Copper*. He gave us a thumbs-up.

"What's the pucker factor?" he yelled. He seemed unaware of what had happened to Captain Harbury.

Harbury nodded vigorously and held up an index finger for "Number One." I tried to grin, but the muscles in my face were rigid.

I elbowed Harbury and pointed to two small holes in the rounded cowling above the open left door beside us. We could see light from the sky shining through those two holes. I hadn't seen them before—granted I didn't do a visual inspection when I got on the chopper—but the bright holes called attention to themselves. They were the first things I noticed after Captain Harbury got back in his seat. I saw no damage to the padding strapped to the ceiling. No puncture holes, no cotton stuffing or nylon fibers protruded from the padding's olive drab canvas. So the line of fire—the trajectory—could not have been on our left because the bullets would have to have been fired from slightly above us. The rounds that made those two holes had to come from the ground on our right—at considerable distance from our flight path— zinging up from the open door on our right, almost nicking the floor's edge, angling across the space in front of us, and through the rounded cowling over the left door. I thought back to whether I'd heard a *tick* or *bap*, but I recalled no sound of that kind.

The bullets had zipped within a foot or two of our noses.

We dropped Captain Harbury off at Tan Son Nhut Air Force Base. He was required to report and deliver his papers to the generals at MACV. He wouldn't dare walk around MACV without something on his head, so he must have borrowed or bought a new helmet or jungle hat before entering MACV grounds.

We lifted off from Tan Son Nhut and flew to Long Binh. Approaching or leaving Tan Son Nhut Air Force Base in our open-door Huey always gave me a squirt of adrenaline. We had to tree-hop under incoming and departing airplanes. Flying that low, we had to move fast so we'd be a difficult target to hit. One time, for a lark, the pilot took us down a base camp access road. We flew tipped forward, about twenty feet above the road, trees flashing past us on either side. We scared Vietnamese motor bikes, pickup trucks, and buffalo carts off the road and into the ditches. We didn't do that often. If we set a pattern doing it, some day we'd fly into steel cables strung across the road between the trees. But oh man, it was a larky ride while it lasted.

We landed at Long Binh sometime around 8:30 in the morning. I disembarked the chopper and immediately began sweating after the chilly ride in the Huey. I rolled up my sleeves and walked in hot sun and humid air to the 85th Engineer Group Headquarters and turned in my papers.

At Long Binh I was now free and on my own until I picked up return papers and caught the afternoon chopper to Tan Son Nhut and then back to Cu Chi. Sometimes we stopped at Bien Hoa, too, but not today.

Couriers were ED, "Exempt from Duty," meaning no KP, no de-drumming at the asphalt plant, no perimeter guard duty, and no CQ runner. Not only was I exempt from extra duty, I had no assigned work at all, except to courier documents early in the morning and late in the afternoon.

I had been assigned my new job while Janice and I were on R & R in Hawaii. While I was gone, the previous courier DEROSED. The top brass didn't know he was going home and he didn't mention it to Adjutant Harris. The guys in personnel and the clerk in Headquarters Company got their asses reamed. They all thought it was somebody else's responsibility to inform the adjutant or the XO about the courier's DEROS date. Adjutant Harris took some heat, too, because he's the courier's immediate supervisor. But Harris saw the guy only once or twice a day for moments at a time, so he wasn't high on Harris's radar.

A substitute courier did the job a few days and then, while I was on R & R, Major Roberts chose me as permanent courier. He told Harris to distribute my awards and typing responsibilities among the other S-1 clerks. When I found out, I was both surprised and offended. Wasn't Major Roberts pleased with the work I was doing in S-1? Nobody could have put in more time and effort, even enthusiasm, on the newspaper or awards jobs.

But my new courier job lasted only three weeks. They found another courier and I was reassigned back to S-1. From then on I served as substitute courier whenever the regular guy was sick or on R & R.

When I returned to S-1, the award recommendations were backed up and the files were scrambled. Several officers and NCOs had complained to Harris and Roberts about not having my help writing recommendations. Hackett wanted me returned to awards, too. He said he missed my editing and screening work. But nobody complained about the one missing edition of *The Road Paver*.

When I was working as courier, I spent my layover every day at Long Binh. It was a major base camp and headquarters complex. It had stores, restaurants, movie houses, swimming pools, massage parlors, and bars. I was told early in my tour that Long Binh had 50,000 personnel stationed there. Seems like a lot. Maybe that figure includes non-military support and supply people. After I dropped off my papers in the morning, I always walked to a place called Jake's Bar.

Jake was a Native American Indian—Apache Tribe—maybe forty years old. He always wore a flannel red-and-black checkered shirt in his super-cooled, air-conditioned bar. His wide-set eyes and high cheekbones were creased in a perpetual smile. Stubby black hair on his broad head looked like bristles on the back of a wild boar. When the bar started filling up in the afternoons, he'd walk among the men and lay his big hand on a man's shoulder, or give a quick rub to another man's back, or trade shadow punches with muscle-bound bozos like a coach giving attaboys to his team. He had a calm sense of masculinity he never had to back up with posturing.

The sign on Jake's door was flipped to *Open*. I pulled the wooden handle on the spring-hinged, wood-slat door and stepped from searing hot sunlight and steaming humidity into florescent-blue, cool air and the fermented smell and smoke of a well-used bar. The cement floor and white Formica table tops, and two-by-fours that ran waist high along the plywood walls, were cluttered with beer cans, peanut shells, and crumpled potato chip bags from the night before. I walked across the littered room and pulled myself up on a stool at the plywood counter that passed for a bar.

"Hey, engineer." Jake's voice boomed from the storage room behind the bar. He walked through the open door and leaned against the rear edge of the plywood counter. "Second pot o' coffee's still brewing, good buddy."

"Thanks, but I've already had a morning wake-up call. I'd rather have a beer if you have one handy."

Jake slid open a Coke cooler and pulled out a Bud and one of the glasses he kept cold for special customers. I sometimes helped him clean tables and sweep the floor.

"Trouble out there this morning?"

"Sniper took a few shots at the chopper. No big deal. Chopper maneuvers were what caught my attention. That and a newbie Tropic Lightning courier playing Mr. Macho. Didn't fasten his seatbelt and darn near fell out the door."

"Damn." Jake whistled.

I popped the can's tab and poured the beer down the inner side of the frosty glass. I wiped sweat from my forehead and drank half the beer in two swallows. It plowed an iceberg down my throat, and chilled my stomach and then my head like crystallizing ice. I shivered.

"Nothing like that first swallow on a hot day in Vietnam." I turned and looked around the room.

A GI was hunched over his beer at a table in the corner. He looked up at me. He had a long, hound-dog face and large ears. I'd seen him somewhere before. His fatigues were clean. He hadn't come in from the boonies.

"How you doing?" I asked.

No answer.

I glanced at Jake. He shrugged.

"I'm in Vietnam," the man said.

I chuckled. "Doesn't get much worse than that."

He was silent. Then low and sarcastic, "Yeah, right."

I tried again. "Between assignments or just laying low for the day?"

No response.

I nodded and waved goodbye. I turned back to Jake, but the GI in the corner spoke again. I swiveled on my stool. "Excuse me, I didn't catch that."

"You stationed at Cu Chi?"

"182nd Engineer Battalion. I'm doing their courier work right now. Ordinarily I'm in the S-1 office." I took a swallow of beer. "Do I know you?"

"We was infantry together when we come incountry. You and me, and twenty-eight other Eleven Bravos that got assigned to the 182nd. But not for long, least for most of us."

I got off my stool and walked toward his table. "What's your name?" I was squinting, trying to recall those early days when we processed into the battalion.

"Martin. Sulley Martin. Pull up a chair if you want."

I went back to the bar and got my beer. I returned to Martin's table. On his shoulder patches he had the white-headed eagle of the 101st Airborne Division.

Martin tipped back his head and looked down his nose at me. "So you took sniper fire on your chopper this morning?"

"A few rounds. No major damage." I held up my glass in a half-hearted toast.

"Must've scared you pretty bad after sitting at a desk half your tour."

I smiled. "Were you in Echo or Bravo Company in the 182nd? Most of the Eleven Bravos were assigned to one of those companies."

"We hauled and dug as best we could," Martin sipped his beer, "but I guess not good enough to stay in an engineering unit." He raised his eyebrows and widened his eyes in feigned puzzlement and wonder. "So what'd you do to stay in the 182nd?"

"I made myself useful to the colonel and the major. When the call came down from the 101st for all the Eleven Bravos, Major Roberts had my MOS records changed to clerical."

Martin's eyes got heavy with contempt. "You're college, right?"

"Yeah."

"You try ducking the draft, too?"

"I stayed in school until I finished—"

"An' sucked ass soon as you got here. An honest-to-God, *Rear Echelon Mother Fucker*. The genuine article! How do you do?" He stuck out his hand as though wanting to shake mine.

I glared at him. "How about you? You sucking anything in Long Binh?"

Martin snorted and dropped his hand. "Been on R & R. Went to Thailand."

We sat for a moment without talking. My face was hot. I wanted to get away from this man. "How were the girls?"

Martin looked at me, puzzled. "What girls?"

"In Thailand."

"Oh. They was okay." Martin crumpled his beer can between his hands. "Hey, Jake," he called, "how 'bout another one?"

Jake was across the room collecting empty beer cans in a clear plastic bag. "You guys get your own beer," he called. "Leave the money on the counter."

Martin got up, tall and large-boned. He pointed at my glass. "You want a reload?"

"Ah ... sure. I'll have another one."

I studied his long angular body while he got our beers and returned to the table. I popped the tab on my beer and topped off my glass.

"You're not too enthusiastic about seven days of boom-boom," I said. "Asian girls don't suit you?"

"Whole time all I thought about was coming back here."

We sat silent drinking our beers. Then he said, "Been AWOL three days wandering Long Binh like a lost dog." He chugged his beer, slap-banged the empty can on the table, and belched a low rumble.

"Pretty tough in the 101st?" It was a stupid question, but I was seriously off balance.

"Ain't been on a base camp more'n eight days since I left Cu Chi." He swiped at the surface of the table, sweeping something I couldn't see onto the floor. "We come in for a day or two and then back out in the boonies for weeks at a time."

"See much action out there?"

"You heard of the A Shau Valley? Near the Laotian border?"

"Can't say I have."

"Ho Chi Minh Trail snakes in from Laos through the A Shau."

I nodded.

"Ever hear of Ap Bia Mountain?"

I shook my head and shrugged.

"You clerks don't know shit about what's going on in Vietnam, do you?"

"You involved in operations up there?"

"Hamburger Hill mean anything to you?" He wagged his head at me.

"Sure. *Stars and Stripes* said it was the worst battle so far. Denounced by Senator Kennedy as pointless carnage."

"I don't know anything about that shit, but Hamburger Hill's in the A Shau Valley. That's what we called Ap Bia Mountain."

"You were at Hamburger Hill?"

He looked at me, sneering. "Other Eleven Bravos from the 182nd was there, too."

"Jesus. I knew you guys went to the 101st, but it never occurred to me…. In May, right?"

"Ten days in May. Took eleven assaults to capture that mountain."

I heard a noise behind me. I turned and saw Jake walking toward our table with his plastic bag of empty beer cans. He was looking at Martin.

"Did I hear you say you were at Hamburger Hill?" Jake set the bag of cans on the floor, pulled out a chair, and sat down at our table, all while staring at Martin. "You must've seen some heavy action."

"More'n I ever plan to see again." Martin's voice was flat, laying down the truth. "I ain't no coward, but I ain't no hero, either."

"No need to explain that to us," Jake said.

"Who said I was explaining anything?" Martin's eyes shifted to me. "I don't need to explain anything to anybody."

"You got that straight, buddy. But right now you're in Jake's Bar." Jake smiled and briefly rested his big hand on Martin's shoulder. "And that's a good place to be. Am I right?"

Martin looked at Jake and nodded his head. "It's a good place to be." His eyes glazed with moisture.

"That's why we pull together," Jake said. He looked at me and looked back at Martin. "If people back home knew half this shit, they'd pull us out right now."

"Well, you tell 'em we took that mountain," Martin said, his voice rising. He pushed back from the table. "You hear me, Goddamn it?" He was yelling, tears in his eyes, jabbing his finger at Jake. "We took that mountain after the bravest man I ever knew got killed up there and the fucking brass give it back to the gooks a week later. Jesus Christ this war's fucked up." Martin suddenly stood up, knocking over his chair, and threw his empty beer can across the room.

"Hey, I hear you," Jake said, looking up at Martin. "The hell with this screwed-up war."

"I'm sorry about your friend," I said. "I'm really sorry."

"Fuck you, suckass," Martin said, glaring down at me. "You don't even know what it's all about."

"Hey, hey, wait a minute," Jake said, standing up, too. "We had a couple beers, okay? And maybe we're saying things we wouldn't otherwise say."

I stayed in my seat, looking at the two men. I tried to appear calm.

"Fuck that shit," Martin said. "He can't be sorry when he sucked ass to get out of it. He let somebody else do his job for him."

Jake looked at me and then back at Martin. He stepped back several paces, picked up a steel-framed chair by its back, looked at us again, and hauled off and flung the chair across the room. I jumped up and watched the chair bounce end-over-end on the tops of two tables before crashing into the plywood wall.

"Let's break some furniture," Jake said. "Here." Jake picked up another chair and held it out to Martin.

Martin's mouth hung open. "You're fuckin' crazy."

"You gonna throw this goddamned chair or pussy out?"

Martin grabbed the chair. Jake and I backed away. Martin, tall and unsteady, whirled like a discus thrower and sailed the chair into a metal post off to his left eight feet away. It clanged and clattered to the floor.

"Okay, your turn, engineer." Jake held out a chair. I grabbed it and whirled like Martin did, but I let go of the chair at too low an angle. It caught on the nearest table and bounced to the floor in front of us. We jumped out of the way.

"Didn't get much altitude, there, engineer," Jake said. He picked up the chair and handed it to Martin. "Show him how to do it." Martin sailed the chair past the post and over the nearest table, and crashed it into the wall.

"Feels good, doesn't it?" Jake said. Martin and I laughed. "Give me some skin," Jake ordered. He held out his hand, palm up, first to Martin and then to me. We each slapped his broad hand and he slapped ours. "Now let's sit down so I can hear about Hamburger Hill."

We pulled chairs from nearby tables and sat down again.

Martin glared at me. "You should've been there."

"How many of our guys went up the hill?"

"Don't know. Eight. Maybe more. They split us up."

"Any casualties?"

"Remember Wilcox? Pimples on his face? Or Ben Grady, the guy with the picture of the naked girl in bed? They got hit. Messed up bad. Dusted off."

"My God." But I did not remember those men. I felt hollow. Exposed.

Jake asked, "Why didn't they just bomb the hell out of that mountain and be done with it?"

"They did. Shelled it. Bombed it. Napalmed it. Looked like the moon in some places. Blown apart trees scattered all over. But the NVA was dug in deep. So the brass said we had to do regular assaults to get 'em out. But when we couldn't do it with a couple assaults, the brass kept sending us back up the mountain 'til we did. Then they walked us off and gave it back to the gooks." Martin's jaw clamped shut. He blinked hard several times.

I examined my glass and quietly asked, "What was it like to be up there? I'd like to know."

Jake suddenly raised his hand as though being sworn into office. "Hey, you know what? I got a CAV unit coming in from the boonies tonight, and if I don't get this place ready I'm gonna be messed-up real good." He stood up. "You guys go ahead and talk."

Jake walked to the front door, opened it, flipped the sign to *Closed*, and locked the door. Then he walked behind the bar and came back with two more beers and set them on our table. "I'll be unloading a truck out back." He nodded his head at Martin. "We'll talk another time." Jake picked up his plastic bag of empty cans and walked past the counter to the back room.

Martin and I studied our beers for several minutes.

"They didn't trust us."

"Who didn't trust you?"

"Guys in the 101st."

"Why not?"

"They been living in the boonies. Seeing bad shit. And we was combat newbies from an engineering unit. Nobody wanted us. Said we was dangerous. Wouldn't talk to us. Wasn't anybody give a rat's ass if we lived or died."

"What'd they assign you?"

"Ammo carrier for a machine gunner named Rodriguez. Everybody called him Roddo. His carrier got hit."

"Was this the man—?"

"Big Mex from LA. Been growin' a mustache for months." Martin laughed. "All thin and straggly. Looked like shit." Martin stopped. Tears filled his eyes. He slapped them away. "He was decent. Looked out for me. Hell, he was that way with everybody."

Martin was silent for a moment. I waited, looking at my beer.

"One of our assaults up the hill, our point man got hit by an RPG. One minute he was walkin' the trail, next minute he exploded. Pieces of him landed near me and Roddo. Everybody up front cut loose, but they stopped firing when Roddo went nuts. He jumped up and charged the bunker by himself. Held 'em down 'til he got on top of 'em. Killed three gooks before he blew through his ammo belt. Bravest thing I ever seen."

Martin glared at me while reaching for his beer and knocked it over. He grabbed the can from the foamy puddle, wiped it on his pants, tipped the can to his mouth, and swallowed the remaining beer.

"Something happen to Roddo?"

Martin looked at me, squinting. "Know what?" Martin belched again. "I'm not talking about this with you anymore. You wanna know what it's like out there, go fight the fuckin' war yourself."

I nodded. I felt sick to my stomach. My face burned. I turned my glass and wiped the condensation off with my thumb. "So what happens now? You going back to your unit?"

"Don't know. Maybe I'll re-up and get a job like yours."

I finished my beer and looked at my watch. "Hey, I got things to do. Gotta go."

I carried my glass and beer cans to the bar. Jake had returned from out back and was taking a break on the far side of the room. He gave me a nod.

I looked back at Martin. He was staring over the far edge of the table at the floor.

I left Jake's Bar and walked around Long Binh for awhile.

I ended up in a library I hadn't known was there. I pulled down a multi-record set of Haydn's London Symphonies I was surprised to find. I stacked the records on a portable record player and listened through earphones while looking at magazines. The next time I checked my watch I was late.

I ran to the 85th Group Headquarters, my .45 semi-automatic flopping on my hip. I signed for the papers and ran to the chopper pad.

The pilot was cranking the rotor for takeoff. I'd barely made it. I scrambled up on the canvas seat closest to the door.

"He's on board," Chief Hot Copper yelled. We lifted off while I fastened my seat belt.

Chief Hot Copper leaned forward, tapped me on the shoulder, and yelled, "Pilot wants to know if you need an appointment secretary or just a wake-up call at the bar."

"Tell him I prefer the secretary," I yelled back, "followed by a wake-up call."

I was out of breath and drenched with perspiration from all the running. I quickly cooled in the rush of air from the chopper's open doors.

I rode that rush to euphoria. I wanted to yell and shout. I wanted to tell somebody—anybody—what I escaped.

And Martin? He would have done the same thing I did if he'd had the chance.

"Pure dumb luck," I said, telling the other clerks in my hooch that night about Sulley Martin and my close escape from Hamburger Hill. "Pure fucking dumb luck."

Monday, Nov. 3, 1969 - Cu Chi Base Camp
Dear Janice:
During my chopper layover in Long Binh I do a lot of reading. I've started reading William James's The Varieties of Religious Experience. *It's the most*

interesting assessment of religion and spiritual experiences I've ever read.

I heard that Chaplain O'Donnell DEROSed and was replaced by another Catholic chaplain, a fellow by the name of Sebastian. I'll miss O'Donnell. He wrote good articles for The Paver *and provided me with thoughtful conversation and visits to fire bases and villages. He was almost as stimulating to talk to as my buddy Jerry Maener in personnel.*

A terrible thing happened back at Cu Chi two nights ago (I'm writing this at Long Binh). A guy walked over to Charlie Company's HQ Office and in front of the office tucked a M16 muzzle under his chin and blew his head off. I was told he fired three rounds before his thumb left the trigger. One round went through the outer office door and damn near hit the clerk. The guy gave no prior indication he was depressed.

The world is a dark and unhappy place. I'm glad we have each other.

> *Love, Andrew*

Friday, Nov 28, 1969 - Cu Chi Base Camp
Dear Janice:

I'm back working in S-1. Adjutant Harris said I'll be the substitute courier when the new courier is sick or on R & R. That's okay with me.

I've come back to the office just as the battalion is moving north to Lai Khe. Everything is packed or getting packed. It's a confusing mess.

We had a good Thanksgiving evening meal. Turkey and stuffing, and pumpkin pie. The cooks did a great job! But I missed seeing one of the cooks. A good guy. Some bad stuff happened not long ago. I'll tell you about it sometime.

I know we talked about this in Hawaii, but I went ahead anyway and extended my tour of duty past December. This way, when I return to the States in March, I can get out of the Army immediately, and I won't have eight months of remaining active duty like I would if I returned home next month. You know how much I hate the Army.

> *Love, Andrew*

RALPH MANTIS

"Wow, that's a big one," Adjutant Harris said. "He won't bite, you know."

"I know that, Sir." I circled the five-and-a-half-inch praying mantis on the floor of the corridor outside the battalion's S-1 office at Cu Chi Base Camp. "But he can sure put the clamps on your finger."

Moments earlier I had picked up the green mantis just below his long, rigid back. The mantis swiveled his triangular head around and looked directly at me with his bulbous, black-dot-centered eyes. Then he turned his upper body and clamped his forearms, lined with needle-sharp spines, on my index finger. I was so startled I flipped him to the floor. We later discovered his arm spines could leave indentations on a wooden pencil.

Harris stooped and slid his hand on the floor, palm down, toward the insect. The praying mantis stepped up on the back of Harris's hand as dignified as a king. Harris carried him into the S-1 office to show Connors and Parker.

We gathered around Harris and poked pencils at the huge insect to see what it would do. At each poking, it reared back and turned toward the offending pencil, arms tightly folded.

Suddenly the mantis took flight.

Everybody scattered. The bird-sized green bug made a buzzing and flapping sound as it flew to the rear of the office and landed on the window screen behind and to the left of my desk and chair. He took up residence on that screen and made it his new home. Harris named the mantis "Ralph" because, he said, it reminded him of a friend back home: skinny and bug-eyed.

Ralph soon became my valued assistant.

My first responsibility of the day as junior clerk in the S-1 office—I was still the "junior clerk" because I was the last man assigned to the office—was to come in early each morning and dust everything, make coffee, and knock down spiders and the webs they spun every night in the corners of our office.

The spiders were big as half dollars, leg tip to leg tip, and had bulbous bodies and thick hairy legs. Hitting one with a fly swatter left an unpleasant mess on the wall I wiped off with a wet cloth, which itself left blotches on the wall. Spider disposal became far more efficient when I used them to fill Ralph's dietary needs.

I would stand on a chair or a desk in front of the spider web with a pencil in each hand and rapidly circle one of the pencils through the anchoring strands of the spider's web. The spider would drop straight down on an escape line from the web now wrapped around my pencil. But I quickly rotated the two pencils around each other like a windlass, winding up the escape line while I stepped down from the desk or chair and walked to the window screen.

Stepping up on another chair I had positioned next to Ralph's screen, I continued rotating the pencils around each other, but now above Ralph. He would rear back in his most prayerful manner, his front arms tight against his chest. Then I stopped rotating the pencils. The spider continued dropping on its escape line, past Ralph, and Ralph snatched it for breakfast.

I found two or three big spiders in the office almost every morning. Ralph couldn't eat them as fast as I supplied them. Even so, he always grabbed a second spider with his free arm before finishing the first one.

Ralph devoured a spider in ten minutes, sometimes less. With Ralph's help, I cleanly eliminated all the spiders in the S-1 office within thirty minutes of my early morning arrival. No more spider guts and splotches on the walls from wet rags. Between spider presentations to Ralph, I made coffee, dusted the office, removed my plastic typewriter cover, and laid out my unfinished work from the previous day.

I kept a little hand broom and dustpan hidden between my desk and the wall for sweeping up crusty leg tips Ralph dropped to the floor. Sweeping up those crusty leg tips and other bodily remains was my last "junior clerk" job of the morning. Sometimes I delayed that job into the work day because Ralph ate his third and fourth spider much slower than the earlier ones, and he didn't eat as much of them.

After breakfast, Ralph always cleaned his face and arms. Then he rested. But he always reared back, ready to attack, if somebody came near or walked past him to the mimeograph room behind my desk.

Occasionally we served Ralph an evening meal. These meals were office-wide projects, and everyone was happy to join in the search for Ralph's entrées. When our late afternoon hunts were successful, we served him *Live Baby Toad on String* (in season). *Live Baby Lizard on Lassoed Tail* was a less eager snatch. Ralph sometimes got kicked by these entrees while he ate them, but he seemed not to mind. For dessert we occasionally served him *Fresh Moth Sans Wings on Pencil Point*.

Ralph became a celebrity. We talked about him in the mess hall, at the EM club, and in the hooches. Soon clerks started coming from personnel and company offices to see Ralph. Even a few sergeants came by. Men promised me beer at the EM club to see how I fed Ralph spiders, but I rejected their offers. I didn't want Ralph's appetite spoiled for morning meals. But when my buddy Jerry from personnel came over to see Ralph, he gave us some stunning news.

"I'm sorry to tell you this, but Ralph is a girl. Whoever named her Ralph was a gender-bigoted lunkhead. Just because it's big doesn't mean it's male. The little ones are the males. I suppose you could change her name to Ralphine." Jerry chuckled.

Adjutant Harris overheard Jerry's chortling comments and was incensed, which was unusual for Harris. "Why the hell would I name him Ralph if he's a she?"

"Maybe because you didn't—"

"Okay, wise guy, prove he's a female!"

"I don't know what kind of genitals they have or where to look for them. I'm just telling you what I've read and remember from biology class."

Adjutant Harris ordered Jerry "back to personnel where you belong" and declared Ralph to be a male "no matter what anybody says."

Despite Ralph's celebrity status, Colonel Hackett was oblivious to Ralph's existence until one morning when I was late for work. That delayed my removal of spiders and spider webs. Within moments of his arrival, Colonel Hackett charged out of his office, his morning cigar clenched between his teeth.

"Why is there a large spider hanging in a web above my wall map?" he demanded.

"Yes, Sir. I can explain that. Our spider-killing machine is overloaded right now, but the spider in your office will be processed within minutes."

Hackett removed the cigar from his mouth and peered at me with deep-set dark eyes. His voice lowered to a purred growl. "What the hell are you talking about?"

Harris, Connor, and Parker, still half asleep, were suddenly wide awake and watching closely to see how much trouble I'd get myself into, because Hackett tolerated no foolishness.

"Sir, I believe I can show you better than I can put it into words. Would you mind stepping to the rear of the office?" I led Hackett between the desks to the window screen behind my desk.

I gestured toward Ralph. "This is our office mascot, Sir." Ralph turned his head in the direction of my moving hand as though saying hello to Hackett. "Isn't he magnificent? He stays on this window screen because we feed him our office spiders. He's almost ready for the spider in your office. The one he's holding right now is his second spider of the morning. He's a cold, heartless killer. He eats his prey alive." I smiled. "His name is Ralph."

Hackett jutted out his jaw and squinted at Ralph and then at me. He shook his head and walked back into his office. I grinned and gave a thumbs-up to the other guys sitting at their desks.

Hackett said nothing when I entered his office a few minutes later, head down, intent on my mission. I stood on a chair in front of the wall map and wound up the spider, worked him like a yo-yo, and carried the doomed creature out the door I hooked open with my elbow.

Later in the day, Hackett came to my desk and demanded a feeding demonstration. I staged it the next morning by leaving one spider undisturbed in its web until Hackett came to work.

After that, Hackett sometimes came into the clerical office and stood behind me and used a wooden pencil to play with Ralph. Ralph's triangular head and unblinking black eyes tracked Hackett's movements with the cold logic of a programmed killer. When Hackett turned to walk back to his office, he always said, "Carry on, soldier." I always said, "Yes, Sir."

In mid-afternoon, Ralph sometimes flew the short distance from the window screen to my shoulder. He would stand next to my ear, perfectly still, and watch me type.

One day he climbed down my green fatigue shirt and hung on my chest, perfectly still. He was watching my fingers on the typewriter. About that time, a visiting high-ranking officer came out of Hackett's office and continued talking to Hackett as he wandered expansively to the rear of the clerical office where I sat typing. He was carrying a manila folder in one hand and a cup of coffee in the other. He looked at my chest, puzzled, and walked closer as he spoke, trying to distinguish Ralph from my green fatigues.

Ralph suddenly reared up for battle, arms folded, and rustled his wings. The officer jumped back, yelled, "Good God," and sloshed coffee all over himself and the manila folder. Colonel Hackett, standing in his office doorway, laughed so hard he started coughing.

"Hate to see you in an ambush," Hackett said, wheezing and laughing.

After that, Connors and Parker brought in two more praying mantises. We thought Big Bertha and Tiny Tim would be happy on the window screen beside Ralph, even though they all acted hostile and rattled their wings when they first met.

A few days later I realized our food resources could not meet the needs of all three mascots. Another problem developed, too.

Tiny Tim was randy. He'd sneak up on Big Bertha with the apparent intent of mounting her. She'd rear back and rattle her wings in a way that would scare any ordinary male silly. But not Tiny Tim. He was persistent.

"He may as well forget it," Parker said. "Big Bertha's a feminist."

"Maybe so," Connors said, "But little guys are spunky. Maybe he'll wear her down."

The fourth night they were together on the window screen, Big Bertha ate Tiny Tim. I found Bertha in the morning with Tiny Tim's little leg in her mouth like a dog with a bone.

Then, after two weeks of low-yield spider harvests, Ralph killed and ate most of Bertha. Proof of this second atrocity was my discovery one morning of Bertha's partially devoured abdomen and wings on the floor below Ralph. This raised our estimation of Ralph. We saw him as a war-hardened killer with a thousand-yard stare.

When our battalion moved from Cu Chi to Lai Khe, we forgot Ralph. It's hard to believe, but we did. We left him hanging on the office window screen. Several days after the move we asked Hurley, the colonel's new driver, if there was any chance he could drive back to Cu Chi and get our mascot.

"You're in luck," Hurley said. "I'm supposed to drive Colonel Hackett to Cu Chi this afternoon. If I get the chance, I'll bring Ralph back in a paper bag."

Early that evening, after returning from Cu Chi and spending an hour dusting and polishing the colonel's jeep, Hurley visited our hooch.

"Hey, guys," he called even before the screen door banged shut behind him. He walked down the aisle between the cots, footlockers, and lawn chairs. "I got bad news."

"What happened?" several of us asked in unison.

"When I got there, guys from the new battalion were moving furniture around in your old office. I asked about the praying mantis and one of them said he'd heard somebody had knocked a big green bug off the back window screen yesterday and stomped it into green goo."

As it turned out, we didn't have a convenient source of food for Ralph anyway. Spiders seldom spun webs in the S-1 office at Lai Khe.

Saturday, Dec. 6, 1969 - Lai Khe Base Camp
Dear Janice:

We're set up and fully functional here at Lai Khe Base Camp.

We have new hooches built by the Vietnamese under the guidance of our men from Echo Company. That now seems wrong-headed to me.

After seeing from up in the choppers the enormous size of our base camps at Cu Chi, Long Binh, Ben Hoa, and Tan Son Nhut Air Force Base, it dawned on me the destructive effect we must be having on Vietnam's economy. We hire thousands of these people to burn our shit, shine our shoes, wash our clothes, and build our hooches, and when we leave, what will these people do? The amount we pay them is enormous compared to the little they can earn in the Vietnamese economy. So after they've adjusted their lives to what we're paying them for being our lackeys, we'll drop them over an economic cliff when we leave.

Don't worry. I'll get back to my normal corrupt self after a while and be upbeat about the good work I'm doing helping get medals for men who shouldn't be here.

All the boxes of hi-fi equipment arrived? That's great.
Love, Andrew

Sunday, Dec. 21, 1969 - Lai Khe Base Camp
Dear Janice:

Colonel Hackett DEROSED today.

I interviewed him a week ago for a newspaper article about "His Legacy." He got pretty chatty.

He said he was lucky he stayed the full year. Most higher brass serve in Vietnam only six months, which is far less than ideal because it takes that long, Hackett said, for a commander to get a sense of his mission's obstacles and acquire commitment from his troops. He thinks the reason for the six-month rotation of higher-ranking officers is so more of them can puff up their credentials with service in a war zone. He didn't explain how he managed to stay a full year. But he said none of this was to be included in the article.

I thanked him for his candor and told him he sounded like a rebel. He laughed.

The new commander, Lieutenant Colonel Clive Forester, is strict. Too bound by rules and regulations. Wears tailored fatigues. I haven't once seen him smile or heard him compliment anybody for good work. He sets everybody on edge. Nobody likes him.

We're all thinking about Christmas.

Oh, yeah. Merry Christmas!

I look forward to being home with you.

Love, Andrew

ROVING GUARD

The night it happened I was assigned as roving guard for our battalion's perimeter bunkers. My job was to walk back and forth on a dirt road behind our eight bunkers and make sure no VC suicide sapper snuck through our stretch of perimeter.

A brightly lit field runs around our entire base camp. Along the inner edge of this field, starting about ten yards in front of our bunkers, coil after coil of razor wire threatens any intruder with being hooked by needle-sharp points sticking out from the sides of hundreds of tiny razors affixed to the wire. Those needle-sharp points hold the intruder while the razor edges slice his flesh as he tries to extract himself. Tin cans, each containing a few pebbles, hang from the razor wire and rattle when jiggled. The wire is held in place by five-foot high metal stakes. Between those stakes, here and there, thin wires stretch to sensitive flares that ignite, when tripped, into brilliant yellow fire that illuminates the position of any person in the vicinity.

Each bunker has four or five claymore anti-personnel mines set up behind the coils of razor wire, but facing outward, away from the bunkers. Electrical wires from the claymores trail back to the bunkers so the guards, if they see anything moving, can detonate a claymore that contains a pound of C-4 plastic explosive that blows 700 steel balls forward in a 60-degree arc, left to right, so any person within that arc will be rendered into chowder. The guards constantly survey the field from bunkers spaced a half city block apart.

Nobody knows how sappers get through all those defenses, but they do. Then they harass us with potshots or explosives, or sometimes they wait around and slit the throats of sleeping guards.

It's a damn spooky business, walking out there in the dark by myself, looking for men so clever and dedicated they can penetrate our perimeter defenses and sneak into the camp on missions they probably won't survive.

I walked along the dirt road behind the bunkers, my helmet on, my flack jacket crisscrossed with two ammo bandoleers, a couple grenades clipped at my shoulders, and my M16 held across my chest, locked and loaded, my thumb on the safety. After calling out the password loud and clear, I stopped at bunkers here and there, bullshit with the guys, and continued my walk under a star-filled sky. The moon was so bright I had a shadow walking behind me in one direction and a shadow walking in front of me when I went in the other direction.

I was not happy about that bright moon. It made me a prime target for a sniper. He'd be aiming at a moving target from half a mile or more away, and he'd be sighting against the glare of perimeter flood lights, but that didn't make me feel any better. I still felt like a mouse walking past a hungry cat.

Around midnight clouds rolled in and obscured the moon. I'd taken a ten-minute break at one of the bunkers and then continued my walk, back and forth, feeling a little more secure. My night vision adjusted to the light filtering through the clouds and I could see quite well except in the shadows. Sometimes I'd stop and listen. Or I'd stare at a point up the road and practice my peripheral night vision by detecting movement by our guys on top of a nearby bunker. Then I'd move on.

Suddenly a short man carrying a glinting, nickel-plated revolver, and wearing nothing but blue-jean cut-offs and tennis shoes, ran out from the base camp toward the bunkers. He couldn't be mistaken for a VC. Even so, I flipped off the safety on my M16. The man had a gun and I didn't know how drunk, stoned, or deranged he might be.

"Halt," I yelled. "What's the password?"

He didn't stop running. He yelled over his shoulder, "I'm gonna kill me one of those little bastards." He was drunk. Stoned guys aren't that aggressive.

I flipped my safety back on and followed him to the bunker.

Forget calling out the password. The men on the bunker heard us and saw us coming. They laughed and did the ass grabbing and poking shit to a drunken man with a loaded gun. I told the stupid fucks I almost shot him and they better get him off the perimeter line or I'd call the Sergeant of the Guard. They said they'd send him back as soon as he sobered up a bit.

"Okay, but keep him out of my patrol area!"

How they'd do that I didn't know. He'd have to cross the road again. Hell, let them deal with it.

I continued walking and looking. I was almost at the turn-around point at the end of our line of eight bunkers when I heard automatic weapons firing.

I dropped to the ground. But then I held my head up to see what was happening. Risky thing to do, but I needed to know what was going on.

I saw muzzle flashes from automatic rifle fire at multiple points along the distant tree line out beyond the perimeter. Sounded like strings of popping firecrackers. Tracers snapped in like green lines drawn straight as a ruler. Snaps and zings. Damn close!

I put my head back down.

I was pretty sure this was harassment, not a full scale ground assault. Otherwise they would have preceded it with mortar fire. It wouldn't last long. The muzzle flashes show where the shooters are, and though tracers show the VC where their rounds are hitting, tracers also reveal the shooter's position. So they shoot and run since they know our Cobra gunships will be after them within minutes.

Our bunker guards made me proud. They turned it around like the Mother of God having her butt cheeks pinched. M60s clattered outgoing rounds at six hundred a minute. M16s sputtered like unmuffled motor bikes. Our red tracers stitched the bunker line to the tree line. M79 grenade launchers blooped grenades out among the distant trees where they exploded sounding like M-80 firecrackers.

Then the VC let fly four or five RPGs like arrows with their feathers on fire. Most of them hit wire or metal stakes and exploded harmlessly. But one RPG skipped along the ground and hit a neighboring bunker, one that wasn't in my unit. I saw it hit from where I was lying on the road.

The VC stopped firing just as suddenly as they started. Their side of the firefight didn't last more than a few minutes. Maybe not even that. Seemed like hours.

Then two Cobra gunships joined the firefight that already ended, but not quite. The Cobras would try to nail the VC before they could retreat to secure ground or jump back in their tunnels.

We couldn't see the Cobras, but we could hear them high above us approaching our section of the perimeter. Then two powerful spot lights blinked on high in the black sky and shined down on the woods behind the tree line. Those two unbelievably bright and narrowly focused spot lights swung back and forth searching for the enemy. I knew, from seeing Cobras fire their mini-guns during the day, they would soon tip forward, suspended in the air, to fire at specific targets and cover them with a carpet of bullets.

Then the Cobras began firing their mini-guns, one to a chopper. Each spinning six-barreled gun fired six thousand rounds a minute. That's one hundred rounds a second. Their streams of tracers, one tracer every fifth round, looked like two clusters of red ribbons with their upper ends gathered and pinned at two points in the sky, while their lower ends widened out in multiple streamers that brushed gently, back and forth, against the ground.

It was so beautiful and gigantic a spectacle I forgot, in the first couple seconds, that those ribbons were puncturing the ground and anything above the ground with death and destruction. Then the sound of the mini-guns reached me.

Unlike automatic fire from M16s or M60 machine guns in which discrete shots can be heard like washboard bumps under a speeding car, the mini-guns emitted a continuous, guttural roar. The sound shook the air and pressed against my chest. It reminded me that men were being chewed alive by the ends of those pretty ribbons. No movie or painting of the glory and wrath of God at the Last Judgment could be so awesome.

The Cobra mini-gun show almost over, I waited a few moments and got up and ran doubled-over toward the bunker that got hit. The rocket appeared to have exploded on the face of the bunker. I knew from the way it exploded it didn't fly through the firing slot and detonate inside, which is what the VC are trying to do when they skip RPGs along the ground toward the bunkers. And I was pretty sure the RPG didn't hit protective fence mesh in front of the firing slot because almost all RPG screens in front of perimeter bunkers had been long ago rolled up by guards so they could see better. But either way—exploding on the fence mesh or on the face of the bunker—if the men were inside and ducked below the firing slot, they'd probably be okay except for busted eardrums.

I stopped on the road behind the bunker, knelt on one knee, and did a visual inspection. I couldn't see anybody on top. I called out the password.

"Waterspout! Waterspout!"

No response. They were probably inside.

If they were inside, they were newbies. Experienced GIs do their guard duty on top of an assigned bunker, behind a waist-high wall of sandbags, so they can see and hear better. Only incoming mortar rounds force them in the bunker. Down there they can't hear anything. And they can't see if anybody is coming at them from the right, left, or rear. They see only through a twelve-inch-high firing slot two inches off the ground where they don't have good perspective and can't see much of anything at a distance. Vision inside a bunker is made even worse by RPG fence-mesh stretched three or four feet in front of the bunker, which is why most guards roll it up.

Bending at the waist, I walked slowly toward the bunker. It looked massive. A big black box half-buried in the ground. I started seeing more details.

No cots or lawn chairs on top. Like I said, the bunker wasn't ours. We have cots and lawn chairs.

I walked cautiously, still bent over, to the entrance at the side of the bunker, and called down the password again. Still no response.

"Hello? You guys okay?"

Then I thought, *Hey, stupid, their ear drums are blown. They can't hear you.*

"Okay," I yelled, "I'm coming down. Don't shoot me!"

I started down the steps. Dust and smoke from the explosion drifted up around me from the entrance hole.

At the bottom of three steps I ducked my head and dropped to my knees. I was surrounded by thick darkness pierced by a wide shaft of faint blue light coming through the firing slot from the brightly lit field out front. It backlit the dust and smoke in the bunker air.

I propped my M16 next to the exit hole. I crawled further into the bunker.

Similar to our battalion's bunkers, the fucking ceiling was so low I couldn't stand up.

I shifted to my left knee and stuck out my right leg so I could reach in my trouser pocket for my flashlight. My boot pushed against something that felt like a leg. Not good.

I knew it wasn't smart to turn on a light inside a bunker because it shines out the firing slot and makes a perfect target for a sniper. But this was an exception. I needed light. So I pressed the rubber-covered button on my flashlight, but it didn't work. I smacked the flashlight against my palm several times and it blinked on.

I directed the beam along the front of the bunker. No wire mesh outside the firing slot. Rifles and clackers askew on the floor. Firing slot stripped to raw wood, slivers sticking out in all directions. I turned the flashlight around to the back wall on my right.

There they were. The RPG must have hit the front wall of the bunker near the firing slot and blown these men to the rear of the bunker. They'd watched it coming at them. Mesmerized. Unbelieving.

My initial response was revulsion. They did not appear human. They were misshapen obscenities. Violations of human nature. No human being should look like that. No man should have this happen to him.

The blond haired man nearest me, on my right, was bare-chested and sitting with his back against the wall, his legs splayed out in front of him. His jaw was blown open and hanging at an angle on his chest. His right cheek hung like torn chicken fat from the side of his upper jaw. His right arm was ripped from his shoulder and hung by blue tendons. I could see white bone sticking out the end of his upper arm. Blood pulsed out his shoulder and down his side.

I turned the flashlight to the left. That man was lying on his right side, his face in a pool of blood. His left arm drooped over his back as though it had no bones. His shirt sleeve was rolled above his large bicep, now soft and flat, and oozing blood from multiple puncture wounds from one-inch splinters. His right arm was underneath him, his right hand and forearm protruded out from under his back. A claymore clacker was half-buried in his forehead. The RPG explosion must have blown the clacker off the bottom of the firing slot just as he ducked.

Most guards store their clackers—hard plastic electric-pulse generators connected by wires to blasting caps in the claymores—on the bottom ledge of the firing slot to make them easily seen and available. Otherwise they're on the floor, in the dark, next to the front wall where they can't be seen but only felt.

I held the beam from the flashlight on the chest of each man. I couldn't tell if they were breathing.

Suddenly the man with the ripped jaw gurgled and his chest expanded with a big intake of air. It startled me. I jerked back and swung the flashlight on him.

His left eye was uninjured and open. The pupil was enormous. A black hole. Empty. Nothing there.

Like an idiot I whispered, "Can you hear me? Are you conscious?"

I looked around for the field phone. It was ripped partway off the wall. I tried to reconnect the wires—my hands shaking—but the wires weren't long enough to patch together.

The Sergeant of the Guard would come soon anyway. He'd miss their sit-com reports. And surely somebody from another bunker saw this happen and would call it in. Or their roving guard would come by.

In the meantime, what should I do? These men were surely dying. And if the guy with the clacker in his skull wasn't dying, he'd be a vegetable if he survived.

I couldn't leave them like this. I had to do something. But what? I had no medical supplies. I wouldn't know how to use them on wounds like this anyway. There was a first aid kit on the back wall in the upper right corner. How would that help? A tourniquet? A bandage? Iodine?

Then it occurred to me. *There is something I can do. I can end this nightmare for these men.*

Wouldn't that be horribly wrong?

No. It's what I'd want done for me. No question about it.

Can I get away with it?

Why am I asking that? If I were laying here like they are ... Why not do what's right in a war that's nothing but evil? End this defilement of their humanity!

I crawled over and grabbed my M16 leaning next to the steps. I crawled back and faced the two men on my knees. I laid the flashlight on the floor and directed it at the man on the right. I was trembling. I tried not to look at his mouth or his eye.

I raised the M16 to my shoulder. I didn't know where to aim. Where should I shoot this man? I lowered the rifle and shook my head.

Wait for the Sergeant of the Guard! Or the roving guard! Whatever battalion maintains this bunker has a roving guard, too.

But these men are my responsibility, too. I have to be strong. They would want this done for them.

So, damn it, shoot the man! Go on. Put him out of his misery! He's almost dead anyway.

But where should I aim?

Not the head. Don't shoot him in the head. Not with his eye open. Shoot him in the chest.

I aimed at the man's chest.

Oh God, he was a mess. Slivers of wood peppered his face and upper torso. He was covered with blood. Shadows hid much of it. His boots and legs blocked the flashlight. But I could see patches of white skin over the sights of my rifle.

Sweat dripped in my eyes. I swiped at my forehead and returned my hand to the rifle's hand guard. I shook so violently I worried I'd miss him entirely or merely increase his agony. I lowered the rifle. Resting on both knees, I bowed my head, closed my eyes, and calmed down. I opened my eyes and raised my rifle.

Aim to my right of his solar plexus. Hold steady! Ready. Aim—

And I pulled the trigger.

Nothing happened.

I quickly tried the cocking lever but I'd already locked and loaded on the road. I pointed the rifle to the side of the bunker and pulled hard on the trigger. Nothing. The trigger must be jammed.

I looked behind me at the floor near the front wall. I could use one of their guns. I laid my M16 on the floor and swiveled on my knees toward the rifles at the front of the bunker.

But what if the explosion damaged their rifles? Their rifles might not work any better than mine!

Then it dawned on me. *My safety is on! I flipped the safety on back on the road.*

I crawled back to my rifle and flipped off the safety. I repositioned the flashlight and raised the rifle to my shoulder.

Ready. Aim—

But now I couldn't do it.

I lowered the M16 and silently begged the man to die. I rocked on my knees at a loss for what to do. He slumped on his left side and stopped moving.

"Hey down there!" yelled somebody at the top of the steps. "I'm coming down. Don't shoot."

A voice of authority. Probably the Sergeant of the Guard. Or the Officer of the Guard. Somebody who knew what to do.

"I won't shoot," I tried to call. But I found myself shaking so badly my teeth chattered. I couldn't form the words.

The sergeant cautiously stepped down and crawled into the bunker. I could see him in the spill light from my flashlight on the floor. He had a .45 semi-automatic in his holster and a flashlight in his hand. He turned it on as soon as he was down the steps and on his knees.

"What the fuck!?" He crawled in further. "What happened here? Jesus God Almighty." He turned to me. "Who the hell are you?"

I tried to tell him who I was and what unit I was from and what I saw, but it all jammed together. I couldn't stop shaking. I gritted my teeth to stop the chattering.

He shook my shoulder with his left hand. "Pull it together buddy!"

I stopped shaking.

"Phone work? Why didn't you call…?" He turned to look.

I shook my head no, the phone didn't work.

"Stay put 'til I drive back with medics and replacements. I'll radio ahead, but it might be ten or fifteen minutes before I return. You okay?"

I answered in a hoarse whisper. "Yes, but I need to get out. I need to—"

"You stay the fuck right here with these men until I get back or I'll have your ass in a sling so high you won't be able to see the ground. I'll be back as soon as I can."

I waited what seemed like a very long time. I debated turning off the flashlight, but I didn't want to be down there in the dark.

Neither man moved. They didn't appear to be breathing.

I picked up my M16 and flipped on the safety.

When the sergeant with two medics and two additional guards showed up, I told the sergeant what unit I was from and my assignment as roving guard. Then I got out of there and started walking the road behind my bunkers.

I was stunned by what I'd seen and by what I'd almost done. I walked the road reliving the nightmare.

A third of the way down our row of bunkers I saw, out of the corner of my eye, a man staggering out from a bunker toward the base camp. I raised my M16 and called, "Halt! Who goes there? What's the password?"

The man stopped. He held his arms out wide and hung his head. He had a nickel-plated revolver in his right hand. He wore blue-jean cut-offs.

I lowered my rifle and walked up to him. All the emotion of the previous forty-five minutes came out as I yelled, "What the fuck are you still doing out here?"

He flapped his arms. Helpless. "Couldn't go back … firefight." He'd had more to drink. I could smell the whisky from where I was standing.

"Give me that pistol," I ordered. He held out the revolver, muzzle first. I took it and popped open the cylinder, dropped the cartridges in my hand and threw them in the field. I handed the revolver back to him.

He said, "Going now. Pleased to meet you." He stepped forward and held out his hand, but then pointed at my pants. "You got shit all over you? Oil? Tar? You …?"

I looked down at my fatigues. My legs were covered with it. It looked black in the cloud-filtered moonlight. *How could it be oil? Or tar? I haven't been….* I reached down and touched my left pant leg. It was wet. Slippery and thick, like melted Jello. I smelled it. Nothing. So I tasted it, like I'd tasted water or gasoline from the garage floor at home.

Copper. Tastes like....

I gagged and started heaving.

When I delayed my walk back to the hooch that morning most of the men had left for work. The remaining men took no notice of me. They assumed I'd been de-drumming or had some other job that entailed getting oil or tar on my pants.

I removed my fatigues, put on clean ones, and threw my blood-soaked clothes in a trash barrel outside the hooch. I'd have burned them if I could. I returned to my cot and looked at my M16. I'd clean it later.

I had the day to sleep, but I was too agitated to try. I grabbed my floppy hat and walked outside. I walked around the base camp the rest of the day. I was so disoriented I eventually got lost, but I didn't, until dusk, ask anybody how to get back to the 182nd.

That night I slept. Physically and emotionally exhausted.

It's been quite some time, now, since that night in the bunker. I still have nightmares. Fewer than before, but enough to tell me I'll be bothered by that night the rest of my life.

The image of those two men haunts me.

I'll be looking at a document or typing at my desk, and I'll suddenly stop moving, immobile, like a statue, and I'll stare unseeing through whatever's in front of me. During those times my attention is sucked back inside that bunker and I'm aware of only the mangled bodies of those two men. Then I replay, over and over, what I tried to do and then didn't do.

I seriously tried to kill those two men. I pulled the trigger. Hard. Repeatedly. Why? Why did I do that? My reasons are no longer clear to me. And then, when I realized my stupid mistake, I didn't follow through and pull the trigger. Why? What happened between the first attempt and the second attempt? I'm not sure.

I wrote this story to objectify my experience. To get it out there so I could more clearly comprehend and evaluate what I saw and did. Maybe create a catharsis for myself. But it didn't work. It's made it worse.

After setting this story aside for many weeks, I've reread it and tried to imagine how others might read it. What I discovered is a misguided monster who tried to kill his wounded comrades. And a fool for the risk he was taking. Maybe a coward, too.

So I've spent hours trying to find some small measure of honor, some redeeming value, in my behavior—something resembling good intentions that would be recognized as such by readers. But I haven't succeeded.

Euthanasia might be a dark business, yet at the same time well-intended. But I now wonder if I wanted to end the suffering of those men enough to pull the trigger. Far stronger, it now seems to me, was an insane desire to obliterate the horror, the deformity, from the face of the earth.

I wanted to yell, "*Stop this! Stop this! Stop this!*"

Hell, stop the world. Annihilate the universe.

And when I work myself up to believing my overriding concern was to put those men out of their misery and stop the disfiguring horror for them, too, I find I'm a coward for not doing it. And a downward spiral of conflicting self-recriminations begins from which I fear no loved one, friend, or counselor will ever be able to free me.

Wednesday, Dec. 31, 1969 - Lai Khe Base Camp
Dear Janice:

I'm doing the courier job again. Just for a week or ten days while the regular guy is on R & R in Thailand. It messes up my awards work, but I don't care. I'll do the best I can and what I can't do … screw it. I don't care anymore.

Allowing the government to send me over here was a big mistake. I should have gone to Canada. Or prison. Or lied and claimed I'm a religious conscientious objector. I was so damned concerned about being honest and speaking with integrity. What a joke.

I was on my layover in Long Binh when Bob Hope put on his Christmas show. I saw some of it, but the humor was so 1940s and filled with cheap one-liners I finally left. That kind of entertainment cannot make this war palatable. It was insulting.

Love, Andrew

Tuesday January 13, 1970 - Lai Khe Base Camp
Dear Janice:

I'm back from being courier. Been back a few days.

Hard to get motivated. Maybe it's the new colonel, new legal clerk, and new adjutant. Adjutant Harris DEROSed while I was gone. The new adjutant knows nothing about editing or grammar or anything else.

Jerry Maener's girlfriend mailed him a newspaper article published by a reporter named Seymour Hersh about a massacre over here. You hear about it?

Apparently an officer named Lieutenant William Calley led his men in a massacre of maybe hundreds of unarmed civilians in March of 1968 at a place called My Lai. Apparently Calley's men suffered numerous casualties from mines they thought the villagers should have warned them about. So Calley and his men killed the villagers. All of them. Including women and children.

Guys in my hooch are sick about it, but they think they understand how it happened and wonder if they might have done it, too, given similar circumstances. If you've seen your buddies blown apart, one after the other, again and again, then maybe ....

But I don't know. Shoot little babies? Pregnant women? Young girls?

Jerry Maener voiced a sobering thought about it. He said, "The only difference between Calley's massacre and what the Army does every day is how close they were to who they killed. We bomb and napalm villages all the time without knowing who's there or how many we might kill. Receive a few shots from a village and patrols call in artillery or bombers and level the place."

Love, Andrew

Sun Jan 25, 1970 - Lai Khe Base Camp
Dear Janice:

You're right. I'm depressed. And I think I have good reason to be.

I was sheltered and nurtured by loving parents, a caring suburban neighborhood, a well-intended evangelical church, and good schools. But I've discovered my country and the world and other people—even myself—none of it is what I thought it was.

Wholesale raping. Killing. Starvation. Slavery. Disease. Disfigurement. Racism and religious hatred. Military subjugation of entire tribes and nations. This stuff is going on every minute of every day in most of the world. I knew about these things before I came to Vietnam, but it was all head knowledge. Something

I read about in books and magazines. But now I've seen some of it for myself. And let me tell you something. I've been living on the clean white rim of a worldwide sewer.

I've walked through villages and driven past Vietnamese people who live in fear and torment and loss of loved ones all their lives—from the colonizing French, the VC, their own corrupt government, and from the good ol' American GI sent to Vietnam to save America from communism. And I've participated in it by allowing myself to be part of the machine that's grinding them down.

This world is fucked up. I'm fucked up, too. I feel guilty for being part of this war, and I feel guilty for avoiding combat. I'm ashamed I allowed myself to be sent over here, and I'm proud of my work helping get tin medals for heroes. How screwed up is that?

What will I be like when I come home? How will what I've learned fit into suburbia and a job for getting nicer stuff? I don't know.

Love, Andrew

JIMMY BEAMIS

Jimmy Beamis looked like a mama's boy in military uniform for a junior high school play. You'd swear he couldn't have survived basic training, but apparently he did.

He had smooth white skin and light brown freckles and sandy red hair. His arms were the fleshy, hairless tubes of a little boy. Jimmy's black framed glasses were always sliding down his sweaty pug nose in the tropical heat and humidity of Vietnam. He often slid his glasses back up by tipping his head back and squinching his nose and upper lip, thereby exposing his front teeth and gums. Unblocked by the rim of his glasses, but only for a moment, his soft brown eyes looked at you with unblinking and unguarded trust. Jimmy Beamis believed anything you told him.

The men in Alpha Company enjoyed giving booze and dope to Jimmy, and he often accepted these gifts with a John Wayne impersonation by turning his shoulders, his hands on his hips, bending at the waist, and saying, "Well now, I'd be the last man to say a stiff drink and a good toke won't improve the morale of the troops."

Jimmy was drunk or stoned night after night. His little-boy antics and tough-guy pretense made men laugh until they fell on the floor.

At the suggestion of one of the men, Jimmy put a large tab of LSD or opium-laced speed—nobody knew what it was, except it was too intense—in a gob of peanut butter and fed it to a mangy black and white toothless mutt that hung around the hooch. The dog and Jimmy kept the men entertained all night long.

The dog's head wobbled after that, and he couldn't walk straight, but it was a good lesson, everybody said, of the dangers of undisciplined use of non-prescription drugs. Always do a little before you do a lot, and know your dealer, so you know what you got.

When drunk or stoned, Jimmy loved to pretend he was a soldier fighting gooks from behind cots and foot lockers. That was what made him so funny. A soldier was the one thing Jimmy would never be, at least in the minds of the other men and maybe in his mind, too. Nobody could imagine going into battle with Jimmy at his side. It would be like going into battle with your kid sister. You'd get yourself killed trying to protect the little shit.

The last time I saw Jimmy was early one morning when he was sitting handcuffed in a jeep with two MPs waiting to be taken to the Long Binh Jail for trial on charges of murdering a Vietnamese civilian. I found out what happened after talking with several men in Alpha Company.

Alex Beamis, Jimmy's forty-nine-year-old father, served as a Marine in the bloodiest battles of Okinawa in World War II and was now working as a grain elevator operator in Salina, Kansas. He had told Jimmy that he wasn't to come home unless he'd shot one of those pinko commie gooks for Dad. And since Jimmy had been assigned to the 182nd Engineer Battalion, he was afraid he'd miss his chance.

So early one evening, when Jimmy Beamis was pulling perimeter guard duty, he got that chance, or so he thought. The time was 1815 hours (6:15 p.m.), according to Jimmy's own account, fifteen minutes into "free-fire" time. He was alone in the bunker because his buddy had snuck back into camp for a portable radio so they could listen to the latest episode of "Chickenman" on Radio Saigon. It was then that Jimmy saw what he thought was a man riding a bicycle on the road outside Lai Khe's base camp perimeter.

The man was not supposed to be there. 1800 hours (6:00 pm) was the deadline for when the road was to be cleared of all Vietnamese who had been working for us on the base camp during the day. They had been warned, time after time, that anyone on that road after 1800 hours would be considered VC by perimeter guards who could fire at them without seeking permission from the Sergeant of the Guard.

So Jimmy locked and loaded the bunker's M60 machine gun and opened fire on the man who was furiously peddling away from Lai Khe Base Camp. Jimmy was surprised at how difficult it was to fire a M60 machine gun and hit such a tiny moving target that seemed, over the bouncing sights of the machine gun, so far away, so he strafed back and forth to get his man. Then he fired his machine gun up and down and back and forth again to ensure a positive body count.

But the man Jimmy cut down turned out to be an eleven-year-old

Vietnamese boy named Mai Thanh. He had illegally come to work on the base camp with his papa-san to help fill our sandbags and help burn shit in our shit cans. He had gotten separated from his father and missed the five o'clock truck that would drive him off the base camp and back to the nearby village. A soldier apparently discovered the boy and gave him a bicycle used by mama-sans during working hours and told the boy to hurry up and get the hell off the base camp.

The case against Jimmy was difficult to contest. Evening light at the time of the shooting was still good enough to distinguish a child from a man, and firing on a single figure on a bicycle in plain view a mere fifteen minutes into "free-fire time" seemed a bit extreme.

But what cinched the case against Jimmy was that he had been drinking beer and smoking grass on guard duty. Several beer cans and a couple roaches were on the bunker sandbags when Sergeant of the Guard Rapelli arrived at the bunker to find out what the shooting was all about.

Sergeant Rapelli said Jimmy was talking nonsense as though he were a character in a Sad Sack comic strip reporting to an imagined officer and saying things like, "Yes, Sir" and "No, Sir" and "Up your thirty thousand bushel silo, Sir."

Once Jimmy was sober and he was told what he had done, he stopped talking. Weeks went by without Jimmy uttering a word, even to his defense attorney.

Mr. Mai, the father of the dead boy, showed up at our battalion headquarters office two days after the killing, and Uncle Sam paid him the equivalent of forty dollars for his loss. I was there when Mr. Mai bowed and thanked Adjutant Harris for the forty dollars Harris handed him, which made us all feel a little awkward because Mr. Mai had been asking for his son's body.

I was also in the office when Mr. Mai came the second and third times. Each time he came, Mr. Mai bowed in thanks for the adjutant's unsuccessful attempts to obtain the boy's body from the Central Intelligence Division at Long Binh.

Central Intelligence wanted the body so they could retrieve the bullets for the prosecution's case against Jimmy. But an earlier U.S. military autopsy of a dead Vietnamese citizen had been publicized in the Saigon press as being illegal and sacrilegious, and that made Army doctors reluctant to extract the bullets from Jimmy's victim for fear of further violating Vietnam's religious beliefs and laws about the sanctity of a dead body.

So a legal investigator was assigned the task of finding out how the boy's case should be handled to assure our Army doctors they would not be embroiled in additional violations of our host country's laws and religious beliefs. In the meantime, the boy's body was stuck in a freezer somewhere in Long Binh until matters could be clarified.

Several weeks later, Jimmy confessed to his crime. Once he confessed, the prosecution didn't need the bullets from the boy's body, and the body could be returned to the father. But when we sent men looking for Mr. Mai, we discovered he had quit his job at the base camp and nobody knew where he was. He apparently moved away from Lai Khe.

Case closed.

What happened to the boy's body? What happened to Jimmy Beamis? I don't know. I assume the boy was buried and Jimmy went to jail. But quite honestly, they've ceased to be topics of conversation around the office and nobody has made an effort to follow up on the story because it isn't unique. Every week battalion headquarters receives reports of civilian injuries we cause while paving the roads, or reports of medics treating civilians for burns and bombing and ambush injuries our combat units inflict.

I showed a bit more interest, initially, because I'd met and talked to Jimmy several times, and I prided myself on being a little more sensitive than the average engineer or grunt in the field. So I tried to go the extra mile and be humane, but I got turned off real quick.

I walked out to the jeep to say good-bye to Jimmy, but he wouldn't talk to me. I even bowed to Mr. Mai when he left our headquarters office after his final visit, but three bows for the adjutant that day was apparently enough bowing for Mr. Mai and he didn't bow back.

So I said, "Fuck it."

I had work to do. I was the awards clerk. I was the writer of articles Major Roberts reviewed for negative attitudes before being approved for the battalion newspaper. And sometimes I was a courier of important documents between base camps.

We all say "Fuck it," at least all the soldiers I know. We get drunk or stoned so we don't feel the cynicism cutting away at our hearts in a war without moral, political, or military direction.

We know what's happening to us. The veil is being pulled aside. We're seeing our country and our world as they really are. Without mercy, without justice, without compassion. Evil and corruption, we've realized, are systematic and monolithic.

We can't cope with it. We've risked our lives and gone to war, and then we stay at war after we see the sham it is. We don't want to disobey orders and be thrown in jail, so we acquiesce. We do all this for the approval of our loved ones and our superiors so we can return to the Land of the Giant PX and resume our lives as contented consumers.

"No evil happens to a good man," Socrates said. But we are not good men. We are the men we've read about in history books.

The bottom line is this. Jimmy Beamis may have pulled the trigger, but he was not the only one who killed that eleven-year-old boy and ushered that boy's father into a lower level of hell.

Friday, Feb 6, 1970 - Lai Khe Base Camp
Dear Janice:

I took your advice and met with Chaplain Sebastian yesterday.

I asked him how he got his name. He said his father, a career soldier, was killed in WWII at Anzio, Italy. In honor of his father, the Captain took the name Sebastian at his ordination and joined the Army's Chaplaincy Corp. Turns out St. Sebastian is the patron saint of soldiers and most often depicted tied to a post and shot with arrows.

I asked Father Sebastian how a man can napalm a village or riddle other human beings with shrapnel and bullets—or arrows for that matter—and not be doing something fundamentally evil.

"God sometimes makes allowances for what ordinarily would be mortal sin," he said. "In times of war against an unholy enemy, God sanctions violence if there's no other way of defeating them. But since men don't retain love for the enemy while doing the terrible things they do in war, they must confess the resulting sin—what you've identified as evil—that arises in their hearts."

Live and learn. If you retain love for the villagers while napalming them you'll be okay. The good chaplain is a brainwashed idiot.

Love, Andrew

SNAPSHOT

Sergeant George Garrett has a long face on a big head. His face has the hollows and ridges of a character actor whose larger-than-life features can be seen from anywhere in the auditorium. The rest of him is thin and taunt with corded muscle, as if his body is a stalk for showing off his head. When you first see Sergeant Garrett you keep looking at him to convince yourself he's real, that a person can look like that. He's not ugly. He's unique. Everybody does a double-take when they first see Garrett.

Personality-wise, he's edgy and aggressive. I'm not sure why. But the way people look at him, as though he just stepped out of a cartoon, triggers his aggression. That much I know for sure.

One time in the mess hall I saw Garrett catch a newbie looking at him a moment too long. Garrett walked across the mess hall, pushed that face of his up close to the kid, and said, "You got a problem?"

Garrett gets into fights all the time. One night he attacked three battalion headquarters clerks at the EM Club. Off-duty sergeants and officers aren't supposed to socialize with the lower ranks, and that includes going to the EM Club, so Garrett had no business being there. But he likes drinking with his fellow medics, all SPC-4s—which is one rank lower than Garrett's—and nobody wants to tell Garrett he ought to leave the bar, especially after he's had a few.

I suppose you could say it was the clerks' fault he attacked them. All three of them were drunk, swaying arm-in-arm between the tables, singing the 1966 hit song by the Seekers, "Hey there, Georgy Girl." Everybody was laughing and looking at Garrett. He sat fuming a minute or two and jumped up and beat all three of them bloody before anybody had a chance to stop him. His fellow medics pulled him off the only guy left standing.

The medics gave the clerks first aide. Two clerks needed bandages for their cuts and bruises. The third guy got a nose splint, but it turned out his nose wasn't broken, only gushing blood.

Nobody reported Garrett. Maybe it was because Garrett was an outstanding medic and we couldn't get an equally good replacement. Or maybe it's because everybody was afraid of him.

So I sat up straight when Garrett walked over to my mess hall table one evening, set his meal tray opposite mine, sat down, and asked, "What are you reading?"

I often saw Garrett in morning formations and in the mess hall, but we'd never said a word to each other. I hung around S-1 and personnel clerks, and Garrett hung around medics and drinking buddies at the EM Club.

I had spent my day in the S-1 office doing my usual routine, and at six o'clock, I was off duty. Rather than head for the mess hall with the other men, I hurried back to my hooch—as I always do—and then out to the wash house for a shower before the water tank was drained. That usually makes me late for dinner, but I enjoy the luxury of being freshly showered and eating my dinner at a table by myself in a quiet, nearly empty mess hall, while reading a book.

While I was eating, Garrett and three other medics had entered the mess hall and walked through the serving line moments before it closed. They sat down two tables away from me. From the corner of my eye, I saw Garrett checking me out, squinting with his large, blue, cartoon eyes. Suddenly he picked up his tray and walked over to my table.

"It's a novel by John Updike called *Couples*," I said in reply to Garrett's question. I creased a corner and closed the book.

"You like that stuff, huh?" He pointed at my book. "Lots of hot sex?" Garrett grinned and made a loose fist with his right hand and bobbed it up and down over his plate of biscuits and chipped beef gravy.

"Well, yes," I chuckled to be agreeable, "but Updike doesn't get too graphic in his sex scenes."

Sergeant Garrett nodded his head and shrugged his shoulders. He said nothing for a moment. Then, accusing more than asking, "You're the guy who puts out the battalion newspaper. Right?"

"It's a poor excuse for a newspaper, but it's my best shot given the time I have. Aren't you a medic? Where you from?"

"California. Near L.A."

"You enlisted?" I set the salt shaker upright from where I'd laid it on its side to prop up my book.

"Yep. Swallowed six years so I'd get the schooling."

"Making a career of it?" I brushed salt off the green plastic tablecloth.

"This is it." Garrett raised his eyebrows in a half-apologetic, what-you-see-is-what-you-get look, and held his arms out to include everything around us.

"Good for you," was the most I could squeeze out.

"That's something you should write about in your newspaper."

"What's that? Do an article on you or on lifers in general?"

"No, not me!" Garrett grinned and bowed his head almost in his food. "Do an article on medics. Write about one of our MEDCAPS. We've been going out to villages near the base camp doing minor injuries, a little dental, stuff like that. We just got back from a MEDCAP at Dong Nho Village."

"What does MEDCAP stand for?"

"Medical Civic Action Program. It's the Army's way of maintaining friendly villages."

I finished off my last bite of rubbery red Jell-O. "Who goes on a MEDCAP?"

"Captain Newlin—he's the battalion surgeon—myself, and the three medics at the table over there." Garrett turned and gestured with his thumb at the other men. "That's Calloway, Jablonski, and Tony Alvino." Garrett turned back to me. "The Vietnamese translator, Phong, goes out, too. And three or four guards in case of trouble."

Garrett spooned up some chipped beef gravy. I pushed the bottle of Tabasco sauce to his side of the table.

"Thanks." Garrett unscrewed the little cap on the standard-issue, extra-large bottle, and squirted hot sauce on every square inch of his biscuits and gravy. Then he covered his boiled beans with it, too.

"When are you going out next?" I asked.

"Two days from now. Heading back to Dong Nho. Five miles east of here. Captain Newlin says a hundred and fifty villagers live out there, but I'd guess more if the men stayed around."

"Who gives the okay for me going out with you guys?"

"Captain Newlin in the dispensary. We leave early Wednesday morning, soon as the mine-sweeps clear the roads."

"I'll have to ask Kellaway about this, but that shouldn't be a problem. It's actually a great idea."

"Kellaway?"

"He's the battalion adjutant. My immediate superior." I pulled a pen from my pocket and opened the back cover of Updike's novel. "Long as we're sitting here, you mind if I ask a few questions?" At the top of the inside back cover I wrote, *Sergeant George Garrett.* I looked up.

Garrett glanced over both shoulders, hunched his back, and squinted at me.

I leaned my head to one side. "You don't have to tell the truth, you know."

Garrett broke into a big smile, as if posing for a snapshot.

"Your dad in the Army?" I asked.

"How'd you know?"

"Guessed. What'd he do?"

"He was a cook. Stationed all over the world."

"Still in the Army?"

"Hell no. Retired from life." Garrett smirked.

I nodded, without smiling, and wrote, *Father—Army cook all over—dead.*

"No, seriously," Garrett waved away the lame attempt at humor. "He retired and moved near L.A. Bought a little restaurant with his savings and married the waitress." Garrett slid his meal tray, the food half eaten, to the side of the table.

"Waitress your mom?"

Garrett nodded.

"How'd your dad do with the restaurant?"

"Screwed it up. Too much booze. Couple years later he died. Liver blew out. I was seven. Left Ma with all the bills. Dad's pension didn't cover them."

I closed my book and looked at Garrett. "Why'd you enlist? And why become a medic?"

"I thought about college, but I didn't have the money. And Ma needed help with the bills." George rolled his eyes and shrugged his shoulders. "So I enlisted and went for something people depend on, something—I don't know—something that makes a difference if you know what you're doing."

I reopened the back cover of Updike's novel and wrote down the quote. I looked up at George. "I can use that in the article."

"This is one of the things we're doing over here that can make you proud," Garrett yelled at me over the wind and noise in the back of the jeep. Tony Alvino was driving us up Highway 13 toward Dong Nho Village. Captain Newlin was riding shotgun.

We squinted behind our sunglasses in the fierce morning sunlight glittering off the asphalt road and rice paddy water flashing by on either side. We had wedged our cloth jungle hats under our thighs so the wind wouldn't blow them away. The rushing air dried the sweat from our hair and faces, and gave us the illusion of a delightfully cool morning that was actually humid and hotter than hell.

Medics Calloway and Jablonski rode with translator Phong in a medic's van behind us. And behind the van, four guards filled a jeep that had a M60 machine gun mounted on a post between the seats.

We all had M16s and bandoleers of ammunition, but nobody except the guards wore a flack jacket. We were visiting a friendly village in a friendly sector with no known enemy activity for months.

From my seat behind the driver, I studied Doctor Newlin. I tried taking a profile shot with my new 35mm camera I bought second-hand from another GI. The background light was intense, so I snapped the picture with the meter needle tight against the top of the viewfinder so Newlin's face wouldn't be underexposed.

Newlin was about thirty-four years old. Soft white skin. Black plastic glasses with clip-on shades. Nose and upper cheeks burnt pink. Forearms pink, too. His black hair was long enough to comb straight back, and was shiny with hairdressing. Garrett told me Newlin would soon DEROS and open a general practice somewhere in Ohio.

I leaned forward and yelled at Newlin, "You like military life?"

He turned in his seat, looked at me a moment through his clip-on shades, and yelled, "I'm proud of my men and I'm pleased you're doing a story about them."

I was pleased, too. It gave me the chance to observe Sergeant Garrett doing something I admired. Ministering to the sick and wounded was a noble thing to do, and seeing Garrett in action might improve my negative attitude toward lifers.

Before I was drafted I hadn't thought much about career soldiers. A soldier was a soldier. But during and after basic training, I began thinking of lifers as slow-witted goons with polished boots and starched pants who needed

240

someone to tell them what to do. I knew that was unfair and prejudicial. I knew I was wrong to prejudge any man. But it was hard not to prejudge lifers when so many of them revealed themselves to be rule-bound, insensitive thugs.

Lifers weren't born that way. The Army trains them that way. Its suppression of questioning, its reliance on authority, its training in violence, and its encouragement of aggression accustom men to think first with their fists and later, if at all, with their brains. This is all summed up in traditional Army advice to new recruits. Don't ask questions. Don't disagree with superiors. Don't show pain. Don't show sensitivity. Do what you're told. Be tough and take pride in the arts of killing and destruction.

There are exceptions, of course, but the majority of lifers I've encountered fit this description. Maybe it's an occupational hazard of being a trained warrior. I don't know. But it can sure make them unpleasant and difficult to be around.

Our caravan of two jeeps and a van drove the last mile to Dong Nho Village on a red dirt road. We arrived at the marketplace in a cloud of red dust.

The marketplace was a roof on posts over a concrete slab similar to a park pavilion. It was empty, the concrete swept clean.

Thatched huts surrounded the pavilion, but we saw no villagers. Not one. We knew they were nearby, because the pathways to the huts were freshly swept and the roof thatching was in good condition, but for now, they were hiding.

I offered to help the medics unload the van, but Garrett told me I'd be in the way. So I stepped back and watched, and took notes on my "reporter's pocket pad."

The medics carted out wooden chests, leather satchels, collapsible tables, and metal folding chairs. Guards Frazer and Kopecky divided the marketplace in half by stretching a rope waist high across the pavilion and tying it to opposing posts. Then they subdivided our end of the marketplace by looping rope between plastic stanchions they pulled out of the van and positioned on the floor.

While the medics were setting up their equipment, villagers started coming out of the huts and gathering around our end of the marketplace. Most were women and children, but a few disabled men and old papa-sans hobbled out, too.

Within fifteen minutes our end of the marketplace was transformed into a diagnostic area, a treatment area, and a dentist's office. By then, sixty or seventy villagers were watching us, most of them wearing rice paddy hats and standing in the hot tropical sun out beyond the shade-line of the tin roof. Captain Newlin, Tony Alvino, and interpreter Phong were the diagnostic and pharmacy team. Garrett and Jablonski were the treatment team, and Calloway was the dentist.

Each of three guards stationed himself, with a M16, at a different corner of the marketplace. The fourth guard sat in the jeep behind the mounted M60 machine gun.

I took a few pictures of the assembled villagers with my camera. But since I couldn't include my photos in our mimeographed newspaper, I let the camera hang from my neck and concentrated on taking notes.

Newlin's first patients were two barefoot boys about twelve years old. One boy wore a short-sleeved white shirt and tan shorts. The other boy wore a baggy red swimming suit. When Newlin asked them, through Phong, what was wrong with them, they both coughed loudly. Newlin checked their throats and ears. He instructed Tony Alvino to give each boy a cherry-flavored cough drop.

Newlin's next patient was a shirtless boy, maybe eight years old, in ragged cut-offs. I assumed the woman who accompanied him was his mother. The boy's right hand was wrapped in a bloody rag. The mother, wearing a faded calico dress, explained through translator Phong that the boy and his friend had been fighting over a bayonet they had found. Newlin called Garrett away from his set-up activities so Garrett could observe the examination.

Newlin unwound the rag from the boy's hand. A gaping wound ran across the palm. Several fingers had wounds cut parallel with the cut in the boy's palm. Newlin inspected the wounds. He asked the boy, through Phong, to wiggle his fingers and open and close his hand. The boy did, but he winced and whimpered. Newlin conferred with Garrett. Garrett then guided the boy and the mother to his own treatment area. I followed them.

Jablonski—brown hair, wide face, and a tiny red and white metal flag of Poland pinned on his pocket flap—prepared a stainless steel basin of warm soapy water from a supply tank in the van. Garrett tried to wash the boy's hand in the steel basin, but the boy cried out and pulled back his hand.

Garrett wasted no time coaxing the boy. He dried his own hands with a towel. He pointed to the boy's hand and then to his own. He curled his fingers and bent his hand into a twisted claw and waved it in front of the boy, explaining in sign language what would happen if the boy continued to refuse treatment. Then he pointed to the exit space between the ropes.

"Didi mau, didi mau," Garrett shouted. "Go on, get out of here."

The boy's eyes went wild. Startled villagers talked excitedly. The boy's mother wailed and grabbed hold of Garrett's arm. Garrett pulled away from her. The mother, waving her hands, turned to the boy and scolded him in staccato Vietnamese. The boy cried but nodded his head.

Garrett went back to work. He washed the cuts with a soft-bristled brush. Tears cascaded down the boy's cheeks. He flinched and cried but didn't pull back.

Garrett prepared a syringe, winked at the boy, and after Jablonski swabbed a couple spots with alcohol, Garrett injected painkiller into the boy's hand. Then he applied antibacterial ointment and sutured the palm wound closed. While Garrett was bandaging the boy's palm and fingers, I walked several feet over to the dentist's office.

Calloway was injecting Novocain in the lower gums of a wrinkle-faced old mama-san wearing a white blouse and black slacks. Her black hair was pulled back in a stringy bun at the back of her head. She sat on a metal folding chair, her hands resting in her lap, her head tipped back.

Calloway's hair was curly and golden. His eyes blue, face open and friendly. Shoulders broad, arms full without body building. A girl somewhere in the States was begging God to bring Calloway safely home to her.

When Calloway completed the injection, the woman didn't close her mouth or move her head. She continued staring, unblinking, at the tin roof.

Calloway washed his hands in a stainless steel bowl, inspected the mouth of the next patient, washed his hands again, and returned to the old woman. He leaned over, grabbed hold of her jaw with his left hand, and with his right he reached into her mouth with dental pliers. He locked onto a molar in the woman's lower left jaw and twisted and turned the pliers and pulled hard. The molar came loose with a "plop." He held up the brown tooth like a trophy. All the villagers in the dental section applauded.

"You do fillings, too?" I asked.

"Just extractions." Calloway bent back, hands on his hips, and groaned.

"What happens if the roots are too long or the tooth breaks?"

"We take those people, if they let us, back to an Army hospital for oral surgery. If the tooth looks rotten, I don't fool with it."

I returned to Garrett's treatment area. This time I stood among the villagers. I watched Newlin and Garrett examine a little girl. She wore faded yellow pajamas and was held by a young woman wearing a rice paddy hat tied to her head with a white scarf under her chin. The little girl—about two years old—was whimpering and crying quietly. Her left eye was missing. The socket looked like the pushed-in toe of a thick brown sock. A gash on the left side of her scalp was infected and swollen.

Newlin completed his examination, spoke with Garrett, and returned to the diagnostic area. Garrett took the crying girl in his arms. She looked at Garrett and cried louder.

"Get the mama-san to sit on a folding chair," Garrett ordered Jablonski. "And get that damn hat off her head."

When the woman was settled, Garrett set the crying child in the mother's lap. He motioned for the woman to hold the girl's arms down. Garrett looked up at Jablonski.

"Don't just stand there. Hold the kid's head still!" Standing behind the woman, Jablonski reached over her shoulders and held the girl's head.

She started screaming.

Garrett began cleaning the girl's head wound. With each gasp of air, the girl let out another steam-whistle scream. Scream after scream after scream.

"You can't inject pain-killer?" I called to Garrett.

"Too risky with a head wound," Garrett called back, "particularly a kid this young."

I couldn't stand the screaming.

"Would it be okay," I called to Garrett, my voice breaking, "if I wander around a bit? Take some pictures of the village?" I held up the camera hanging from my neck.

"Put your valuables in your shirt pockets," he replied without looking up. "Don't be out of sight too long."

I stuffed my wallet and watch in my left shirt pocket and my pen and pad of paper in my right shirt pocket and buttoned the flaps. I checked my M16's safety and ammo magazine, slung the rifle over my shoulder, and walked away from the marketplace.

Within minutes a dozen children were walking with me. Three or four on each side held my hands and arms. Children behind me pulled on my uniform. Several walked backwards in front of me, keeping their eyes fixed on me, smiling and giggling. I felt little hands in my pockets, front and back.

Thieves in miniature. These happy, excited, tawny little bodies, some of them trying to rob me, took me on a tour of their village.

They tried to take me inside a hut, but an old mama-san appeared at the entrance and shooed us away. The children guided me past several more huts to a wooden cage the size of two orange crates side-by-side. It contained a scrawny little pig. I had seen no dogs, monkeys, or chickens in the village. Translator Phong later told me the animals had been eaten.

"Dong Nho very poor," he said. "VC scare men away long time."

We looked at the pathetic animal a few minutes, and then the children pulled me toward the rice paddies at the edge of the village.

We stopped thirty feet from a huge water buffalo tied to a post. It was resting on its stomach in grass two feet high. The children talked quietly and pointed at the animal with awe and admiration. I assumed the water buffalo was used for plowing rice paddies. The children were showing me an essential and respected member of their community. Its horns were fifteen inches long, its eyes dark and intense.

I walked closer. I wanted to get a frame-filling photo, but when I looked through the viewfinder, the buffalo looked too far away. I took a few steps closer while looking through the viewfinder. No luck.

So I walked to within ten feet of the beast. I got down on one knee, and composed my shot so I could get tall grass in the foreground and the buffalo in the background. Then the water buffalo snorted and rose to its feet.

I grinned and turned to my left and right to see the reaction of the children. They weren't there. I looked behind me. They were standing back where we first stopped. They weren't smiling. They were looking at me with a mixture of fear and admiration.

I stood up and turned back to the water buffalo. It was massive. Taller at the head than I was. I snapped a quick shot, unsure I even had the camera focused. The buffalo took several steps toward me and lowered and raised its head and pawed the ground.

Then I saw the thin cord that tethered the buffalo to its post.

I turned and dashed back to the children. They squealed and danced with laughter. The buffalo, no longer threatened, settled back down into its grassy bed.

Late that afternoon I returned with the MEDCAP team to Lai Khe Base Camp. The next day I wrote the MEDCAP article for our battalion newspaper and submitted a copy of it to *Stars and Stripes*. Several weeks later the editors sent me a note that said my article was rejected because they had already published numerous articles of a similar kind.

My MEDCAP article read like the rankest form of propaganda: it was a laundry list of minor medical procedures the Army performed for Dong Nho village while we bombed, burned, and relocated other villages. Major Roberts loved it. When I mimeographed and distributed the January edition of *The Road Paver*, which contained the article, Sergeant Garrett asked for eight extra copies.

———

I extended my twelve-month tour in Vietnam by two months to take advantage of a deal offered by the Army. If a draftee volunteered to extend his tour by two months, the Army canceled his remaining six months of active duty. Otherwise a draftee returned home after twelve months in Vietnam and served an additional eight months to fulfill his two year obligation (which included, of course, the initial two months of basic training and two months of AIT). Those eight months would be served under stateside spit-and-polish discipline. Boots and shoes shined to a mirror finish. Uniforms spotlessly ironed and starched into flat boards and crisp edges. Insignias positioned just so. Saluting like a robot. Mindlessly showing deference to half-brained NCOs and officers no matter how moronic their directives might be. The thought of living that way infuriated me.

If I returned to the States and an officer upbraided me for dusty boots or unpolished brass, I'd tell him to go to hell, or worse. I'd heard many draftees in Vietnam—all rear echelon—voice the same concern. After a year incountry, the last thing we wanted was to go back to strict military rules and regulations we'd learned to live without.

As a battalion S-1 office worker, my additional two months in Vietnam would be spent on a secure base camp where threats to my safety were minimal: random mortar rounds and occasional sappers, snipers, or ground assaults were the dangers I faced. It was worth the risk to get out early.

At the beginning of February 1970, the second month of my extended duty, my good friend Jerry Maener and I were promoted to Specialist 5th Class. Our promotions were not something we worked for or even wanted.

Our battalion automatically scheduled our promotions to SPC-5 when we extended our tour of duty beyond the standard twelve-month assignment. In clerical ranking, SPC-5 is the beginning of professional military status, equivalent to sergeant, but without much authority to boss anyone around.

The good part was that our promotions eliminated our eligibility for de-drumming detail, CQ runner, KP, guard duty, and provided us with increased pay. Otherwise, being a newly anointed SPC-5 meant nothing to us. Actually, it embarrassed us. The promotion ceremony and shoulder patches made us look like lifers. And that was the last thing either of us wanted.

Sergeant Garrett was promoted to Staff Sergeant at the same time, and he and several other lifers threw a party for the three of us who were promoted in Headquarters Company. I was on my cot in my hooch reading a book around nine o'clock in the evening when I heard Garrett calling to me through the hooch screens from the raucous party between the hooches. The party had been going on for several hours.

"Hey, Newspaper Man, you comin' to the party?"

I yelled back, "Thanks, but I've got reading I want to do."

Twenty minutes later the hooch door flew open. Garrett staggered in with a beer can in his hand. He weaved around the empty hooch. I hoped, if I kept quiet, he'd leave without seeing me. Everybody was at the party between the hooches or drinking at the EM and NCO clubs—everybody except me and my friend Jerry Maener who bunked in another hooch. We decided we'd "celebrate" our promotions by reading rather than by getting drunk or stoned.

Then Garrett saw me on my cot. He bent down and peered at me from halfway across the hootch. His eyes were bloodshot. He spoke like a parent pleading with a spoiled child.

"You need to come … party. Everybody there." He lurched past my footlocker and stopped next to my cot. He leaned against the metal siderail of the cot and looked down at me. "You wanna celebrate, don't you?"

"Not this time, Sergeant. Drink one for me. I'd rather stay in my hooch and read."

Before I could make a move to defend myself, Garrett jammed his right knee against my chest, grabbed my right wrist with his left hand and pressed it to the mattress. I was pinned like a bug to my own cot.

Garrett's remarkable face, hanging over me, contorted into a show of rage unlike anything I'd ever seen. Big bloodshot eyes bulging with fury. Curled back purple lips. Face flushed with red blotches. Trembling with anger, he crushed his beer can—a full one—with his right hand. Beer cascaded over me and my cot.

"You don't come out … join us … so help me …." He pulled back his fist, the one with the crushed beer can. But that backward motion carried his torso with it and he almost lost his balance. He swayed and quickly righted himself.

I realized I could knock Garrett off me, but it would lead to a fight that would go on until one of us was unconscious. Likely me. But I had more reason than that for not wanting to fight Garrett.

I didn't want to hit him. The thought of hitting him in the face was inconceivably foreign and wrong to me. I wanted only to avoid associating with him and most of the men around him. I wanted, just once in my short military career, to announce my independence from all this shit I'd had crammed down my throat. I loathed and despised every bit of it.

"George," I wheezed with his knee on my chest, "why make such a big deal out of this?"

"Goddamn you." Garrett swung his head from side to side and almost fell again. "Don't you understan' anything?"

"George, what difference does it make whether I go to the party? You celebrate your way and I'll celebrate mine."

"You college fuckers turn everything …." He swayed and pulled back his fist again.

"Okay, okay, I'm coming."

I followed Garrett outside. At least ten men, each with a beer can in hand, were out there laughing and telling jokes in the faint light coming through the screens of my hooch and the hooch thirty feet further down the dirt road. Some of the men were sitting on the waist-high walls of sandbags around the hooch and other men leaned on the sandbags or sat on the ground. None of the men were buddies of Jerry's or mine. Then I spotted Jerry without a beer in his hands. Apparently he'd been coerced out there, like me, and refused an offered beer.

"What the hell does it matter if I want to get drunk or read a book?" Jerry yelled at the men around him. "Why can't you respect a difference of opinion?" Jerry looked fragile, even scholarly, in his gold rimmed spectacles.

One of the men crouched behind Jerry. Another man pushed Jerry backward, toppling him to the ground.

I yelled and moved in Jerry's direction, but several men stepped in front of me and roughly pushed me back. More men gathered around me, including Garrett.

"You stay here, College Boy … this happy circle," Garrett said, and he palm-punched my shoulder and staggered backward.

The cluster of men around Jerry wouldn't let Jerry get to his feet, so he relaxed and sat on the ground. Then several men poured beer on us.

"That's all?" Jerry asked from his cross-legged position on the ground. "Don't we get more beer than that?"

Everyone laughed while several men poured more beer on us. Our hair and clothes were drenched.

"I hope we're happy, now," Jerry said.

"That was fun," I said. "Thanks for the good time."

"Fuck you, Office Boy," Sergeant Garrett shouted. "Fuck you. Fuck you. Fuck you." He staggered into me and pushed me away. "Go back in the hooch, fucking asshole. Don't want you … anyway. We're havin' a party. We're havin' a *party!*" Garrett bumped into another man and fell to the ground laughing.

They let Jerry get up, and the men who circled me drifted away.

"And a good time was had by all," Jerry said to me, shaking his beer soaked head as we left the drunken men behind. He paused and smiled at me. "Know what I think?"

"What?"

"I think I can't wait to get the fuck out of here."

Jerry returned to his hooch and I returned to mine. Water at the wash house was exhausted by this time of night, so I couldn't take a shower. I threw my fatigues under my cot, toweled off, and put on clean underwear. My hair and skin were sticky. I changed the sheets on my cot, but the mattress was still wet with beer.

I lay on the damp cot and tried to read, but I couldn't concentrate. My emotions were churning and so was my stomach. I was angry. Humiliated. And not just by the behavior of the other men. I didn't feel right about myself either, but I couldn't identify why.

The party disbanded around two o'clock and I finally fell asleep.

In the morning I was covered with malt-slimy night sweat. I smelled like a beer hog after a weeklong binge.

Friday, Feb. 27, 1970 - Lai Khe Base Camp
  Dear Janice:
  A little kid, in a field near one of our 182nd road repair crews, stepped on an anti-personnel mine. A foot popper. It blew his foot off.
  Foley, part of the road crew, carefully walked across the field to the kid. Foley was sure he'd trigger a mine, too, but he said he couldn't leave the kid alone in the field.
  Foley got to the kid, tied his green T-shirt around the boy's leg up by the knee —stones, dirt, even weeds were blown into the kid's calf, bulking it up—and carried the stunned boy back to the road. The crew's RTO had already called for a dust-off.
  The kid lived. Minus one foot.
  The officer in charge of the road repair crew came into S-1 in the late afternoon to tell Colonel Forester about it, but Forester wasn't in his office and hadn't left word where he'd be. The officer gave me a summary of the story and said he wanted to submit an award recommendation for Foley. I offered to help write it, but the officer said he'd do it himself. I was glad. I didn't want to help.
  Another day in a war zone.
                                              Love, Andrew

Sunday, Mar 15, 1970 - Lai Khe Base Camp
  Dear Janice:
  My replacement arrived today. That gives him a few days to learn the ropes before I DEROS on March 20. That's more break-in time than I had.
  Cecil Miguel. Nice fellow from Arizona. Attended college until he ran out of money. That's when the draft caught him. He'll do fine with awards work. Smart. Types well. I took him over to meet the guys in personnel.
  I'll hang round the office a couple hours in the mornings while he finds out what he doesn't know. Then I'll go read for awhile. Come back in the afternoon. See if he has more questions for me. Then back to the books. Or a good smoke. Probably a good smoke.
  I won't write again. I'd be home before the letter reaches you.
  I look forward to seeing you and being with you.
                                              Love, Andrew

GETTING OUT AND GOING HOME

Two hundred of us sat shoulder to shoulder in a DC 707, our seatbelts buckled, waiting for takeoff. We felt naked without our weapons and helpless without an avenue of escape. We worried the plane would be hit by a mortar round or RPG while still on the tarmac. A lone voice from the rear of the plane expressed our one and only thought: "For Christ's sake, let's get this thing off the ground."

The air conditioning was off. The fans were off. Our newly issued jungle fatigues—stiff with sizing—were black and soggy under every arm and down every back. The whole plane smelled of ripe funk and wet canvas.

"Sorry for the inconvenience," the pilot announced through little speakers above our heads. "We won't be turning on the air conditioning until we're at a predetermined altitude which we hope to reach quickly. Good to have you on board. We'll be on our way shortly."

When our Silver Bird of Paradise finally lifted off the tarmac at Bien Hoa Air Force Base, a few men whooped, but most of us held our breath. The pilot banked the plane hard to the right, then pushed full-throttle at a sharp angle into the sky. My chest vibrated with the roar of the jet engines. The sides of the cabin trembled. After a half a minute that seemed like an hour the pilot reduced our angle of ascent, backed off the throttle, and turned on the fans and air conditioning.

For the remainder of the trip, we sat dumbstruck. Head-whacked. One minute we were soldiers in tropical heat and humidity worrying about incoming rockets and mortars or an ambush out of nowhere, and the next minute we were sky high in air-conditioned comfort on a commercial aircraft smelling the perfume of round-eyed stewardesses in short skirts handing us cups of fresh coffee and cellophane-wrapped sandwiches.

Men all around me shook their heads and said things like, "I don't believe it" and "This is unreal." Our sense of unreality was far more complex than a year-long dream come true or the surprise that our tour in Vietnam was finally done and we survived.

When we stepped through the doorway of that plane, we stepped back in time to a way of living and thinking now foreign to us. Memories of our civilian lives could not compete with Vietnam memories of such intensity and surreal flash they robbed all other memories of reality.

Living in a war zone had forced us to expect dismemberment or death, if not today, then maybe tomorrow. So we were always tense—our muscles tight, often without our conscious awareness—and we were attuned to sounds and alert to signals of any threat to our survival. That slowed the passage of time to a crawl, for when danger was eminent, we lived every minute as though it were an hour. And when danger was not eminent, we experienced things with greater appreciation—veins in a blade of grass, a cooling breeze across the face and arms, bright stars in a sky of infinite darkness; even the gray plastic weaving of sandbags was marvelous to behold—each thing revealed to us, in what might be our shortened lives, its singular beauty and the wonder of existence. Living life with such intensity turned days into weeks, weeks into months, and months into years.

But it wasn't only our memories of civilian times that seemed unreal by comparison to our Vietnam experiences. How we saw ourselves and who we were—our very identities—had changed from what they had been a year or so ago.

We were state-sanctioned killers, willing or actual; some of us were vicious abusers and torturers; still others were annihilators of entire villages with one radio call to napalm bombers or Puff the Magic Dagon flying high in the sky. Basic Training began the changes, but Vietnam completed them.

Stepping into that plane, we faced the expectations of those who waited for us to return home as the men we were before, but maybe with a few bad experiences we'd set aside as we began living again our previous lives. But we could not live up to those expectations. We were not the naïve, idealistic youth we once were. The thought of getting jobs and joining our loved ones in maintaining a well-painted, plasterboard and plastic world seemed like a comedy fit for a stage.

Then a gestalt shift would occur and we'd see our current selves as prior selves would see us—coarse, angry, dark with guilt, contemptuous of our country's leaders—and then nothing at all seemed real, including ourselves.

Who am I? Who will I be when I get back home? How will loved ones see me and how will I see them? In what, in a fucked-up war, can I take pride? How can I hold my head up after being such a fool as to believe my country's leaders spoke the truth?

Prior to boarding the Silver Bird of Paradise, I spent a full day at 90th Replacement Facility at Long Binh Base Camp. Homeward-bound GIs drove and flew to the 90th from all over South Vietnam. Many of us had not slept the night before. Some got drunk, others stoned. Since few of us knew men outside our immediate units, and since few men in a platoon or a company departed Vietnam on the same day, we were strangers to each other at the 90th.

Hundreds of us milled around the compound. There was no sequence to follow for many of the things we had to do, and other things required a precise but unfamiliar step-by-step procedure. Sergeants yelled instructions, but we weren't familiar with the names of the documents or the names of the buildings they shouted at us. Men waited in lines in front of every building and Quonset hut, but few signs indicated or explained what was going on inside, and those signs were sun-bleached beyond reading. So we'd choose a line, ask the men in front of us what the line was for—"Fuck if I know, but it's good as any"—and wait our turns to fill out forms and hear briefings.

After hours of confusion and form-filling, I was told I needed new boots and new fatigues, and I would not be allowed on the plane without them. Why I needed a new uniform was beyond me, but I wanted on that plane. So I waited in a long line at a warehouse for new clothes. In the warehouse I was told I wouldn't be allowed on the plane unless I got a haircut. Apparently the Army wanted its returning soldiers to look shiny and new, ready for patriotic reunion photos with mothers, wives, kids, and the family dog.

Wearing my new boots and fatigues, I joined the long line of men waiting for a haircut. I waited thirty minutes and only ten or twelve men were ahead of me when the two barbers went to lunch. An hour-and-a-half later I got my haircut. Then I stood in line to exchange my Military Payment Certificates for American dollars. After that I waited in line with my duffel bag for a contraband shakedown. Finally, late in the evening, twelve hours after my arrival at the 90th Replacement Facility, a sergeant bellowed a flight manifest for the next plane, and he called my name.

I hadn't eaten all day, but I didn't care. I was going home.

Our flight to the States was boring and emotionally exhausting. Every time I thought about seeing Janice and holding her in my arms, my stomach clenched, my muscles stiffened, and I'd get an erection. But imagination carried me no further. Other than going to bed with Janice, nothing else materialized in my mind. I could not imagine what I'd do the day following my return home. Or the day after that, or the week or month after that. Nothing other than seeing Janice seemed a real possibility.

Even arriving in the States would be a bummer because I'd need to go through out-processing—"might take a whole day," a sergeant told me—and then I'd board another plane for a five- or six-hour flight from California to Detroit where Janice would be waiting for me.

But when our plane landed at Travis Air Force Base in California nineteen non-stop hours after taking off from Bien Hoa Base Camp, everybody cheered and I did, too. In a wonder-world delirium of dissociation and fatigue, we filed off the plane and boarded busses headed for Oakland Army Discharge Center. Nothing seemed real. Blink and we'd be back in Vietnam.

At the Discharge Center a staff sergeant—a brush-cut pretty boy with bleached hair—told us where to pile our duffel bags. Then Pretty Boy directed us to the center of a gymnasium and instructed us to count off into groups, twenty men to a group. He assigned a number to each group. While he was talking, my mind went blank from exhaustion. When I refocused, he was telling us to find a place on the bleachers extending from three walls of the gymnasium. The fourth wall, the one without bleachers, had a double door that led to another large room. Three hundred men, maybe more, were already sitting on the three banks of bleachers.

As we walked to the bleachers I asked a GI walking next to me what Pretty Boy said near the end of the briefing. I explained I'd blanked out. The GI told me someone would call out our group number. When we heard our group number called, we should go through the double doors into the adjoining out-processing room. "The sergeant said if we don't hear our number and our group goes in without us, we won't be processed until they finish with the guys on the next incoming plane."

We all assumed our numbers would be called within several hours, so nobody made an effort to organize us into sitting together so we'd be sure somebody in our twenty-man group would hear our number when it was called. You might think that was foolish of us, and it was. But most of us were draftees, and we'd grown to hate any expression of Army authority that told us, hour after hour and day after day, what to do. So any draftee who attempted to take charge, or suggest a system of organization and cooperation, would have been asked, "So who the fuck are you?"

Disdaining "herd" mentality, we scattered over the bleachers looking for seats that didn't encroach upon the space of men already there. I climbed the center bleacher and found a seat opposite the double doorway leading to the out-processing room. I figured whoever called out the group numbers would be coming through those doors. I asked several men sitting near me how long they'd been there.

"I come in yesterday," said a thin GI with red hair, bad acne, a southern drawl, and three day's worth of spotty pink whiskers.

A chubby black guy sitting next to me—wide nose, thick lips, purple shaving bumps on his double-chin—said, "I been kickin' it so long I don't remember when I started kickin' it."

Thumping sounds under the bleachers caught my attention. I looked down between the benches and saw a GI in only his undershirt and boxer shorts. He was banging his head on the wood frame of the bleacher where it was bolted to the wall. Looked and sounded like it would hurt like hell. The men around me ignored him.

"My God, look at that guy," I said. "Shouldn't we go down there and stop him before he injures himself?"

"Don't do it, man," said the red-haired GI. "That guy's crazy. Some of us went down earlier and he went nuts. Must of seen some heavy shit."

"Or done uppers on the plane," said the black guy next to me.

"Either way, can't help a man doesn't want help," said the redheaded GI.

Two MPs standing near the double doors started walking across the gym toward the man banging his head. The man stopped as the MPs approached him under the bleachers.

"Hey, I told you before, keep the hell away from me," he shouted. The MPs moved closer. The man screamed, "Hey, I'll kill you, I swear I'll kill you."

"Leave him alone," a GI yelled from the far-left bleachers. "Why don't you guys go cruise a bar for drunks?"

One MP called out, "You mind your own business, smartass. We don't need any help from you."

"You cocksucker," the man on the bleacher yelled back with a chuckle. He was giddy, over the edge.

Everybody sat up to see what would happen. One of the MPs turned and was walking toward the guy who'd yelled. But the guy was on a roll and wasn't half done.

"If that soldier wants to knock his head against a post or wall or whatever the fuck it is, he won't be doin' no different than what he's been doin' all year long. So you get the hell out of here before every grunt in this room helps me stomp you ass-wipes in the ground. An' you wanna call more MPs in here? Well, you go right ahead, you shit-for-brains. Bare-knuckled we'll take on the whole fuckin' goddamn mess of you, so help me God, you buncha piss-ants."

The whole gymnasium erupted with the joy of releasing long-suppressed frustration. Every one of us was on his feet yelling and stomping. The ceramic-surfaced brick walls of the gymnasium bounced back thunder. The bleachers trembled and shook. We stomped and hooted, whistled and cheered. Once started we couldn't stop. The two MPs looked at each other, their faces turned white, and they walked double-time back through the double doors.

The MPs' exit gave us another reason to stomp and cheer. Several men near me had tears in their eyes. Men were slapping each other skin and giving each other high fives. We continued the ranting and stomping another three minutes.

It was one of the best times I'd had since I was drafted. If those MPs had made a dismissive wave of their hands or flipped us the bird, we would have run down those bleachers and torn them limb from limb.

But after sitting down, still laughing and joshing and making jokes about MPs, we settled into more waiting and mindless boredom.

But then one of the men yelled, "Hey, anybody who's a medic, go down there and check out that head-banger. Looks like he's unconscious. Got blood on his head."

Four men jumped up, presumably medics. Now everybody was engaged and ready to help each other. The four men, from different parts of the gymnasium, started down the bleachers and were about to run to where the head-banger lay bloody and unconscious. But they stopped when two MPs came jogging in with a stretcher and headed for the guy under the bleachers. But they weren't the only MPs who came back in the gymnasium.

Six more MPs, including the two guys who left the gym a few minutes earlier, came double-timing in and stood at modified parade-rest, three MPs on each side of the double door. Each man held a M16 at waist level, the muzzle pointed down, one hand on the pistol grip and the other hand on the barrel's hand guard. Then an officer walked through the door and stood with his feet spread apart and his fists on his hips. Six more MPs entered through the double door on my left, the one we'd used to enter the gym. They also stood at modified parade rest, each man holding a M16 at waist level.

This was definitely an "oh shit" moment.

"Okay men, I want your attention and you better listen up real good," yelled the officer. He kept his fists balled and on his hips. He was red-in-the-face angry.

"I'm Captain Lawrence James. What just happened in here will not happen again without the most severe consequences. I understand you men are tired, frustrated, and you've come back from Vietnam with a lot on your minds. But you threaten one of my MPs again or you stage some kind of brainless insurrection, and this is what will happen. The men at these doors will close and lock them from the outside. Then we'll toss in two CS gas grenades. When we're sure you're totally immobilized, we'll open the doors and carry you out on stretchers and court-martial you on charges of insubordination, insurrection, and threatening a superior. You'll spend most of the rest of your life at hard labor at Fort Leavenworth. What you just did carries heavy legal implications, and I have full power and authority to take the measures I've just described. Good day, gentlemen,"

Nobody made a peep while Captain James was talking. Then he swiveled an about-face and left the gym. The twelve MPs, however, remained stationed by the doors at parade-rest.

We all sat looking at each other. Stunned. Suddenly everybody was talking, but quietly. Nobody stood up. Nobody declared contempt of James's threat. And nobody had any doubt that James meant what he said. His description of our behavior as being an "insurrection" was sobering. It put our angry "uprising" in a legal context nobody around me had thought about. And the threatened punishment was serious.

We calmed down and began waiting, again, for our group's number. After a while, as I was dozing, the twelve armed MPs left the gymnasium

Every forty-five minutes or so—but it was hard to tell because I kept nodding off and couldn't remember to check my watch or even remember what time it was after I did check it—Sergeant Pretty Boy walked through the double doors and shouted the number of the next group for processing. He shouted the number twice. But the size of the gymnasium, the undercurrent of noise from the men, the southern drawl of Pretty Boy, and the few seconds it took to wake up, combined to make the shouted number unintelligible. Several men yelled, "Why not write the number on a chalkboard?" Pretty

Boy ignored them.

My thoughts drifted into dreams.

I woke up when I fell onto the head and shoulders of the man in front of me. I asked the chubby black guy next to me if we could take turns sleeping while the other man listened for our numbers. He agreed. We exchanged group numbers. He said I could sleep first and he'd stay awake. I stretched out on an empty bench and fell asleep.

When I woke up, my buddy was slumped over snoring. I kicked his boots and moved to another area of the bleacher. I asked several guys in the new area if T-6 had been called. They said they didn't know because they listened only for their own numbers.

"Anybody from T-6?" I called out, but not loud enough to startle dozing GIs. "Any T-6s here?" No response.

I went down to the double door. I asked the new staff sergeant, who replaced Pretty Boy and smelled of Aqua Velva Aftershave, if T-6 had been called.

He glared at me. "We announce the numbers two times, loud and clear."

"Just tell me if T-6 was called and I won't bother you again. Please."

He sighed. "Okay. You caught me in a good mood at the beginning of my shift." He looked at the list on his clipboard. "T-6 has not been called and it'll be awhile before it is." He looked at his watch. "We'll break for dinner soon. You'll eat in the mess hall. But while you're eating, another planeload will come in and they'll have an even longer wait. That satisfy you?"

"Thanks."

The bleacher seats were getting unbearably hard. My clothes stunk. My eyes stung from oily sweat off my face. My stomach felt like a crimped tin can of sour milk. My legs ached. My back ached. And every ten or fifteen minutes I found myself dreaming with my eyes open.

It wasn't until seven o'clock the next morning that yet another staff sergeant called my group's number. I made my way down the bleachers on stiff legs, heading toward the double doors. I leaned on the shoulders of seated men to keep from stumbling. I saw other men working their way down the bleachers, too, but I was too adrift in my mental haze to remember them.

In the out-processing room, the new staff sergeant waited for the last man to join us. Then, in a loud voice he said, "Listen up. Any of you who want to claim a major medical or mental problem that developed while you were in Vietnam, step forward and form a line over at the blue desk. You'll be processed slower than the other men so we can determine the legitimacy and extent of your claim."

Slower? Nobody moved.

"Nothin' wrong wit' me but two missing arms and a bad case of syph," said the guy next to me, shaking his head.

The staff sergeant broke the twenty of us into four-man units, gave us paper forms, and told us to line up behind a variety of booths and tables and have our forms initialed after we completed the exam at each station. My group started at the heart station.

"Anybody with a bad ticker from humping the rice paddies? No? Okay, take off your shirts and stand facing me on this white line." The medic walked past us while he touched each man's chest with a stethoscope. He could not have heard more than one heart beat per man.

All of us passed the heart exam.

About an hour later, our physicals completed, a staff of men and several women measured and fit us with new dress greens, sewed on our insignias, and machined our plastic name tags. The GI next to me asked the workers who were fitting us, "So why'd we need new fatigues for the flight home?" Nobody answered.

The last form we filled out was typed for us by a clerk. It was *Form DD 214: Report of Transfer or Discharge.* For draftees who extended their tour in Vietnam, this was our ticket out of active military service. The clerk asked me, "What's your service number?" I was so exhausted and flustered by the question I couldn't remember the number without looking at my dog tags. The clerk said, "How'd you get through Vietnam without getting killed?"

I was instantly furious. I wanted to bash the man's head in with his typewriter. I forced myself to calm down.

"Here's your DD 214 buddy," the clerk said. "Sign at the bottom and you're out."

A large group of us was briefed on veteran's benefits. Then we stood in line for our severance pay and another line for our flight tickets home.

And that was that. One hundred of us picked up our duffel bags, and with our DD 214s in our pockets and our flight tickets in our hands, we walked outside into California sunshine.

Yellow taxi cabs and brown military buses were waiting for us along the curb up and down the road. Most of them displayed the same destination sign: *San Francisco Airport.* The buses were free. The cabs we paid for ourselves.

I stood a few moments savoring my freedom. I was anxious to get home and hold Janice in my arms, but other thoughts crowded in and held my attention.

Men carrying their duffel bags walked past me and boarded the buses. After they dropped their duffel bags on the seats, they shouted and gave each other high fives. They rocked the buses like football players who'd just won a game, but they weren't celebrating victory. Far from it. I could hear them whooping and hollering, "I'm done with this shit" and "Fuck Vietnam" and "Don't make no never-mind."

I stood there a good five minutes watching my fellow GIs vent, like steam escaping from a high-pressure cooker. Then I shook myself and walked to the curb and dumped my duffel bag in the open trunk of a yellow taxi and climbed in the cab.

Two other servicemen walked up to the taxi and looked in at me. I nodded yes. A taxi driver pushed off from the grill and fender of the cab behind us where he'd been talking with another driver. He grabbed the two duffel bags, one in each hand, flung them with a "thump-thump" into the trunk, and motioned for the two men to join me in the cab. One man rode shotgun up front and the other man climbed in back with me. Within minutes we drove two or three city blocks and accelerated down an entrance ramp onto an expressway.

It occurred to me that I could stop the cab and get out. I could go to a bar and stay all day if I wanted. I could go anywhere and do anything.

I looked out the windows and studied the passing scene. All thoughts of arriving home and holding Janice left me. I was mesmerized by what I saw.

Signs. Thousands of signs. On roadsides and overpasses, buildings and trucks. Signs on buses. Then I noticed signs on our cab seats and floor mats. Signs everywhere.

The Biggest, Brightest Color TV You Can Buy.
Silva Thin, The One That's In.
Coke. It's The Real Thing.
Feel More Important On TWA.
It Looks Expensive and It Is.

Billboards displayed pictures of girls in swimming suits and tight sweaters, their breasts like balloons, their eyes boldly looking at me looking at them. Other billboards were razzle-dazzle come-ons for booze, restaurants, soda and shaving cream, new subdivisions and fancy furniture.

Then I focused on the eight-lane concrete highways. Fields of concrete and asphalt bordered by huge glossy-mirrored buildings. Multi-level overpasses. Little patches of mown grass like green velvet.

And cars. Thousands of cars. Racing. Swerving. Changing lanes.

Semis speeding past like walls on wheels.

Everybody moving fast. On the job. Making money. Here in the USA.

I was home. In the States. My country.

Then it hit me. This is the face of my culture. Maybe the soul of my nation. This is why I was sent to war. This is why my fellow soldiers died. To protect all this.

GLOSSARY

AIT: Advanced Individual Training is given to recruits after Basic Training: it's two months of training in a special type of service, e.g., mechanic, clerk, artillery, infantry.

AK47: a Russian designed, semi- and fully automatic 7.62mm assault rifle; heavier rounds are fired at lower velocity and fewer per minute on automatic than the M16 rifle, but it's more rugged and dependable; used by the North Vietnamese Army and the Viet Cong.

APC: a tank-sized Armored Personnel Carrier mounted with M60 machine guns or quad-fifties, i.e., four .50-caliber machine guns, two over and two under.

Army Enlisted Ranks (lowest to highest):

Private (PVT)	Staff Sergeant (SSGT)
Private 2 (PV2)	Sergeant First Class (SFC)
Private First Class (PFC)	Master Sergeant (MSG)
Corporal (CPL)	First Sergeant (1SG)
Specialist-4 (SPC-4)	Sergeant Major (SGM)
Specialist-5 (SPC-5)	Command Sergeant Major (CSM)
Sergeant (SGT)	Sergeant Major of the Army (SMA)

Army Officer Ranks (lowest to highest):

Warrant Officer (WO1)	Lieutenant Colonel (LTC)
Chief Warrant Officer (CW2-5)	Colonel (COL)
Second Lieutenant (2LT)	Brigadier General (BG)
First Lieutenant (1LT)	Major General (MG)
Captain (CPT)	Lieutenant General (LTG)
Major (MAJ)	General (GEN)

Army Unit Organization (smallest to largest):

Squad: (4 to 10 soldiers) led by a sergeant or staff sergeant.

Platoon: 3 to 4 squads (16 to 45 soldiers) led by a lieutenant.

Company: 3 to 4 platoons (100 to 200 soldiers) led by a captain.

Battalion: 3 to 5 companies (500 to 1000 soldiers) led by a lieutenant colonel.

Brigade: 3 or more battalions (3000 to 5000 soldiers) led by a colonel.

Division: 3 brigades (10,000 to 16,000 soldiers) led by a major general.

Corps: 2 to 5 divisions (20,000 to 80,000 soldiers) led by a lieutenant general.

Field Army: 2 to 5 corps; (40,000 to 400,000 soldiers) led by a general.

Article 15: gives commanders authority to administer a range of punishments without resort to court-martial. Punishments for the lowest level Article 15 can be up to 14 days extra duty, 14 days restriction to quarters or base, and oral reprimand.

ARVN: Army of the Republic of Vietnam; South Vietnam's army controlled by Saigon.

Automatic Grenade Launcher: most often seen on Cobra attack helicopters; four to five barrels spun by electric motor that fire 40-mm grenade rounds (same as for an M79 grenade launcher) at 400 rounds a minute; the most commonly used rounds for an AGL are high-explosive or fragmentation grenades that have a five-meter casualty radius.

Beaucoup: Vietnamese/French/GI slang term for "a lot" or "many" (pronounced by GIs as boakoo).

Big Red One: U.S. 1st Infantry Division headquartered at Lai Khe. Has approximately 14,000 troops attached to it.

Blooper: slang for the single-shot, 40-mm M79 grenade launcher; term derived from the sound the M79 makes when fired; looks like a pregnant shotgun the length of a man's arm; carried by a strap slung over a shoulder; fires fragmentation grenades with a five-meter casualty radius; also fires high explosive, heavy buckshot, smoke, and illumination rounds.

Boom-Boom: sexual intercourse.

Boom-Boom Girl: a prostitute.

Boonies: jungle or rice paddy fields; almost anywhere off a base camp.

Bouncing Betty: an anti-personnel mine that pops up from the ground chest high before exploding and sending shrapnel in all directions.

Bunker: a protective shelter, partly or entirely below ground; constructed of heavy timber and covered with sandbags and/or ammunition boxes filled with dirt.

Butter Bar Louie: a second lieutenant; called a "Butter Bar Louie" because the single gold bar indicates he's the lowest grade of officer and soft with inexperience.

Bush Hat or Floppy Jungle Hat: broad-brimmed, green cloth hat worn by many American troops instead of safer, but far heavier, sound-distorting steel helmets.

C-4: plastic explosive that can be shaped and molded like putty to direct the force of the explosion; comes in one-pound cellophane-wrapped sticks; field troops burn small pieces of C-4 to heat food rations.

CAV: cavalry that use armored road vehicles and/or helicopters rather than horses.

Charlie: the enemy; the term is derived from the radio operator's designation for the Viet Cong: "Victor Charlie."

Chickenman: a radio series broadcast on American Forces Radio Vietnam that spoofs comic book heroes and the *Batman* television series; Chickenman is a shoe salesman who fights crime on weekends; his yellow crime-fighting car is called Chicken Coupe.

Chief Warrant Officer: see Warrant Officer.

Chinook: large, twin-rotor CH-47 cargo transport helicopter.

Chopper: any helicopter.

Clacker: hard plastic, handheld electric-pulse generator to which wires are attached from blasting caps or other electrical devices for setting off explosives, frequently claymores.

Claymore: a concave, plastic-covered paperback-size anti-personnel surface mine that's set on its edge on metal fold-out feet; when detonated by a trip wire or a handheld electrical detonator, a one-pound layer of C-4 plastic explosive blows seven hundred steel balls forward in a 60-degree, fan-shaped fifty-yard kill zone; the concave backside of the claymore cancels out much of the backward blast.

Cobra: a sleek attack helicopter (36 inches at its narrowest) armed with two or four rocket pods, an automatic 40-mm grenade launcher (400 rounds per minute), and a 7.62-caliber mini-gun (6000 rounds per minute); the Cobra's lower front is often painted to look like white jagged teeth in a red mouth.

Concertina Wire: (also called razor wire) considered an improvement on farm-styled barbed wire designed to restrict animal passage; comes in large coils that can be expanded like a concertina musical instrument; secured to the ground or the top edge of a wall to form a barricade to human passage; protruding from the wire every inch or two are razor-sharp cutting edges that, at each end, project needle-sharp points that catch and hold a man's flesh while the razor edges repeatedly slice a quarter inch deep as long as the man struggles to free himself; will cause sufficient blood loss for death to ensue if entanglement is severe.

Commo-Wire: electrical communications wire.

CO: commanding officer.

Court-Martial: a military court set up for trial of military personnel charged with offenses committed during their military service; trial and punishments are in accord with the Uniform Code of Military Justice; rather than a jury, the court is made up of military officers appointed by a commander; three levels of court martial (summary, special, and general) deal with increasingly serious charges and punishments.

CQ Runner: Charge of Quarters Runners are men in ranks below sergeant and Specialist-5 grades who are assigned from rotating duty rosters to stay awake at night in unit headquarters offices to take phone calls and radio reports and alert everybody to any adverse conditions or enemy activity that might endanger the unit or base camp.

Crew Chief: a helicopter crewmember who maintains daily operational chopper status and fixes minor mechanical problems; usually the left door gunner on Hueys.

CS Gas: riot control gas stronger than tear gas.

Cu Chi Base Camp: located approximately twenty-five miles northeast of Saigon; home of the 25th Infantry Division (Tropic Lightning); area surrounding camp is heavily infiltrated by Viet Cong and a known site of underground tunnels used by the Viet Cong; located southwest of the Iron Triangle (see Iron Triangle).

DEROS: Date of Expected Return from Overseas (the day a soldier goes home).

Det-cord: explosive cord (looks like plastic clothesline) that explodes at five miles a second; for stringing together and simultaneously detonating multiple explosive charges.

Deuce-and-a-Half: a standard two-and-a-half-ton dump truck.

Didi-Mau: Vietnamese for "move away quickly!"

Dinky-Dau: Vietnamese-GI slang for "crazy."

DOD: Department of Defense.

Don't Make No Never Mind: purest expression of cynicism and depression in Vietnam GI lingo; believed to be first used by grunts as a way of expressing pessimistic and despondent acceptance of the death of buddies who died for no good reason (i.e., the Vietnam War) and the need to continue doing the very thing that killed their buddies.

Doo-Rag: (also spelled "do-rag" or "dew-rag") a head covering comprised of a single layer of cloth that covers most of the forehead and down almost to the ears; particularly popular among blacks and Latinos.

Door Gunner: a machine gun operator on a helicopter (usually a Huey).

Downdraft: the forceful downward blowing of air by the spinning rotor(s) of a helicopter.

Dust-off: nickname for medical evacuation by helicopter because the helicopter creates a dust storm when it lands and takes off; also called "medevac."

Earthmover (290): a long cavernous metal container on wheels connected by a universal hitch to a diesel cab; below the metal container a wide, adjustable cutting blade hangs at a slant, facing forward (like a vegetable slicer), that cuts swaths of dirt into the metal container when the blade is lowered and pulled across the ground.

Eleven Bravo: nickname for a trained infantryman; based on the numerical designation of an infantryman's military occupational specialty (MOS), that being 11B10.

EM Club: Enlisted Men's Club; provides beer and entertainment for soldiers under the rank of sergeant; NCOs and officers have their own clubs, but NCOs in Vietnam often drink at EM clubs; see NCO.

Firebase (or Fire Support Base—FSB): usually a small encampment having six or more howitzers (105-mm and/or 155-mm) that provide artillery support for patrolling units and other encampments.

Flack Jacket: a thick, heavy, fiberglass-filled vest worn for protection from shrapnel; offers protection from small arms fire, too, but not as effectively.

Frag or Fragged: murder or injury of an officer or NCO by use of a fragmentation grenade.

Gook: derogatory term for a Vietnamese person.

Grunt: an infantry soldier serving in combat operations.

Gunner: a machine gun operator on a helicopter; see Door Gunner.

Gunship: a heavily armed helicopter; also a heavily armed C-130 Hercules Airplane with three or four mini-guns that fire out an open side of the plane's fuselage—nicknamed "Puff the Magic Dragon."

Hand Grenade: see M26 hand grenade.

Hooch: a Vietnamese house or hut; also GI living quarters.

HQ: headquarters; often used as an abbreviation for a headquarters building, as in "Bravo Company's HQ" or "Headquarters Company's HQ."

Huey: UH-1 helicopter, its side doors usually opened or removed; used for troop transport, medical evacuation, and fire support for ground troops; the workhorse of the Vietnam War.

IG Inspection: an inspection by representatives of the Office of Inspector General, once every six to twelve months, of every aspect of a major Army unit; military units prepare for months before its occurrence.

Incoming: enemy mortar rounds, rockets or small arms fire coming in on your position.

Incounty: short for "in Vietnam."

Iron Triangle: a triangle of heavily forested land about ten miles northeast of Cu Chi and twenty-five miles northwest of Saigon; between the Saigon River on the west and the Tinh River on the east; the site of a large underground complex of tunnels used by the VC; U.S. and ARVN military units that ventured into the Iron Triangle experienced extensive VC resistance.

Jesus Nut: helicopter rotor nut that holds the main rotor on the mast; if the nut comes off while the chopper is in the air, the rotor flies off, the chopper drops like a stone, and people on board meet Jesus.

Jungle Hat or Floppy Bush Hat: broad-brimmed, green cloth hat worn by American troops instead of heavy, sound-distorting steel helmets.

KA-BAR Knife: the standard KA-BAR knife has a wooden handle and a seven-inch steel blade with a two-inch indentation along the shank to reduce weight (popularly called a "blood groove" but technically called a "fuller"); designed for combat by KA-BAR Knives, Inc.; adopted by the Marines in 1942 as a standard-issue weapon and utility tool.

KIA: Killed in action.

Klick: short for kilometer; one klick is a little over half a mile or 3280 feet.

Lai Khe Base Camp: northeast of Cu Chi about forty miles from Saigon on Highway QL-13; a major base camp and headquarters for the 1st Infantry Division (Big Red One).

Land of the Giant PX: America, where you can buy anything.

Laterite: reddish soil found in the tropics (rich in iron, quartz, and hydrates of alumina); can be spread, watered, and compacted into a hard surface for use as road bed; older tunnels dug in laterite soil, like many tunnels under Cu Chi, have walls hardened like concrete from humidity.

LAW (M72): a Light Anti-tank Weapon weighing 5.5 pounds; fires a four-pound rocket from two extended telescoping tubes balanced on the GI's shoulder; the rocket's propellant is fully expended before the rocket leaves the tubes, the exhaust blowing out the open end of the rear tube; the blast from the shaped explosive in the rocket can penetrate a foot of armor; this is the American version of the RPG (rocket propelled grenade) used by VC and NVA soldiers.

LBJ: the Long Binh Jail; also the initials of Lyndon Baines Johnson, U.S. President from November 1963 to January 1969 when Richard Nixon became president.

Lifer: (1) a person committed to the military as a career; (2) a derogatory term used by draftees for career soldiers; (3) anybody who puts unrealistic emphasis on military rules and regulations above care and concern for the men themselves.

M14 Rifle: U.S. Army semi-automatic rifle; fired 7.62mm bullets; replaced by the M16.

M16 Rifle: U.S. Army rifle that replaced the M14 rifle; semi- and fully automatic; weighs about 7.6 pounds with a full magazine; fires high-velocity 5.56mm bullets at 650-700 rounds per minute; copper-covered M16 rounds are designed to tumble on impact, creating a large irregular wound, thereby violating the spirit and intent of the Geneva Convention's ban on break-apart or mushrooming bullets.

M26 Hand Grenade: a twenty-six ounce fragmentation grenade with a smooth outer surface shaped like a large lemon; a chemical, non-smoking fuse is activated by a spring-loaded hammer; the hammer is held back by a handle (or spoon) extending the length of the grenade and locked in place by a pin; when the pin is pulled out and the grenade is thrown, the handle flips off and the hammer hits the fuse; four or five seconds later the explosive is detonated; the explosion causes a long, serrated wire—coiled between the explosive and the inner surface of the grenade's outer casing—to fragment into pellets that blow outward in a killing radius of ten feet and a wounding radius of forty-five feet.

M60 Machine Gun: U.S. Army machine gun; fires 7.62mm bullets in linked belts (100 rounds to a belt) at 550 rounds per minute; effective range about one mile; designed to be manned by a gunner and one ammo carrier/assistant.

M72 LAW: see LAW.

M79 Grenade Launcher: single-shot, 40-mm grenade launcher carried by troops; looks like a pregnant shotgun the length of a man's arm; fires fragmentation grenades with a five-meter casualty radius; alternate rounds include high explosive, heavy buckshot, smoke, and illumination rounds; see Blooper.

MACV: Military Assistance Command Vietnam is central headquarters for all U.S. forces in South Vietnam and is located at Tan Son Nhut Air Force Base; General William Westmoreland, stationed at MACV, was in command of all U.S. military forces from June 1964 to July 1968 when he was replaced by General Creighton Abrams.

Mama-San: a Vietnamese woman, usually older.

MARS: Military Affiliate Radio System, or, Military Amateur Radio Services; a network of ham-operated, short-wave radio connections that allow troops in Vietnam to converse with friends and loved ones back in the States.

MEDCAP: Medical Civil Action Program; free medical treatment for Vietnamese villagers provided on-site by traveling U.S. and ARVN medics.

MEDEVAC: Medical evacuation of wounded by helicopter; see "dust-off."

Military Payment Certificates (MPC):   "Funny money" issued to GIs in place of U.S. currency so U.S. dollars cannot accumulate and be used by the NVA or VC to buy military supplies on the black market from manufacturers in other nations; the design printed on the MPC changes every four to six months—the day before the change occurs, troops are notified that on the following day they should exchange their old MPC for new MPC since the day after that, the MPC bearing the old design will be worthless.

Military Time: Like civilian time, military time starts the new day at midnight, which in military time is written as 0000 hours. 1:00 a.m. is written as 0100 hrs ("oh one hundred hours"); 2:00 a.m. is written as 0200 hrs ("oh two hundred hours"), and adding one hundred for each remaining hour of the 24-hour day. So noon is 1200 hrs ("twelve hundred hours") and 1:00 p.m. is 1300 hrs ("thirteen hundred hours"). Midnight, if counting goes no further, can be designated as 2400 hrs ("twenty-four hundred hours"); but if counting goes past midnight into the new day, midnight should be designated as 0000 hrs.

Mini-Gun: a machine gun with five or six rotating barrels driven by an electric motor; fires 7.62mm bullets at 6,000 rounds a minute.

MOS: Military Occupation Specialty is the kind of work in which a soldier is trained, e.g., an infantryman's MOS is 11B10 (commonly called "Eleven Bravo"), and a clerk/typist's MOS is 71B30.

MPC: see Military Payment Certificates.

National Liberation Front: a South Vietnamese national and political organization created in 1960 to attract support for overthrowing the South Vietnamese government of Ngo Dinh Diem and unifying the country (north and south) under communist rule; it tried to hide its communist intent; its military arm was the People's Liberation Armed Forces (PLAF), most commonly referred to in the West as the Viet Cong (VC).

NCO: Noncommissioned Officers are sergeants (all categories) who move up in rank by promotion; by contrast, lieutenants, captains, and colonels, etc., receive their ranks by commission.

Newbie: anybody newly arrived in Vietnam.

NLF: see National Liberation Front.

Number One: slang for "most," "best," "highest," "greatest."

NVA: the North Vietnamese Army controlled by communist Hanoi.

Papa-San: a Vietnamese man, usually older.

Parade-Rest: heels twelve inches apart; legs straight and rear edges of heels touching imaginary line running behind all men in that formation row; hands held at back, right hand in left palm unless a weapon or other device is held, in which case device is held in front of body, arms hanging loose, hands holding device at waist or groin level.

Personnel File (201): Official Military Personnel File (OMPF); file folder that contains a soldier's records; when he moves from one military unit to another, he carries his personnel file with him; once assigned to a military unit, his 201 file is stored in that unit's headquarters' personnel office.

PIO or PIO Clerk: Public Information Office or PIO officer or clerk.

Point Man: the leading GI of a squad or platoon walking in the boonies; he discovers trip wires and potential ambushes and warns buddies who are following him.

Poncho: a square nylon sheet for protection from the rain; has a hole and a hood in the middle for a soldier's head, and snaps on the edges to fasten the sides of the sheet around the soldier's arms in baggy sleeves.

Pop Smoke: a smoke grenade is "popped" or released to give a predetermined sign that a landing site is clear or something was seen, etc. Various colors of smoke are available, e.g., red, green, yellow, and white.

POW: Prisoner of War.

PRC-25 Portable Radio: the "prick 25" is a backpack radio for communication in the field; weighs about 23½ pounds; the squad or platoon's radio-telephone operator (RTO) carries it strapped to his back; the high aerial makes the PRC radio operator a prime target for snipers.

Pucker Factor: a measurement of the tightness of a person's asshole when he or she is experiencing fear, thus a measurement of fear; #1 is considered the tightest or greatest possible fear.

Puff the Magic Dragon (also Puff or Spooky): A Douglas AC-47D transport plane converted to a gunship by instillation of three or four 7.62mm Gatling Mini-guns (each firing 6,000 rounds a minute, a tracer every fifth round) mounted in the port side of the fuselage; approx. 16,500 rounds are carried on a typical mission; flying in a circle with the plane tipped toward the center and firing out the side of the plane will produce, due to the tracers, a visual effect called "the cone of fire" where the cone's tip is on the ground.

PX: Post Exchange (general store for military personnel).

Quad-Fifties: four .50-caliber machine guns mounted two over and two under, often on an armored personnel carrier (APC); capable of firing all at the same time.

Razor Wire: see concertina wire.

R & R: Rest and Recreation (or Rest & Relaxation); every soldier in Vietnam is allowed one week of R & R at approved locations—Bangkok and Hawaii are most popular—plane tickets free of charge.

Ready Rolls: originally a name used in the early 20th century for commercial cigarettes rolled by machine rather than by hand; the name was adopted by GIs in Vietnam for marijuana cigarettes made and sold to GIs by the Vietnamese; a Kools cigarette is rolled vertically between a worker's hands until all the tobacco falls out leaving a tube of paper with a menthol-flavored filter at one end; the worker then fills the tube with finely cleaned top quality pot, twists the end of the paper tube shut, collects twenty of them in the original Kools package, reseals it, and sells it for the equivalent of two American dollars, a lot of money in the Vietnamese economy.

REGS: official Army regulations or Department of Defense regulations.

REMF: an acronym for "rear echelon mother fucker," a derogatory phrase used by grunts in the field to describe men working as support personnel on safe and secure base camps and seldom exposed to the dangers of combat. Four-fifths or more of all soldiers who serve in the Vietnam War are REMFs, which is also true of most other wars.

Re-Up: re-enlistment in the armed forces; provides bonus pay and sometimes one's choice of assignment.

Revetments: sturdy, free-standing walls five or six feet high and fifteen feet or more long; designed for protection of choppers against mortars and rockets.

Round: one bullet, shell, or projectile (fired or unfired).

Roving Guard: an armed guard on the perimeter of a large base camp who walks back and forth behind assigned bunkers looking for sappers or other enemy who sneak through the perimeter defenses.

RPG: Rocket Propelled Grenade; fired from a variety of handheld devices; the rocket is similar to that of the LAW and has a shaped charge for punching through armor.

RTO: Radio-Telephone Operator; most units in the field have one or more RTOs; in the field, RTOs carry PRC-25 radios for communication with other field units and base commanders, and for calling in artillery and air strikes as well as dust-offs. See PRC-25.

S-1: a battalion's central legal and administrative office.

Sappers: VC or NVA who sneak through U.S. base camp defenses and plant explosives they've carried with them or commit other acts of aggression.

Satchel Charge: an explosive carried in a canvas satchel by infiltrating sappers.

Short: having few days left before DEROSing (going home).

Short-Timer: a person with only weeks or days left before DEROSing (going home).

Short-Timer's Calendar: a cartoon figure (often Yosemite Sam from Bugs Bunny cartoons) drawn so short his head rests on his combat boots; picture is divided into 365 numbered spaces (like a paint-by-the-number picture) and each day the soldier colors in another numbered space, starting with space #365 and then space #364, etc., until only one space is left—space #1, DEROS day—the day the soldier leaves for home; most commonly used by REMFs who have a locker, next to a cot, on which to hang their calendars.

Silver Bird of Paradise: the name Vietnam GIs give the commercial, silver-winged passenger plane that takes us back home.

Sit-Reps: Situation Reports; term most often used for reports received over the radio.

Slope Head: derogatory term for Vietnamese people.

SOP: Standard Operating Procedure.

SPC-4 & SPC-5: pronounced "speck four" and "speck five"; clerks, cooks, mechanics, engineers, and other men with non-combat training are ranked in the Army as Specialist Four or Specialist Five; SPC-5 is equivalent to the lowest grade sergeant. (See "Army Enlisted Ranks.")

Spooky: see Puff the Magic Dragon.

Stars and Stripes: a newspaper published by the Department of Defense that claims to be editorially separate from the DOD; reports on all matters affecting military personnel and is provided to them around the world free of charge.

Stract: behaving strictly by military regulations; being overly concerned about military appearance and conduct at the cost of common sense and camaraderie with fellow soldiers.

Tet: beginning of Vietnamese New Year determined by Vietnamese lunar calendar; Tet on our Western solar calendar varies, year to year, between January 21 and February 19.

Tracer: a bullet that leaves a momentary visible trail in the air from a phosphorus-packed rear end; U.S. tracers leave red trails; Chinese and Russian tracers supplied to the NVA and VC leave green trails.

Tropic Lightning: 25th Infantry Division headquartered at Cu Chi; has approximately 13,000 troops attached to it.

Tunnel Rat: a GI who specializes in exploring VC tunnels and killing any VC he finds there.

VC: Viet Cong (South Vietnamese guerillas sympathetic to North Vietnam's political and military goals); see National Liberation Front.

Vietnamization: "new and revised" U.S. policy announced by President Nixon in June 1969 that attempts to turn the conduct of the war over to the South Vietnamese military and thereby end America's involvement in Vietnam, something we've supposedly been trying to do all along.

Warrant Officer or Chief Warrant Officer: an expert in certain military specialties (e.g., office administrators, trainers, helicopter pilots); they serve under warrant from the Secretary of the Army and rank above enlisted grades and below commissioned grades. Warrant officers have five ranks: the lowest is WO1 and the next four (CW2 to CW5) are called "chief warrant officer."

"Waste him": to waste a person is to kill that person.

XO: Executive Officer, second in command to the commanding officer (CO).

QUESTIONS FOR REFLECTION

Andrew's Military Training

1. What were some of the events and movements in our country during the years 1968 to 1970 that contributed to social and political unrest, and led to concern about the well-being and even survival of the nation?

2. What incident first compelled Andrew to take his military training seriously? Talk about why you think it had that effect on him.

3. What reasons did Andrew give for doing what his military superiors and his government told him to do? Do you agree with his reasoning?

4. By what criteria can we distinguish a lawful command from an unlawful command issued by a sergeant or officer during a time of war? Are there examples we can cite of obviously lawful or unlawful commands that could be useful for developing guidelines for a soldier?

5. Andrew's wife and family members apparently believed that if his country called him to war—drafted him—he had no choice but to go. Do you agree?

6. Was Sergeant Akeana's treatment of Duchek purely sadistic or could he have had some remotely justifiable reason for it? What about the platoon's treatment of Duchek? Might there have been a legitimate rationale behind Akeana's encouragement of that behavior?

7. What are some of the methods the drill sergeants used to coerce trainees into doing what the sergeants wanted them to do?

8. Do you approve of Lieutenant Kilmore's treatment of Private Jason Tilson and Private Cunningham? Please explain.

9. What drew Andrew to Carson? Did Carson help Andrew understand what it takes to be a soldier? Or was Carson simply a reckless fool and a bad example?

10.   In the Escaped POW Course, was Andrew a coward for running from the ambush? By what criteria might we fairly judge a person a coward?

11.   Why would *any* trainee who was threatened by the guards in the Escaped POW Course pretend, along with the guards, that they had loaded guns? In other words, why wouldn't any trainee run from a phony, "let's pretend" ambush, as did Carson and Robinson, as well as Andrew?

12.   In the "Escaped POW Course," what reasons might the sergeant have had for giving Andrew directions to friendly lines? How might the three POW guards who ambushed Andrew on the gravel road describe their encounter with Andrew?

13.   What was going on in Andrew's mind immediately prior to the POW guard saying, "Whoa, fella, we don't want any trouble"?

14.   Why were Andrew's jaws aching, eyes burning, and arms "thrumming" after the transport truck arrived at the barracks from the POW exercise? What did Andrew learn about himself?

15.   While polishing their boots in the barracks, Andrew and his friends made a pact together. What was the nature of that pact? Why might someone say their pact was idealistic and sentimental? How might it have affected Andrew's behavior in the story titled "Roving Guard"?

16.   When Andrew was on the land mine course, what do you suppose contributed to his delusion that he was on a real battle field suffering from a sucking chest wound?

"Ugly Truth, Ugly Justice"

17.   Andrew explains his battalion's policy of not informing family members of the unfortunate and ugly manner in which a surprising number of men die in a combat zone. Do you agree with that policy?

18.   After hearing Archie Armstrong's account of Hackett killing the mama-san, Andrew, having had too much alcohol, fell asleep beside the sandbags and the bunker just as Armstrong did. What might the author be suggesting?

19.   Was Colonel Hackett justified in executing the mama-san he believed planted a booby trap that injured and killed some of his men?

"Bronze Stars and Purple Hearts"

20.   What was Andrew's opinion about medals in general? And his opinion

about Bronze Stars for excellent non-combat work? Talk about why you agree or disagree with Andrew.

21.	Andrew's comments about "lifers," in "Bronze Stars and Purple Hearts" and in "Snapshot," make some readers uneasy, even angry. What do you think about those comments? How might Andrew have come to such opinions?

22.	Andrew visits Raymond Landers, and his buddies Nitro and Marvin Simmons, to acquire more information so Andrew can write a better Bronze Star recommendation for Landers. Simmons doesn't seem as impressed with Landers as is Nitro. Why might that be?

23.	When Raymond Landers reflects on his act of bravery, he says about the woman he saved, "Got hit in the leg .... I mean, I saw her ... watched her dragging around. But I thought the gooks with me in the ditch, I don't know .... Or maybe ... but that's stupid, with the kids ...." Why is he verbally stumbling around like that? What is he insinuating about the "gooks"?

24.	Nitro tries to explain and defend Landers by saying, "Those fuckers are dedicated .... Nobody knows what they might do." Why do you suppose Nitro said that? What did he mean?

25.	Simmons responds to Nitro's comment ("Nobody knows what they might do") by saying, "'Some' my women I know is like that," and then chuckles and looks over his shoulder at men passing around photographs and "hee-hawing together." What might be the significance of Simmons's comment?

"De-Drumming"

26.	Derek Waller cuts loose on Andrew: "If you're so righteous, why are you in Vietnam? Nobody even knows why we're here. You came over here ready to kill women and children because otherwise you'd go to jail. Right? And now you get high and mighty because I fucked a prostitute ... At least I'm not a fucking hypocrite." Do you agree with Waller? Might there be a more middle-of-the-road judgment of Andrew?

"Perilous Foundations"

27.	Reeko, sitting at the edge of the excavation, told Markowski, "When my company discovers a tunnel? They call me." Markowsky asked, "So you're ordinarily out in the boonies with an infantry unit?" In response, Reeko looked contemptuously at him. Why did Markowski ask that question? And what reasons might Reeko have had for responding the way he did?

28.　How might someone argue that "Perilous Foundations" is a metaphor for the planning and execution of the entire Vietnam War?

"R & R"

29.　When Jerry continues speaking of Andrew as though he's Watson to Jerry's Sherlock Holmes, Andrew says Jerry is doing "the worst kind of posturing, because it's true." To which Jerry says, "Touché," and Andrew shoots back "a fake smile." What's going on here?

30.　Explain Jer y Maener's reasoning about why the soldier who fell into the bed of his truck and was buried under hot asphalt would be judged by most soldiers in Vietnam as a "dumb fuck" or an "asshole."

31.　After worrying that they all might be drowning in jasmine tea, Andrew says, "I don't care. It's all so beautiful." Why does Andrew say, "I don't care"? Obviously he does. And why does he say "It's all so beautiful"? It's obviously not. What's going on here?

32.　Try unpacking a few similarities (and differences, too) between REMF Andrew Atherton's comment, "I don't care, it's all so beautiful," and the comment sometimes made by grunts out in the boonies after seeing yet another buddy killed: "Don't make no never mind."

"Intervention"

33.　Gallagher tells Andrew the old man who was terribly burned spoke "words of forgiveness" to Gallagher. Why did Gallagher feel he needed forgiveness? Was he correct about that?

34.　Andrew warns Lieutenant Paddington, "… if the full story of the Sáng Mât Trâng fire were picked up by *Stars and Stripes* or the press back home, your medal winners might appear foolish despite their obvious heroism." Why?

35.　Imagine yourself as an avant-guard newspaper reporter writing an article about the Sáng Mât Trâng Village fire. What might be your first sentence?

36.　In what way(s) might "Intervention" be interpreted as a metaphor for the entire Vietnam War?

"KP with Bruno, Tweeze, and Berry"

37.   If you've been in the military and assigned KP duty, was your experience similar to Andrew's? In what ways?

38.   Have you ever worked in a job where the boss thought he or she could treat workers anyway he or she wanted? What effect does that environment have on a person?

39.   What is Berry's "connection" to Sergeant Major Mollema? Do you think, as Dretchler did, that a white person would get a less speedy repair of the dishwasher?

40.   What is the primary issue a higher authority would consider when reflecting on Berry's request to the sergeant major?

41.   What are your thoughts about "Berry-Ain't-Cherry"? Do you find him compelling? Offensive?

42.   Talk about Berry showing Andrew and Tweeze how a black jazz and dance enthusiast would dance to the music of Billie Holiday. What was Berry giving Andrew and Tweeze?

"Riding High With Mangus"

43.   Mangus tells Andrew, "Don't mess with me, man. You got a college education and you're working at battalion headquarters, right?" To which Andrew says, "I'm not walking down that road, Mangus." What road does Andrew wish to avoid? Do you suppose he's walked it before?

44.   How does Andrew win Mangus over to answering Andrew's questions?

45.   During the Vietnam War, many soldiers like Andrew, Mangus, and Jerry Maener smoked marijuana and used other drugs. What do you think about that practice?

"Going Out in Trucks"

46.   Captain Blaine instructs the assembled perimeter guards, "If you men in those bunkers [that have cut phone lines] see movement beyond accurate firing range, pop smoke and I'll send a runner for details. Otherwise, the roving guard will keep you tied in with info." Explain what Captain Blaine is talking about.

47.   Why do you suppose Sergeant Tibbot ordered the reserve guards out to the perimeter in trucks?

48. If you were asked to assess Tibbot's military performance, what would you say is his primary fault? His primary virtue?

49. Do you agree with Andrew that a soldier is justified in killing an officer or a sergeant who is unnecessarily dangerous to the welfare of the troops?

50. When Tibbot was on the phone and the reserve guards were standing in the underground bunker ready to walk defiantly up to ground level, why did they delay their departure? Was it because Andrew said, "Hold off …"?

51. Do you think Andrew rigged the booby-trap grenade in Tibbot's desk? What reason(s) do you have for thinking that?

52. Was Tibbot responsible for Berry's death?

"Pure Dumb Luck"

53. Sully Martin claims Andrew "let someone else do his job for him" on Hamburger Hill. Is that true? Did Andrew "suck ass" in order to shirk his responsibility? Is he deserving of blame?

54. Andrew asks Sully Martin what fighting was like on Hamburger Hill. Martin answers, "You wanna know what it's like out there, go fight the fuckin' war yourself." Martin's answer made Andrew sick to his stomach and his face burn with embarrassment. But why? As Andrew says, if Martin had the chance, he would have done the same thing Andrew did.

55. Was it, indeed, only "dumb luck" that provided Andrew an escape from the fighting on Hamburger Hill?

"Ralph Mantis"

56. Anything in "Ralph Mantis" that especially amuses or puzzles you?

"Roving Guard"

57. What do we know about Andrew that might have contributed to his decision to euthanize the two wounded men?

58. Was Andrew a moral monster for trying to kill those two wounded men? Was he a coward for not killing them?

59. How might Andrew's struggle over what to do about the wounded men resemble the moral struggle some men have over participation in the Vietnam War? Or any war? How might protesters who went to Canada in

opposition to the Vietnam war judge mercenaries who, for money or a job, will fight in whatever war the American government orders them to fight, my country right or wrong?

60. Suppose Andrew had shot those two wounded men as he initially intended. What might have been the consequences if he had been caught by the Sergeant of the Guard? If he had not been caught?

61. Is euthanasia ever justified in war?

"Jimmy Beamis"

62. At the end of the story, Andrew says Jimmy "was not the only one who killed that eleven year old boy …." Who else then? How?

63. Andrew says Jimmy's killing of the boy "ushered that boy's father into a lower level of hell." Describe the hell Andrew presumes the father is aleady in. What risks might the father be taking? What compromises? What hardships might he be enduring?

64. What might Andrew have meant by writing, "… we were not good men. We were the men we'd read about in history books."

65. In "Jimmy Beamis," what has Andrew come to believe about himself and the world of human affairs?

"Snapshot"

66. How does Andrew describe "lifers"? Might he be partially correct? Or is Andrew's description due simply to a clash of civilian and military cultures?

67. How would you describe Andrew's behavior toward Sergeant George Garrett at the table in the mess hall?

68. The reader is led to believe that "Snapshot" will be a portrait of George Garrett. But who else is profiled in "Snapshot"? Is that portrait flattering?

69. Why didn't Jerry and Andrew want to join the celebration of their own promotions?

70. Why did Jerry yell, "Why can't you respect a difference of opinion?" at men who will surely dismiss the question as naively high-minded?

71. After leaving the party, Andrew returns to his hooch and tries to read, but he can't concentrate. "I was angry. Humiliated. And not just by the behavior of the other men. I didn't feel right about myself either, and I couldn't identify why." Why didn't he feel right about himself? Why couldn't

he identify what was wrong?

72.   What could the buffalo symbolize?

"Getting Out and Going Home"

73.   Andrew describes the sense of unreality the men experienced on the plane flying back to the States. What are some things he mentions that brought about that sense of unreality? Might this be true for soldiers coming back from other wars?

74.   At California's Oakland Army Discharge Center, what motivated an entire gymnasium full of returning GIs to behave in what the MP captain described as an insurrection?

75.   When Andrew was looking out the window of the taxi taking him from the Oakland Army Discharge Center to the airport, he says, "This is the face of my culture. Maybe the soul of my nation. This is why I was sent to war. This is why my fellow soldiers died. To protect all this." What mixed feelings might Andrew have had as he said this?

ACKNOWLEDGEMENTS

I would not have had the confidence or courage to start and complete this novel if it had not been for the support and guidance I received, above all, from Jacqueline, Gaynell, and Kristina, but also from Phillip, Harvey, and Amira. From the bottom of my heart, I thank you.

CPSIA information can be obtained at www.ICGtesting.com
Printed in the USA
LVOW13s0449240514

387205LV00007B/10/P